Wilhelm, Kate.

Defense for the devil.

$24.95

DATE			

DEFENSE FOR THE DEVIL

ALSO BY KATE WILHELM

The Good Children (1998)
Malice Prepense (1996)
A Flush of Shadows (1995)
The Best Defense (1994)
Justice for Some (1993)
Seven Kinds of Death (1992)
Naming the Flowers (1992)
And the Angels Sing (1992)
Death Qualified (1991)
State of Grace (1991)
Sweet, Sweet Poison (1990)
Cambio Bay (1990)
Children of the Wind (1989)
Smart House (1989)
The Dark Door (1988)
Crazy Time (1988)
The Hamlet Trap (1987)
The Hills Are Dancing (with Richard Wilhelm) (1986)
Huysman's Pets (1986)
Welcome, Chaos (1983)
Oh, Susannah! (1982)
A Sense of Shadow (1981)
Listen, Listen (1981)
Better than One with Damon Knight) (1980)
Juniper Time (1979)
Somerset Dreams and Other Fictions (1978)
Fault Lines (1977)
Where Late the Sweet Birds Sang (1976)
The Clewiston Test (1976)
The Infinity Box (1975)
City of Cain (1974)
Margaret and I (1971)
Abyss (1971)
Year of the Cloud (with Theodore L. Thomas) (1970)
Let the Fire Fall (1969)
The Downstairs Room and Other Speculative Fiction (1968)
The Killer Thing (1967)
The Nevermore Affair (1966)
The Clone (with Theodore L. Thomas) (1965)
The Mile-Long Spaceship (1963)
More Bitter than Death (1963)

KATE
WILHELM

DEFENSE FOR THE DEVIL

St. Martin's Press New York

Library of Congress Cataloging-in-Publication Data

Wilhelm, Kate.
Defense for the devil / Kate Wilhelm.
p. cm,
ISBN 0-312-19854-X
I. Title.
PS3573.I434D44 1999
813'.54—dc21 98-44576
CIP

First Edition: February 1999

10 9 8 7 6 5 4 3 2 1

Designed by Kathryn Parise

For Jon, Kitte, Mo, and Roxanne—sharers of hearth and home.

And special thanks to Julie A. Stevens for her continuing support and advice in legal matters. Any mistakes (of course, and alas) remain mine alone.

Every man before he dies shall see the Devil.

—OLD ENGLISH PROVERB

MITCH

1

Eddie carries, you handle the paperwork. Have a shower, eat something, relax, just be sure to call this number exactly at one.

Using the name on the credit card and driver's license—R. M. Palmer—Mitch signed for two steaks, fries, beer. He ate his steak with a towel wrapped around him, his hair dripping. At one he made the call. "Mitch," he said. "We're here." *Here* was Miami, not even the beach, just Miami.

"Let me speak to Eddie for a second."

He handed over the phone. Eddie's end of the conversation was a series of grunts. Eddie was six feet three, and nearly that broad, with a brain that would have left empty space in a peanut shell. Eddie handed the phone back to him.

"Her plane gets in at four, Swissair from Zurich. Let her make the first move. If she doesn't, return to the motel and call this number at seven. You remember the rest of it?"

"Sure," Mitch said.

"Good. I'll be waiting to hear from you."

After he hung up, Mitch pulled the spread off one of the beds and lay down. "We'll head out at two-thirty," he said. "I'm going to snooze." Eddie grunted, watching a ball game on TV. When he got up to go to the john, he took the suitcase with him; when he sprawled again, he kept it at his side. It looked like an ordinary twenty-six-inch suitcase, except for the keypad lock. The first time Mitch and Eddie had done this, Palmer had said, "Pick a number, Mitch, see if you're lucky." When he touched the keypad, a little red light had come on. "Message is, don't touch," Palmer had said. His was the scariest voice Mitch had ever heard.

The problem with Eddie was that he slept like a cat, dead out one minute, wide awake the next. He had gotten plenty of sleep while Mitch drove from New York. Mitch had slept little when they switched places, and he felt sore now, but the adrenaline was pumping; he was primed.

At two he got up and took his duffel bag into the bathroom. He brushed his teeth and then took out a length of weighted pipe and a six-inch-long leather holder that slid over the end. He swung it, nodded, and kept it in his hand under the towel when he went back to the bedroom. He moved around a lot; he went to the window, checking out the sun, grabbed his slacks from a chair and shook them. Eddie scowled and hunched lower, closer to the television. When Mitch began to whistle, Eddie reached over to turn up the volume. Mitch swung the pipe hard, catching him in the temple.

Eddie went down to his hands and knees, and Mitch hit him again, harder, and then again. Eddie slumped to the floor.

When Mitch left at two-thirty, he hung the DO NOT DISTURB card on the door, and he carried his duffel bag and the black suitcase.

Park the car and go in together. Buy a red rose and slip it under the strap on the suitcase, then go to the customs section and wait. Don't stay too close together, just keep each other in sight. Give it time, there might be a delay in customs; but if no one approaches by five-thirty, go back to the motel.

He arrived at Miami International at three-twenty, and by a quarter to four he was near customs, waiting, with what seemed to be a million other people. All he knew was that it was a woman this time.

She was short and plump, forty maybe, expensively dressed in a beige silk jacket and skirt, carrying a big shoulder bag and a briefcase. She looked around anxiously—amateur—then spotted the suitcase with the rose and walked toward him.

"Eddie?"

He nodded.

"I thought there would be two of you." Scared.

"He's over there," Mitch said, nodding toward a man leaning against a post.

She reached for the suitcase tentatively; he moved it back. "We have to make a phone call first," he said.

"Oh, of course."

He led the way to a bank of telephones. She looked alarmed when the man leaning against the post left it and walked away in the opposite direction and was lost among the hordes in people. "Don't worry about him," Mitch said. "He'll keep us in sight." He used the phone card and punched in numbers. The telephone rang once at the other end. He made a grunting noise. No one expected Eddie to talk much on the phone.

"No problems?"

"No."

"Let me speak to her."

He handed the phone to the woman. She listened a second, then after a quick glance at the suitcase, she said, "No problems. They're here. Everything is well." After another pause, she said, lowering her voice, "Of course. Penelope. Wait a second." She fumbled in her shoulder bag, found a notebook and a slim gold pen, and jotted down something. Then she handed the phone back to Mitch.

He listened to the instructions he already had memorized, and the line went dead. He continued to hold the phone to his ear. "Yes," he said. "Sure. Right." He nodded, listening to a dead line, then hung up.

"Change of plans," he said. "I've got to drive you to a hotel. He's afraid for you to drive back alone. You've read the stories about carjacks along that route?" He looked around, as if searching for his partner. "Wait here. Don't move a step. Be right back." He strode off, carrying the suitcase. The area was packed with arrivals, piles of luggage, people milling about. He mingled a minute or two, then returned to her. "All set," he said. "Let's go."

Her anxiety had returned. She eyed the suitcase, gave him an appraising look, then glanced around for the other man.

"Look," he said irritably, "I don't like this any more than you do. You don't have to register at the hotel. Once we get there, I hand over the suitcase and the car title and keys, you give me the briefcase, and you're on your own." He looked past her into the crowd, nodded, as if to his partner, then said, "Let's move. I've got to be back here in time to catch another plane. My partner will keep us in sight until we get to the car. And we'll both hope and pray I get back in time to make the flight. Let's move."

"He should have told me," she said.

"Yeah, but he didn't. Now, are you coming or not? Lady, I don't give a fuck one way or the other." She looked at the suitcase. When he started to walk, she did, too.

As soon as Eddie makes the transfer, he'll take her to the car, give her the title and keys, and you're done with her. While he's doing that, you pick up your tickets at the Delta counter. Someone will meet your plane at La Guardia. Right.

The car was a black two-door Lexus. The sight of it seemed to cheer her up a little. He tossed the suitcase into the back, but she kept her bag and the briefcase with her. The lead pipe was under the driver's seat. Traffic was fierce. It was five-fifteen, rush hour.

When he exited the freeway, she seemed unaware that they were nowhere near downtown yet; her alarm didn't go off until he turned onto a mean little side street. She clutched the briefcase harder. After another minute or two, she asked hoarsely, "Where are we going?"

"Not far," he said, making another turn. There was little traffic in this section of the city; a hurricane had hit hard a year before, few repairs had been made and a lot of the buildings were uninhabitable, but he knew people were watching the expensive car. This part had to go fast. He pulled into an abandoned convenience-store parking lot and stopped. She was trying futilely to open her door when he hit her with the lead pipe. It was a backhanded blow without much room for the swing, even with his seat all the way back, but it was a heavy pipe, and his arm was strong. Carefully he pulled the briefcase from her limp hands, then he grabbed her bag and riffled through it swiftly, searching for every scrap of paper, her airline ticket folder, receipts. . . . He took out the notebook and her wallet. He pulled out a couple hundred-dollar bills and the smaller ones and dropped them back into the bag loose, kept the wallet. Then he undid her seat belt, released the lock, opened the door and pushed her out, tossed her bag out after her. Let the local greaseballs have a few bucks to play with; by the time someone got around to calling the cops, there'd be nothing to find but another unidentified stiff, and nobody would have seen anything.

Hours later when he gassed up, he jotted down the name she had said on the telephone: Penelopy. He searched through the notebook for the message she had written and found it near the end, the code for the suitcase lock.

"Message is, don't touch," he said.

MAGGIE

✧ 2

It was four in the afternoon, muggy outside, and Barbara Holloway had been rushing for an hour and a half by the time she rang the bell at Martin's restaurant. He was closed at this time of day, she knew, and probably he was busy doing prep in the kitchen, but he opened the door almost instantly. He was so big that seeing him in an open doorway was always something of a jolt; he seemed to fill the entire space. And he was so black that the glare of his white beret was blinding and appeared to her sun-dazed eyes to be floating. He couldn't wear a chef's high hat, he had explained a long time ago, because ducking all the time killed his back.

"Is she here yet?"

He shook his head. "Look at you, dripping wet. You been running races or something?"

"Or something. I got two luscious salmon steaks, and lettuce and spinach for a salad. I washed it and have it in the fridge. And little red potatoes. Is that enough? Oh, and green beans."

"Sounds like plenty. You want some lemonade or iced tea? We're having iced tea."

"That would be wonderful." She sat at her usual table and pulled a cookbook from her briefcase. “Salmon is easy, isn’t it? And quick?” She glanced up at him as he was entering the kitchen; she could see that his shoulders were shaking with laughter. The problem was, she thought glumly, that people who knew how to do things had no sympathy for people who didn’t. And she didn’t know how to cook.

She should have been out of here by three with the whole afternoon ahead of her, plenty of time to think, to plan, to try things and toss them if they didn’t work out. But at two or a little later a frantic woman had called and begged for an appointment, now, today, as soon as she could drive over from the coast. And she, Barbara, had agreed.

She and John had explained to her father at dinner on Saturday night the arrangement they had come up with. “What we’ll do is take alternate days, John one day, me the next. Then over here on Saturday, as long as your invitation is still good, and a restaurant one night a week.”

Frank had turned to John, who nodded and said, “I have six dishes that are incomparable. Two weeks before I have to repeat.”

Barbara had not missed the amusement in her father’s eyes. He knew as well as she did that she had three dishes in her repertoire: steak and baked potatoes, canned soup, and frozen entrées.

Anyone can cook, she told herself frequently, anyone who can read a recipe and understand the directions and follow them without fail. Of the three necessary skills, she was very good at one. She was reading more than she wanted to know about salmon when Martin brought out iced tea. A fat fish? Rolls of fat around the waist? What waist?

“Salmon’s easy,” Martin said without a smile. “You going to put a sauce on it? It’s good without sauce,” he added quickly, “just a squeeze of lemon juice, a little butter.”

It needed a sauce, she understood, with a feeling of desperation, remembering the one time she had tried white sauce and it had come out with little gooey lumps like hard library paste.

The doorbell rang and he turned to go answer it.

She shoved the cookbook back inside her briefcase and watched as he admitted a man and woman, both dressed in jeans and T-shirts and running shoes, exactly the way Barbara was dressed. The woman was carrying an oversized tote bag with a picture of a whale. She was thirty-something, he a little younger. Both good-looking, fit.

"Thank you for seeing me on such short notice," the woman said. "I'm Maggie Folsum." She held out her hand. "And this is Laurence Thielman."

"Barbara Holloway," Barbara said, shaking hands with her first, then with him.

"Laurence will wait out in the car," Maggie Folsum said. "He just wanted to make sure everything was okay first."

"Too hot out there," Barbara said. "You could hang out in a booth."

Laurence Thielman looked at Maggie. She glanced back at the booths, then nodded.

"You folks want some iced tea? Coffee? Coke or something?" Martin asked.

They both said iced tea and he went back to the kitchen. Laurence settled himself in the most distant booth, not very far away in this small restaurant, but out of hearing.

Not hysterical, Barbara decided, studying Maggie Folsum, but either exhausted or ill. She had deep shadows under her eyes, and the drawn appearance that came with sleeplessness. About as tall as Barbara, slender and muscular, with long dark hair pulled back on her neck loosely with a ribbon. No makeup. Her eyes were lovely, brown with thick lashes, very steady as she submitted to the scrutiny without embarrassment or shyness.

"While we're waiting for your tea," Barbara said, "tell me how did you know about me? Why me?"

"My daughter is your devoted fan," Maggie said. "She wants to do what you do, work with poor people in a ghetto somewhere. As a doctor, not a lawyer, though. She's seventeen," she added.

"You have a seventeen-year-old daughter?"

"And an eighteen-year-old daughter," Maggie said. "I'm thirty-five."

Martin came out with a tray and put her glass down, glanced at Barbara's, went back to Laurence Thielman with another glass, and returned to the kitchen, all without a word.

Maggie said apologetically, "There's really no way I can get into it without going back to day one. I'm sorry. I'll try to make it brief."

"Day one it is," Barbara said. She sipped her tea and waited.

"I live at Folsum, over on the coast," Maggie said. "I grew up there, and the Arnos lived there until recently. I've known them all my life. I was sixteen when Mitch Arno swept me off my feet. He was twenty-two. His nickname, which I didn't understand until much later, was Mitch the Cherry Picker. Anyway, same old same old. I got pregnant, and his family and my parents got together and made him marry me. My mother was mortified, my father furious, Mama and Papa Arno outraged, like that. Mitch took off as soon as I started to show a lot, by May. Then, in February, six months after Gwen was born, he showed up again. I was living with my parents, they were both gone when he came, and he roughed me up and raped me. I was seventeen."

Her voice was steady, but she had to pause to sip tea often.

"My folks came home and found me bruised and crying, and him in the kitchen. There was a lot of yelling." Her voice faltered and she drank again, then continued almost in a monotone. "My mother called Ray, Mitch's brother. He came with Papa Arno, and they dragged Mitch out to the yard and Ray beat him up. Really beat him up. They took him to town and put him on a bus to Portland. I never knew what all was said, but probably everyone else in Folsum knows. Papa disowned him publicly."

Very faintly then she said, "Karen was born nine months later. I was eighteen, with two daughters. I divorced Mitch. I took my maiden name back and changed the girls' names to Folsum. End of day one.

"Day two," Maggie said, in a near whisper. "Last Thursday." Her hands were on the table, shaking. She looked at them, then put them in her lap, drew in a deep breath, and let it out slowly. "Okay. I own and manage Folsum House, a bed-and-breakfast inn, and I decided months ago to throw a big family reunion, a birthday/graduation party for Gwen, and make it something she'd never forget. She'll be going to the university in the fall, here in Eugene. I wanted it to be very, very special for her. And Mitch came back." She closed her eyes hard.

When Maggie opened her eyes and started speaking again, her voice was even lower. "It was late, after eleven. We'd all been busy, there had been guests in the inn, and one couple was still there, planning to check out the next morning. I was expecting sixty or seventy people. Anyway, I had just put some pies in the oven when he walked in through the kitchen door as if he'd never left. He smelled bad, was road dirty, unshaven, rumpled, as if he had been driving for days without sleep. He came in carrying all his stuff—suitcase, briefcase, a duffel bag, a sport coat over his arm—and just let it all drop inside the door. I told him to get out or I'd call the police. He . . ." She shrugged. "He came at me and said he'd break my arm if I gave him any lip, and he grabbed my wrist. I hit him with the first thing I could grab, the rolling pin from the worktable." She shook her head, and a very faint smile appeared and vanished. "What a cliché, hit him with a rolling pin. Anyway, he went down and didn't make a sound or move, and I thought I had killed him."

She drank thirstily then and wiped her mouth with the back of her hand. "I had to get him out of the kitchen. One of the girls might not be asleep yet, come out for water or something. I kept thinking he had come back to spoil Gwen's party. Crazy. Anyway, I ran out to the shed and got a wagon we use to haul firewood, and got an old beach blanket from the garage. I rolled him up in the blanket and dragged him to the wagon outside the back door, and I took him to the garage and got him inside the house van, wrapped up like a mummy. I locked the van so no one would get inside. I really was crazy, but it was all I could think of. I couldn't call the sheriff. They'd arrest me . . . Gwen's big day ruined, my mother could have a heart attack, more scandal, all those people on the way. They'd come for a party and attend a wake. And my daughters . . . I was crazy." She stopped again, longer this time.

"I hid his gear. I cleaned up the kitchen and took the pies out of the oven, and I remembered he must have left a car somewhere. It was in the drive near the garage. I had to get rid of it before people started to arrive the next day. That day. It was after one by then. All I could think of was to drive the car to a day-use park about two miles away and leave it there. Just before dawn that's what I did, and I waited in the park until there was enough light to walk home on the beach, where no one would see me."

She drank more tea, gazing past Barbara. "I made breakfast for the two customers, we cleaned their room, my housekeeper was there by then. . . . My parents arrived in time for lunch, and Mama and Papa Arno got there in the afternoon. I had a reservation for an early dinner for all the grandparents, the girls, and myself; by eight or nine, others would be pulling in, and we had to be back by then. There wasn't any time to do anything about Mitch. Then the Arnos decided to let me have a couple of hours with my folks—they said they would visit friends in Folsum—and we left them and went to dinner at about four. Mother wanted a little walk on the beach before dinner, and there's easy access down in Folsum, so we left early. When we got home Dad wanted to put his car in the garage, so I had to back my car out first, not the van, a little Nissan. I looked in the van to make sure nothing showed, and it was empty. I nearly fell down in relief; I felt as if I had been living a nightmare all day and finally woke up. He had come to and left, that's all I could think.

"On Sunday," Maggie went on, "most of the guests left, but a few stayed over until Monday. We had arranged for me to ride up to Portland with my brother and his wife Monday morning, and we'd leave right after my mother and father did. They took the girls down to California with them to spend a month. They adore their granddaughters. Irene and her crew came early to clean up the place; high-school kids would be around to collect chairs and tables I'd borrowed from the school, and everything would be ready for customers on Tuesday. So I went to Portland and spent the day with Laurence. He had a show in a gallery that I wanted to see; he's an artist. Anyway, we took all day, had dinner on the way back, and got home about eleven. Irene and her husband met us at the door. Tom's a deputy sheriff. My house had been torn apart.

"He had ripped open mattresses, chairs, couches, dumped things out of drawers, torn clothes out of closets, broken things. Every room was a disaster." Her hands were clenched hard and her voice was vehement now. "That bastard destroyed everything he could get his hands on."

"Easy," Barbara murmured. "Back up a second. How? When? I thought the place was crawling with people?"

Maggie shook her head. "Irene said she got through at two-thirty, and the kids were done loading stuff in their trucks before that. She left a lot of windows open to air the place out; she said people had been smoking, and I guess they had been. Anyway, she left it airing out at two-thirty, went back at eight-thirty to close up, and found the mess. She called her husband, and he brought in the sheriff. By the time we got home, no one was there except Irene and Tom, who was going to spend the night and make sure no one did any further damage. Tom said I couldn't stay, and Laurence couldn't. Even his apartment was a wreck! We would have to go to the hotel in Folsum. I couldn't move anything or touch anything until the insurance adjustor inspected it all and the sheriff's office investigated. They said it was malicious vandalism, and I didn't tell them about Mitch. I was too . . . I couldn't say anything," she said. "I actually couldn't speak. We all went to my room, and suddenly

Irene shoved me into the bathroom and I threw up. I could hear her telling Tom to leave me alone a minute. I looked in the hiding place where I put Mitch's stuff, a little space you can get to from the bathroom. Everything was still there." She started to pick up her glass but pushed it away instead. "That was yesterday."

"Intermission," Barbara said quietly. "You want a glass of wine?"

Maggie nodded. Barbara stood up and went back to ask Laurence if he wanted wine, beer, anything else. He didn't. He was drawing in a small sketchbook. Taking her time, she went to the kitchen, where Martin and Binnie were hard at work preparing entrées. "Sorry," she said. "Martin, could we have a couple glasses of chardonnay?"

"You got it," he said.

She returned to the table. Maggie was standing at a window, gazing out over dazzling white café curtains. Barbara watched her for a moment, then made a noise moving her chair, and Maggie jerked and returned from wherever she had been.

"All right," Maggie said as she came back to the table and sat down again. "Today. I was up really early making phone calls to head off customers; Tom let me take the reservation book. And I had to find rooms for my guests. The insurance adjustor couldn't get there until ten or eleven, and I couldn't touch a thing at the house, so I was still in the hotel, in the coffee shop, when a man approached me and said he wanted to talk to me. I told him some other time. I really didn't have time."

Martin brought out their wine, and she said thank you and sipped hers gratefully. "The man said his name was Trassi, and he wanted to talk about Mitch. I hadn't told a single person that I had seen Mitch. No one. I still haven't, until now," she added.

"He said Mitch worked for a company in Southern California, and he had been sent to their Seattle branch with important papers. He said Mitch had mentioned that he might stop off and see his ex, that he had a debt to pay, but everyone assumed he meant on the return trip and had thought little of it. He was due to arrive in Seattle on Friday and never showed up. Instead, he called and at first claimed that his car had broken down, but when his supervisor told him to rent a car and get to Seattle, he said his ex had thrown him out and he couldn't get back in to collect the stuff until Monday because there were a hundred or more people around. When he didn't show on Monday, the company sent Trassi, the company lawyer, to get the papers and find out what was happening."

Maggie stopped there and sipped her wine again. Her eyes were narrowed and a slight frown creased her forehead. "He told me they would give a thousand-dollar reward for the suitcase and briefcase, and the company would cover the damage Mitch had done to the inn. He described the briefcase and suitcase."

Barbara drank her wine and waited the few seconds it took for Maggie to resume. There was no point in prodding her; she knew what she wanted to tell, what she had to tell, and her report was as clear and precise as Barbara's would have been.

"I was tempted," Maggie said. "Really tempted. My insurance is pretty limited, the minimum that I have to carry. So there's a big deductible, and partial coverage. Anyway, before I could even ask a question, Mama and Papa Arno and Ray came rushing in, over from Eugene. I told Trassi I had to leave. He tried to keep me another minute or two, but the Arnos were all over us, and he saw it was useless. I left with the Arnos. We drove up to the inn, and Mama was crying, Papa cursing, like that." She flashed her fleeting smile again. "It begins to sound like a farce here," she said, almost apologetically.

"They were all talking at once," she said. "But what happened on Friday was that Papa Arno saw Mitch getting a drink from a hose near a shed, and he thought it was a bum who had stumbled out from the woods. Then he saw it was Mitch. He ran over to him and told him to turn around and beat it, but Mitch was muttering that he was going to kill me, and Papa Arno knocked him down. He thought he had to hide Mitch or someone would be killed that weekend. He shoved him inside the shed and told him to stay or he'd have him arrested. Mama and Papa Arno got together to decide what to do, and they called Ray and told him to wait at his house for them. When the rest of us went to dinner, they took Mitch to Ray's house, here in Eugene. Ray told him to clean himself up and they'd talk on Monday, that if he showed up at the inn, he'd beat him to a pulp. Then he came over. But on Monday when Ray got home, Mitch had left. He broke some lamps, spilled beer, left a mess; we think he might have broken into Papa's house, too, but he didn't do any damage there. Then he hit my house," she said furiously. "What if I'd been there with the girls?"

Her hands were shaking again. Barbara patted one and said, "Easy. You weren't, they weren't. So he tore up the place, no one got hurt."

"Right," Maggie said after taking another of her calming, deep breaths. "Anyway, Monday when I got home from Portland, there was a message on my phone machine from Ray, for me to call him back that night. And I called him from the hotel later. He told me Mitch had been there and was gone, and I began to cry, I guess, and I told him about the inn. He wanted to come over then and hang out, just be there if Mitch came back, but I told him that Tom Lasker was on guard, and he wouldn't be allowed in. That's why Mama and Papa came over the next morning with him. We got to the inn and Mama went to pieces again, but Irene kept saying it was her fault, for leaving the place open to air out, and Tom was there telling everyone it was simple vandalism. I really wanted to tell them, at least to tell Ray that Mitch had been there, get his advice about what I should do, but Mama was crying, and everyone talking at once, and Mama and Papa so upset. . . . I didn't mention that I had seen Mitch. No one mentioned Mitch. I got Ray to take Mama and Papa back home. No one could do anything until the insurance man finished. Then, the first chance I got, I really looked at Mitch's stuff. The suitcase looks very expensive, leather, with a keypad lock. And the briefcase is leather, with a keypad lock. It's really heavy. His sport coat is silk, with a New York tailor's label." Her voice dropped to a whisper. "He had seven hundred dollars in his wallet and eighty-two hundred dollars in a money clip. And I remembered something I hadn't thought of again. When I went to back my car out of the garage on Friday, I saw something shining on the floor and picked it up. A watch. I just put it in my pocket, and when I went inside the house again, I put it in my bag and forgot it." Now she rummaged in the big tote bag and drew out a Rolex and laid it on the table.

Martin stepped from the kitchen and stood in the doorway. "Barbara, you and your friends are welcome to sit as long as you need, but I have to warn you that in a few minutes I got to unlock the door and let customers in. It just won't be as private."

Startled, Barbara looked at her own watch. It was ten minutes before six. "We'll be done by six," she said. "Thanks. Maggie, tell me something about Ray. He keeps figuring in what's happened. Do you suppose he knew Mitch was coming back?"

Maggie shook her head hard. "No way. It's just that we all rely on him for so many things, he's the one we all call if the car won't start or the furnace makes weird noises. He was the first one I told when I got pregnant; he and Lorinne were engaged, and they offered to take me in, take care of me. For a while I was afraid my parents would kick me out. He's just always been there for me, for my daughters." She shrugged. "He's my pal and my big brother."

Barbara nodded, and Maggie leaned forward and asked, "Will you handle this for me? Have I told you enough?"

"Exactly what do you want me to do?"

"I want to track down Mitch and make him pay for all the damage, make him help send the girls to college, collect back child support. I don't know! But he must have gotten rich somehow. And my daughters have gone without a lot of things over the years. I don't want him to get away with this again. I want you to take all Mitch's stuff out of my house and put it away in a safe place, and keep that, too." She pushed the expensive watch toward Barbara.

"I don't want to touch anything of his. And will you deal with Trassi?"

"You're on," Barbara said. "As of right now we have a verbal agreement that will have to be put into writing, but later. A few quick questions. Is his car still in the day-use park? And what kind of car is it?" She slipped the Rolex into her bag.

"It's gone. It was gone on Monday when I went up to Portland with my brother. We drove past the park and I looked. I don't know what kind it was. Black, with leather seats, is all I know. Expensive."

In the next few minutes they agreed that Barbara would go to the inn and collect Mitch's stuff and put it in a safe-deposit box. Maggie gave her a brochure about the inn, where it was, how to get there. Barbara said she would bring out an agreement to be signed, and Maggie wrote a check for five hundred dollars, a retainer.

"I'll bring a detective with me," Barbara told her. "I'll want pictures of the damage. And you're not to say a word about any of this to anyone, and don't talk to Trassi at all. Not a word." She gave Maggie two cards, one to be handed over to Trassi, and they both stood up just as Martin walked out to unlock the door.

"By the way," Barbara said, beckoning Laurence to join them, "if you and your friend need a recommendation for dinner, you can't do better than right here."

Then she muttered, "Oh, God! Dinner! So long, Maggie, Laurence. I just remembered something I have to do. See you tomorrow." To Martin she said, "I'll settle up tomorrow or the next day. Okay?"

"Hold it just a second," he said. He went into the kitchen and returned with a paper bag. "Sauce for the salmon. Seven minutes an inch, under the broiler. Got that? Let it rest a minute, then sauce it. And a nice vinaigrette for the salad. Don't use that bottled stuff. I think Binnie tossed in something, don't know just what."

She hugged him and took the bag, feeling guilt and relief in equal measure. The last glance she had of Maggie and Laurence was of rather bewildered expressions cast her way, before they reseated themselves. They at least would eat very well.

3

Where had May, June, and July gone? It was not amnesia, because if she put her mind to it, she could fill in the weeks and months, most of them anyway. Although the first few weeks were a blur of lovemaking, eating, swimming, and more lovemaking. Then Aztec ruins. After she and John Mureau had spent weeks in Mexico, an earthquake had struck and John had been drawn to it irresistibly, and they had climbed rocky places so he could examine the wreckage, lecturing her on the physics of earth movements all the while. They had flown to New York and spent a few days, then on to Wheeling, West Virginia, so she could meet his two children. Barbara understood very well that part of her confusion about time was due to the fact that there were periods she had put away out of mind, to be thought about later.

She imagined that in her mind was an infinite file cabinet where she could store things that needed considering someday, but not right now. The meeting in Pikeville, Kentucky, with his mother and other family members was tucked away there, too.

Eventually they had flown to Denver, where he had stripped out a large four-wheel-drive camper van. As a geologist working as a mine-safety consultant, he spent a lot of time out in the field in the camper. She had been dismayed at the amount of stuff he had to move from his apartment, and more dismayed when she first saw his office. The desk alone would have filled her living room back in Eugene. He needed it to spread maps on, he had said. It had taken many days for him to pack up the things he would take in the camper, and then to arrange for movers to come for the rest.

Days and days in Denver had been followed by a slow drive to Eugene in the overloaded camper that struggled on hills in a way that made him clench his jaw hard enough for his scar to flare.

For more than a week they had stayed at Frank's house after they finally arrived in Eugene. A frantic search had started, a race to beat his belongings that were then in transit, a race that had ended here. And here was too small by half. A three-bedroom apartment that had looked good when it was empty. Now it was jammed with boxes, with *things.* Rolls of maps, file cabinets, big mover's boxes, some opened, some still taped, the camping gear he had taken out of the camper . . .

They ate on a card table that had to be folded up again when they were done. Two of the bedrooms were big enough for offices, they had thought at first, when the rooms were empty; the biggest bedroom would be theirs. And the little ones, after they were organized, were big enough for cots when the kids came to visit, he had said. Very carefully, wordlessly, she had stored that item away in her secret mental file cabinet.

That morning she was drinking a cup of coffee, standing by the sink with it, since the table was already folded up against the wall. Bailey was due any minute. She watched John finish cutting the tape on another box; he groaned.

"Only thing to do is open a window and start heaving stuff out," he said.

"Promises, promises."

Grinning, he crossed the few feet of space between them and took the cup from her hand. "Be back early?"

"As early as I can."

He nuzzled her neck.

"I'm sorry I said no," she said softly. "It turns out there was time."

"You'll pay, and pay, and pay," he murmured.

She laughed and pulled free, aware that if he kept it up, by the time Bailey arrived she'd look as sappy as little Mary Sunshine. The doorbell rang.

"And pay," John said ominously, and went to admit Bailey.

Bailey Novell came in, carrying an old denim daypack that he claimed held his junior detective kit. He said hi, and gazed about noncommittally. If Queen Elizabeth sashayed in with a rose between her teeth, he would look noncommittal, Barbara thought, picking up her briefcase and shoulder bag. Bailey was the best detective on the West Coast, her father sometimes said, and she had no reason to disagree, but he looked like a tramp in old hand-me-down clothes that never fitted right. John blew her a kiss and they left.

"Your car or mine?" Bailey asked outside the apartment building.

"Mine," she said, thinking of his expense account. Not only the best detective but one of the most expensive, that was Bailey.

"Okay, but you know your driving puts me in heart-attack territory."

She gave him a look. The apartment was at Fifteenth and Patterson, a nice walk to downtown and the office and courthouse, but too far to walk to Martin's, another annoyance. They got in her car and she headed for Eleventh, and westward.

"You might give a guy a little more warning next time," Bailey commented, slouched down in his seat.

She had not gotten around to calling him until almost ten-thirty last night. "Sorry," she said.

"You going to tell me why we're going to the coast, and why you wanted me to bring a gun?"

"Okay, just the highlights first. A woman's ex is on the rampage, he tore up her bed-and-breakfast place, and he may be crazy. I want a lot of pictures of everything. We're going to pick up some stuff and put it away in a safe-deposit box, so we have to get back before the bank closes. That's why the early start." It was then nine-thirty.

"Where's the place?"

Barbara bit her lip. She had not gotten around to looking at the brochure. "Somewhere between Florence and Newport. There's a brochure in my purse, with directions. You want to root around and find it and guide me in when we get to the coast?"

She pretended not to notice his swift glance at her; she was afraid the deadpan Bailey might be smiling.

He found the brochure and began to read, then he whistled. "It's only seven rooms to rent out, but pretty fancy. The lady loaded?"

"With seven rooms? Not likely. I think she must work pretty hard at it."

"Says her breakfasts are four-star events."

She sighed. She might have known Maggie would be a great cook.

"About ten miles south of Newport," Bailey said. "You should have gone up and out through Corvallis. Quicker that way." He put the brochure on the dashboard. "You going to give me any more than that?"

Traffic picked up; it was always heavy in the summer, and it would be worse coming back. The road was still straight, here on the outskirts of Eugene, but it would start snaking around hills, then mountains in the Coast Range, up and over and around for thirty miles, posted anywhere from ten miles an hour all the way up to thirty. She began to fill Bailey in on the details. When he began asking questions, she had few answers.

"Bailey, I just took her on as a client yesterday. Late yesterday."

"Be nice to know," he said gloomily. "See, the car could have been stolen. But if the ex got the car, and there was a gun locked up in the glove box, that's something else."

Her hands tightened on the steering wheel.

It was twelve o'clock when she pulled into the drive to Folsum House. Another time, she wanted to come back and explore the little town of Folsum, but not today. A white three-story building came into view, gleaming in the sunlight. There were several cars in front of the building, and as she got closer, she could see mattresses stacked at the top of several stairs that led to the open front door.

Maggie came out to meet them. She was hot and sweaty, her hair was tied up in a high ponytail to keep it off her neck; she looked years younger than the thirty-five she had admitted to. The deep shadowed hollows under her eyes were less noticeable, as if she had gotten some sleep the night before.

"Let's start at the top and work down," Barbara said after introducing Bailey. Two young men emerged from the house with another mattress. Bailey was already taking photographs.

A woman came toward them from a long hallway when they entered the building. She was muscular and lean, forty or forty-five, dressed in chino pants and a plaid shirt. "Irene Lasker," Maggie said. "This is the lawyer I told you would be coming. Ms. Holloway and her associate."

Irene Lasker nodded. "I told her not to trust that insurance man," she said. She stalked away again, muttering, "I hope they catch them and nail their hides to the wall, that's what I hope."

"Well, upward?" Barbara said, eyeing the stairs. Two men were starting down, carrying an upholstered chair; the seat, arms, and back had all been slashed, the stuffing pulled partway out.

"We'd better use the back stairs," Maggie said faintly, watching the men wrestle the chair down the staircase.

It was carnage from attic apartment all the way through. Paneling in the halls had been broken, storage spaces under eaves and stairs had been emptied, closets ransacked, drawers dumped, overturned. Worse than Maggie had described. Finally Maggie took them to her room, and closed and locked the door. Part of the room had been outfitted as an office; there was a twin-size bedframe, and clothing scattered everywhere. Papers were on the floor, drawers overturned on them.

Maggie went on to the bathroom, a large, oddly shaped room with hyacinth-blue and white tiles, a blue oversized tub, with a blue tile ledge in a sharply angled corner, blue cabinets. . . . Evidently a large flowerpot had been on the ledge; dirt, greenery, shards, were in the bottom of the tub. The cabinets had been emptied, hair dryer, towels, cosmetics, bowl cleaner. . . . A second door led to the girls' room, Maggie said. On the wall opposite the window were floor-to-ceiling open shelves that had been swept clean, and a lighted mirror over a vanity table and small chair. Maggie went to that wall.

She moved an upturned clothes hamper out of the way, moved the chair and then the vanity. Then she opened a panel in the wall. "Dad added the bedroom and bath when my mother got pregnant the first time. She didn't want an upstairs room and she wanted an adjoining room for a nursery. They angled it out for the view," she added. "And that made the bathroom this shape. They squared off some of the corners, but still there was space left where the pipes come in, and it was unusable, I guess, so they walled it off but left access to the plumbing."

She stood aside to let Barbara and Bailey get to the opening. It was too dark to see much. "Let's get pictures first," Barbara said, moving out of Bailey's way.

While he was getting the photographs, she glanced inside the girls' room. More carnage, more clothes strewn about. This room was lavender, and now she saw a painting of lavender flowers on the wall, a graceful spray of lilacs, and she recalled that every room had a flower painting. Lilacs, roses, sunflowers . . . She examined the painting; it was Laurence's, and it was very fine. Each room was decorated with colors that matched the colors he had used. The lavender bedroom, blue tinged with lavender in the bath, rose in Maggie's room. It must have been a very elegant bed-and-breakfast.

As soon as Bailey was done, he dragged the stuff into Maggie's bedroom and took more pictures of everything.

"Tape and seal the suitcase and briefcase, will you," Barbara said to Bailey. "I'll get the paperwork out of the way. Not over the key-pad locks," she added. He scowled; he knew that, she understood. Maggie cleared enough space on her desk for the laptop, and very quickly Barbara filled in the information on the fee agreement, and then quickly keyed in another agreement, her obligations and Maggie's. She finished almost as soon as Bailey was done.

"I want a look in the duffel bag," Barbara said.

Very quickly Bailey said, "We should find something to dump it out in, something smooth."

Maggie rummaged in the tangle of clothes and brought out a white blouse, which she spread on the floor.

After Bailey dumped the bag, they all gazed at a lead pipe and leather holder. "What . . . ?" Maggie said, reaching for it. Bailey caught her hand.

"Don't touch," he said. He found a plastic bag in his gear, and latex gloves that he pulled on; then he carefully picked up the pipe and holder and put them inside the bag. He held it by the top and let them look. "Hair, fibers, blood, all that expert detective stuff." He put the plastic bag back inside the duffel. No one commented as he picked up the other items and replaced them in the duffel bag. Dirty shirts, underwear, socks, shaving kit . . . After that, he made a note of the tailor's name in the silk coat, then he counted the money in the clip. "Eighty-two hundred." Maggie nodded. In the wallet they found $728 and identification in the name of Gary Belmont. Driver's license, insurance card, Social Security card, all in Belmont's name.

Barbara picked up a little notebook. "Okay if I keep this with me? Could help track him down."

Maggie shrugged, and Barbara slipped the notebook into her bag and brought out the Rolex, which she added to the duffel bag.

"Is that Mitch?" she asked then, handing the driver's license to Maggie.

"Superficially it resembles him. Dark hair, at least. The statistics are almost right: six feet two, a hundred ninety-five pounds. Mitch is six one, and not that heavy."

"Okay. I'll write up an inventory of the stuff you're turning over to me, explain the various agreements, then a quick look outside, and we have to beat it."

It didn't take long. She explained the various papers to Maggie and was pleased to see that Maggie was actually reading them. She feared for clients who didn't read what they signed. A few minutes later they were ready.

"This end of the house can be closed off from the paying guests," Maggie said at an outside door near her room. "We have a little privacy that way, and use this as a private entrance."

"How close can we get my car?" Barbara asked.

"The driveway is over there, past my room," Maggie said, opening the door to a terrace. "You can't see it from here."

Barbara could see why the room had been angled as it had been. One wall with many windows faced northwest, one faced southwest; the view in either direction was magnificent—ocean, beach, cliffs.

"Be right back," Bailey said; he started around the house toward the garage.

"I want to walk out there a bit," Barbara said. She left Maggie in the doorway. The house was two hundred feet in from the edge of the rocky cliff, which was like a peninsula jutting out from the mainland. At the edge she stopped to gaze down. It was almost a straight drop from here to the beach, about seventy-five feet down, although on both sides the cliff sloped in a scalable fashion. A rustic split-log fence outlined the edge in both directions. She followed it to a break, where a trail zigzagged downward.

When she returned to Maggie, she said, "Wow! It's great!"

"Yes," Maggie said. "It is. When there's a storm, a real gale, spray comes up over the fence."

Bailey came around the corner of the house. "Both cars torn apart," he said morosely. "Walk over and look around. I'll bring the car back to pick you up, and while you're looking, I'll load the stuff. What did you do with his car keys?" he asked Maggie.

For a moment she looked blank, then she paled. "Oh, God, I forgot all about the keys. They're in my jeans. The jeans are—they were in the bathroom hamper."

They all went back to the bathroom. Maggie pulled the jeans out from under other things and felt in the pockets. "They're gone," she whispered.

When they left the bed-and-breakfast, Barbara headed north and drove slowly past the day-use park. It was jammed full, and the cars were visible from the road, which was no more than a narrow access road to the park and the inn. A mile farther up, it joined the coast road, 101. At Newport, Bailey told her to pull in at a drive-through fast-food place. Then, eating hamburgers, they headed out of Newport, back toward Eugene. It was ten minutes to three. She waited until Bailey had finished his second hamburger to ask, "Well? Comments? Observations? Anything?"

"Two guys. They were searching and being fast and careless about it. One's a lefty," he added.

"How do you know one's a lefty?" she asked, passing a truck. He groaned.

"Close your eyes and imagine—God help me, I didn't say that! Just imagine, open-eyed, how you'd go about yanking stuff out of a closet. Which hand you open it with, which one you grab stuff with, how you toss it."

She had no trouble visualizing it, but she had not seen it herself. "Gotcha," she said.

"And he's got the car keys," he said gloomily.

A little later she said, "See what you can dig up about Belmont. Could be Arno's alias. And if Mitch has a record. You know the drill."

"Barbara, Belmont's from New Orleans."

"So? I don't expect you to go there and pound on doors. Just dig a little." She drove for a minute or two, thinking, then said, "Maggie will stay at the hotel for a while, and no doubt Trassi will get to her. He'll probably give me a call tomorrow. It would be helpful if I had a little information before I talk to him."

"Wish for the moon. Tomorrow?"

"It's a thought."

They got to her bank in Eugene ten minutes before it closed at five-thirty. There had been a log truck on the Corvallis road with traffic lined up behind it for miles. She parked illegally out front long enough to carry the stuff from the trunk inside the bank, then handed the keys to Bailey, who would move the car. When she was finished with the safe-deposit rental business, she made a Xerox copy of Maggie's check and deposited it and two other much smaller ones, and she was done.

Bailey was waiting for her. "Now the notebook," she said, but hesitated. He had to look through it, but where? Her office at the apartment was impossible; she couldn't even close the door. Not her father's office; the firm was closed by then, and she didn't want to use her key to get in. "How about a drink?" she said finally.

"How about that," he said with more enthusiasm than he had shown all day.

"Where's the car?"

"Two-hour parking slot. It's okay. Let's walk over to the Park Bar and Grill."

They crossed the street and walked through the small urban park with its big fountain, walked one more block and entered the cool, dim bar.

There, in a booth with a gin and tonic before her, a double bourbon on the rocks before him, they sat side by side and looked over the notebook.

"What the hell?" he said. "Foreign telephone numbers?" He flipped the page to find more foreign numbers. Not written by a European, Barbara thought; the sevens were all American, not slashed. Bailey flipped to the next page. "These I know. Seattle area codes. San Francisco." He copied all the numbers in his own notebook.

There was a long string of numbers without any notation to indicate what they were for. Under them was a flight number. The letters *f* and *l* and the number.

A woman's handwriting, Barbara thought, studying the two letters. At the bottom of the page, printed in capitals with a different pen, a felt tip, was the word PENELOPY.

Bailey closed his notebook and stowed it away in a pocket, and she slipped the other one back into her bag. They finished their drinks and walked to her car, and she drove to her apartment.

"I'd offer to give you a call," he said at the car door when they got out, "but damned if I know where to call."

"Shit! Look, I'll see Trassi in Dad's office. When he makes the appointment, I'll leave a message on your machine. If you can get there half an hour or so before him, that should give us time enough."

Bailey saluted and slouched away toward his own car, and she thought, Goddamn it! She would have to use the office, after all. There wasn't any other place where she and Trassi could have a private talk.

When she opened the apartment door, the fragrance of spicy enchiladas hit her. The card table was set, with an unlit candle, a bottle of wine, and a rose in a glass, and John was hurrying from his office.

"You said you'd be home early," he whispered into her ear, drawing her in close.

"I said as early as I could," she murmured, setting her briefcase down, letting her shoulder bag slide to the floor.

 4

When she closed the bedroom door without a sound the next morning, she saw the clutter that she had overlooked the night before. It was worse than ever. At her office door she stopped, rigid with rage. He had moved her desktop computer to the side and put two of his file drawers on her desk. She went to shower and took a long time, willing her anger to ebb and flow out with the water.

He had to work, he had said days ago. It had been months since he had done any serious work. He would get to the stuff as soon as he could; every day he would get more of it stowed away, but he had to work.

Every day he unearthed more junk, and nothing vanished.

The shower had helped some, she thought, wrestling the card table out from behind a box. She set up the table in the kitchen space, started a pot of coffee, and retrieved her laptop from the floor where she had placed it the day before. In spite of herself, she had to smile at the briefcase and purse just inside the door. *All right,* she told herself, *just go with it for now.*

She had finished her notes and was working on a plan of action when John came from the bedroom, naked.

"How can it be? You look as good at eight in the morning as at midnight." He kissed the top of her head and was in the process of turning her chair toward him when she pushed him back.

"Working," she said as lightly as she could.

"Can't it wait?"

"No. Go take a shower."

"In a minute. You know that Staley mine I told you about? The assholes are challenging my findings! I spent hours trying to find my original notes and pictures."

She looked at her monitor. Her hand had been on the keyboard; nearly a whole page of *F*'s filled the screen. "Shit!"

"My thought exactly," he said, pouring coffee. He carried it out with him through the little hallway to the bathroom. She heard the shower.

After cleaning up the *F*'s, she sat staring at the last work she had keyed in, *Trassi,* then had to backtrack in an attempt to recover her train of thought. Where was his office? Who were his clients?

John returned with a towel around him. Water dripped on her arm as he passed her. Very carefully, she saved her work and closed the laptop.

"Don't go," he said. "You're not in the way. Want some scrambled eggs?"

Standing up, keeping her voice calm with great effort, she said, "What's all that stuff on my desk?"

"What stuff?" He went to look, then said, "Oh, God, I'm sorry. I was looking for that Staley file. I'll get it off today."

"But you thought it was perfectly all right to put it there. I can't go in my own office and use my own desk, close my own door. And you say I'm not in the way."

"Hey," he said softly. "I'm sorry. I shouldn't have done it. Can't you use the downtown office today? Or your father's place?"

Still unnaturally quiet, she said, "I've tried hard to keep my private business out of the office. Today I *have* to go there because I don't have anywhere else." Her voice rose and she stood up. "And I hardly think it's my father's responsibility to provide me with working space."

"Barbara, Christ, what else can I say except I'm sorry. Can't you put off working until we get things better organized?"

"My office *was* organized, but I can't use it." She picked up her briefcase and purse. "I have to go."

She started for the door, then stopped and spun around to face him. "Oh, my God," she said. "We're fighting."

He nodded miserably, and this time when he tried to hold her, she did not resist. "I'm sorry," she said. "Frustration, I guess."

"My fault. I just kept thinking of that damn Staley file. I'm really sorry."

"Okay." His arms tightened around her. "I really do have to go." Drawing back from him, she touched his lips with her fingertip. "Not much of a fight, slugger. We'll do better next time."

He shook his head. "No next time. Back early?"

"As early as I can."

She sat in her car for a minute or two. Go, but where? Eventually she had to go to the courthouse and do a little research, and she had to get to a phone and call Ruthie at Frank's downtown firm, and she had to call her father, and . . . *Oh, cut it out,* she told herself then. She headed for her father's house.

When he met her at the door, a huge smile crossed his face instantly. "Bobby! Just in time for some breakfast."

Not *How are you? Is anything wrong?* Just *Come on in and eat.* She smiled back gratefully.

In the kitchen a few minutes later, she eyed him suspiciously. "Is that oatmeal?"

"You betcha. Good, too. Maple syrup on it. Cyrus tells me I eat too much high-cholesterol food." Cyrus was his doctor.

She felt a pang at the reminder that her father was considered elderly, was elderly, and a possible candidate for a heart attack or plaque-clogged arteries or something else. Frank was seventy-four, seventy-five? Somewhere around there.

"Where are the monsters?" she asked, watching him spoon oatmeal into a bowl for her.

"Backyard. They can't come in. Fleas. Later on I intend to walk over to the garden shop and see if they have any of those nematodes you can use on the lawn. Just spray it on and the little buggers knock off all kinds of pests. Then I'll give the cats a bath. And hope for the best." He didn't sound hopeful.

The oatmeal was good. They ate in silence. Then she asked if she could use his downtown office sometime during the day for about an hour or two.

"Honey," he said reproachfully, "that's your office, too. You know you can, anytime you want. What's up?"

"Another lawyer, maybe from California, maybe not. I want to make him believe I'm for real."

Frank laughed. "You going to look him up in the ABA reference? Quote his own lies to him?" He felt about Los Angeles attorneys the way most people felt about all lawyers.

"Something like that. And would you mind if I park in the upstairs office for a time? Our place is still uninhabitable."

She was well aware of his shrewd appraisal, but he made no comment, asked nothing, just said sure.

One of the golden coon cats started to scratch on the screen door. She no longer could tell them apart, just Thing One and Thing Two. The other one pounced on the first one and they both rolled across the porch and tumbled down the few steps to the ground.

She told Frank in vague terms about a "he said, she said" case she had taken on; he told her about Mrs. Gillespie's new will. She called Ruthie at the office and told her to set up an appointment with Trassi anytime after two, and to call back here. When she hung up, she caught Frank's gaze on her. He was smiling.

"It's good to have you here like this, shooting the breeze," he said.

"Yeah, it is. I'll wash up. You can go about your business," she said.

"Just don't let those fool cats in." He went to his den to collect his own briefcase and notes.

Barbara worked awhile, paced, worked some more. Ruthie called, and Barbara called Bailey's number and left the message on his machine: "He's coming at two. I'll get there at one. See you."

By the time she entered the offices of Bixby, Holloway, and a couple dozen others, she had done all her chores: laptop work, courthouse records, notes, a game plan for "he said, she said" . . .

One o'clock was slack time at the office; nearly everyone was off to lunch. One of the stenographers was filling in at the reception desk; Barbara asked her to send Bailey on back when he got there, and went down the corridor to Frank's office.

It was spacious with high and wide windows, a lot of fine paneling, glass-fronted bookcases, forest-green leather-covered chairs and couch, a very nice coffee table—the kind of room where you could tell your lawyer your deepest, darkest secret without fear.

Bailey arrived ten minutes later. "Hi," he said. He glanced toward the bookshelves that concealed a bar.

"Help yourself," she said, and watched him go straight to the shelf with the *T*'s, open it, and stand considering the choices. "You could start talking," she suggested sarcastically.

"Oh, yeah. Forget Gary Belmont. Dead. Mugged, killed with the good old blunt instrument down in New Orleans during the night of July twenty-three. Found on the twenty-fourth by a biologist pursuing the mating habits of alligators." He poured bourbon, then seated himself in one of the client's chairs. "That one was easy, New Orleans newspaper, on the Web. Nothing on Arno. Clean, or he uses some other alias. The telephone numbers. Two restaurants and a pharmacy in Zurich, Switzerland. A restaurant and a hotel in Paris. A deli and a bookstore in Seattle. A hotel in San Francisco." He shrugged. "There are a couple of others, but you get the drift. All places like that—bookstores, restaurants, nothing personal, no individual." He sipped the bourbon straight and eyed her over the glass.

"I'm afraid your guy might be wanted for murder."

"Tell me about it," she said, frowning. "Anything else about Belmont?"

"Born and raised in the area, live-in girlfriend. Worked the docks, hit the bars and nightspots, gambled. Last seen in a bar in the Quarter. Arno might have cruised looking for a good-enough resemblance, then hit. Or maybe he knew the guy. However that goes, he ended up with the ID."

And added a whole other dimension to the case, she thought glumly. She couldn't conceal evidence of a felony crime. She remembered a saying a friend of hers had quoted once: "Heaven is high and the emperor is far away." She said, "Back burner. At least for now."

Bailey shrugged and finished the drink. He rummaged in his bag and brought out some folded papers, his reports. "The flight number is United out of Miami, a daily nonstop to San Francisco."

She watched absently as he regarded the glass for a moment, as if considering. He set the glass down and waited.

"Look," she said, "Trassi's due in a few minutes. Can you hang around to get a peek at him? And I might have something after he's gone. Can do?"

"Barbara," he said reasonably, "it's my job, what I get paid for. I'll mosey back in when he's gone. See ya."

"Take that with you," she said, pointing to the glass.

By the time Ruthie called her to say Trassi was there, she had put Bailey's report in her briefcase and spread some yellow pads on the desk, one of them opened with her notes. She left them and walked out to meet Trassi.

"Barbara Holloway," she said at the reception desk. "Mr. Trassi?"

"Yes." He was slightly built, fiftyish, with sparse hair carefully combed over a bald spot, and he was very pale and gray—hair, eyes, expensive suit, all gray. His handshake was perfunctory, hardly more than a touching of her hand.

"The office is this way," Barbara said. He was looking around at everything; people had returned from lunch, some were still trickling in; there was a murmur of voices, a laugh from the stenographer's room.

In the office, with him in the chair Bailey had used, and her behind the desk, she asked pleasantly, "Would you like a cup of coffee? Tea, perhaps?"

"No."

He had examined the office with the same careful scrutiny he had shown in the corridor. Now he sat primly with his feet together, his hands on the arms of the chair in what looked like a very uncomfortable position.

"I don't know why your client thought it necessary to employ legal counsel for what is a very simple request," he said.

Barbara glanced down at the open legal pad and closed it. "As you see, however, she did seek counsel," she said.

"Mitch Arno is basically a messenger," he said, "a courier, no more than that, but a highly trusted courier until this incident." He told the same story she had heard from Maggie. When Barbara did not comment, he said coldly, "Arno left our material at his ex-wife's inn. We need to recover it."

Barbara nodded. "So they sent you. Why you?"

"Because I can identify the bags, and I can open them. I can identify the contents. We assumed I could reason with Ms. Folsum, explain the situation to her, and compensate her for any trouble this has caused."

"Have you requested police help in locating Mitch Arno?"

"No! Absolutely not! We are constrained by the nature of the papers he was carrying. It must not be known that such sensitive material was out of our hands for even a second. This must be kept confidential."

He leaned forward. "What we propose, Ms. Holloway, is a meeting with Ms. Folsum, long enough for me to demonstrate that I have the combination to both of those locks. I shall show her enough of the papers to prove my point. In your presence, of course. We are willing to pay her five thousand dollars, and to cover any uninsured losses to her inn."

Barbara shook her head kindly. "I'm afraid that won't work," she said. "Ms. Folsum doesn't have anything of Mitch Arno's lying about, nothing less than eighteen years old, from the time he abandoned her. Of course, you could get a court order to force anyone who might have happened across your material to release it. With the proper identification, verification of employment of Arno, a statement from him, certified authorization from your company, you know, all those petty details, you might gain possession. No doubt everything would have to be opened in a judge's chambers to verify the contents of the bags, in such an event."

"What do you want?"

He had not shown any anger and showed none now. Ah, she thought, he had been kissed by the Snow Queen. He could neither laugh nor cry.

"I was working on that earlier," she said, and opened her legal pad. "At five hundred a month for child support for the older child, for eighteen years, I arrived at one hundred and eight thousand dollars. For the younger daughter, the figure is one hundred and two thousand. Seventeen years," she said, looking up pleasantly. "The damage to the inn has yet to be determined, as has the cost of the loss of business."

His eyes narrowed, his only reaction.

"We want to talk to Mitch Arno and arrange a settlement with him," she said, closing the pad again. "If we can't reach an agreement with him, we are prepared to institute garnishment proceedings, in which case a third party who happens to hold property or money belonging to the defendant would be ordered by the court to retain such property awaiting due process. An investigation, of course, would follow—full disclosure, proof of ownership, and so forth." She stood up. "Is that all?"

"For now," he said, rising.

She went to open the door for him, then watched him walk down the corridor and out of the reception area.

She was deep in thought when she heard Bailey's characteristic tap on the door. "It's open," she called.

He shambled in and took his chair.

"Get a look at him?"

"More. I tagged along after him. He headed for the pay phone in the lobby downstairs, changed his mind, and used one half a block up the street. Called two numbers, one probably long-distance. At least he used a card on that one. One local. I had to keep back because he's got smarts. He was watching his tail. Then he went to the Hilton."

She nodded. "Can you get those two bags open? The suitcase and briefcase?"

"Sure. I'll bring a hacksaw."

"I want a look," she said. "Now, today, tonight."

He nodded, then said, "But I'd like a little reassurance that my hand isn't going to be blown off."

She told him about her meeting with Trassi, and finished saying, "He doesn't want cops, and he never batted an eye when I said two hundred ten thousand. I want to see what's in them. I think he believes we've already opened them. He'll consult with his client and come back with a better offer."

"Where?" Bailey asked then. "Not at the bank."

"No. Here. We'll have to get the stuff over here, preferably without his knowing, just in case he's keeping an eye on us. And Maggie will have to be present."

He reached down and pulled a glass from his bag, then held it up inquiringly. It was her father's glass, the one Bailey had taken out with him. When she motioned toward the bookshelves, he went over, opened the bar, and poured himself a drink. Bailey was polite; he never helped himself without permission.

She waited. At last he said, "Can you get Maggie over here by seven-thirty?"

Barbara said yes, and hoped it was true. She was aware that everything she was doing was involving her father deeper and deeper in whatever it was she was mixed up in. She had to involve him. She couldn't put that stuff in his office safe without his knowledge and permission.

"Use your phone?" Bailey asked. She nodded and went to sit on the couch; he pulled the phone around to him and dialed. She heard his greeting: "Sylvia, how's things?" His voice dropped then and he talked, listened, even laughed once, but finally he hung up and came to sit in an overstuffed chair across the coffee table from her.

"Okay, all set," he said.

 5

At ten minutes past three Barbara decided that Frank was not home, and she stood undecided what to do next.

Finally she unlocked the door, then entered his house, and heard him cursing. She followed the sound through the wide hallway, past the living room and the dining room, and found him in the downstairs bathroom on his knees at the bathtub.

"Goddamn it, you do that again and I'll wring your neck."

There was a tremendous splash, and water sprayed from the tub all over him. "You little fucker, you misbegotten son of a bitch!"

Grinning, she backed away and went to the kitchen, then called out, "Dad, you around somewhere?"

Now she heard a cat's furious yowling. Frank yelled, "Be right with you." The bathroom door slammed.

She stood at the back door, laughing. He came out in a few minutes, and one of the Things streaked past the kitchen and up the stairs, yelling. It was soaked to the skin.

"Turn on the sprinkler and those fool cats play in it like kids.

Roll around in the birdbath. A real bath and they turn into maniacs," Frank said. "But I did them, both of them, blast their eyes."

He went to the sink and washed his hands, then got a glass of water and drank most of it before he turned back to look at her.

"Are you going to go get dry?" she asked.

"No. Feels good this way."

"Can we talk a little?"

"Sure. Coffee? Something else?"

"No, thanks. It's about private business, a case I've taken on at Martin's, but I've already used your office, and I have another favor to ask. I need to use the safe."

"Okay. So use it. You going to fill in more than that?"

She told him about it. He whistled when she said $210,000.

"And he didn't bat an eye," she said. "I'm convinced he thinks we've already gotten inside that suitcase, that we know what we're talking about. But we don't."

"Drug money? Drugs? Secret plans to take over the world? New and better Pentagon Papers? Maps to militia caches? Could be anything. Industrial spying, national security stuff . . . Corporate plans to conquer the stock market. It could be FBI or CIA business." He shrugged. "Could even be what he claims it is, legitimate company business. You on contingency?"

"Of course not."

"Okay. Wishful thinking. So you and Bailey will get the stuff to the office around five. I'll drop in, check my mail, cheer up Patsy. She thinks I spend too much time somewhere else." Patsy was his secretary.

"Thanks," she said. "I've got to run. Bank at four-thirty. Bailey said he and Sylvia would be there waiting."

"Sylvia? He's bringing in Sylvia?" Frank laughed. "You'll love her."

"You know her?"

"Oh, Lord, yes. Sometime when you have an hour, I'll tell you about Sylvia. Beat it now, or you'll be late."

Get there at four-thirty, Bailey had said, *and go to the safe-deposit boxes.* She did that, and her bank escort used her key to open the box, then watched as Barbara inserted hers and turned it. The door swung open; the escort withdrew and pulled the vault door closed behind her. Barbara brought out the suitcase, the briefcase, and duffel bag, shut the drawer, and rang the bell for her escort. She had forgotten how heavy the briefcase was.

"I'm ready," she said.

Her escort was careful not to glance at the things Barbara had, but they both turned to look toward an open door outside the safe-deposit area, where a woman was saying in a quarrelsome way, "I told you I wanted to put the earrings in there. Why didn't you watch?" Another escort was standing at the door, gazing fixedly at her shoes, as if this has been going on for a while. "Now I have to get back in." The door swung open all the way, and a man pushed a wheelchair out of a small private room. Barbara blinked. Bailey, in a black suit and tie. The woman was grotesque, orange hair frizzy about her face, big dangling earrings that looked like emeralds, a long multicolored skirt, and a garish red filmy top; one leg was in a cast. She looked to be seventy or older.

"Barbara! Barbara Holloway! You remember me! Sylvia Fenton, we met at some silly luncheon. My dear, you look wonderful."

Bailey gazed at the ceiling with a wooden expression; both escorts looked at the floor.

"How are you?" Barbara said, feeling inordinately stupid. The old woman had a broken leg, that's how she was.

"Not too bad, considering. My dear child, you surely don't intend to carry all that by yourself, do you? Ridiculous! Ralph, help her."

"Oh, I couldn't impose," Barbara said hurriedly.

"We'll deliver it wherever you say," the old woman said. "Ralph, put it in the office here, while I go get rid of those earrings. Miss," she said to her escort, "I'm afraid we have to open the door again. If it's not too much bother. Ralph, where's my key? Put this bag somewhere and help me with my crutches. If you'd been paying attention, we wouldn't be having all this fuss."

Bailey took a large paisley print bag from her, carried it back inside the office, and came out with crutches. They all watched anxiously as she got up and supported herself on the crutches. "Put that damn chair back in the office and stay with my bag," she told Bailey. Then she said to Barbara, "Just tell him where you want the stuff delivered, dear. I won't be a minute, then we'll drop it off on our way home."

"Centennial Bank," Barbara said. "I was going there from here." She looked at Bailey, who appeared bored unto death. "If it's really no bother—"

"No, ma'am. No bother. I'll just put your things in here with her bag. And stand guard," he added.

"Thank you," Barbara said, and shrugged at her escort. "I guess that's all."

She left the bank and walked the two blocks to the other bank, where she rented a box exactly like the one she had just emptied, and ten minutes later Bailey entered, carrying all three bags. "She said I should carry them down for you," he said in a patient voice. They were escorted to the vaults by a male this time.

Bailey put the bags down, and she handed him a ten-dollar bill. "You've been so kind," she said.

"Thanks. Appreciate that." He left, and she put the bags in a drawer. Ringers, she realized; they looked all right, but were subtly different, and also empty, and lightweight.

Afterward, back in her father's office, she paced. Frank sat on the couch, grinning. "Now what?" she demanded.

"I wouldn't spoil this for anything. Relax, he'll be along in a minute or two."

In a few minutes Ruthie buzzed them; Bailey had arrived. Barbara ran to open the door and saw Bailey pushing the wheelchair down the corridor toward her. Mrs. Fenton's big paisley bag was on the seat, and Bailey was smiling.

"Nothing to it," he said.

Barbara watched as he opened the paisley bag and drew out the duffel, then opened the back of the wheelchair and took out the briefcase, and finally removed the seat and brought out the suitcase. "See? Slick as a whistle. Sylvia was great." He reassembled the chair.

"Where is she?" Barbara asked, imagining the woman hobbling down on the street, giving orders right and left.

"Talking to her broker on the first floor, making a scene, I bet. I came up the service elevator. Gotta run. Take her home, get a bite to eat, back here at seven-thirty. See ya."

Oh, God, Barbara thought in dismay. Eat. Again. She waited impatiently as Frank took his time opening the wall safe tucked way behind the bookshelves. As soon as everything was put away, the safe locked up, she said, "Dad, I have to go. Seven-thirty."

He watched with a faint smile as she snatched up her bag and ran out. Under his breath, he said, "Ah, Bobby."

Maggie was late; she had borrowed Irene's car, she said, and it was cranky and slow. After Barbara introduced her to Frank, they gathered around the coffee table and the suitcase and briefcase. Bailey touched a key. A tiny red light came on in the upper corner, blinked once and went out. He scowled.

"You understand that there are people who can get into them without destroying them," he said darkly. "I'm not one of those people." He looked at Barbara, who shrugged. Then he turned to Maggie.

"Break them open," Maggie said. "I don't care."

"Right. Over at the desk." He carried both cases to the desk and picked up his denim bag. When Barbara started to move around the desk to watch, he said, "Beat it."

She went back to the couch with Maggie and Frank.

When everyone was settled, Frank asked, "Has Folsum House been an inn a long time?"

"Ten years," Maggie said. "That was another reason for the party, to celebrate my tenth year there."

"You started it?" Barbara asked, surprised again by this young woman. "At twenty-five?"

"I had some help," Maggie said. "Laurence's father made it happen. After Mitch left for good, Papa Arno got me a job at Cliff Top Hotel. Mama Arno baby-sat the girls while I worked, and gradually I was learning something about how a hotel is run. Then Mr. Thielman bought Cliff Top. He does that, finds a hotel with potential and buys it, renovates it and trains local people, then sells it to a chain. He trained me."

"All this leads up to how you became an innkeeper at twenty-five?" Frank asked. Barbara pretended she was not watching Bailey.

Maggie nodded. "About then, my mother began to talk about moving to California to be closer to my brother Richard, and then one day they told me they were putting our house up for sale. I was still living with them with the girls; it was all I could afford. Everyone just assumed I would go, too. Then Mr. and Mrs. Thielman asked me to come into his office for a talk, and he asked me if I wanted to move to Los Angeles, and I said no. He made a proposition. Why didn't I buy the house and turn it into a bed-and-breakfast? He had trained me well; I knew everything there was to know about how to run it, and it would provide a living for me and my children as long as I wanted it to. I nearly laughed in his face. I didn't have a penny to my name."

Across the room Bailey muttered something unintelligible. Of course, Barbara thought, it was a metal case and the lock was probably an integral part of the frame. She wanted to call out for him to use a blowtorch.

Maggie was still talking. "Mrs. Thielman said Laurence was unhappy about their coming sale of Cliff Top and moving on, this time to Singapore. He refused to go. He was in art school in Chicago and wanted to finish, and then live on the coast and paint. She said they both understood his need to prove himself, but on the other hand he was so young, only nineteen then, that if he did manage to find a suitable apartment, he would never keep it. It would be robbed in his absence or he would spend rent money on art supplies or a trip somewhere or something else." She smiled faintly. "Their offer was incredible. If I would let Laurence have the attic apartment, they would pay his rent in advance every year for ten years. They had already sent someone out to look over the house and see if it could be converted, and Mr. Thielman had an estimate of what it would cost. Mrs. Thielman said they would be relieved, knowing that Laurence had a home to return to, where his belongings would be safe, where he could paint, and after ten years he would be on his own.

"They made it happen. I had no credit and I couldn't borrow the kind of money it would have taken, but they bought our house, and the next day they sold it to me. They carry the mortgage. I've never missed a payment, and next month Laurence has to start paying rent or get kicked out."

"Hats off," Frank said quietly. "You did it and you did it alone."

"Not altogether," she said. "The second year I was about to go under, and Papa Arno came to my rescue and loaned me money. If it hadn't been for his and Mama Arno's trust and faith, and Mr. and Mrs. Thielman's belief that I could do it, it wouldn't have worked."

There was a loud snapping from the other side of the room. They all watched as Bailey pushed the suitcase aside and pulled the briefcase around.

A little later Frank and Maggie were discussing whether commercial art, illustrations, could be considered real art. Laurence hated doing commercial art, she said, although he was very good at it, but he refused to do more than enough to scrape by. Evidently that was a sore point in their relationship.

Just then there was another snapping noise and Bailey said, "Done."

They hurried across the room to the desk.

"They're unlocked," Bailey said. "Tape's still in place. Whose move?"

"I'll do it," Barbara said. No one stirred or spoke as she peeled the tape off the suitcase, then lifted the lid. Maggie gasped. Barbara let out a long low whistle. Money, stacks of money bundled in neat rows.

"Don't touch," Bailey said. He got a pair of latex gloves from his kit and pulled them on, then he lifted out a bundle of hundred-dollar bills and riffled through it, replaced it, and pulled out a second one. "Ten thousand in the bundles." He counted. "Two hundred fifty thousand, looks like, except one's been tapped." He counted that one. "Ten grand missing. Two hundred forty thousand bucks. Used bills. Not in sequence. If they're marked, it's going to take a real examination to see how."

Silently, leaving the suitcase open, Barbara peeled off the tape on the briefcase and opened it. Papers. A thick stack of papers. Bailey, still wearing the gloves, lifted the stack out and set it on the table. Computer printouts, hundreds, perhaps thousands of sheets of flimsy fanfold printouts in computerese, totally meaningless to Barbara. The print was so small, it appeared almost illegible.

Bailey examined the briefcase; nothing else was in it. After a quick look at Barbara, then Frank, who both nodded, he returned the stack of printouts to the briefcase; Barbara closed it. Then, more slowly, she closed the suitcase.

Bailey left soon after that, saying he'd be in touch.

Maggie sat on the couch with a dazed expression. "Where did that money come from?"

Barbara shrugged. She was thinking it was no wonder that Trassi had shown no surprise at the figure she had arrived at for child-support arrears.

"What we should do," she said, thinking out loud, "is keep all that in the office safe until we know where it came from, whose money it was, and why Mitch had it. And he's the one who can tell us those things." She looked steadily at Maggie. "He'll have to get in touch with you. He doesn't know about me. Don't stay at the inn at night for the time being; stay down at the hotel, with a lot of people around you. If he calls, give him my name and number, and if he shows up, the same. Tell him you'll meet him here, but don't talk to him alone anywhere." Maggie was wide-eyed and pale. She moistened her lips.

"If he tries to get rough," Barbara said matter-of-factly, "scream, yell, make noise to get others to gather around. Just don't go off alone with him for even a minute." She waited for Maggie's nod. "Okay, then. We'll put everything back in the safe. Bailey's running down what he can, and until we get some answers, or see Mitch himself, there's nothing else we can do except sit tight and wait. And don't talk to anyone, not a word. Agreed?"

"Yes," Maggie said.

Then Frank said, "Maggie, you can't drive home alone, not at this hour. I have three upstairs rooms going to waste, without a living soul in them, unless it's a cat. Cats in my house are bootable. Stay over and drive back in daylight."

"He's right," Barbara said. "You shouldn't be out alone at night, not until we know more than we do now. I left gowns and things in the closet and drawers. Please help yourself."

Maggie hesitated only briefly, then said thanks, she would be glad not to drive out now. After putting everything back in the safe, they left; Maggie followed Frank home, and Barbara hurried to her own apartment.

In his house, after showing Maggie the upstairs rooms, turning on lights for her, Frank went to his own bedroom and eyed the coon cats at the foot of his bed, well aware that they had not forgiven him.

He admired Maggie quite a lot, he reflected. Courage, good sense, determination, all admirable qualities that she had in abundance. He understood her need to throw a big party, to demonstrate to everyone that she had done it. He had great sympathy for young women like her, working so hard to prove their worth to a world that was either disbelieving or indifferent, or both. Even when they succeeded, the world tended to say, So what, can you cook?

He realized he had switched tracks and was considering his own daughter, who was also struggling to prove something. Of the two, Maggie and Barbara, Barbara's self-appointed task was the harder. She had a tougher critic: herself.

"Okay, you monsters," he growled then. "Move over." Usually when he turned down the bed, the cats moved, took up their positions like two warm guardians, one on each side. Tonight they looked at him with golden eyes and did not move. When he took them in to have them neutered, they had not forgiven him for a week. He wondered which they considered worse, having a bath or having their balls cut off. He squirmed into bed and pushed one with his foot until he had room enough, and although usually he promptly fell asleep, that night he lay thinking about the suitcase and briefcase, thinking about Mitch Arno. Why hadn't Mitch Arno called or come back?

He didn't like the answer he was getting.

6

"Hot," Barbara murmured when she and John returned home from a hike up Spencer's Butte on Saturday. John fiddled with the air conditioner, and she hit the MESSAGE button on the phone, then began to unlace her boots. She stopped moving when Maggie's voice came on.

"Barbara, it's Maggie. Are you there? Please pick up!" she sounded panic-stricken. "Please. Okay. I'm coming to town and I'll go straight to Martin's. Please, if you get this, be there. I need help!" The machine voice said, "Saturday, August tenth, eleven forty-five A.M."

"I've got to go out," Barbara said, retying her boot. It was ten minutes past one. She looked up to see John regarding her with a hurt expression. All the way home they had been talking about a shower, a little nap. . . .

"John, I'm sorry." She sounded desperate. "I have to go."

"Sure."

"When I get back, I'll tell you what this is all about." She picked up her bag and hurried from the apartment. So much for weekends together.

If Martin was surprised to see her at the restaurant, it didn't show.

"I'm sorry to barge in," Barbara started at the door. Past him she saw Binnie at one of the tables, the remains of a salad, a pitcher of something still in place. "A client said she was coming here. I'll take her to Dad's office when she shows up."

"What for? We were just waiting for the kitchen to cool down before we get to work. It has by now."

Just then a car pulled up with a squeal; Maggie jumped out and ran toward Barbara.

"Have a seat," Martin said, stepping aside to let Maggie enter. "We're out of here." Binnie was clearing their table.

"Mitch is dead," Maggie whispered. "The police had Ray identify the body, and they asked him questions and sent someone to Papa Arno's to question him. What am I going to do?"

"Three deep breaths, first thing," Barbara said calmly, feeling anything but calm. Dead! Police! Good God!

The long breaths were not working as well as they had before when Maggie first talked to her, but she was more coherent when she said, "Ray called me, just before I called you. He said the police asked him to go downtown to try to identify a body. It's Mitch. Someone killed him. Ray said he was beaten up and killed." She drew in another futile breath, let it out too fast. "They kept Ray and questioned him; he told them the truth, that he left Mitch in his house on Friday and he was gone on Monday. That's all he could tell them. He doesn't have anything to lie about! But what will I tell them?"

"The truth," Barbara said sharply. "After Ray told you Mitch was back, you retained me to deal with him."

"I told Ray I'd come right over, as soon as I could get a ride. He'll be expecting me."

"Let me think a minute," Barbara said. She got up and walked the length of the restaurant and back again. Martin came from the kitchen with a tray of iced tea, silently put the glasses on the table, and returned to the kitchen. Barbara sat down again.

"Maggie, you have to stay calm and not go to pieces. I need some information. Did the police question Ray downtown or at his place?"

"Both. He said they kept him in the living room and two men went all over the house. They scraped something from the floor."

"Is his wife back from her parents' place yet with the children?"

"No. They'll come home tomorrow."

"Did the police fingerprint the house?"

"I don't know. He didn't say."

"That probably means no. You told me that someone had knocked things around there; you assumed it was Mitch. And you said someone had broken into Papa Arno's house but hadn't done any damage there or stolen anything. Remember?"

"Yes," Maggie said in a faint voice. She was calmer now, paying close attention.

"Has it occurred to you that there's more than one possible scenario to account for the breaking and entering at Papa Arno's house, then for things being knocked over at Ray's, and Mitch being gone?"

Maggie's eyes widened, then narrowed as she thought. After a moment she said, "Someone could have been looking for Mitch; they could have taken him away."

Barbara nodded. "Remember, you said that, not me. It could become important. Another thing to consider, Maggie. The police did a scraping, but they didn't fingerprint the house."

"They didn't believe Ray," Maggie said. "They won't bother to look beyond him."

"Good," Barbara murmured. "Anything else?"

"No." When Barbara remained silent, Maggie closed her eyes hard. Finally she opened them.

"Someone should fingerprint the house before Lorinne gets home tomorrow. She'll clean things."

Barbara wanted to hug her, but she remained silent, waiting.

"I don't know what else you want," Maggie cried. She studied Barbara for a moment, then closed her eyes again, and this time when she opened them, she asked, "Would the detective you use do it for me?"

"You could ask him," Barbara said. She wrote down Bailey's name and number on the back of one of her cards and handed it to Maggie, then pointed to a phone on the cashier's desk. Maggie hurried to it.

In a moment Maggie said, "He isn't home. A woman said he'll be back any minute." She was holding her hand over her mouthpiece.

"Leave your name and this number, and ask her to tell him to call, that it's important."

Maggie spoke into the phone again, then came back to the table.

"We need a couple of minutes to talk," Barbara reassured her. "Maggie, you absolutely must not say a word about seeing Mitch, about the stuff he left at your house. Not a word. If you even breathe that you saw him, you could be compelled to tell it all. At this moment, we don't know anything about this murder, or even if it was a murder. Not how, when, where—nothing. If he was killed when all of you were at your place, there's nothing to worry about, and the police will look further. But if it turns out that Ray was back home when Mitch was murdered, and if the police seriously suspect Ray, then if a large amount of money surfaced, it could be seen as a motive. You can't tell Ray or anyone else anything. If they ask Ray to take a lie-detector test, he has to be free to tell the exact truth, or he'll be in serious danger." She paused. "Do you understand?"

"Yes." She was very pale.

"All right. If the police ask you if you saw Mitch that weekend, tell them the truth, you didn't. It isn't a lie. You didn't see him after Thursday night."

Maggie started to say something, but stiffened as the phone rang. Martin picked up in the kitchen, then, after a moment, opened the door and said from the doorway, "It's for Ms. Folsum." His voice was very gentle. She ran to the telephone.

"He'll do it," Maggie said when she returned to the table. "I told him I'd meet him at Papa Arno's, that's where Ray was going, and I'll take him over myself. I'll tell them all what I think happened, that some men got in the house and took him out."

"Will you have a reason for saying it?" Barbara asked.

"Sure. Ray told the truth, and Mitch didn't have a car and wouldn't have left on foot."

It would do, Barbara decided. She jotted down phone numbers on one of her cards and handed it to Maggie. "Whatever happens, keep in touch with me. Try my place first, then my father's, then the office, and if all else fails, call here. Someone will know where I am. I'll find out what's going on, and we'll talk again soon."

Maggie started to walk to the door, but she wheeled about and rushed back to the table, where she grasped the tabletop with both hands and leaned forward, her face close to Barbara's. Her voice was low and harsh when she spoke. "I told you Ray was the first to know when I got pregnant. It was more than that. I was down on the beach, in a little cove that gets cut off at high tide, no exit if there's a heavy surf. I was waiting for the ocean to come get me. I wanted to die, an accident in the ocean, something that would be regrettable but not scandalous, for my mother's sake. It was all I could think of, to die, be done with Mitch, with my life, with the baby. All right, teenage angst, but it's real, Barbara. It's real enough to kill yourself. And Ray spotted me from the cliff, and he came down and got me. I fought him, but he carried me out, climbed up the cliff with me over his shoulder and waves crashing over both of us. We could have been killed, both of us. He took me home with him and gave me a hot bath; I couldn't stop shaking I was so cold. He poured hot cocoa down me and talked to me. Really talked to me. He promised that my baby would not be a bastard, an illegitimate baby that people would scorn and hate and mock, but a respected member of the Arno family, complete with grandparents who would be silly about it, and three big Arno uncles who would protect it, and I would inherit three brothers and in-laws who would welcome me like a daughter. He made me believe it all. And it was all true," she said, her voice dropping to a whisper. "It all came true." She straightened up then, drew back from the table, and said very precisely, "We know other people were looking for

Mitch, and why, but the police don't know that. If I have to tell them, I will. Ray, all of the Arnos, they're my real family. I can't let anything happen to them."

"I can't stop you," Barbara said. "Promise me this, though. If you make such a decision, you'll tell me first."

"I'll tell you first," Maggie said, and hurried out.

As soon as she was gone, Barbara went to the phone and hit the redial button. Bailey answered. "It's me," she said, and he said he thought it might be.

"Right. Maggie hired you to do some work for her, and you bill her directly, not through me. Got that?" He said sure. She told him what little she knew, and then said, "Find out what you can about it. And while you're with the Arno clan, keep your eyes and ears open. Okay?" He asked if she wanted to teach him how to tie his shoes. Ignoring that, she said, "I'll be at Dad's tonight, and you're welcome to drop in for dessert and coffee, if you'd like. And if you have anything for me."

He laughed. "You're hitting a new low. In my books that's bribery. See you around."

She drove home deep in thought, and only when she entered the apartment and John emerged from his office, still with a distant, hurt expression, did she remember that she had promised to tell him what was happening.

"I made some tuna fish," he said. "I'll fix you a sandwich while you get the boots off and wash up. You look hot."

He wasn't going to ask anything, demand anything, she understood, yet this would be between them, her silence, her abrupt departures, staying out past office hours with no explanation, and it would fester and grow.

The card table was in the kitchen with the two folding chairs in place. She sat down and started to unlace her boot. Not looking at him, she said, "If I talk with my clients about legal matters, no power on earth can make them or me reveal what was said, but that doesn't apply to you. If you know anything about a case and you're put under oath, you would have to testify, or possibly be held in contempt of court, possibly even go to jail. There's no protection, not even spousal protection in our case."

She finished with the boots and wriggled her toes; her feet were hot and sweaty, she thought with disgust.

He had stopped moving at the tiny counter by the sink. "You think I'd reveal a confidence," he said flatly.

"No, I don't. It's just that you could be at risk." She pulled off her socks. "I want to spare you any possible problem."

"Is a problem going to come up? Spousal protection. You mean one spouse can't be forced to give evidence that might be incriminating to the other, don't you? Are you involved in something that's going to cause you trouble?"

"There could be trouble down the road. Sometimes things that start very simply turn complicated. A pretty simple case just went postal."

He finished making the sandwich and put it down in front of her. "Wash your hands at the sink here and then tell me about it. And eat something first."

She ate first and then told him about it.

He was silent a moment when she was done, then he asked, "Can I comment?"

"Sure."

"She can't collect from a dead man, and the bum's dead apparently. Why not hand the stuff over to the cops and let them deal with Trassi, get to the bottom of it?"

"She has a child who wants to go to medical school," Barbara said. "She'll come out with a hundred-thousand-dollar-plus debt to pay back. That's for openers. But worse, suppose the police come up with a different story. Mitch arrived and told her about the money, maybe showed it to her. She killed him and hid his body and called Ray for help. Or Ray killed him for a share of the money. I have to stall for now, until we know more about Mitch Arno's death."

"Barbara," John said thoughtfully, "granted that you like Maggie Folsum, but has it occurred to you that maybe she hasn't told the entire truth?"

"It's always a possibility that a client's been lying. They often do. But let's drop it now. I'm so sticky and stinky, I can't stand myself a minute longer. I have to have a shower."

It did not surprise her at all when he joined her beneath the spray a few minutes later.

Frank's dinner was mainly garden vegetables, all crisp and tender and brightly colored, done to perfection in a way that Barbara decided could only be magic. His halibut was moist and flaky, with a luscious lemon-and-garlic sauce. Her salmon had been tough and dry; she had forgotten to set a timer. She had told him when he admitted her and John that Bailey might join them for dessert. He had raised his eyebrows. "Always plenty."

Then, at the dining room table, he began to talk about Sylvia Fenton. "You know who Joe Fenton is, don't you? The jewelry-store owner?" Barbara nodded. "Yes, well this started back, oh, thirty or thirty-five years ago, when this rich bachelor was on a jewelry-buying trip to New York. Can't say he was handsome, he never would have won a beauty contest, but he was rich and eligible. Every gal in the county was after him. Anyway, he was in New York and someone took him to an off-Broadway show, and he saw Sylvia. She was a bit player, did character roles—the Irish waif, the saucy French maid, tough honky-tonk dancer. You know what I mean. But something hit Joe hard that night. He came home with a bride."

He was grinning. He helped Barbara to another serving of spinach salad with feta cheese, talking all the while.

"Well, Joe's mother tried to have a heart attack, and his father threatened to disinherit him. But a funny thing happened. In just a couple of months the mother-in-law was Sylvia's champion; she took her everywhere and introduced her as 'my daughter.' And the father-in-law began talking about doing it right, a real wedding with no expense spared. Joe was the happiest man in the county. She has a way, that Sylvia." Frank looked at John then. "Now, I know a few things about folks around here. Barbara knows more, I'm sure. Bailey knows just about everything. And Sylvia knows more than Bailey.

"She fitted in, kept busy, volunteer work, stuff like that, but it wasn't quite enough. Then one day she came to see me and brought a maid in with her, and the maid's story was that a nursing home had killed her mother through neglect, wrong medication or something. Sylvia believed her, but there wasn't a shred of evidence. Inspectors never found a thing out of line. Bailey said he might be able to get a ringer, someone to send in undercover, and Sylvia said she'd do it herself. Right before my eyes she changed from queen of high society to a barely literate, ignorant drudge. So she went in and got a job emptying bedpans and scrubbing; she took a camera with her, and she nailed them. The usual thing, sugar pills instead of prescription drugs, and pocket the money, a lot of things like that."

He laughed. "Thing is, Sylvia loved doing it, and Joe was so proud, you'd have thought she just invented heaven. Sylvia told Bailey she'd be available if something else came along. And, by God, every now and then something does come along." Very softly he added, "Everybody loves Sylvia, and no one more than Joe. He's still the happiest man in the county."

They all cleared the table, and Frank brought out a raspberry torte and a carafe of coffee. As if on cue, Bailey arrived at that moment.

Finally even the dessert was gone, and Bailey put sugar in his third cup of coffee and said, "You tell him anything yet?"

"I told John about it, but not Dad." She told Frank then about

Maggie's visit, Mitch's death. "What did you find out?" she asked Bailey afterward.

Frank's face had been jovial, a look of fond reminiscence had softened his features; now he was grim-looking.

With a reproachful look Bailey said, "You sent me straight into bedlam. Three sons—Ray, James, and David—two wives, a thousand kids, Maggie, the old man and old lady all talking at once. Nobody listens, everyone talks."

She shook her head impatiently, and he continued.

"Okay, okay. Problem is, you ask Ray a question and while he answers it, so does everyone else, a chorus of answers, and no one seems to notice. I fingerprinted the whole crew, even little kids wanted their fingerprints made, so I did them, too."

John looked bewildered. "Why?"

"Elimination. Match up what I can, and anything left over goes to the FBI lab for identification," Bailey said. "So, no point in doing that house, not with people swarming everywhere like they were. Maggie, Ray, James, and the old man, we all went to Ray's house and I did that one. Got a nice footprint in the bathroom, and another one on a hassock in the living room. Looked like someone had put his foot against it and shoved it across the room."

No one moved as he talked. "Okay, out at his house, I asked Ray to show me around the property, alone. And I got to ask him some questions without the Greek chorus helping out. Ray says that the old man showed up at seven or a little later on Friday, hauling Mitch in with him. The old man took off in his truck, and Ray told Mitch about the party at Maggie's place and warned him if he showed up, they'd make the last beating look like practice. Then he took off, collected his brother James, and they went to the coast.

"On Monday when Ray got home, the living room looked like Mitch had gone wild. Two broken lamps, a can of beer spilled on the floor. Mitch had shaved with Lorinne's razor, and he had eaten and left dishes on the table. He had showered in the big bathroom and left a footprint. He had put on a pair of Ray's jeans and a shirt with the shop logo on the pocket. Mitch was gone and so were his own clothes. That's all Ray knows about that.

"This morning at seven two cops come to the house and seem a little surprised to find Ray. They might have thought he was the dead man. Anyway, they split up—one goes in with him to identify the body, and the other one tags along behind. They're being helpful, they'll help him with parking, show him the right place to go, and generally be of assistance. He's grateful, and after he identifies Mitch, he tells them everything he knows."

Barbara groaned and he nodded. "Right. I doubt it would have occurred to him to clam up, get some advice, not his style. They ask questions, he answers, and they send a couple of detectives back to the house with him. They send someone out to talk to the old man, and the questions are getting tougher with Ray. The way he sees it, they're doing their job and he'll help any way he can. Simple."

"What do the police have?"

"Last night they got a tip about a body up at a cabin around Blue River. The caller said it was behind a place that's for sale. He was hiking with friends and they spotted a foot sticking out of the ground and did their duty and called. And hung up. The cops went out last night and found him, buried, except for one foot. The cabin had been broken into, and he had been beaten and probably killed inside. And they found the name *Arno* in blood on the floor, so tracking Ray down was easy enough, that and the shirt."

"Jesus Christ!" Frank muttered in a low, savage voice.

Barbara asked, "Anything else?"

"They've been up there today poking and prying. No time of death yet, no direct cause of death. Hell, the autopsy hasn't been done yet, more than likely. But the police will be all over Folsum asking questions, and if they don't already consider Ray their prime suspect, they will soon. Who else?"

John was watching her so closely, she felt almost as if rays were being emitted from his eyes, burning her. "Are you going to take him on if he asks? Get involved in another murder case this soon?"

"Even if I wanted to, and I don't, I couldn't," she said. "Conflict of interest." She stood up. "Excuse me. Right back." Outside the dining room door she paused, listening to her father's voice.

"See, John, she already has a client, and it's her duty to protect that client, to fulfill her obligation to her, and not bring harm to her."

"Wouldn't that be a criminal offense, to withhold information in a murder investigation?"

"Now you see the problem."

She hurried to the bathroom, where she gazed at herself in the mirror. "Oh my, yes," she whispered. "Certainly a criminal offense."

7

Sunday was going to be another hot, bright day; at ten in the morning it was already too hot to be carrying the camping gear from their apartment down a flight of stairs that collected heat and stored it. By the time all the equipment was beside the van, sweat was running down her back, down her legs. John was unbearably cheerful; she suspected he had been more oppressed by the cluttered apartment than he had admitted, and now they were doing something about it. He regarded with satisfaction the piles of bedding, the stove, refrigerator. . . . There was so much, it seemed impossible that it would all fit into the van.

"Go on and cool off," he said. "This will take a couple of hours."

Thank God for air-conditioning, she thought as she returned to the apartment. And thank God for silence, she added. She felt desperate for time without distraction.

She took her briefcase to her newly cleared office and sat down to think. Already dates and times were slipping away; she had not made sufficient notes to set them in her mind.

John came back; she heard him moving boxes in the living room, and she put down her pen. In a moment there was a very soft tap on her door, as if a low noise would be less intrusive than a real knock. John pushed the door open and asked, "Have you seen a box about like so? Tools in it." He held out his hands to indicate size; she shook her head, and he withdrew.

It took a long time for her to remember something she had started to jot down. She finally got it back and wrote: *What if Mitch had not recovered his car, and instead some kids had hot-wired it and taken it joyriding? Had it turned up wrecked anywhere? If so, what was found in it?* Bailey work.

If there was any way she could keep Maggie out of the murder investigation, she would do it, she had decided; something in the car might drag her in anyway.

The phone rang and she went to the kitchen to listen. "Ms. Holloway, I have to talk to you. It's imperative that I talk to you today."

She picked up the phone. "Barbara Holloway," she said.

The caller let out an audible sigh. "Thank God," he said. "My name is Brad Waters, in San Francisco. I'm catching the first flight I can get, and I'll go to the Valley River Inn. Can you talk to me this afternoon? At four? It's about Mitch Arno and what he was carrying?"

"Hold on, Mr. Waters—" She hit the CALLER ID button and quickly jotted down the number that came on the display.

"I can't. I have to run to make that flight. In the lounge at Valley River Inn, at four. Please be there." He hung up.

"Shit," she said under her breath. The number she had written down had a Seattle area code. She tore the page off the pad and took it to her office, where she compared it with the numbers they had found in the notebook from Mitch's bag. It didn't match any of them. More Bailey work.

Barbara walked into the lounge at exactly four. "I believe Mr. Waters has a table already," she said to the woman at the reservation stand.

The woman checked her list and smiled. "Oh, yes. He's here." She beckoned a waiter. "Mr. Waters's table."

The waiter led Barbara to one of the dimly lighted tables on the upper tier, not down by the wide windows overlooking the Willamette River. The lounge was very busy, every table filled on both tiers. Waters was sitting facing the wall. He rose instantly when she drew near.

"Ms. Holloway? Brad Waters."

There was not enough room for the waiter to get behind her chair to adjust it, but he hovered. "Can I bring you anything?"

"Iced coffee," she said. She shook hands with Waters, then seated herself.

The light was dim, especially after the brilliant sunshine outside, but as her eyes adjusted, she could see that Brad Waters had dark hair and was smooth-shaven, and from what little she had seen, he was athletic, with broad shoulders. She couldn't tell the color of his eyes, just dark. A tall glass of beer was in front of him; it looked untouched.

"No trouble getting on a flight?" she asked. "Sometimes, this time of year, it's difficult."

"No problem. I checked in here at two. Then I did a Web search on Barbara Holloway. I'm glad I had time to do that."

"How did you come across my name in the first place?"

"I called Ms. Folsum's inn early this morning, and someone there gave me another number to try. Then Ms. Folsum referred me to you and gave me your number."

She understood that they would kill time waiting for her coffee, and he seemed to have the same understanding, but it was irksome.

He was saying, "—afraid you might be tied up with a client at the diner—" when the waiter reappeared and placed the coffee before her.

As soon as the waiter was gone, Waters leaned forward. "Ms. Holloway, I'm the head of security for a large computer company. What I'd like to do is give you a little background and then make a serious request, so please, be patient for just a few minutes. And please be understanding if I don't mention real names just yet, including my own." He was watching her closely. She nodded. "All right. My company is big, not as big as Microsoft, but big, and the principals, a man and a woman, are, or were, the company. The two of them started it as partners, and they produced some very important programs over the years, working as a team. A few years ago, we had a major theft of a program in development; a rival company introduced it weeks before we were ready. We were able to track down the guy who sold us out and promised him immunity if he would tell us how the theft had been worked." He leaned back and began to move his glass of beer in circles.

"It was a simple scheme," he said flatly. "How they worked it was to have a lawyer draw up papers to have a car brokered and delivered to the guy. The driver was to deliver a large sum of money along with the car, and he was to receive the program. Simple. The transfer of an automobile was aboveboard, not suspicious in any way. How much the broker knew, anyone's guess, but the lawyer was in on it, and so was the driver. That driver was Mitch Arno. We pieced it together bit by bit, and tried to track down Arno, with no luck. And there was no way to prove a theft had taken place, that it hadn't been parallel research. We tightened security, did what we could to prevent it happening again."

He finally tasted the beer and set the glass down again, as if the taste had not registered. "Okay," he said then. "That's the history, the background you need in order to understand what comes next. My two bosses had a big falling-out; they had been lovers for more than fifteen years, but they fought and split in a very public and very ugly way. It was bad. He started to date pretty young things. She was not a pretty young thing, and it hit her hard. She got back by stealing the new program that was in development and selling out. She had access to everything I had found out about the first incident, including the lawyer's name."

He drew in a long breath and shook his head. "They were both my friends. I saw how hurt she had been, but I never imagined this. Anyway, the last day she showed up at work, she left with a new fancy briefcase with a keypad lock and she got on a plane for the States. The next day she was found dead, murdered. The police said she had ordered a car, a Lexus, and the broker furnished the names of two delivery men; one of them was found dead in a motel room, the other one vanished. He was using a different name, but the description fits Mitch Arno. The briefcase did not turn up, and neither did the suitcase. The police think the missing man killed them both for the car, and for the cashier's check for the balance due—forty-two thousand dollars. What we think happened is that Arno grabbed our programs and the check, as well as the suitcase of money, and took off, probably planning to get bids on what he had. Other research groups have bits and pieces of the program; she had it all."

As he spoke, Barbara felt as if the chill from her iced coffee had entered her hand and traveled throughout her body, until she was chilled all over. He continued to push his glass back and forth in a distracted way.

"Why are you here now?" she asked. "How did you track Mitch Arno here?"

He rubbed his eyes. "As soon as we learned she was dead, and a Lexus was involved, we started a continuous-search program for him. His name came up when he was reported murdered. His name, his former wife's name, the trashing of her inn."

"Why do you think the other company doesn't already have the program?"

"Because Trassi's hanging around. I've been having him followed. I knew when he flew into Portland, rented a car, and came here to Eugene. I just didn't know why, until we got Arno's name. The stuff hasn't come to light, or Trassi wouldn't be here. Folsum still has it, or turned it over to a third party. If there's a suitcase like the one they used before, it has a fancy keypad lock on it. The briefcase has another one. I hope and pray the program is still intact, hidden away where it's safe." He added, "But whoever has it isn't safe, Ms. Holloway. If Maggie Folsum and her kids had been home when her place was torn up, they'd all be dead."

Carefully Barbara asked, "If what you believe is actually true, would these people be less dangerous if they learned the program was in your company's hands once more? Wouldn't they go after the suitcase?"

He shook his head. "Such men will kill if they have to; they killed Mitch Arno, but they don't kill out of revenge. Once they know we have the program back, they'll vanish into the slime and move on to a different project. The last thing any of us wants is an official investigation and publicity. As soon as they know we have the program, this matter will wind down, finis. You know the saying 'All's well that ends.'"

"Maybe," Barbara said. "I understand why they wouldn't want an investigation, but what about you, your company? Why haven't you gone to the police?"

He began sliding his glass around again. "I can't. My boss is shattered. He takes complete responsibility for what she did, blames himself for everything up to and including her death. He said if her reputation is damaged, he'll give away everything he has, kill me and then himself.

"Ms. Holloway, I said that I had a request. Two, actually. All we want from you is the program. We're not interested in the suitcase, or anything else Arno might have had, just the briefcase, our program. That program is the biggest and most important thing they ever produced together, and that's the only complete program in existence; she destroyed the tapes, the backups, everything else. If our competitor brings it out as his, that will be the last straw for my boss."

"The other request?"

"Your silence. An agreement of confidentiality. If a single question arises, my boss will deny everything—the original theft, any knowledge of a new program, everything."

"I see. Are you going to be staying here at the hotel?"

"Yes. I doubt anyone would recognize me; I keep a very low profile. But they might. I'll hang out around here. You have to understand that they are very clever. They'll get to you through Folsum, threaten her children, force her to back out of whatever arrangement you have with her. And you have to understand that it's not just Folsum who might be in danger. Anyone with that program is at risk, and if they learn that I'm around, the risk would become uninsurable. I know you have to discuss this with your client, but don't take too long to reach a decision, Ms. Holloway."

Abruptly she stood up. "I have a lot to think about, as you are aware. I'll be in touch, Mr. Waters." She left him signing the tab for the drinks neither of them had wanted.

She walked out into the blinding sunshine. Maggie's children at risk? She had thought of them safely tucked away in Southern California, but how safe were they?

8

The next morning she sipped coffee in Frank's kitchen, watching him eat a bran muffin that looked terribly healthful. "Wait for Bailey and tell us together," he had said when she told him there was a new wrinkle.

One of the coon cats approached, rose to its hind feet, and put its paws on the table to look over breakfast. "My God, how big do they intend to get?"

"I've been reading up on them," Frank said complacently, ignoring the cat. "Don't reach full growth, fill in bulk and such, until the second year. He's still a kitten." The kitten weighed in at eighteen pounds now.

The Thing rubbed his cheek against Frank's arm, dropped lightly to the floor, and strolled away to his own food.

When Bailey arrived, Frank motioned toward the coffee. Bailey helped himself and joined them at the table. "Got the prints separated out," he said. "I'll send them in when I leave here. You know it's going to take two, three weeks to get a report back?"

She knew. "What about the murder? What do you have?"

"Thought I'd wait until your dad finishes eating," he said.

Frank pushed his plate away with a half-eaten muffin still on it. "Done," he said.

"Someone really worked him over," Bailey said gloomily. "Good old blunt instrument. They're saying maybe a baseball bat, something like that. One arm broken, some fingers broken. Back of his head caved in, that's what killed him. And someone doused both his hands with lighter fluid or gas or something and set him on fire."

"Christ," Frank muttered. He stood up and went to gaze out the sliding glass door.

"Time of death?" Barbara asked after a moment.

"No word yet. Maybe Sunday, no later than Tuesday. They're working on it."

She was silent, thinking, when Bailey added, "Thing is, he should have stayed buried. The hole was deep enough to cover him, but one foot was poking out of the ground. They're saying an animal started to dig him up and got spooked or something."

"Shoes?" she asked, remembering the barefoot print he had recovered at Ray's house.

"No shoes. They roughed him up in the cabin and burned him inside. Maybe they meant to burn down the cabin itself, but he kept going out."

Barbara glared at him. He shrugged. "Sorry. He managed to scrape the letters *A-R-N-O* in blood on the floor."

Frank sat down again. "Was he burned before or after death?"

"Don't know. Maybe they don't know yet."

"They'll go for aggravated murder," Frank said. "Maybe torture and murder."

Bailey said he might be getting information about Trassi later on, then Barbara told them about her meeting with Brad Waters. "It shouldn't be too hard to find names," she said. "How many female partners in a computer company got killed recently?"

"Barbara," Bailey said, "you realize that if Mitch Arno killed his partner and the woman, they probably have his prints on file. And if I send in my batch of unknowns, they're going to find his among them."

"Shit." She thought a moment. "I'll see if Maggie has anything with Mitch's prints on it. About the car, we know a little something about it now. A forty-two-thousand-dollar black Lexus. The other day you said maybe it was stolen. If some kids took it joyriding, what next?"

"They finally wreck it, or take it to a chop shop," he said promptly.

"If they wrecked it, someone must have found it. See what you can dig up. Especially what was in it. And the broker who arranged the deal. Who is he, where?"

He was eyeing her with a detached expression. He never questioned strategy or asked why about anything; they had their jobs, he had his. But he always asked if the client was prepared to pay his expenses. He asked now.

"I'll find out," Barbara said. "But for now, the answer is yes."

"Okeydokey." A few minutes later he left her and Frank at the table.

Frank began to clear the few dishes, and she went to stand at the door. The two cats were engaged in what looked like a battle to the finish; they were distracted by a hummingbird and started a new game of catch-me-if-you-can. "Do they stray off?" she asked.

"Some. But they come back when I whistle. Bobby, what are you planning? What's on your mind?"

She turned around. Almost helplessly she said, "I don't know. I feel as if I've been sucked into a whirlpool and more and more junk gets pulled in with me until I can't tell flotsam from jetsam. I haven't had time to think."

"You're just reacting. Things are happening too fast, and all you can do is react. Find yourself a quiet spot and sit there and think a long time."

"Okay. I can take the money and the program in to the police right now. Today. Then what? Even if we knew the names of the companies fighting over the program, they'd both deny everything. Trassi would be horrified that Mitch had a sideline that no one else knew about. Waters would disappear back into his high-security cubbyhole, which he can prove he never left. Nope, he was never in Eugene, never met me or discussed anything with me. All I would give the police is a whole lot of money and a program that no one seems to know anything about." She drew in a breath, then added, "And a powerful motive for either Ray or Maggie or both working together to have murdered Mitch. A motive everyone understands."

"Maybe some significant fingerprints," Frank said.

"Maybe. We don't even know that yet." She shook her head. "No matter how much bait I toss out for Trassi, he comes back for more. How far will they go? And the other guy, just keep all the money. Hah! I have to keep stalling until I have more information."

"If a single damn one of them is telling anything near the truth, I don't think you're going to have much stalling time. I'm going to mosey down to the office for an hour or two."

All right, she thought then, someone who had information and would give her straight answers: Lou Sunderman, the firm's tax expert. She called him and made an appointment for eleven. In succession she called Maggie and arranged for a six or seven o'clock meeting, then John.

"Hi," she said. "It's me."

"On your way home?"

"Nope. Up to here. Want to drive over to the coast this evening, fourish?"

"You just don't want to make dinner."

She laughed. "I know a great seafood restaurant over there."

"Cheap?"

"On me."

"You just talked me into it. Be home early?"

"As early as I can."

She was smiling when she hung up. One last call, she told herself after a moment. She gritted her teeth and called Wes Margollin, king of the nerds. He was a computer consultant who had set up the systems at the office, and talked.

"Jeez, Barbara," Wes said aggrievedly, "you guys got another problem? I'm really busy."

"No, no. I just want to open your brain case and take a quick peek inside. Information. Can you spare a little time today?"

"No way. Like I said, I'm really busy. Lunch? We gotta eat, right?"

Not only was he a talker, he was a moocher. They agreed on lunch and she hung up. Then it was time to go talk with Lou Sunderman.

He was only five feet six, possibly weighed 120, and no doubt was the most valued member of the law firm.

"A hypothetical problem," Barbara said when she took a chair across his desk from him. "If a woman collected back child-support payments for eighteen years for two children, and the sum came to a very big number, would it be taxable?"

"No. The amount is unimportant."

She restrained herself from uttering, "Hah!" then she asked, "Could she collect from his estate in the event he died before he paid up?"

"Much would depend on circumstances. Did he have a will? Are there other children from a different marriage? Did he leave large medical bills? And so forth. If he died intestate, probably the best she could hope for would be for her children to inherit whatever would be left after all accounts are settled. That money would be taxable."

"What if he paid her and soon afterward died, before she had a chance to do anything with the money?"

Lou looked as if his patience was nearing an end. "If it can be proved that the sum due her was transferred to her before his death, that money is no longer part of his estate. It is hers and it is not subject to seizure by his creditors, if she can prove delinquency in his support payments. The Internal Revenue Service would conduct its own investigation and issue a closing agreement before she could claim the money legally."

Pushing her welcome, she asked how long it would take. He said, "Months," and looked pointedly at his watch. She thanked him nicely and walked out to meet Wes Margollin.

She groaned when she saw how packed the Greek restaurant was that Wes had chosen. He was standing at a table across the dining room, waving a menu at her.

"Hey, Barbara, how you doing?" he called before she reached him. "You know what I'm up to my nose in? See, everyone's got a modem, everyone's surfing the Net, everyone's got to have a Web page. Shoeshine boy, bank president, janitor, they all got to have a Web page, and not a one of them knows diddly about HTML. You want a Web page?"

She shook her head. A harried waitress came and took their order and rushed away. The noise level was decibels above comfort, but it didn't slow Wes down a second.

"See, you tell me what you want, how fancy you want it, music, bells, dancing bears—"

"Tell me about a company started fifteen or twenty years ago by a man and woman partnership. She died recently."

He didn't even change gears. "You mean Major Works. You want to buy stock, go for it. Imagine Einstein with two heads, that was Major and Wygood, and she got herself mugged and killed. Everyone's watching to see if he can hack it alone, but it won't matter to the company. With what they already have, they'll coast a long time. You never thought of just Major, or just Wygood; it was like one word, you know. Major/Wygood. He began showing up places with babes on his arm, and she took off."

Barbara listened, confirming item by item what Waters had told her. Their lunch came and she ate her Greek salad and he his kebabs, and he never stopped talking. It was awesome, his talking, eating, drinking wine all at once, and just a bit disgusting, too, she thought, looking away from him.

Finally she interrupted. "What will the next big breakthrough be?"

"Lots of stuff," he said promptly. "First, AI—that's artificial intelligence—but not this century. Next, TV, computer, telecommunications combo, big bucks, big brains, big-power machine chugging in the background. Big, really big fights. Then, a voice-recognition system. You know, like Dick Tracy talking to his watch and his watch answering. Right now it's like speech-class training, you know. Ev. Er. Y. Syl. La. Ble. has to be enunciated clearly. We gotta train people how to talk all over again. And people don't train too good. Not just that, either. It's how we talk. 'That guy's a beanpole.' What's a computer supposed to do with something like that? Or 'He's sawing logs.' Or 'She's pickled,' or 'He's a real lady killer.' But that's not even the worst of it. What about the homonyms, the synonyms, dialects, accents, not even touching yet on irony or symbolism? Nobody understands symbolism. People from Boston don't understand Mississippi. No one understands Texans. What about Brooklyn? It's a headache. See, there's another one. But, Barbara, baby, you get that and you connect it with telecommunications, you just bought yourself a key to heaven. For a while people thought Major/Wygood was working on it, but nothing came out, so if they were, they got mired down just like everyone else. I saw Wygood on a panel once talking about the problems, and suddenly she got real quiet, but she flashed a funny look at Major first. I was there, I saw it."

The waitress came back and Wes ordered baklava. They both had coffee. Barbara let him ramble on about Major/Wygood until he had his dessert, then she asked, "What would a workable program like that be worth, do you suppose?"

He snorted. "Can't even put a price on it. Millions? Lotsa millions." He wagged a finger at her. "But it's got to work on the platforms out there. And that's the rub. You need more memory, more RAM, more speed, more everything than we've got."

He finished his coffee and stood up. "More Web sites, more home pages, more, more, more. You decide you want a page, give me a buzz. Of course, you'll have to get in line. . . ."

"Thanks, Wes," she said to his back as he hurried away. She had forgotten the noise in the restaurant, she realized then when it hit her as a cacophony. She put her credit card on the table; the waitress was there almost instantly, and soon Barbara was back outside. It had grown many degrees hotter; she crossed the street to keep in the shade, and walked slowly, thinking of what Wes had told her.

A block from the office, as she crossed the open, downtown plaza where food vendors were doing a brisk business—tacos, Scandinavian pastries, ice cream, espressos—she saw Trassi, the gray man, who looked out of place here in his gray suit and sour expression. He rose from a bench and watched her approach.

"I want to talk to you," he said curtly.

"All right."

"Not here. There's a little park up there." He pointed toward Park Street, a block away.

"Fine."

Neither spoke again as they walked to the little park. An ice-cream vendor was set up and busy; people were sitting on several of the benches, others strolling aimlessly, a few with quick purpose. Shade from the tall fir and pine trees cooled the air magically. Barbara slowed her pace and let Trassi select a bench. There were only two choices.

He nodded toward the one closer to the fountain, and they went to it and sat down.

The fountain had a twenty-five-foot catch basin with a broad outer lip. Water flowed into it from a center pipe, then over the lip to a second, wide return basin, almost soundlessly. The sheen of water as it overflowed made it look like satin at times; when the lighting was just so, it looked like mercury; other times when the wind was blowing a certain way, the overflow was disturbed in such a manner that it looked bunched up, uneven. Barbara had spent many hours on this bench, gazing at the fountain, considering her next move, her next witness, the last witness. . . . Now she gazed at the water and waited.

"My client is prepared to pay a fifty-thousand-dollar finder's fee for the return of our material," Trassi said without preamble. "Plus whatever damage costs the insurance doesn't cover."

She shook her head. "I told you what we want," she said. "Did you forget? Two hundred ten thousand, for the past-due child support, and so far the damage is up to forty-five thousand, and counting." She paused, then said musingly, "I haven't even considered yet the intangibles—fear, worry, loss of goodwill." Her voice became very brisk again. "We want it aboveboard, without the IRS or other creditors seizing any of it. Child support isn't taxed, I understand."

"That's impossible! The man's dead! You can't collect from a dead man who didn't have anything. He never saw the kind of money you're talking about."

"Oh, I don't know," Barbara said thoughtfully. "What if he was a private contractor who earned a lot of money and didn't trust banks? In addition to working for your company, of course. There could be a number of safe-deposit boxes with hundred-dollar bills tucked away inside. Could be that he worked under several different names, lived frugally, saved his money."

Contempt was thick in his voice when he said, "You'll end up with nothing. A dream of riches, that's all, a fairy tale. Go back to your law books, Ms. Holloway. You can't start garnishment proceedings against a dead man; all you can do is present your claim to the probate court and get in line with his other creditors. We are prepared to prove that the material he was carrying belongs to our company, that he was on a legitimate business trip acting as a courier. What he was carrying will be returned to its owners; it will not be included in his estate, believe me. And no matter how many creditors line up, they'll all get exactly the same thing: nothing. He didn't have anything. Nothing divided among three or three hundred is still nothing."

"The way I see it," Barbara said, "Mitch Arno got religion and decided to pay his ex-wife for the many years of neglecting to support his children. You know; he told you he had a debt to pay. He decided to make a grand gesture, pay her in cash, and came here on a side trip to do so. You arrived to make certain it was all legal, with authorization to deliver the suitcase to Ms. Folsum or her attorney. She told you to talk to me, which you did, and after you delivered the suitcase, your mission was accomplished. I, of course, immediately put the suitcase in a safe-deposit box until I had time to determine the legality of the procedure." She paused, then continued in a thoughtful way, "Of course, if that scenario were true, there would be records, payment records, a document to show that he intended to pay his ex-wife what he owed her, an attorney agreement. You know, papers and records, the bane of civilization.

That's what I want, Mr. Trassi, all the paperwork that proves it was his money and he retained you to deliver it, and, further, a statement that you carried out his instructions faithfully before he died. When it's ready, call the office and set up a meeting with our tax attorney, Mr. Sunderman, and he will contact the IRS to arrange for a closing agreement with them."

"You are proposing an illegal action that could get you disbarred. We would never agree to such a scheme." He stood up.

"Okay. So we could auction off what we have and call it quits."

"What you have is valueless to anyone except my company."

"So we won't make much with it. Scan a page or two and put it on the Internet, with a plea for help, might work. Something like 'Found, pages from someone's manual. What does it mean?' Maybe someone would make an offer."

He did not move.

"One more thing," Barbara said, keeping her gaze on the water. "I moved things from my own bank to the safe-deposit box the firm rents, one that requires two senior members to open. I've given instructions that in the event I am incapacitated, those senior members will turn over everything they find in the box to the police. And if I hear that Maggie Folsum has been pressured in any way, I'll turn them over myself. You see, when you start out with nothing, there's little to lose. Is there?" She looked up at him. "And, Mr. Trassi, I see no advantage in further dickering. When you're ready, call Mr. Sunderman and set up a time."

"I'll be in touch," he said. He walked away like a marionette with an inept handler.

She turned her gaze back to the fountain. A thin cirrus cloud had dimmed the sun slightly, turning the smooth water into molten gold that was just out of reach.

9

"When I was a little girl," Maggie said, "I named all these rocks."

They were walking on the beach, where fog was gathering and the surf was gentle for the moment. The rocks were basalt, John had said, old volcanoes sailing out to sea on a raft of tectonic plates. Now John and Laurence were walking ahead, out of hearing.

"This one's the Black Knight," Maggie said, patting a smooth columnar monolith that rose ten feet high. "He saved my life when I was about eight or nine. An erratic wave caught me. He held me, or I held him. Never turn your back on the ocean," she added. Laurence turned to look at them and waved, and she waved back. Her voice became strained. "I remember how my mother used to handle my brothers when we were kids. If they got on her nerves too much, she'd send them to town for a loaf of bread or something."

"Send him on an errand," Barbara said. "Let him go buy the chairs and love seats and things."

Maggie looked surprised, then she nodded. "All I could think of was that it took me two years to find the furniture I wanted; you saw, oak in one room, wicker in another, cherry. . . . He could do that." Suddenly she grinned. "He could do that."

"Okay," Barbara said brusquely. "Do you know when the funeral will be, and will you bring your daughters home for it?"

"We don't know yet when they'll release Mitch's body. I talked to Mama and Papa Arno, and we agreed not to drag the kids home now. I'm not even sure where they are, Mom and Dad had a lot of things planned. The Arnos will have a very small private service, and later on I'll take the girls to the cemetery."

"Good. I'll need a copy of the divorce decree, and do you have anything with Mitch's fingerprints? Bailey needs to eliminate him, the way he did with the rest of the family."

"Mama Arno gave me his birth certificate and the prints they made in the hospital when he was born."

"Next, about that money. You could just keep it and burn the contents of the briefcase. You'd have to destroy the papers in the briefcase if you decided to go that route. Keeping them would be dangerous. They are very valuable, and there are powerful people who want them." Maggie started to say something, but Barbara said, "Let me lay it all out first. The next option is to turn everything over to the police and tell them what happened. The downside is that you'll give yourself a motive for killing Mitch, and you'd never see a penny of the money again. You would put not only Ray in danger but yourself as well. Or you could deal with either Trassi or another man who may have a legitimate claim; Trassi's upped the offer, and he will again, and the other one has no interest in the cash. You'd end up with a lot of money, perhaps all of it." Maggie gasped. Barbara continued. "The downside is how you would then handle the cash. If you put it in your bank, the bank would inform the IRS; it's the law. And then you'd have to account for it, and there would be an investigation. Word would leak, and there's a motive for murder again. You could stash the money in a safe-deposit box and spend it little by little without ever saying a word about it. It's risky, and the chance that your sudden affluence would be noticed is very high."

"What you're telling me is heads I lose, tails I lose," Maggie said. "Where did that money come from? How did Mitch get it? What are the valuable papers? Who are those powerful people? I can't make choices in the dark."

Barbara was always grateful when her client was intelligent, but sometimes, she would also admit, it complicated her life. Slowly, picking her words with care, she said, "I can't tell you a lot because we are still checking out various stories, and I'm stalling everyone until we have hard facts. It could be a case of industrial espionage.

Two competing companies, one stole a product from the other one, using Mitch as the delivery man who was to have paid off the thief and receive the product. He double-crossed them all and ended up with everything."

"Then *they* killed him," Maggie exclaimed. "The police would understand that much."

"Neither company would admit a thing," Barbara said patiently. "We don't have a shred of proof. We don't even know for sure the names of either company. I'm afraid the police might decide that Mitch had acted on his own and was involved in something yet to be determined; meanwhile, a quarter of a million dollars in cash would be irresistible as cause for murder."

They became silent, walking slowly in the packed sand. The fog had thickened; it was like a misty rain defying gravity. Laurence and John had turned, were coming their way.

"Barbara," Maggie said tiredly, "you've told me the things I can't do, but what's left? What can I do?"

"Let's wait until they get past and let them lead the way back," Barbara said. She looked at the sea; only a hundred feet away the fog eclipsed it wholly and hushed the sound of invisible waves breaking over invisible stacks out in the water.

"Hey," Laurence said, still dozens of feet from them, "can we stop being pariahs yet?"

Barbara shook her head. "Nope. Girl-talk time." She could see water droplets sparkling in John's hair.

The men walked past them, and after giving them a good lead, they followed. Then Barbara said, still speaking carefully, "You remember our agreement, what I agreed to do?" Maggie nodded. "That's what I want to do, Maggie. I want to get you all the back child-support payments that are owed you. I want to do it in a way that won't compromise the money or you, and won't jeopardize either Ray or you. But to do that, I need your confidence, your trust. I need to know that you won't decide that you have to go to the police until I say so, and then we'll go together. I promise, we will go. Further, I have to know that you won't talk to Trassi or anyone else, including the family. I need to have the same kind of trust in you that I'm asking from you. Also, to do that, the expenses might run up more than you anticipated."

Maggie put her hand on Barbara's arm and stopped her. "What kind of money are you talking about? And expenses? I have to know before I can agree."

"I'm talking about two hundred and ten thousand dollars, and expenses will go to several thousand, at a minimum."

Incredulity swept over Maggie's features. She laughed, a bitter, choked sound. "I don't believe you."

"That's what I'm going after, if I have your permission and cooperation."

"Did you tell me all the things I can't do so I'd jump at this?" Maggie asked, her voice subtly different now; she spoke as a businesswoman who had learned some things along the way.

"I told you why you shouldn't do the various things you've been contemplating, and the one thing you didn't contemplate."

"That's for sure," Maggie said. They started to walk again. After a moment Maggie said, "I won't talk to anyone and I'll do what you advise me to do." She looked at Barbara. "Shake?" They shook hands solemnly. Then Maggie said, "The police came here to ask questions. They already knew about the party and the vandalism. It was like you said, they just asked about Friday and afterward. They've been all over town asking questions. They know all our past history by now." She paused, then asked, "If they arrest Ray, will you defend him?"

"I can't. It would be a conflict of interest."

Maggie kicked a clump of seaweed. Then she said, "If they arrest him, his trial won't be for months. Could you take him later?"

"Maggie, you'll be my client for months. Ray needs an attorney now, before he talks to the police again. I have several names for you to give him, if you choose. All people my father and I would recommend."

"What if I decide I don't want you to represent me anymore, then could you take Ray?"

"No."

"Why not?" Maggie demanded.

"Because if I were defending him, you'd be at risk."

"You'd use what you know about me?" Maggie stopped again.

"Yes," Barbara said. "Nothing that was confided when we had an attorney-client relationship, but anything that developed afterward. If I had to use it, I would."

Maggie stared silently at her, then abruptly started to walk. Neither spoke again until they were back at the inn.

They dried themselves while Maggie went to get Mitch's birth certificate, the fingerprints, and the divorce decree. She handed Barbara an envelope, without comment, and Barbara gave her the paper with attorneys' names. She said she would keep in touch, and she and John left and drove to Newport.

At Mo's Seafood Restaurant, eating clam chowder, she asked John what he had made of Laurence.

"He's thirty, going on twenty," John said judiciously. "He complained that Maggie treats him like a kid much of the time." They both laughed. Then John said, "He thinks he wants to get married; she doesn't. He wishes there were dragons around so he could kill one for her. I know the feeling," he added.

For a time they sat holding hands, not eating, not talking, but when the waiter came to remove the soup bowls, Barbara said, "Not yet." She pulled loose from John and picked up her spoon. "Not another word about me or my client's problem child. What's happening with the Staley mine?" He had not brought it up for many days, she realized with a twinge of guilt.

"The usual bullshit," he said. "The miners lodged a complaint, unsafe working conditions. The commission hired me. The company hired its own experts, and now we snap and snarl at each other."

He was being too flippant; the little twinge of conscience was replaced with a stab of fear. "You'll go back, won't you?"

"Finish your chowder," he said. "I'm ready for halibut and the works." He looked around the restaurant. "I like this place."

The tables were picnic tables, with plastic tablecloths, and benches that were to be shared with whoever wanted to sit down and eat. The food was delicious, perfectly cooked seafood; the house specialty was clam chowder for which people traveled many miles. Outside the windows was a dock on Newport Bay, where people were fishing, children playing, seagulls swooping. Fishing boats were returning, riding the incoming tide, racing the fog.

By the time they left the restaurant, fog had shrouded all of Newport, turned lights into multicolored glowing clouds, made distances unpredictable, and played optical-illusion tricks with moving vehicles. "We could check into a motel," Barbara said doubtfully; she knew they would not find a room so late in the evening during the season.

"Let's go home," John said. They went to the car and he drove.

She could feel John's relief when the fog cleared and he picked up speed. She well knew that for many miles this road wound its way up and down, around and around, and each time it went down, it would be smothered by fog again, probably all the way through the Coast Range, possibly all the way home. They started down the hill they had just climbed, and before them lay a white lake of fog. John eased up on the gas and crept ahead cautiously.

And so it went, up into clear air, down into fog, mile after mile after mile. Neither spoke. Other cars were on the road; approaching they appeared to be formless glowing clouds that became defined slowly, then vanished. Now and then someone passed them in a suicidal rush, and their taillights were clouds on fire.

She should have driven, Barbara thought; she knew this road, not in a way that was communicable, but her hands, her reflexes knew it. Soon they would reach Mary's Mountain; when they curved around it, descended again, they would enter the broad Willamette Valley. Usually summer fog didn't get beyond that point, although winter fogs recognized no boundaries. If she were driving, she would know without question whether she should drive on east to I-5 or turn south onto Highway 99, a crooked narrow black road. It was her preferred route because it was twenty miles closer to home that way, and it didn't have the din and roar of an interstate with its countless trucks. But not in fog. She breathed a sigh of relief when they left the mountains and the valley lights shone clearly ahead.

"Good job," she said when John turned south on 99.

"Hairy," he said. "Thanks."

They were quiet until they reached their apartment, pulled off their sweatshirts, and had drinks in their hands. John had cleared out enough stuff so that they could sit in the living room, she in the good chair she had moved from her previous house, he in a new chair that they both suspected was not quite right but had bought anyway.

"Something's got to give," he said tiredly. "I didn't want to tell you about the Staley mine like that, in a public place. I wanted to talk it over, explain."

"No explanation is called for. You said the mine is unsafe, and you'll go back in it to prove your point. What's to explain? Besides, did I say a word? Did I scream or faint or throw a tizzy fit?"

"You screamed, all right," he said. "Inside you were screaming your head off, and it showed all over you."

"Well, shee-it," she said. "I'll just have to learn to hide my feelings, won't I?"

"Goddamn it! Don't do that! I told you up front what I do. And you said you weren't going to get involved in anything yet, not until we've had some time to sort things out about us."

"What do you want? A pledge that I'll sit home and not worry when you're in the field? Make dinner and do the laundry and be the sweet little housewife with nothing on her mind? If that's what you want, you should have stuck with Betty! You knew up front what I do, too."

His face twisted in anger at the mention of his ex-wife. "I know, all right. I know you hate what I do as much as I hate what you do. That's a given. But you don't have to get involved the way you do, that's what's different, everything on the line—professional life, personal life—all hanging out. Obsessed. You get obsessed with what you do, and it goes on and on until it's your whole life."

Shocked, she drank deeply of her gin and tonic. Then she said, "Surgeons get obsessed with the cut-open patient; I guess firemen get obsessed with a raging blaze; I know you get obsessed looking for a crack in a rock wall that might bring a mine down on your head. But I can't get obsessed with my work. I see. Now I understand. Of course I hate what you do. It's the test-pilot's-wife syndrome. But I didn't understand before that you hate what I do." She glanced at her glass but didn't pick it up again. She stood up. "I'm going to bed."

"Wait a minute, we're not through."

"I don't know. Maybe we are."

"Well, ask yourself why you have to identify with every client who comes along. Why you have to make them all personal crusades. What are you trying to prove?"

She walked from the room to the bathroom and brushed her teeth, and then went to bed. She was still awake much later when he got into bed beside her. They were careful not to touch.

In the morning she was ready to leave when John came from the bedroom. Before he could speak, she said, "I have to go. I think from now on, for the time being, neither of us should talk about our work. If you have to go somewhere and I'm not around, just leave a note. I'm not sure where I'll be all day."

"Fine," he said.

He didn't ask if she would be home early.

10

Barbara realized, driving to Frank's house, that the secret file cabinet in her mind had sprung open overnight, and all the things she had tucked away to be considered later had surfaced.

John's mother hadn't liked her; his children had been silent and watchful, resentful of her presence. His ex had become a burden, worrying about him; Barbara had filled in details silently. His ex had become the test pilot's wife, unable to still or conceal her fear. Now Barbara was playing that role.

Well, she demanded savagely, *what did you expect? That those problems would evaporate, vanish?* Maybe, she thought, and maybe she could have dealt with them a little at a time. Maybe there wasn't enough time in the space-time continuum to deal with the fact that he hated her work, what she did, probably who she was when she did it.

When she pulled into Frank's driveway, Bailey's car was close behind her. Frank opened the door.

She and Frank exchanged good mornings. "Two with one blow," he commented. "Coffee's on the table."

She went past him to the dinette and sat with her back to the glass doors. He had cleared away his breakfast; there were cups and the coffee carafe on the table, and the newspaper folded open to the editorial page.

"Hiya," Bailey said cheerfully, coming in with Frank. They took chairs, and Bailey began to go through his denim bag. "You get some prints for me?"

"Yes. His hospital birth record, hands and feet." She pulled the document out of her briefcase and passed it over.

"Good. I'll start with Wygood. You hit the jackpot with those names, Barbara. Thelma Wygood ordered a car from a broker in

New York, to be delivered in Miami. Two guys drove it down, Eddie Grinwald and a guy called Steve Wilford. They were supposed to deliver the car and collect a cashier's check for forty-two grand and take it back home. They never got back. The police found Grinwald's body in the motel they used, and the next day they found Wygood's body. Car, cashier's check, and Wilford were all missing."

Bailey pushed a folder toward Barbara. "It's all in there. Wilford's clean. Grinwald has a record from twenty years ago, manslaughter. Did four years. Funny coincidence, though. Wilford's description fits Mitch Arno to a T."

He pulled out a second folder. "Another coincidence. Happened that a second customer ordered another Lexus coupe, just about like the one headed for Miami. And this time Mitch Arno was supposed to deliver it, drive out from New York to somewhere up in Washington. On Saturday, August third, three A.M., Corvallis police found the Lexus in a ditch. All the goodies were gone—stereo, CD player, like that—but in the glove compartment they found a title transfer with the customer's name not filled in; the transfer was by the delivery company, R. M. Palmer Company. They get in touch with Palmer, and lo and behold, happens his attorney is on the West Coast, and he'll handle it. Enter Trassi on Saturday, August third."

"Story number three," Barbara commented.

Bailey grinned. "Cops are figuring Mitch picked up hitchhikers, kids who never even saw the title, didn't realize the car was up for grabs. They drove him around on the coast, he got away within walking distance of Maggie's place on Friday, and old man Arno found him. They have it all figured out."

"Let them figure," she said. "Anything else?"

"Major Works," he said. "Seems to be common knowledge that Russ Major's had a nervous breakdown, or is having it. Wygood left just about everything to Major, except for a few bequests for family, friends, like that, and she was buried on his island hideaway with only the family members present. He hasn't left the island since. Jolin, his security guy, has been everywhere. No one knows where he goes, when he goes, when he gets back. He reports only to Major. Not there now, though."

She gave him a dark look. Jolin, calling himself Waters, was at Valley River Inn, which he well knew. "She was buried on his island?"

"Seems it was in her will, written years ago, and she never got around to changing it. When you're her age, you're not too worried about kicking."

"Anything new about Mitch's murder?"

"Not much. They're digging through history, and they think they have the answers. It's not a big deal for them. Just another family feud."

Barbara stood up and went to the door to gaze out at Frank's immaculate garden and the two golden cats stalking shadows. That summed it up, she thought, shadow dancing, what she was doing.

She returned to her chair and gathered together the various reports Bailey had produced. "Okay," she said. "Go with the prints. I may want something later, but I can't think of anything right now."

And that summed it up, too, she thought bleakly; she couldn't think, period.

After Frank took Bailey to the door and returned, he asked bluntly, "What are you planning to do?"

"Don't know. Something's bugging the bejesus out of me, though. I feel like I'm stuck in the briar patch, and everywhere I look, the thorns are big and sharp."

"And poisonous. Keep that in mind, too. I've got stuff to plant in the garden." He watched her shove papers inside her briefcase, refill her cup, and walk out slowly to go upstairs.

When they came home from their prenuptial honeymoon, he had seen her walking around so lightly that she wouldn't have left footprints in snow. And now her feet were shod in lead. "Old man," he told himself sharply, "butt out. You knew it was going to happen."

He picked up the seed packets and went outside.

Upstairs, Barbara read through Bailey's reports, as meticulous as ever, and not helpful.

She picked up a magazine article Bailey had dug up about Major and Wygood. She didn't read the article, but studied their pictures. In one they had been posed waist deep in computer printouts arranged like waves and hills around them. They were both grinning like idiots and were as stylish as turnips. His hair was longer than hers, and he wore oversized glasses that had slid down his nose. Her hair had been cut with little regard to her plump face. She wore no discernible makeup, no jewelry except a watch. They both had on company T-shirts. The other picture had been taken at a trade show; he had on a business suit and tie, and running shoes; she had on a suit also, the skirt too short for her figure, and flat shoes, and her hair had been pouffed unbecomingly. They were holding hands in that picture. Barbara wondered if either of them had known the other was not pretty, not handsome. When he started dating models, Thelma would have come to know it, she thought sadly.

She began a Web search for Major and Wygood, and found thousands of entries. It was a familiar story, their rise from poverty, developing a program in a bed-sitting-room, the new programs, the company. Einstein with two heads, always Major/Wygood, or Wygood/Major, always paired, one as good as the other in their field, until he had become distracted by pretty young things.

So Thelma went to Europe to plot her revenge. Not for the money, but to hit hard where Major was vulnerable, probably the only place he was vulnerable. If she'd been after money, it would have been to her benefit to finish the program, put it on the market, and watch the cash flow in. She had been a full partner, after all. Not for money. In fact, she had spent money—

"Where's the damn cashier's check?" Barbara said under her breath.

She found the inventory of things from Mitch's belongings, then reread Bailey's account of the police report about the wrecked Lexus. No cashier's check for forty-two thousand dollars. Mitch might have cashed it; she rejected the idea. Not with all that money in the suitcase.

She started to pace again.

When Frank finished his garden chores, he looked at the two cats, both with muddy feet and bedraggled muddy tails, and shook his head. "You guys can't come in," he said. "Clean yourself up." He went inside the house, fastened the latch on the cat door, and cleaned himself up. He started up the stairs then to see what Barbara wanted for lunch, but halfway up, he stopped. He could hear her pacing, the way she did when she was engrossed in a puzzle. He hoped it was the Folsum dilemma that was making her move, not her own personal dilemma. That problem, he was certain, would not yield to logic and reason, no matter how many gray cells she put into action. Quietly he returned to the kitchen. She would eat whatever he fixed.

She ate salad, but he knew she was not tasting it. "Are you due over at Martin's at one?"

She blinked, then said, "Oh, God. I forgot." She looked at her watch. "It won't take me long. It's that 'he said, she said' business. Wrap that up, and then hand over a check to a couple of kids who got robbed by a car dealership. . . ."

He recognized the signs; he had done exactly this many times, thinking out loud, juggling people, happenings, things.

"Oh," she said then, still thinking, "are you going out? I'll pick up stuff upstairs if you are."

"I'm not going anywhere. Leave it."

"Thanks. I've got to run. I won't be long."

❖

She had finished her business at Martin's and was preparing to leave when a couple walked in hesitantly.

They were both in their forties, she guessed; the woman looked it, but he didn't at first glance. She was about five feet five and a little overweight, with a round face and pale blue eyes. Her hair was light brown, almost frizzy, it was so curly, and she looked terrified. He was over six feet and lean, with black hair and eyes.

"Ms. Holloway?" he said, still hesitant. "Ray Arno, and this is my wife, Lorinne. Can we talk to you?"

"Of course," she said, trying to hide her dismay. "Please, sit down."

Ray was anxious, but he looked more puzzled than frightened. He cleared his throat. "We know you're helping Maggie," he said, "and we've read about you before, the cases you've worked on, I mean. And my family keeps telling me to talk to a lawyer." He glanced at Lorinne. "She said we should at least talk to someone."

Lorinne nodded vigorously. "They might arrest him! They keep asking questions. You know about his brother Mitch, how he was murdered? They think Ray did it!"

"We had a fight nearly twenty years ago," Ray said patiently. "They're just doing their job, asking everyone questions. No one holds a grudge for nearly twenty years. Kids fight, but it doesn't mean anything when they're older. They know that's—"

"They do think it! All those questions! Maggie thinks they'll arrest him, too! Everyone thinks it except Ray. They think they had another fight and Ray killed him. That's what they think! You can tell by the way—"

"Honey, take it easy," Ray said. Almost apologetically he said to Barbara, "If you could just reassure her a little that it's just a routine investigation, something like that?"

"It isn't! Tell him it's more than that!"

There had not been a gap wide enough for Barbara to get in a word yet; now she did. "Mrs. Arno, please, I know how afraid you are, and you have cause, but it's very important that you keep control. And, Mr. Arno, you have to understand the situation, or you could do yourself damage. Please, both of you, just listen a minute," she said swiftly when it appeared that both of them were going to start talking again. "Mr. Arno, I can't act as your attorney, but I can give you some advice—"

"Why can't you," Lorinne cried. "We don't have much money, but the whole family will pitch in." She was near tears.

"It would represent a grave conflict of interest," Barbara told her, "because I already agreed to be Maggie's attorney in another matter. If the two cases came into conflict, I would have to withdraw from both of them. And no one knows when such a conflict might arise, especially when both cases involve a single family."

"But—"

"It's the law, Mrs. Arno. There's nothing I can do about that." She looked at Ray then and said soberly, "And you, I'm afraid, have not accepted the seriousness of the situation. They might arrest you and charge you with murder. Statistically, they know that murders are frequently committed by family members. And the fact seems to be that you were the last person who saw your brother alive, other than his killer or killers. You should have your own attorney. I gave some names to Maggie to pass on to you. Has she done that yet?"

He had gone pale with her words. "No."

Lorinne took his hand and held it, wide-eyed, panic-stricken.

"Call her and get them. My advice is for you to retain an attorney immediately and to refuse to answer any more questions except in your attorney's presence. Everything you say will be noted, and if there is a contradiction, they will seize upon it and use it in a way that could be damaging to you. People contradict themselves; they misremember; they leave out details. That's human, but it can look incriminating months later."

He looked more puzzled than before. "Ms. Holloway, there's nothing for me to leave out, or misremember. I've told them the truth. I don't have anything to lie about. There's nothing—"

"He can't lie! He's never told a lie in his life! He can't even fib a little. He's a good man, Ms. Holloway. A really decent man. He never learned how to lie because he's never needed to hide anything."

Studying Ray Arno's face, Barbara believed every word Lorinne was uttering. She said, "Mr. Arno, I'm on your side, I believe you, but that's beside the point now. Get a lawyer and take his advice. And please, accept that very good people, innocent people, sometimes get charged, put in jail; sometimes they get convicted of crimes they didn't commit. It happens, Mr. Arno."

"We've taught our kids that if they tell the truth, no harm will come to them," he said slowly. "It always seemed a good lesson to pass on."

"It is a good lesson," Barbara said. "The best. And you must keep telling the truth, no matter what."

He stood up and held out his hand to Barbara when she and Lorinne also got to their feet. "Thanks," he said. "I was deluding myself, wasn't I?" He grinned and looked boyish for a moment. He put his arm around Lorinne's shoulders and gave her a squeeze. "Time to march. I'll get a lawyer, Ms. Holloway. I'm grateful to you. I needed a swift kick, I guess. Thanks."

They walked out with his arm around his wife's shoulders.

When she returned to Frank's house, she told him about the Arnos' visit. "They're good people, fine people. You'd like them. Oh, shit!" She went upstairs.

Dinner for three, he thought, watching her out of sight. She was too troubled to give food a thought. He'd go round up John himself, if that's what it would take. Barbara's efforts toward domesticity had both amused and alarmed him. His alarm button had gone off only when he saw how important Barbara considered it, how she equated failure in the kitchen with something a hell of a lot more meaningful than that.

A little later he lifted the phone to call a fish market and was startled to hear Barbara saying, "That's right, Sally Bronson. My Visa number . . ." She rattled off a string of numbers and gave the expiration date, then said, "May I have a confirmation number?" The other person gave her a different string of numbers, and Frank hung up. What the hell . . . ?

When he tried the phone half an hour later, she was on it, again reciting a Visa card number. He started up the stairs to see what the hell, but he resisted the impulse; she would tell him when she had something to tell. Then he called up to her, "I'm going dinner shopping." He had to say it once more before she came to the top of the stairs.

"I'm sorry? What did you say?"

He said it a third time. "Won't be long. Everything's locked up down here."

"Oh," she said vaguely. "All right."

After shopping, he dropped in at the Patterson Street apartment. John opened the door, looked past him, then at him, not hiding his anxiety at all.

"Is something wrong?"

"Nope. I was in the neighborhood, came by to invite you to dinner. Bobby's at the house, working, not a thought in the world about the next meal."

John's face tightened. "Thanks, but not tonight."

"Well, it will be there, a plate out for you. Six-thirty, if you change your mind."

"Thanks again," John said stiffly. "You should have called, saved yourself the trip."

"Couldn't," Frank said. "I think she's into telemarketing or something. Kept the phone tied up all afternoon. Sometimes, watching her when she's hot after something, I wonder how the hell my wife put up with me for more than thirty years. Never thought to ask her, never guessed she had anything to put up with."

John grinned slightly. "She's like you were?"

"Yep. Not saying it's admirable, just that it's how she is. I recognize myself over and over. It's a little uncanny. Well, I've got to hustle some nice fat tiger prawns home and do interesting things to them."

Barbara came down the stairs as he was washing snap beans. "Wine for a dying-of-thirst voyager," she said piteously. He pointed toward the refrigerator, and she helped herself. He then pointed to a small glass dome covering an assortment of cheeses, and she helped herself to a bit of cheese, too.

"I've run up a terrible phone bill," she said then. "When it comes in, let me know how much. See, I got to thinking about the cashier's check, but of course Wygood never had one, not for forty-two thousand. The car was part of the payoff. But why would she want to be paid off? She was filthy rich already. Then I got to worrying about all those telephone numbers, the other numbers." She was wandering in and out of the kitchen. When she paused, she sipped wine or nibbled cheese.

"Okay," she said. "What if that long string was a hotel confirmation number? So I began calling every hotel number in her notebook—Zurich, Paris, San Francisco—and I made reservations each time and got a confirmation number each time. They'll check the credit card and know it's a fake, but meanwhile, I have what I was going after. It's a confirmation number, all right, for the Hilton at Miami International. Then I called United and said I was trying to clear up a credit card misunderstanding, and an obliging man told me that Thelma Wygood had had a reservation for the flight to San Francisco on July twenty-third, that she was a no-show, but unfortunately they had not received a cancellation, and the charge would have to be paid. I said I understood."

Frank studied her; she showed not a trace of embarrassment or guilt. She caught his searching gaze and grinned, lifted her wine glass and drained it.

"Then I started to wonder about the other phone numbers—bookstores, and a deli in Seattle. Why? A long way to order a pastrami on rye, don't you think?" She poured more wine. "I called the Seattle numbers to find out where they're located, a bookstore and a deli, within half a block from the Major Works headquarters. Useful, if you happen to be working in Seattle, but from Zurich?"

She was pacing again, her voice rising and falling as she moved close to the sink, then farther away. Frank turned off the water and dried his hands.

"I began to do some heavy thinking about Thelma Wygood," she said. "Looked up things about her on the Internet, and found out a lot. She and Major were equals in every way; her name came first as often as his did when they released a new program. She wasn't shy about taking credit for her work, either. She knew damn well what she had done and what it meant. I'm getting ahead of myself," she said apologetically, returning to the kitchen.

"I tried to put myself in her place. I'm in Zurich, and leave carrying nothing but the briefcase with the program and my purse, maybe with a toothbrush and a nightgown in it. I have a reservation for the Miami airport motel, and a flight out early the following morning. What do I plan to do with the car and the money? I can't get through airport security with a metal suitcase full of money, and I sure as hell wouldn't check it through. So what? Why the stopover in Miami? Why not a connecting flight on to San Francisco if that's where I wanted to be?"

She paused. "Putting myself in her head made me realize that in many ways Maggie Folsum is like her. She had her party to show her family, her parents and brothers, that, by God, she had done it and done it alone. Rub their noses in it a little. Women like that are fed up with achieving a lot and having the credit go somewhere else."

Her voice had become a bit hard-edged.

"If I argued a case and won it before the Supreme Court, do you imagine for a second that I'd go all demure and shy and say, 'Daddy told me what to say'?"

Frank burst out laughing, and she grinned again, broader. "Anyway, you can see where my thoughts were taking me. I just don't believe Thelma Wygood would have let someone take her program and claim it as his own. And if that wasn't the case, then she and Major might have done something extremely foolish. And, as it turned out, fatally dangerous."

Frank's eyes narrowed, and now he poured wine for himself. "Let's have a seat," he said, motioning toward the dinette. He carried the bottle in with him.

"Okay," Barbara said. "I can imagine how bookstores would be useful if you're conspiring. A simple message left with a secretary: The book Mr. Major ordered will arrive on the third, something like that. But it would be limited, don't you think? But a deli that's open until two in the morning, all day, that offers more possibilities, especially if you own the building, the deli, all of it. I haven't checked it out, but I'd put down money that Major owns that whole block."

"You're suggesting that she might have planned to turn over the car and the money in Miami to private investigators, FBI, something like that?" Frank said. "Then fly to the West Coast. Another trip to the island next? Maybe." He drank his wine, deep in thought, then said, "It's a stretch, Bobby. You're speculating a lot, and assuming a lot, too."

"Yes," she admitted. "It just makes sense this way. Nothing else does. Would they have had a fight in public that everyone seems to know about? Then the elaborate separation, all the way to Europe for her. And for him to have sported Barbie dolls in public? I bet they scared him to death. None of that's in character with anything I've been able to find out about them."

"But what's that program she was selling, then?" Frank asked after a moment.

"I don't know. I want to ask Major."

"If Major's in seclusion, occupied with having a nervous breakdown, that step might be in the range of hard to impossible."

"I know. I'm going to try something. First I wanted to air it all, and have a bit of wine." She drew the notebook from her pocket. "Dave's Deli, my next move."

She went to the kitchen phone; Frank followed, then stood nearby as she dialed. When a man said, "Dave's Deli," she said, "I have an urgent message for Mr. Major."

The man on the other end said, "Hold on." Then he yelled, "Dave, you want to take this?" There was a lot of background noise; apparently the deli was busy.

"This is Dave," a different man said after a moment.

"I have a message for Mr. Major. It's urgent. Tell him it's about Thelma and Penelope." She gave Frank's number, and Dave hung up without another word.

"Now we wait," she said, then let out a long breath.

11

When Frank mentioned that he had invited John to dinner, Barbara momentarily looked startled, then she shrugged. "I'm not telling him any of the new developments," she said. "I think it's best not to involve him further."

"Okay," he said, but he had mixed feelings. One day he would be the one kept in the dark, and he knew very well how that would sit; on the other hand, John was curiously innocent about a lot of things. Also, the fewer people who knew about this matter, the better. Still, there would be injured pride. None of your business, he reminded himself, and turned the shrimp in the marinade of garlic and oil.

Barbara went to the door when the bell rang at six-thirty. John was holding a bottle of wine. She had a flashing memory of the first time he had come here to dinner, and had brought flowers and a bottle of Grand Marnier. The flowers were for her father, he had said gravely when she reached for them.

"Hi," he said, his gaze sweeping over her—up, down, then fixing on her face. "No flowers, no coals to Newcastle."

Her voice was husky when she said, "Come on in."

Inside, he set the bottle down on the side table in the hall and took her in his arms. "I missed you."

She nodded. "Me, too."

Frank stopped at the other end of the hall when he saw them, and backed up again, returned to his food preparation. It might just be a temporary truce, but truces were good. They led to negotiations, which sometimes led to compromises and even agreements.

The truce lasted through dinner, although neither Barbara nor John had much to say. They listened to Frank's stories and laughed at the right places. Twice the phone rang and Barbara jumped up from the table with a hasty "Excuse me." Each time she returned and did not say a word about the caller.

After dinner, John washed the pots and pans the way he always did at Frank's house; Barbara dried them and put them away. Then there was an awkward moment.

"You're waiting for a phone call?" John asked.

She nodded.

"Any idea when to expect it? How long you'll wait?"

"No. It might not even happen."

He regarded her without any expression for a time, then said, "I better get on my way. It's a long walk."

"You walked over?" She realized that he had expected them to drive back in her car.

"Give you a lift," Frank said.

John thanked him and said no. "I need the exercise."

Barbara walked to the door with him. "You could hang out for a while. The call might come any minute, and we'd both leave."

"And it might not. See you later."

He didn't ask if she'd be home early.

She paced while Frank read, then she played with the cats, then she paced again. She sat down and stood up many times. She should see a counselor, she thought; no, John should see one. They should both see one. But he wouldn't. She realized she was chasing her own tail and stopped, then went over her reasoning about Thelma Wygood again.

At eleven she said, "Dad, go on to bed. I'll just read for a little while. He isn't going to call this late."

Wordlessly Frank left the living room; he returned with a sheet, which he draped over the back of the couch. He knew she would go nowhere until that call came, or morning came, but maybe she would stretch out and get some rest.

At fifteen minutes before twelve the phone rang. She ran to pick it up before the machine took it. "Hello."

A hoarse voice demanded, "Who are you? Did you leave a message for me? I'm Russ Major."

"I called," she said, and sank down into a chair. "My name is Barbara Holloway. I'm an attorney in Eugene, Oregon. I think I have something that belongs to you."

"How much do you want?"

"Just to talk."

"How do you know anything about Penelope? What do you know about Thelma?"

"Not on the phone, Mr. Major. I have to talk to you in person."

"Get up here to Seattle. I'll have you met." To someone else he said, even more hoarsely, "Shut up. I'm handling this."

"I can't do that," Barbara said. "Mr. Major, there's an attorney in town who works for the Palmer Company. I don't want them to know I'm in touch with you, and if I leave, they might follow me. You'll have to come here."

At the mention of Palmer, there was a strangled sound, then a different voice said coldly, "I don't know who you are, or what game you're playing. We'll get back to you. In the morning. Nine o'clock. Be at this number." He hung up.

When Barbara got home half an hour later, John was asleep in the living room, sprawled out in a chair. He would be stiff and sore, she thought in dismay. He roused, rubbed his eyes, and peered at her.

"Can we go to bed now?"

She held out her hands to pull him upright.

12

Frank was in his robe and slippers when he let her in the next morning. He picked up the newspaper, led the way to the dinette, where he tossed the paper on the table, and walked out.

"We have to come up with a good place to put Major where we can talk to him," she said to his back. He vanished into the hall to his bedroom and closed the door hard.

The doorbell rang and she went to admit Bailey, who looked as out of sorts as her father. "Eight o'clock!" he grumbled. "Jeez, Barbara."

"I've been up for hours," she said. "Where can we hide a guy, maybe more than one?"

He shook his head. "It's eight o'clock," he explained.

"Oh, right." After pouring coffee for them both, she filled him in. "So, they'll call back at nine. And I want to be able to tell them where to hole up."

"And maybe they won't call," he pointed out. "And if they call, maybe they won't come down here."

"Let's pretend they will."

Frank came in then, with wet hair but dressed. "I've found that what helps digestion is silence until after breakfast," he said coldly. "You guys want to eat? Just a simple yes or no."

"Yes," they said simultaneously.

Frank busied himself at the refrigerator, pulling out things, setting them down on the counter.

"Well?" Barbara said. She began to drum her fingers on the table.

Bailey scowled and said, just as coldly as Frank had done, "That's no help."

Frank was folding an omelette when Bailey said, "Sylvia's place."

For a moment Frank stared at him, then he nodded.

Bailey made the call from the wall phone. He had to get past two people before Sylvia was on the line. "Hiya, Sylvia. Want to play cops and robbers?" He grinned broadly. "Yeah, right. A guy or maybe two—hell, I don't know, maybe more—need a place for a private conversation."

He listened, nodded to Barbara, and said, "I'll tell them. And I'll call back with some details."

After he hung up, he said, "Okay. They're houseguests, but they'll never know anyone new has arrived, way that place is set up. And they should come in a limo if possible, so they won't be conspicuous," he finished, absolutely deadpan.

Major called at five minutes past nine. Barbara snatched up the wall phone. "Holloway."

"We're coming. Tell me where to meet you."

She gave him the Fentons' names and telephone number, then said, "I'll turn this over to my associate, who can give you driving instructions. Can you come in a limousine, with darkened windows, perhaps?"

"Yes." He said something to someone else, then said, "Here, you do this part."

Barbara handed her phone to Bailey.

Later, in his downtown office, Frank opened the wall safe and brought out the briefcase. Barbara removed a few sheets of print-out and put them in her own briefcase; he returned the other one to the safe and locked it.

At twenty-five minutes after twelve Barbara went out to Bailey's car, and they left. At twelve-thirty, Ruthie buzzed Frank to tell him Mr. Fenton's driver had arrived to pick him up.

"Anyone tailing us?" Barbara asked Bailey as he headed out Franklin Boulevard.

"Nope. But they're watching the office, two of them. Local guys."

They drove out Franklin, past the university buildings, past the I-5 cloverleaf, over the river, and then turned south. The road became narrow and winding. An overloaded hay truck crawled along in front of them. Strawberry fields, farms, a miniranch or two, more subdivisions . . . Bailey turned again, onto a county road that began to snake up into the hills. He turned once more, and they were driving along a high stone wall. When they came to a gate, he stopped and rolled down his window. "Ms. Holloway to see Mrs. Fenton," he said into a speaker. The gate opened soundlessly; he drove through, and the gate closed again. There was a wide meadow all around them now, with horses and cattle grazing, and no fence in sight. Barbara knew she was gaping, and couldn't help it. A real, by-God ranch twenty-five minutes out of Eugene! Dense forest was in the distance, on this side of the stone wall; a bridge over a creek; gardens, fenced off from the cattle.

"How big is this place?" she asked.

"Eight hundred acres. A thousand. Somewhere about that. Jeez! Can you imagine what the property tax is?"

When the house came into view, at first glance it seemed small, then wings began to appear, and the wings had their own wings.

Part of the building was two-story, most of it was one. The closer they got, the bigger it grew. They passed a swimming pool with half a dozen people lounging about, no one in the water. Bailey followed a curve around the house and stopped at a side door, at least two wings removed from the front entrance.

"We are here," he said cheerfully. "And there's Sylvia herself. What a doll!"

The limousine with Frank inside pulled up behind them as they got out of the car.

Sylvia was more garish than she had been before; she was wearing lime-green silk pants and a pink overshirt with a blue sash. She glittered with jewelry. Her hair was more yellow than orange today, and her earrings were dangling rubies.

Her broken leg had made a miraculous recovery. She rushed to the limousine door and opened it herself. "Frank, you beautiful hunk! Come on out." As Frank climbed out, she said to Barbara, "I've warned him fair and square, the day Joe kicks, I'm coming after him. Haven't I warned you, Frank?" She threw her arms around Frank and kissed him on the mouth. To Barbara's amazement, he hugged and kissed back. "Of course," Sylvia said, disentangling herself, "Joe enjoys perfect health, so it won't be tomorrow, but I want Frank to take good care of himself, so when I'm ready, he'll still be full of piss and vinegar. This way, this way."

The door was only steps from the car; they entered a spacious hallway filled with art: paintings on the walls, sculptures on the floor and on stands, tables adorned with gilt and inlays of mother-of-pearl, red-velvet-covered chairs. . . . The result was one of clutter, expensive clutter, but too much, too mixed, too crowded, the worst taste Barbara had ever seen west of Versailles.

"There are a couple of bedrooms," Sylvia said, gesturing, "and a sitting room, and a little dining room. A soon as Mr. Smith and company arrive, lunch will be brought in to the dining room. If you need anything, there's the telephone." She looked around for it, then said, "Maybe it's in the sitting room. It's somewhere. You'll find it. The Smith party will be met at the gate and driven around by one of my boys. Well, enjoy."

She started to walk down the hall; Barbara walked with her. "Mrs. Fenton, this is so very generous—"

"Dear, if I'm going to be your stepmother someday, I insist that you call me Sylvia. I wish I could work more with Bailey. But he holds back. Well, this is better than nothing. . . ." She continued to talk until she reached the door, and left.

When Barbara turned around, both Frank and Bailey were laughing. She grinned, then said, "Well, you beautiful hunk, let's look over the sitting room." Bailey went out to move his car and wait for Major and company.

Frank and Barbara were in the sitting room, exclaiming over the excessive art, when Bailey knocked on the door, then entered with three other men.

Barbara stepped forward. "How do you do, Mr. Major. I'm Barbara Holloway, and this is my father and colleague, Frank Holloway." Major's handshake was limp. Barbara turned to the next man.

"Garrick Jolin," he said. His handshake was almost too hard. "This is our driver, he'll wait outside."

"As will our driver," Barbara said, nodding to Bailey. He left with the other man. Her thoughts were swirling; if this was head of security for Major Works, who was that man at Valley River Inn?

Major was exactly what she had expected, bespectacled, unruly long hair, nervous. Jolin was stoop-shouldered, with a receding hairline, and a hardness that was very much like the hardness Bailey showed sometimes. He had a perceptive gaze that was direct and wholly skeptical.

"There's a washroom, second door down the hall," Barbara said. "Mrs. Fenton said she would have lunch brought in."

"Ms. Holloway, we didn't come here to party," Jolin said rudely. "What do you have? What do you know? And how do you know anything?"

"Let's sit down and I'll tell you."

Major was moving around the room as if examining the various objects—a Ming vase next to a crude pottery vase with some cattails in it, a Miró surrounded by what looked like calendar art. . . . He didn't stop at any one thing long enough to take it in, though, just kept moving. Now he perched on the edge of a chair. He looked ill, haggard.

"I have your program, and a suitcase with over two hundred thousand dollars in it," Barbara said. "I know who killed Thelma Wygood and why. I think I know what she was doing and why."

Major jumped to his feet and started his aimless walk-around again. Jolin said in a hard voice, "Don't play games. What do you want? How did you get anything? Can you prove what you say?"

She opened her briefcase and withdrew the sheets of printout, handed them to Jolin. Major made a soft moaning sound and sat down again, his gaze fixed on the printouts. Jolin handed them to him, and after no more than a cursory glance, he nodded.

"Just tell us what you know," Major said thickly. "How did you get them?"

"I can't tell you everything," she said. "I have a client involved in this, but I'll tell you as much as possible. Afterward, will you fill in some blanks for me? Quid pro quo?"

Major nodded. Jolin was impassive.

"Some time ago an employee stole a new program from you, and you staged a charade to catch the people responsible. Ms. Wygood played her role brilliantly and the trap was set, but the delivery man got greedy, killed his partner and Ms. Wygood, and then he came here to Oregon, no doubt to hide and contact a high bidder. However, he himself has been murdered. And the money and the program ended up in my hands. An attorney named Trassi has been in touch with me to negotiate a sale, and I've stalled him."

Major was on his feet again, with both hands clenched hard. "Wilford's dead? Who killed him?"

"His name wasn't Wilford, and he's dead. I believe Palmer's men tried to force him to reveal where the money and program were hidden, and then they killed him."

"How did you get your hands on anything?" Jolin asked then. His eyes were narrowed to slits, and he looked as tense as Major.

"For now, it's enough that I have the items, and Trassi knows I have them. There's another man in the picture, and he has made a generous offer also. I don't know where he fits in, but he knows all about this."

Jolin looked surprised, then his face became expressionless again.

"It's your turn," Barbara said then. "Was the scenario I gave pretty accurate? You were deliberately baiting a trap?"

Major nodded. "God help us all, we did." He went to stand by a window, facing out. "For nothing," he said in a choked voice. "Nothing."

There was a light tap on the door. Frank went to open it. A pretty young woman in a maid's uniform said lunch was in the dining room.

Briskly, Barbara said, "Why don't you both go wash up, and then we can pick at lunch. We all have things to think about."

After they left together, Barbara said, "I might as well tell them more; Jolin's going to start digging and find out anyway."

Frank agreed. "But who the hell is Waters? Let's go see what kind of a spread Sylvia sent our way."

There was gazpacho in a crystal bowl set in a second bowl of crushed ice, surrounded by crystal cups. There were several pâtés, and baguettes and crusty brown bread, little sandwiches, flutes of paper-thin pink ham. . . .

Jolin and Major joined them in the dining room a few minutes later. Major didn't even glance at the table but started roaming. Jolin spread pâté on brown bread, ladled out gazpacho, took them both to Major, and practically forced them into his hands. Major looked as if he didn't understand.

"Try it," Jolin said, and returned to the table. No one sat down; they moved around the table and picked at lunch.

"You guessed it almost exactly," Jolin said. "It was a trap. We had men in Miami at the motel, waiting for Thelma to get there with the car and the money. We had an FBI number to call when it happened. There wasn't any reason to suspect violence would occur. There hadn't been any violence in the Palmer deals we were able to learn about; simple business transactions, that's all they were." He sounded very bitter. "The plan was to turn over the cash and the car to the FBI, put a tail on the delivery men with the program, and go after Palmer and his client. We know who he is, but there's no proof. Thelma would have been our star witness; she kept a meticulous diary from day one." He drank some gazpacho and set the cup down hard. "It was all worked out. For nothing. We've spent all this time chasing after Wilford."

Across the room Major had put his food down, untasted.

Jolin ignored him. "How did you come into it? Who told you about the theft?"

She gave a bare-bones synopsis of her talk with Waters. Jolin didn't move while she spoke, but Major prowled aimlessly about the room.

"It's almost right," Jolin said when she concluded. "A few details are off, but it's close enough. Our version of what took place," he said harshly, then told about the theft three years earlier. "So we knew the guy had bought a car from the Palmer Company; it was delivered by Steve Wilford and Eddie Grinwald, who flew back to New York afterward, and our guy headed for California and within a few months started his own company. No proof, parallel research, back luck, bad timing—there wasn't a damn thing we could do. The other company brought out the program, and that was that." He glanced at Russ Major, who was standing at a window, possibly even gazing out. "Russ and Thelma knew in a second it was theirs; they told me, and none of us ever mentioned it to anyone else. Our research teams suspected, of course, but since no one talked about it, the matter died. We tightened security, and tried to ferret out the spy."

"Do you know yet who the in-house spy is?" Barbara asked.

"Yes. The day after Thelma was reported dead, a woman left without warning, terrified." He scowled. "A little late to find out, though. Anyway, about eighteen months ago Thelma came up with the scheme to trap the thieves. It looked good on paper," he added, bitter again. "She reasoned that if it had happened once, it would happen again with the next big program, and she was determined to stop it. She didn't call Trassi or make any movement in that direction. Instead, she and Russ both let out a leak about an exciting new program that was coming along, and, of course, our spy informed our competitor. We tightened security again, as if we intended to guard our work to the hilt. Then they staged the first of their fights. The fights became nastier and more public; they separated, and she finally took her research team to Zurich and waited for someone to make the first move. The last time she flew home, she and Russ went to the island, then came back to Seattle and threw a big party, a celebration party, not to announce anything, but to suggest the last bugs had been worked out. Russ showed up with a model draped on his arm, and Thelma took off that night for Zurich. Our spy was probably on the phone before she got to SeaTac. Two weeks later a man approached her and the opening gambit was played out."

He studied Barbara, then said, "I don't quite understand how Waters knows as much as he does, what his game is. Can you describe him?"

"Smooth and personable, six feet tall, broad-shouldered, a good voice, dark hair and eyes. He claimed he was head of security for the company involved and he was persuasive and believable."

"Gilmore!" Major said suddenly. "That son of a bitch!"

"Maybe," Jolin said. "Stuart Gilmore is the man who approached Thelma in Zurich. He's an ex-actor turned con man who's worked for the Palmer Company for a dozen or more years. He makes the first move. It could be him. But why tell you as much as he did? Too much maybe."

"Probably several reasons," Barbara said. "They had no idea how much I already knew, what all Mitch might have had with him. He could have kept Thelma Wygood's ID, her wallet or something that would have led us to her murder and eventually sent us to the police. He made a special plea that I not go to the police, that the affair be kept confidential. But also, I think, to give me an alternative choice, one that appeared honorable and just. And lucrative. His offer was all the money, no questions, and justice served. To cover the possibility that we had her name, he had to make it authentic and detailed enough for me to accept. He was good," she added.

"Why didn't you take his offer?"

"I didn't trust him. And after I read about Thelma Wygood, I came to disbelieve she would sell out her company. Also, I really do have a client to protect." She looked at Major again and said very sharply, "Mr. Major, I need your attention. What do you want me to do with your program?"

"Give it to Palmer's lawyer," he said in a low voice.

"It's a setup, isn't it? How long before they'll know it's a phony?"

He looked helplessly at Jolin. "We worked for more than two years on it, Thelma and I, before we knew it was all wrong. It will take them longer. Our teams never found out, and no one else ever had access to the entire program. Everyone was excited. It would have revolutionized the telecommunications industry, but it was wrong."

"After you knew Thelma was dead, why didn't you go to the police?"

Major looked agonized.

Jolin answered. "What was the point? We didn't go to them beforehand, too afraid of a leak. And afterward? We had no proof, the diary of a dead woman, unsigned, coded, no names in it. Not even a real diary, just pages that she sent on as she wrote them. It would have been pointless, but the rumor would have spread that she had sold out. We weren't willing to do that. We didn't have anything," he said bitterly. "No car, no money, no witness—nothing!"

Barbara could no longer contain her impatience with Major and his ceaseless movements. "Mr. Major, please sit down so I can talk to you."

He stopped walking and looked at her with a bewildered expression.

"Please, just sit down a minute." She waited until he did so. "Do you have any interest in that money? It's two hundred forty thousand dollars."

He shook his head and looked as if he was ready to move again, but Frank spoke now. "Would anyone pay out that kind of money for a program sight unseen, without a demonstration or something?"

Jolin and Major exchanged glances. Jolin said, "You know what vaporware is?"

"Not a clue," Frank admitted.

"Okay. A company announces a new program that's to be released at some future date. The day comes and goes, and the product doesn't appear. It's so common in our field that there's more vaporware than software out there. Major Works has never in twenty years announced a vaporware product. Never. And people know that. Thelma let out a hint early on that they were working on a voice-recognition system; not a blatant hint, but enough, and then she and Russ clammed up. They both let their research teams in on the fact that they were interested in the telecommunications problems and were tackling them. Then they had the big party to celebrate; and another, final, hint was dropped: they would have an announcement for the fall trade show. That was last spring, just before their last big battle. The other company had to bite."

Frank shook his head. Rumors and rumors of rumors. A crazy business.

"All right," Barbara said. "However that went, they did pay out a large amount of money and they don't yet have what they paid for. Mr. Major, your people can't go after Palmer now or the person who hired him. Neither can you get involved with Trassi or Gilmore. The minute they detect your presence, they'll know you're onto them, and they'll cover their tracks thoroughly. There's no way you should know about any of them, is there?"

He looked at Jolin, as if for help, then said, "No. They think we don't know anything."

"Right," she said. "The man who killed Thelma was Mitch Arno. His ex-wife is owed just about the amount in the suitcase for past child support. I intend to get it for her, in a way that will satisfy the legal requirements. But I'm talking about justice more than law, Mr. Major. Ray Arno very likely will be arrested for the murder of his brother Mitch, and he is innocent. I don't intend to stand by and see him get the death penalty for that murder."

"You'll throw Thelma out for them to gnaw on," Jolin said heavily.

"No, I won't. You can't punish her killer, and you can't go after Trassi and Palmer; I can. But I'll need your cooperation, and Mr. Major's cooperation."

"Why would you?" Jolin asked.

"My client is due that money, but she'll turn it over to the police along with the program before she'll let Ray Arno hang for Mitch's death. They wrecked her bed-and-breakfast inn and would have killed her, no doubt, if she had been home. They threatened her children, and me. They tortured and murdered Mitch Arno. An innocent man is at deadly risk. I think they've gone far enough." She knew that was only the surface of her reasons, but she would not have been able to explain herself to these two men, since she could not explain it even to herself.

Jolin continued to study her, his face as expressionless as stone.

Major was up again, on his feet, on the move. "We'll do whatever you say," he said, going to the window. "If you can keep Thelma out of it." He swung around to face her. "I intend to destroy Dan Frisch; getting the program into his hands will do it. It will take time, but he'll be ruined, he won't steal another program. Can you keep your client in line? Will she cooperate, not hand anything over to the police? Ms. Holloway, I want Frisch and I want Palmer, even more than the tools they used."

"I can't defend Ray Arno until my client and I conclude our business, but at that time I want to step in. I want the men who killed Mitch and tore up Maggie Folsum's inn, and I want Trassi, who was more than likely directing the killers. To get them, I'll have to involve Palmer. I can't work out in the open yet, but there's a lot I can start with in the background."

Jolin shook his head. "You can't get them. They've been too careful too long."

"Maybe not," she admitted. "But I have a chance, and you don't. It's that simple. And for openers, I'll want everything you've learned, and then for your people to back off, or work under the direction of my own detective."

He pursed his lips and looked at Major, who nodded. "She's right. She has a chance. Tell us what you need."

"Can I hold out some pages of printout until Trassi makes good on promises? Would that satisfy the person behind all this?"

Major's expression changed, became almost demonic. "Yes! Keep out the first hundred pages, and the last fifty or so. Frisch's team will go crazy trying to fill in the missing pieces. They'll have enough to do to keep them busy for six months, longer, but Dan Frisch will be driven to finish it himself." Abruptly he swung around to face out the window, where he stood rigidly with his hands thrust into his pockets.

Watching him, Barbara realized he wanted to destroy Frisch, his rival, competitor, thief, and he knew how to do it, because whatever it was that drove Frisch drove him as well, just as it had driven Thelma Wygood.

"Let's iron out some details," Jolin said then, and for the next two hours Barbara and Jolin worked on their plans.

Suddenly Major participated again. "Ms. Holloway," he said bleakly, "you know the expression 'Money is no object'? Usually no one really means that. I do. Just get them, any way you can, legal or not. Just get them. If you can't, I'll get them myself. I wanted to. He stopped me." He gave Jolin a bitter look. "But he won't stop me again if I have to do it."

13

Major and Jolin left as soon as they finished; Frank left with the Fenton driver, Ralph, and Barbara with Bailey.

"So you got real backing," he said after she told him about the meeting. "Good work."

"They have an airstrip they use out of Vancouver, Washington. They'll drive there, then fly back to the island, and by eight or so, Jolin will start faxing me all the stuff they've gathered so far."

"Tonight? Barbara, remember Hannah, my wife? You know, I've got a whole other life?"

"You don't need to be there. But I've been thinking. If Waters really is Gilmore, he's going to fly away free as a bird. He romanced a lonely woman in Switzerland, so what?"

She was well aware that Bailey had gone into his hard-listening attitude. He said sourly, "But you've got an idea."

"I may have an idea," she said. "What if a failed actor turned con man met a foolish, rich old woman who longed for the roar of greasepaint and the smell of the crowd, and above all else her own theater, a return of glory? How much do you suppose he'd try to take her for?"

There was a strange sound from Bailey; she glanced at him and realized he was chuckling.

"You want Sylvia to work a sting," he said. "Jeez, she'd love it!"

"Could she pull it off?"

"Barbara, she looks and acts like a nut, but she's as shrewd as they come. And Joe indulges her. She'd love it, and Joe will play along and be happy as a clam. And when the time comes, they know every judge in the state. If she goes for a sting, consider him stung."

"Would she be willing to testify, go the whole distance?"

Bailey laughed out loud. "Are you kidding? Jeez, I wonder what getup she'll wear."

Very softly, Barbara said, "They'll send Gilmore's picture. I'll let you know if he's calling himself Waters."

She had Bailey drop her off a few blocks from her apartment at a Safeway, where she studied the gourmet section of frozen entrées, picked two, and lettuce and tomatoes, and thought with relief that dinner was under control. She walked home.

The truce was still holding. John laughed when she unloaded her bag of groceries. "Look in the freezer," he said. She found half a dozen more frozen entrées there.

He didn't ask what she had been up to all day, and she didn't ask about the Staley mine. After they finished eating and washed the few dishes, she said, "I left my car in the office lot. I'll go over, pick up some faxes, and drive home."

"I'll walk over with you."

Neither had been truly relaxed, but a new tightness appeared on his face, sounded in his voice.

"There's no point in that," she said.

"I'll come," he said.

She shook her head, and suddenly he grinned. "See, you're still doing it. You get impatient and shake your head like a dog with a bone. But, impatient or not, I don't think it's a good idea for you to be out alone at night when you're dealing with the kind of people you seem to gravitate to."

She signed in exasperation. "I've been a big girl for a long time—"

"I'll tag along a few paces behind you," he said.

"Jesus!" she muttered.

"You have any idea how much like your father you just sounded? When do you have to be there?"

They walked to the office together. Half a block from the apartment, he reached for her hand.

The next morning she started to read the faxes. At eight-thirty a special-delivery parcel arrived: Gilmore's picture from his acting days, and two snapshots that Thelma Wygood had taken. Gilmore was calling himself Brad Waters these days. He had been blond in Zurich. There was also a photocopy of Thelma's diary, starting with June fourth. "A blond man introduced himself as Brian, and bought me a drink at the Hilton Bar. His first words were 'God, you look like an American. Please be American. A Kansas drawl would sound like heaven.' It was a very good way to start. We talked a few minutes, nothing of consequence."

Barbara flipped through the pages; some of the entries were quite long, and there were a lot of them.

Bailey arrived a few minutes before nine, and Frank a few minutes later. They both started on the faxes. Bailey concentrated on Gilmore's dossier.

"A snap," he said after a few minutes. "Sylvia will chew him up and spit him out."

"If Trassi actually calls Sunderman to set up a time for a meeting,

I'll call Waters and make a date. It won't take me long to shake him, and he might be in a rush to get out of town afterward, once his role is played out here. I'll let you know when."

Frank looked up sharply. "What the devil are you conniving?"

When Barbara told him, he looked troubled, then grudgingly he nodded. "It probably will work. But you're cutting it pretty close, Bobby."

"I know." She motioned toward the faxes. "I'll go through all this stuff and wait for Trassi's call." She was relieved that no one asked what her backup plan was if Trassi didn't call.

"Word is, they're going to arrest Ray Arno today," Bailey said.

"I know," Barbara said morosely.

She made copies of all the Gilmore material, and Bailey left to talk to Sylvia. Barbara and Frank settled in to read. At eleven Frank wandered down the corridor to Lou Sunderman's office to tell the tax attorney that he had an interesting problem for him. He was humming under his breath; he and Lou regarded each other as members of alien species. Frank thought anyone who liked spending all his time studying new tax laws and trying to find ways to get around them was straitjacket material. And he well knew that Lou thought anyone who chose to hobnob with criminals, possibly murderers, was a seriously deranged pervert.

When Frank returned an hour later, he handed Barbara a sheet of paper nearly covered with his heavy scrawl. "Lou says that's what he'll need from Maggie. Marriage license, divorce decree, kids' birth certificates . . . He's probably being fussy, but he says the more he can produce at the first meeting with the IRS, the better."

She called Maggie, who sounded terrible, frantic with worry. She would get the documents together and bring them over the following day.

"They'll arrest Ray, won't they? He has a lawyer, a man named Bishop Stover, someone who comes in to the sports shop now and then. I told him to try one you recommended, but he said a lawyer he knew would be better. . . . Barbara, I'm so scared for him."

"Take it easy," Barbara said. "Don't go to pieces. We'll talk tomorrow. When will you get here? You might as well come to the office."

When she hung up, she cursed. "Stover! For God's sake!"

"Maybe he'll shake himself for a friend," Frank said. Stover was not a bad man, not evil; he was lazy, and too many of his clients ended up going for a plea bargain. No doubt, most of them were guilty of something or other, everyone was, but a plea bargain should be used as a last resort, not the first.

At three-thirty Trassi called. "I told Mr. Sunderman to arrange a meeting with IRS as soon as possible," he said curtly.

"Good. I shall remove a couple hundred sheets of printout and hold them until the Internal Revenue Service signs a closing agreement. That will take several weeks, no doubt. Meanwhile, you will have enough of the material to satisfy your clients."

"You don't know the people you're trying to outsmart," he said in a low voice. "You don't know what kind of danger you're inviting."

"Maybe not, but I have a very good idea of what my bargaining chips are."

When she hung up the phone, she had to wipe her hand, suddenly sweaty on the phone. Good God! she thought in wonder, Trassi was going to do it! He was going all the way.

At four-thirty she arrived at Valley River Inn, asked for Mr. Waters's table, and was led to the same table they had sat at before.

Waters/Gilmore jumped up. "I thought you might not make it," he said. "I've been trying and trying to reach you." The waiter was hovering. Barbara waved him away. "Russ is really losing it," Gilmore said. "It's really bad. He's threatening to throw himself off a cliff. Ms. Holloway, Barbara, please . . ." He reached across the table and took her hand. "For God's sake, please. I'm begging you. Let me tell him I have his program."

She pulled free and shook her head. "Sorry, Mr. Waters. I'm going with Trassi."

He leaned back in his chair, as if stunned. "Why? I thought you were an honorable woman, a decent human being. Why?"

"Because he can give me what I need, and you can't. Not just the money, but legal justification for it."

"We'll find a way," he said. "If that's all, we'll fix it. Russ will make it legal as hell."

"I don't think so," she said. "Trassi can do it easily in a way the tax people will understand and accept. So, sorry. I have to run."

"You're like the rest, after all," he said harshly. "A lawyer through and through. Don't let decency get in the way of a buck. You'll be directly responsible if Russ does something desperate, if he kills himself. It will be on your head."

"I don't believe your employer's emotional or psychological distress is any of my business. And if two giants nibble each other to death, let them." She walked away.

In the lobby a small group of women were standing under a banner: GRANDPARENTS' RIGHTS ADVOCACY ASSOCIATION. Most of them were silver-haired with a touch of blue here and there, and most of them were extremely well dressed with discreet jewelry. Sylvia stood out like an orange in a snowbank. Her hair was bright orange, frizzed in an Afro; she was wearing leopard-spotted silk pants, and a gold lamé top, and every finger was dazzling with diamonds; diamond pendants dangled from her ears.

Barbara walked past her. In a moment she heard Sylvia's carrying voice: "Excuse me, Lucy. I'll be damned if that isn't Stu Gilmore!"

✧

14

Frank strolled into the office at nine in the morning. Barbara would drop in around eleven, she had said, and Maggie was due by eleven-thirty. There were a few things for him to attend to, nothing of great importance, no matter how Patsy regarded them.

She scurried from her office as he drew near his own. Patsy had coal-black hair she tended so carefully that no white root had ever shown itself. He was very fond of her.

"Mr. Bixby asked you to give him a buzz as soon as you arrived," Patsy said.

He grinned amiably at her. "All right." He entered his office and gave Sam Bixby a buzz. "What's up, Sam?"

"I'd like a few moments, if you have time," Sam said. "I can come over if you're not tied up."

"Come on over."

Moments later Sam arrived. He knocked and waited to be invited in, the way he always did. They exchanged pleasantries and seated themselves in the comfortable chairs by the coffee table.

"What's on your mind?" Frank asked.

"I heard that the Fentons sent a car for you," Sam said, not quite nonchalantly. "I thought it was agreed that if we took on a new client, we would discuss it."

"I didn't take them on," Frank said. "A little advice, no more than that."

Sam looked disappointed. "Oh," he said. "But there's something else. I hear that Barbara's been in and out a lot this past week, even working late. Has she taken on someone we should talk about?"

"Sam, knock it off," Frank said. "You know as well as I do that we're consulting with Lou Sunderman, and yes, it's going to involve him and the office. A tax matter, Sam."

Sam looked uncomfortable. At one time he had worn a hairpiece, but he had given it up and, in fact, had been ridiculous in it; but his head did gleam, and it was very pink. Frank suspected that Sam was a little jealous of his, Frank's, abundant hair, gray as it was.

"What's really bugging you?" he asked bluntly.

Sam took in a deep breath, then said, "I don't believe you're unaware of how this whole office has changed over the years. Drastically. The day you retire, we no longer will be concerned with criminal cases, for example."

"Ah," Frank said. "You haven't forgotten that my cases kept us in chow for a good many of those years, I hope."

"Of course not. But things change. Our image has changed. And criminal cases do not enhance it."

"So when I walk out, you assign this office to whom? Got that far yet?"

Sam turned a shade redder. "No, no. Frank, I'm not suggesting you leave, for God's sake. I haven't forgotten anything. But things change. That's all I'm saying. Things change. High-profile cases alienate people. They take sides. People associate the firm with unsavory publicity, with a lack of discretion. It isn't good for us as a firm. That's all I'm saying."

"I give you discretion. You handle more crooks in a month than I see all year, but discreetly. Now I get it."

"No, you don't! I know you aren't pulling in those cases yourself anymore. But you let Barbara drag you into the middle of them. She uses this firm when and how it suits her. She's a maverick like you. There was a time when we needed that, but we don't any longer. Let her open her own stable of criminal attorneys if that's what she wants. I don't want us to get involved in another murder trial, Frank. Now, do you get it?"

Frank laughed. "Sam, if I decided to take on Manson, there's not a damn thing you could do about it."

Sam jumped to his feet. "Don't do this, Frank. This isn't just my opinion. I told you, things change. This firm, without exception, does not want to get involved in another high-profile criminal case."

Very silkily Frank said, "Oh, you've had meetings? Is that it? Anything else on your mind?"

Wordlessly, Sam Bixby left the office. His scalp was cherry red. Frank knew very well that when he retired, this office would go to one of the associates, and from then on the firm would handle trusts, corporate business, wills, matters guaranteed not to alienate important clients. And the only criminals who would be free to come and go within these august walls would have clean hands, manicured nails, white collars. And their crimes would only affect hundreds, thousands, possibly millions of other people, not the simple one-on-one that he preferred. But, he told himself, things change.

Maggie arrived soon after Barbara, and they all went down to Lou Sunderman's office, where the gnomelike man looked over the documents Maggie had brought and pronounced them satisfactory.

"Very well," he said. "Our next step is to transfer the money to an escrow account and obtain a court order to keep it there until we finalize a closing agreement with Internal Revenue. If Mr. Trassi produces the appropriate documents, we should have no trouble arriving at a closing agreement; however, it will take several months, more than likely. There is no need for you to be present at our initial conference, Ms. Folsum, although your presence will be required at the closing-agreement formality. Also, I think it is in everyone's interest to have this matter kept confidential, and I shall so stipulate in the court order and at the conference. Otherwise, you may find yourself inundated with requests of various kinds, and, of course, there would be unwanted publicity which might make much of the fact that Mr. Arno has been murdered, arousing unnecessary speculation."

He stood up. They would need a separate agreement, he said, since the one Barbara had drawn up was for her, not the firm.

Frank said they'd be in his office and to send it around when it was ready for Maggie to sign, and they left the little man.

Maggie stopped just inside Frank's office, staring in disbelief at Barbara. "You're getting it for us? Is it going to work?"

"Looks like it," Barbara said.

"But what if they ask me questions?" Maggie said.

"You answer." She was watching Maggie closely. "The only thing you have to conceal is that you saw Mitch or even knew he was back before Ray told you."

"You make it sound so simple," Maggie said.

"Just listen carefully to any question put to you, and answer it as briefly as you can. Don't volunteer anything and don't stray from the question. You'll be fine."

Maggie looked at Frank, who nodded.

"When we get the fingerprint report, do I give it to his lawyer, or to the police, or just to Ray himself?"

"What's your instinct about that?"

"Both the police and his lawyer," Maggie said after a moment.

"I think you should pay attention to your own instincts," Barbara said. "Have you accepted that if Ray's arrested, there's nothing you can do or should do immediately?"

"Yes," Maggie said. "I'd just make it worse for him if they knew so much money might be involved. I understand that." She looked miserable.

"That's exactly right," Barbara said. "As soon as we have a formal statement from Trassi that the money is legally yours, we'll go to the D.A. and I'll try to get them to drop the charges against Ray. He's in for a bad time, so is his family, and so are you. It can't be helped now. He'll be frightened. They'll tell him the penalties for various degrees of murder, for manslaughter. They'll tell him his cooperation and a statement of remorse can lighten his sentence, and they'll pretend to assume he'll be convicted."

There was a tap on the door; Lou Sunderman's secretary was there with the agreement for Maggie to sign, and she didn't stay long after that. She would reopen the inn on Sunday, she said; she had to.

Barbara let herself into the apartment quietly, then stopped with her hand on the doorknob, the door not closed all the way yet. John was talking to someone. She hadn't realized how sound traveled in their small apartment; his words were quite audible.

"Yes, vaguely familiar with it. When would you need a report?" After a moment he said, "When do you expect it to start snowing?" Then, "That's cutting it pretty fine. Look, fax me what you already have, and I'll get back to you later today."

She finished closing the door, and called out, "I'm home."

John stepped out of his office, holding the telephone. He waved. He said into the telephone, "Right. I'll call back as soon as I have a chance to look it over. Might be late this evening."

She went in to wash her hands, and when she came out of the bathroom, he was in the kitchen, peering into the refrigerator.

"Time to go out for a hamburger?" she asked.

He shook his head. "Waiting for some faxes. We have some tuna fish, or soup. Flip a coin."

They had soup, and Barbara found herself biting her tongue when she started to ask what was up. He went back into his office, and she went to hers and closed the door. But she could hear his fax machine, and a few minutes after it stopped, she heard papers rustling, a noise she couldn't identify, more rustling.

Finally she stood up and began to gather her things to return to the downtown office. John's door was open; he was bending over a map spread out on his mammoth desk.

"Leaving again," she said.

He looked up, then came around the desk and kissed her. "Short visit."

"Way it goes. I think I'll be out from under all this mess soon. Then back to routine stuff."

He nuzzled her earlobe. "I'll be waiting."

She left and as she drove to the office she thought how different they were. He could leave something he was doing in the middle of a word, then get back to it as if he had an on/off switch. If she became distracted, it took a long time to recapture whatever she had been thinking. Not his problem, she told herself, hers. When his kids were around, it would be just like that, too. He would do things with them, and return to work. On/off/on. Simple. It was as if he could turn his focus into such a narrow beam that what was immediately at hand was all that he was aware of, but her focus wanted to take in everything. Again she told herself, sharply this time: not his problem, hers.

She was in the office, reading more of the Jolin material, when Frank entered. He went to his desk and sat down. "They arrested Ray Arno, charged him with aggravated murder."

There was nothing to say.

"Lou met me in the hall outside," Frank said after a moment. "He's getting a court order for Monday to transfer the money to an escrow account. I'll be glad to get it out of here."

There was still nothing to say. She returned to the report she had been reading about the Palmer Company and finished the last page. "Palmer probably delivers for the Mafia," she said. "Never arrested, never seriously questioned about anything, but there are rumors."

Barbara picked up the copy of Thelma Wygood's diary. She had found it hard to read, and not because of the handwriting, which was small and precise. They were still in the getting-acquainted period—early seduction period, she corrected. She read: "I told him I can't dance and he was delighted. He will teach me, he said, not in a public place where I might feel shy, but somewhere without an audience. 'But you can dance. Anyone who walks like you do, with the natural grace of a princess, was born to dance. Let me teach you. . . .'

"June 15. I met him at the Hilton Bar, as usual, and he said he had a car waiting. There is a restaurant he wants to share with me. I said no. . . . He said, 'You won't heal until you have struck back, stop feeling beaten, fight back' . . . I had my drink and walked out. He did not follow, as I thought he might. He is clever in a reptilian way. I won't make another move until he does.

"June 17. Tonight I took a walk, then sat at a little café and had coffee. He found me there. He said he had a present for me. He left the present on the table. It's the book *Don't Get Mad, Get Even.* I think things will pick up speed soon."

The phone rang, and Barbara turned over the last page she had read and stood up as Frank answered. "Right, Ruthie, she's here." He held out the phone.

"Mr. Trassi is on the line," Ruthie said.

"Put him on."

"Ms. Holloway?"

"Yes, I'm here."

"Next Thursday afternoon at three, same place as before. I'll have the material you require."

"And I'll bring the material you need," she said. He hung up.

She let out a long breath. If anyone had told her just a couple of weeks ago how close she would be to the edge today, she would have laughed. If anyone had told her the bomb would explode and in the fallout there would be obstruction of justice, withholding evidence, trying to pull a fast one on the IRS, the real conflict of interest represented by Maggie and Ray, possible charges leveled at her, Barbara . . . She shook her head in bewilderment; at no time had she planned any of it to work out the way it was moving. But Thursday would see her take a step back from the abyss, not in the clear yet by any means, but not hanging by her fingernails, with any luck. She knew very well she would be at risk until after the IRS signed an agreement with Maggie, and Ray was set free by a trial of his peers or his case was thrown out of court or the cops took off their blinkers and found the killers. . . . But Thursday was a step in the right direction, away from disaster. She turned from the phone to see Frank regarding her; he averted his gaze swiftly.

"Thursday, three o'clock," she said. "Federal Building."

Going home, she considered the coming days and weeks. They would have Saturday and Sunday free, and next week, on Friday, maybe they could drive out to the coast together in the camper and spend the weekend after she talked to Maggie. She began to hurry.

This time when she entered the apartment, she called out instantly, "I'm home."

He came from his office. "All wrapped up?"

"Pretty much. A little tidying remains, that's all."

"Great! Want to take a trip?"

"You've been reading my mind," she said. "When, where?"

"Up to the Canadian Cascades first. It's an all-day drive, get there Sunday night, do a little work for a few days, hike, camp, then swing down through Idaho for a couple of days."

"I have a meeting I have to attend on Thursday," she said, deflated. "Could I get to an airport from where we'd be?"

"No. It was just an idea." He started to turn away, then stopped and faced her again. "Is it okay with you if I leave? You're sure that other problem is settled?"

"Of course," she said. "Just another afternoon meeting or two, and it's over for now."

"I have to make a phone call," he said, and reentered his office. She could hear every word when he told someone he'd drive up on Sunday, arrive before ten at night, and hope the weather didn't change.

One day to drive up, three or four days in Canada, a day to drive to Idaho, three more days, then a day to drive home, ten days at least. And the Staley mine was in Idaho.

⟡

15

Frank grilled dinner on the back porch that night, and he had set up a table and chairs out there. The weather was turning hot again; it was pleasant in the shade scented by a blooming jasmine vine that spiraled up a wire mesh. Thing One and Thing Two apparently considered it an adventure, having the big people eat outside. They took turns trying to climb up on the table.

"Grilled veggies are the best," Frank said contentedly. He had prepared eggplant, zucchini, brilliant orange peppers, new potatoes, tomatoes . . . all touched with a hint of garlic, olive oil, oregano, basil, a faint tang of lemon. There was a whole salmon with a spicy sauce.

She could do this, Barbara thought, then admitted to herself that, no, she couldn't. There were secrets about cooking food to perfection. The secrets were jealously guarded by a cabal, a guild of cooks who had sworn never to tell all.

"How did you fix on geology?" Frank asked John. He poured more wine and leaned back in his chair, in no hurry to start clearing things away and get on to dessert.

"When I was a kid," John said, as relaxed as Frank now, "one day it hit me that we were burning rocks. We had a coal stove. Most people around us did—coal was cheap, free for the taking if you knew where to go dig. Filthy fires, with clouds of sulfurous fumes, creosote in the flues, sooty dust in the house, but we burned it. What was available was low-grade bituminous coal, more junk than coal actually, but it was cheap. Anyway, I was putting coal in the stove, and it hit me, we were burning rocks. I tried to burn other kinds of rocks, until my dad made me stop, and when the fire was out, he made me clean up the mess I'd made. So I got to see the rocks that didn't burn—some had exploded—and the ashes and clinkers. I thought it was a miracle that some rocks would burn and others would explode. Magic." He laughed a low amused rumble of a chuckle. "It never occurred to me until years later that you could go out and study rocks. I just liked them and began picking them up everywhere I went."

"When I was about nine I knew I'd be an Arctic explorer," Frank said. "All that snow, the wilderness, Jack London, Byrd . . . That's what I wanted to do."

"When did you get sidetracked?" John asked.

Frank didn't answer immediately. He drank his wine, and put his glass down first. "I was about thirteen. Back in the thirties, a bad time, a very bad time. My father was lucky, landed a job with the Corps of Engineers, building dams in the West, and we were living in a small town in Oklahoma. Well, there was a killing and a black man was arrested, followed by a speedy trial. They hanged him. A few weeks after the execution there was another killing, same method, same everything. Same killer. I'd followed that first trial, just like everyone else, and it hadn't occurred to me that the guy might not have done it. There was a big town party the night he was hanged. Soon after the second killing, we moved on and I never found out if they got the real killer, but after that I went around picking up trials the way you picked up rocks. I didn't have any idea what I'd do with them, but I couldn't leave them alone, either."

Frank changed the subject then by asking John what he would be doing up in the Canadian Cacades. Barbara had not asked a question, refused to ask a question, but she listened intently to the answer.

"A mining company is trying to pull a fast one, get an approval during the winter months when no one can get near the mine they want to open. An environmental group got wind of it, and they've been lining up experts to investigate—a hydrologist, a forester, a biologist, geologist. I'll tramp around the hills and pick up rocks, take some pictures, look at the hole in the ground, and by January, when they hold the hearing, we'll have our reports ready to present. With any luck," he added. "If it starts snowing, and it could, we'll be limited in what we can find."

Barbara and John didn't stay long that night; he still had things to get ready, and he wanted an early start in the morning, by dawn. It was going to be a long drive.

After she saw John off on Sunday, she went back to bed, on his side, and dozed, fantasizing about being a photographer, taking the vital pictures for him, developing and printing them in her own darkroom. She drifted into sleep again.

Later she read the for-rent ads in the newspaper. All they needed was more space, she had come awake thinking, more separation while they worked, a place where words didn't carry from room to room. Four bedrooms. Not too far from the university library and the public library. Not too far from Frank's house and the courthouse, and Martin's.

Frank called Monday morning to say he would wander over to the courthouse, see what was going on; she understood he would hang out, gossiping with old pals, and learn all there was to know about the arraignment of Ray Arno. "Also," he said, "Lou tells me his escrow officer and the judge's clerk will be here around three to take charge of that loot."

She had a few things to attend to that morning. A visit to a Realtor, another to a rental agency, and last, a bookstore to buy a cookbook for beginners. There was no point in trying to start anywhere else, she had admitted to herself; she had no idea of the basics, how to make white sauce without lumps, for instance. Or what a roux was.

By the time she arrived at Frank's house, she was grumpy. The sales clerk had asked how old the child was who was showing an interest in cooking. Young teens, Barbara had said, feeling stupid. Although the cookbook was insultingly simple, it was exactly what she needed. How to make a stuffed baked potato. How to roast a chicken. How to steam vegetables. Four simple pasta sauces. Easy stuffed peppers. Just what she needed.

When Frank arrived, he was as grumpy as she was.

"Goddamn that man," he said. "They had a meeting in chambers—assistant D.A., Stover, Jane Waldman—and among them they decided there wasn't any reason not to set the trial date for December second. It was that or late February. December!"

Barbara groaned. December second! Not enough time to prepare a decent case. "Who's prosecuting?"

"One of the new guys, Craig Roxbury. It's a low-priority case: do it fast, send the guy up, or to his death, and be done with it. Speedy justice."

"Bail?"

"No."

"Shit! Stover must think there's no defense; he'll let Arno sweat it out in jail for a couple of months and then press for a plea bargain. He doesn't think it will ever get to trial."

Lou Sunderman and the escrow officer and clerk arrived; they counted money, examined bills closely, then made out receipts, which everyone signed. There were two rent-a-cop uniformed men waiting to escort the escrow officer back to his building.

"That's a relief," Frank commented when it was done. "Bailey called. If we're free around four-thirty or so, he'll drop by the house and tell us a funny story."

She drove him home. He changed clothes, back into his slouch shorts and shirt, and they sat on the back porch watching the cats try to catch butterflies.

"May be the best present I ever had," Frank said.

She had gotten him the cats for Christmas the previous year.

When Bailey arrived, Frank brought him to the back porch, and they sat in the shade, sipping wine.

"Full report from superspy Sylvia," Bailey said. He was grinning broadly. "She snagged Gilmore at Valley River Inn and practically dragged him back into the lounge, and demanded a window table, which they managed to provide, no doubt canceling someone else's reservation. I wish I had seen her, how she was dressed."

Barbara told him, and his grin broadened even more. "Isn't she something else! I'd love to know what he thought. Anyway, they reminisced about the good old days, off-Broadway theater, directors, other actors, God knows what all. Then she suddenly remembered Joe, and dinner at seven-thirty, and things like that. So she dragged Gilmore home with her. Gave him an eyeful."

He helped himself to more wine. "Gilmore didn't say anything about why he's in the area on the first day. She had Ralph drive him back to the hotel at about eleven or so. He must have done some homework then, and found out a lot about Sylvia and her past career as an actress, because he called her on Saturday and suggested lunch, and on Saturday, he talked about her acting, how great she had been, plays he had seen her in. And he confided that he's here on a mission. A famous director is looking for a good location to launch a small intimate theater, like the good old off-Broadway theaters used to be. He's had no luck finding the right place. Boulder, Austin, Taos, Ashland . . . now Eugene. The place has to be just right, you see, not too big, not too small, with a good sophisticated audience, a nearby university. Eugene looks good to him, so far." He laughed. "Sylvia gets all fluttery just thinking about it."

"What's the scam?" Barbara asked.

"Matching money, probably. He's being cagey. He hinted that his director, who might be Woody Allen, or maybe not, has to be kept out of preliminary searches. No names. But he'll go for whatever Gilmore recommends, if the conditions are right. What he'll probably come up with is that if Sylvia can put dough into a special account, to demonstrate strong local support, his director will more than match it, and they're in business. He was talking about *Arsenic and Old Lace* as a possible production."

"But that's so blatant! Surely no one would really go for it," Barbara said, somewhat awed.

"Honey, you've seen Sylvia," Frank said. "Doesn't she look ripe for the picking? And to dangle a part in a grand old play under her nose. If Sylvia was what he thinks she is, she'd be in his pocket by now." He looked at Bailey. "Any idea when he'll take the next step?"

"Soon, a day or two. Work it fast and get out of town, that's the way to do it. Tomorrow, next day."

"Then what?" Barbara asked.

"See, she'll put the money in the special account, which he will have access to, of course, so he can deposit the director's money. Sylvia will bring it up with her lawyer, one of her other lawyers, and if he doesn't smell a rat, she'll guide him to the rathole very gently. He'll get in touch with the bunco squad, and they'll watch Gilmore clean out the account and hightail it to the airport. They'll wait until he's ready to board the plane and grab him. He's got a record; he's done time. They'll get him and throw the book at him, a smart New York con man trying to take our own Sylvia Fenton. Meanwhile, Sylvia's having a ball! I might not be able to hold her back after this."

Sitting alone on the porch later, Frank was wishing that Barbara had accepted his invitation for dinner. He would be in there now cooking happily, knowing he had an appreciative guest, but he had no inclination to start anything for himself just yet. He was troubled more than he had realized at the time by the talk he had had with Sam Bixby. Again and again he had found himself going over Sam's words: things change. They do, he conceded.

He suspected that a good part of the problem Barbara and John were having arose from her working habits, maybe the work itself. Many people despised criminal lawyers even more than other lawyers.

Because he was methodical, Frank separated the Barbara problem into parts now. That was one. Not his business, he reminded himself. The other part was his business. Sam wanted her out.

Frank had no illusions about what would happen the day he retired, or fell over dead, whichever came first. If she was kicked out, would she leave the law again? She had left once and he had dragged her back in, but if he couldn't play that role, then what? She would still have Martin's restaurant, but that was child's play, something she would never give up, but not what she was meant to do full-time.

Then he thought, Sam was right after all: she should have her own office, her own people, her own stable of lawyers. Sam would have a fit if she brought in another murder case, especially a Cain and Abel case, which Frank knew she would do, if she could get out from under the Maggie Folsum business in time. And if she wasn't clear of that, she would do something very foolish, he felt certain. What she wouldn't do was let a lazy son of a bitch like Stover allow Ray Arno to be found guilty either by a plea or by a jury.

So there was a double-barreled shotgun getting primed for her, he thought with deepening gloom. Sam would not hesitate to fire. And the other barrel was one she might prime herself, and end up being kicked off the Folsum matter as well as out of Arno's case. And possibly face charges before the bar. She was withholding information, obstructing justice in a murder case, a serious charge. She had made it all but necessary for another attorney to commit perjury, and there was the question of how that money got into her hands. If she was asked directly, would she lie? He thought not, but, he admitted, he didn't know. If she had deliberately set out to cause herself serious trouble, maybe serious enough for disbarment, she couldn't have done a better job of it.

Or, he thought bleakly, had she done it not altogether consciously to achieve exactly that? The idea filled him with such disquiet that abruptly he stood up, too abruptly; for a moment the porch floor tilted. He didn't move until it was stable again, then shakily he reentered his house.

At that moment Barbara was scrubbing out a skillet for the third time. "Goddamn it," she muttered. "You can make a goddamn pancake, for Christ's sake!" But she couldn't. No matter what she did, they stuck to the skillet. She went back to the recipe: *If the batter is too thin, thicken it with a little flour.* She had done that and ended up with what looked like German pancakes, thick ugly things that she couldn't roll, no matter how carefully she tried. If she followed the recipe to the letter, the batter looked like cream and stuck to the skillet. The illustration was of crepes filled with a spinach-ricotta mixture. She washed out the bowl and started over. The batter looked like cream. "Butter the fucking skillet." She buttered it, then added just a little more, then poured in some batter. "Don't stick, damn you!" It stuck to the skillet.

She flooded the bowl with water to dilute the rest of the batter in order to pour it down the drain, scrubbed the skillet one more time, and opened a can of soup.

16

Over the next two days Barbara looked at rental properties, then in desperation at houses and townhouses and condos for sale. Wrong place, wrong room arrangement, especially wrong price.

On Thursday she and Frank prepared to go to the Federal Building for the meeting with the IRS representative. Barbara tore off the top hundred or so pages of printouts, and the last fifty, which she returned to the safe.

At the Federal Building they were kept waiting in a desolate room with wooden chairs occupied by dejected-looking people awaiting their turn with auditors, no doubt. Mr. Chenowith would be with them in a minute, the woman behind the information counter said, but he would be with them only when the entire party had gathered, they understood. Trassi was late. Lou Sunderman looked quite happy.

At ten minutes past two, Trassi hurried in, carrying a suitcase, and he looked as if someone had been tramping on his corns. He nodded curtly to Barbara and did not offer to shake hands with Sunderman or Frank when she introduced them. A door opened and a tall thin man appeared.

"Good afternoon, Lou," he said. "Thomas Chenowith." He shook hands all around as they introduced themselves.

"Please come in." The room he showed them to was marginally less desolate than the anteroom. In here was a round, much-scarred wooden table and too many chairs and nothing else.

After they were seated under a harsh white light, Chenowith said genially, "Now, what can I do for you?"

"Well, Thomas," Lou Sunderman said, "we have a pretty little tax situation that needs clarification." He outlined the situation as he drew papers from his briefcase. "So the money is in the escrow company's keeping, under court order. But all we really need is a closing agreement, and we'll be out of your hair." He smiled, but Chenowith's geniality had vanished; he appeared to be battling with a pain. "Here I have Ms. Folsum's agreement with Ms. Holloway. . . ." He described the documents as he pushed them across the table to Chenowith, who did not touch them. "I believe Mr. Trassi has a statement to add to my account," Lou said.

"My statement, as you insist on calling it, is quite simple," Trassi said coldly. He took a paper from his coat pocket and read from it. "On July nineteenth I happened to meet Mitch Arno in the outer office of the Palmer Company in New York City. I was there on business, as he was. He overheard Mr. Palmer bidding me a safe trip to Oregon, and approached me and drew me aside. He asked if he could retain me for a private matter he was concerned about. I found that I could accommodate him, and I did. I asked one of the girls in Mr. Palmer's office to type out a simple agreement between Mitch Arno and myself to the effect that he would deliver into my hands on July twenty-fifth a suitcase containing valuables, which was the property of his ex-wife, Margaret Folsum.

"I met him as planned in Portland, and he gave me the suitcase and told me again that it belonged to his ex-wife and that I should give it to her and inform her that he would be there in time for his daughter's birthday. As soon as I delivered the suitcase, my duties to him would be concluded, and he would open the suitcase himself at the proper time."

"Why didn't he just deliver it himself?"

"He said he had to deliver an automobile to an out-of-the-way place and would then take a bus back to Portland, where he would rent a car. Evidently he was uncomfortable carrying anything of value on a public bus."

"Did he at any time say what the valuables were?"

"Yes. He said it was a large sum of money, long overdue."

"No more than that, it was overdue?"

Trassi said impatiently, "He said a great deal, but what pertains is that he had not paid his ex-wife for child support over the years, his children were now of college age, and the money was theirs. Also he wanted to regain the favor of his father."

Chenowith remained impassive, but now and again his face twitched in a way that suggested an ulcer was paining him and he was being brave about it. "When did you deliver the money?"

"Not as quickly as I desired," Trassi said. "My other business in Portland took longer than I had anticipated, and I was still in the city on Friday, August second. I called Ms. Folsum to make an appointment for Saturday or Sunday, but the person who answered the phone said she would not be available until Monday or Tuesday. So I postponed going to Ms. Folsum's inn. On Monday, August fifth, I finally drove to the coast, but no one answered my phone calls all evening. On Tuesday, I was horrified to learn that hoodlums had vandalized her inn severely, and when I finally saw her and tried to deliver the suitcase, she was too harried and distraught to talk to me. The following day she referred me to her legal counsel, Ms. Holloway. A day or so later I contacted Ms. Holloway and concluded my legal obligation to Mitch Arno." He hesitated a moment, then passed the statement over to Chenowith.

If she had an Oscar, Barbara thought, she'd hand it over on the spot. Instead, she said, "I put it in a safe-deposit box immediately and left it there until I could talk to my client and decide what the legality of the situation was. We decided to do nothing until Mitch turned up to explain it all. After we learned of his death, I consulted with our tax attorney, Mr. Sunderman, and subsequently turned the matter over to him."

His ulcer was hitting him again, Barbara thought sympathetically, when Chenowith looked at Lou Sunderman.

"I, of course," Sunderman said, "realized that Ms. Holloway couldn't simply release the money to her client, not without a closing agreement from the Internal Revenue Service, even though the money was legally hers from the time Mitch Arno handed it to Mr. Trassi, who was acting as his agent. Mr. Trassi kindly agreed to cooperate, to furnish Mitch Arno's address and other information that would be pertinent to settling this matter. Hence this meeting."

"You have that information regarding Mitch Arno?" Chenowith asked Trassi.

"It's all in here," Trassi said, sliding a file folder across the table.

"Gentlemen," Barbara said then, "since Mr. Sunderman is Ms. Folsum's counsel of record in this matter, if you have no further need for my presence, I do have other business to attend to."

"We'll be in touch with you," Chenowith said.

"Before you leave," Lou Sunderman said. "One more little item. I request that this meeting be held in confidence, by court order, if necessary, until the matter is settled conclusively."

Trassi nodded, and after a moment Chenowith did also. "I'll get an order," Chenowith said, then looked at Barbara and Frank in turn. "You both agree to hold this meeting in confidence pending such an order?"

They said they did. "With one exception," Barbara said. "As an officer of the court, it's my duty to report this matter to the district attorney, since it could be of material interest as that office investigates the death of Mitch Arno. The district attorney will, of course, be under the same court order regarding confidentiality as the rest of us."

For a moment it appeared that Trassi might turn into a leaper before their eyes. His body tensed and his expression was disbelieving and furious. She met his gaze coolly. "If I don't, Mr. Chenowith will. Not to disclose a matter of this significance could be construed as obstruction of justice."

"The district attorney's name will be added to the restraining order," Chenowith said.

Barbara and Frank stood up and walked out.

She had to fight an impulse to hop, skip, and jump her way through the anteroom toward the outside door.

At the door, they stopped when Trassi called out her name. "Outside," he snapped. He was carrying the suitcase.

They stepped out, away from the door, and she handed him the briefcase, which he put inside his suitcase, and without a word turned and reentered the building.

"Round one," she said in a low voice.

Back at the office they found Bailey waiting for them. "Sylvia opened the account at ten," he said. "They went out for a cup of coffee. At twelve Gilmore cleaned out the account. The vice president was in on it, and he called bunco. They nabbed him at the airport, and he's in the county jail. He called his lawyer. Another funny coincidence, happens his lawyer is named Trassi, who gave him holy hell and hung up on him."

Frank nodded. "They won't let him stay in jail long, too risky. Someone will show up and bail him out."

"Trassi is scurrying," Bailey said. "Canceled a flight out of town, making a lot of phone calls. Mad as hell."

"Guess Gilmore knows how Adam felt," Frank said. "Just couldn't resist that one little bite, and here comes the sky down on his head."

He would jump bail, Barbara thought, and there would be an arrest warrant issued. He was of no further use to Palmer, Trassi, any of them. He would go to jail or be a fugitive. "I wonder how long it will be before he realizes his life isn't worth very much," she said.

Frank shrugged. "You want some dinner tonight?"

"Love it, but I might be a little late, after John calls at seven or seven-thirty. And I have to set up a meeting with the D.A. Maybe for Monday."

"You going out to Maggie's place tomorrow?" Frank asked.

She nodded. "I might stay over a night or two, walk out some kinks."

She and Maggie talked in Maggie's bed-sitting-room. Maggie gazed out the windows at the ocean as Barbara recounted the meeting with the IRS. "Do you think they'll accept that story?" she asked when Barbara finished.

"Hope so. No real reason for them not to."

Maggie turned to Barbara then. "Is it extortion or blackmail? You're selling them the printouts, aren't you?" She looked pinched and cold, and years older than she had before. "I've been thinking a lot about this and I've decided I can't go along. I can't start my kids out in life with dirty money. I've been tempted before; there are opportunities for a single woman, as you probably know, but never quite so much money." She laughed, a bitter, harsh sound. "I dreamed about what all we could do with so much money, what it would mean, then I'd wake up and wonder how I could explain it if they ever ask hard questions. Give the printouts to their owner, get rid of the money. I don't care what you do with it." She stood up and crossed her arms over her breasts. "Just don't keep tempting me with it."

Startled, Barbara shook her head. "I want you to believe me when I say this. I'm not doing anything I'm ashamed of or that would shame you." Maggie was like a statue, remote and unreachable. "Sit down, Maggie. It's an ugly story, and you have to promise me that you won't reveal it to anyone now, possibly never."

"I can't make such a promise in the dark," Maggie said.

"If you trust me, you can."

For a long time Maggie didn't move; her gaze on Barbara's face was intent, searching. Finally she sat down. "All right."

"I can't tell you names," Barbara said then. "I'm sworn to secrecy. But I'll give you the rest of the story. Mitch was working for a company that acted as a go-between in serious industrial espionage. . . ." She told it briefly, leaving out only the names. Maggie turned very pale when Barbara said that Mitch had killed at least three people. "Company A authorized me to turn the bogus program over to Company B and to keep the money. That's what I'm doing. What I've done. The money is yours, or will be in a few months."

"And everyone's letting it go at that?" Maggie asked incredulously.

"No," Barbara said. "One day I will tell you the rest. When Ray Arno is free, exonerated, and this is really all over, then I'll tell you everything."

"Is he going to be free?" Maggie asked. "His lawyer doesn't believe that."

"He's going to be free," Barbara said.

Maggie continued to study her face, and finally nodded.

Barbara told her about the meeting being arranged for Monday with the district attorney, and they started going over the questions that might come up.

When they were done, Maggie said, "Would you like to see the rest of the inn, restored more or less to normal?"

It was beautifully furnished, beautifully decorated, with Laurence's flower pictures serving as palettes for each room.

"He did a good job," Barbara said in the Sunflower Room, where a small couch and two chairs were covered in a rich umber fabric, the curtains were pale yellow, and drapes a deeper golden yellow. Red-brown cushions on the couch, and one on each twin bed finished the scheme. Perfect.

"He's good at many things," Maggie said. "There's an art walk in Portland this weekend, or he'd be at my elbow. He keeps hovering," she said with a sigh.

Barbara gave her a swift glance.

"You might as well ask," Maggie said. "Everyone else does. Why don't I marry him?"

"Do you answer?"

"Sometimes. See, the problem is, I can't afford him. I have my daughters to consider first. Maybe when they're both done with school, if he's still around, if he's grown up yet, maybe then. He doesn't really want to be married. We have an . . . arrangement, but if he had a free ride, he'd take it. He really thinks the world owes him that much." She gave the lovely room a last glance and turned toward the door. "I told him I'm serious, that he has to start paying rent or get out, and he took off in a temper. He might stay away for days, weeks, even months, and all the time he's gone, I doubt he'll give me a thought. When he's here, he's like my shadow. That's how it is."

After leaving Maggie, Barbara drove north on 101, through Newport, nearly to Yachats, where she had managed to book a room, on the wrong side of the highway and in a simple motel, but sufficient. She checked in and found no surprises. Then she went down to the beach.

Later, sitting on a massive driftwood log, she watched the play of light on the ocean as the sun set. No flamboyant sunsets here, not like in Hawaii or Florida, or even out on the desert; the sun just rode its path down to the horizon, turning redder as it sank, until it was an orange globe that quietly dipped into the sea and the afterglow turned violet and very gradually darkened.

She was thinking of the women in this affair: Maggie, who was so clear-eyed about what she had to do, and strong enough to do it. And Sylvia, who knew the kind of world she wanted to live in and had arranged it to suit herself. Even Thelma Wygood had done what she had to do from her earliest years.

If she were as clear-eyed as Maggie or Sylvia or even poor Thelma Wygood, she would know what she had to do, but she wanted two mutually antagonistic things: she wanted to live with John and be his love, and she wanted freedom to work her own hours in her own space.

Abruptly, she stood up to climb the trail back to the highway, then return to the motel, and in a little while drive out somewhere for dinner. Tomorrow, she promised herself, tomorrow she would think more clearly.

Tomorrow she would think of the implications of what John had said, that he hated her work. She had tried to think through that many times and had always been distracted by something or other. Tomorrow, she promised again, and started up the trail.

17

When Barbara went home on Sunday, she listened to the phone messages, one from Frank, one from Bailey. She called Frank.

"Want some dinner?" he asked.

She said sure, and then sat gazing at the apartment. It looked like a bachelor's pad. Her good chair and a lamp were the only possessions of hers in sight. Everything else she owned was put away in her little office or in the bedroom; she felt like an intruder here. "A room of one's own," she said under her breath. Then, *an apartment of one's own.* She jumped up and hurried to her office to find some photocopies of apartments and houses one of the real estate people had given her. She stared at the one she had been looking for.

"Rose Garden Apartments, lovely two-bedroom apartments in three groups of twelve units, each group with its own swimming pool. Easy access to the bike trail by the river. Walking distance to town. Ready for occupancy October first . . ."

That evening, while Frank prepared dinner, she explained. "See, this way we'll have four bedrooms, and two baths. Plenty of space to spread out our stuff, for both of us to work at home. And when his kids come, they'll fit, too."

"You signed up for two apartments?"

"One definitely, one conditionally." She added, "I can't breathe in our apartment. Even if we could divvy up the space equally, it's too small. I can't move in it. You know as well as I do that in December I'm going to need breathing room."

He knew. "I say it's a grand idea." He didn't ask the next question, the one she had been asking herself ever since signing the rental agreement: What if John hated the idea?

As Frank sliced tomatoes, he thought that maybe she had found a fine solution to a problem that would only have grown worse. Two adjoining apartments, not the usual mode for live-together lovers, but it would do. And he decided to postpone mentioning his reason in asking her over tonight. He had planned to bring up the idea of her forming her own group, getting her own office space, a secretary, the whole works, now, before she found herself tangled in a mare's nest in December. He didn't believe any more than she did that the D.A. would drop the charges against Ray, and he was more than a little worried about how she planned to work it later.

"I've got a long list for Bailey to start on," Barbara said, "but I wasn't sure where to tell him to meet me. Here?"

"You know here," Frank said.

It was a bad night; she alternated from imagining John in a mine he had declared unsafe, to stewing about how to tell him she wanted separate apartments, to refusing to look down as she balanced on a tightrope across a bottomless chasm. . . .

By nine in the morning, she was at Frank's house ready for Bailey, aware that her father had noted the effects of not enough sleep.

"Okay," she said briskly as Bailey stirred sugar into coffee. "Let's go over some of the things I want us to follow up on." Bailey nodded and took out his notebook; she opened her legal pad, and Frank leaned back in his chair to listen.

Later, she put down her pen. "That's for openers," she said. Bailey was still writing; she waited for him to finish, then said soberly, "I've been stewing about the lead pipe and holder. I want to get them to the New Orleans police, along with the Gary Belmont stuff."

Bailey scowled. Ignoring that, she continued, "The stuff should be packaged up and mailed to the cops with a New Orleans postmark. And you should call the cops with an anonymous tip—you saw Belmont get in a Lexus coupe with this guy who could have been his brother, they were so alike."

Bailey's scowl was ferocious. "You want me to fly down to New Orleans with a lead pipe in my hip pocket!"

"I didn't think it would be that easy," she said. "But you're the expert. If you think that would work . . ."

He turned his glare toward Frank, who simply shrugged.

"We handled the license and other items," Barbara murmured. "I suppose it would be a good idea to clean off our prints."

He didn't even bother to respond, just gave her a murderous look.

She glanced at Frank. "Anything else?"

"Maybe," he said. "I've been thinking about something you said the other day, that Gilmore's life might not be worth much these days. They'll set bail this morning, more than likely, and he'll be out and gone. But he's had time to consider his ways, I suspect. It might be that if someone like my old friend Carter Heilbronner got a tip that Gilmore knows something about big-time espionage, carrying illegal stuff around the country, or anything like that, the FBI might get in touch with him. They could make a deal. Course, we wouldn't know anything about it; they play it too close. But it could be a way to get to Palmer."

Barbara nodded thoughtfully. Then she said, "But we would know. They would want Sylvia to drop the charges against Gilmore. They'd have to guarantee him that much up front, wouldn't they?"

Bailey snorted. "Sylvia working with the FBI! Jeez, where will it all end?"

"Is Gilmore smart enough not to bring in the Major-Wygood deal and her murder?" Frank asked. "Would he have anything else to give them? That's the question."

They all thought about it. Finally Barbara said, "I doubt that he would say anything that would implicate him in a murder, not Wygood's, or Mitch's, either. He's worked for Palmer a long time, twelve years or longer. There must be a lot of things he could talk about." She frowned; then, thinking out loud, she said, "Gilmore could become a threat to Palmer; he's faced with a prison term and he might cut a deal with the state or the feds. He'll be a fugitive, a convict, or hidden away in a witness-protection safe house; in any event, no longer an asset. I wonder if Palmer would be worried enough to want him removed? If so, when? My guess is, sooner rather than later. Later he might be whisked away out of sight.

Heilbronner isn't likely to put a lot of effort into a tip without any foundation, but if Gilmore got knocked off and he has the tip in mind, he might then stir a finger and poke around."

She looked up at Frank, who was frowning also; he nodded. "Or Gilmore could go to ground and hide out for the next few years," he said, "which also might make Heilbronner curious about Palmer."

Abruptly she stood up. "Mind if I put on some more coffee?" she asked. It had occurred to her that John would consider this conversation evil, that this was what he hated about what she did. She, Frank, and Bailey were looking at the situation dispassionately, knowing a man's life might be at risk but also knowing that if it was, the machinery was already in place, the lever already pulled. No one's past could be undone. Gilmore's past had made it impossible for him to walk away from a soft touch like Sylvia; he had not resisted the apple. Although he couldn't have known he was leading Thelma Wygood to her death, he had done nothing about it after the fact, except take on yet another role, well aware that his boss had had Mitch Arno killed. But, Barbara thought bleakly, none of this would be understandable for John, for others like him. And perhaps, she thought then, those others were right, after all. How guilty would she feel if Gilmore got killed because she baited a trap he found irresistible?

"Does he have enough sense to know that maybe his only chance is to cooperate with the FBI?" she said, returning to the table.

"A con man gets pretty good at figuring the odds," Frank commented.

She recalled Gilmore's implicit threat to Maggie's children; he had known the threat was real, or could be made real. "Can you tip off Heilbronner in such a way that he won't come sniffing around us?"

Frank said to leave that part to him.

They discussed some of the points Barbara had raised earlier, and afterward Bailey and Frank agreed on a time for him to pick up the lead pipe and the Belmont material.

"Just give me the fucking stuff. I'll think of something," Bailey said.

Barbara and Frank both raised their eyebrows; Bailey never used such language.

18

Craig Roxbury was not intimidating in any way, she decided when they met on Monday. Not the district attorney, just an underling, the one who would prosecute Ray Arno, he was clearly uncomfortable here in Frank's office, and clearly suspicious. She knew a good bit about him already: thirty-one, divorced, no children, in town less than a year, after three years in the Indianapolis district attorney's office. Methodical and unimaginative, a good worker, conscientious and thoroughly unremarkable, the kind of man who would pass through life leaving little trace. He had dark brown hair cut short and neat, and a clean, freshly shaven appearance. His hands were large and rough-looking, the hands of a man who had worked at hard labor for many years, which fitted the biography she had read. He had worked his way through school as a carpenter's helper. He seemed very earnest.

After the introductions, they all sat down in the visitors' end of Frank's office, Maggie on the couch by Frank, Barbara and Roxbury in the facing chairs. Barbara leaned back and said, "Thanks for agreeing to come, Mr. Roxbury. We really wanted to keep this as informal as possible, but we feel that we have information that may prove vital to your investigation of the murder of Mitch Arno. As you are aware, Ms. Folsum and Arno were married many years ago. . . ."

His suspicious glance toward Maggie said that indeed he was aware. Barbara continued, starting with the Monday after Maggie's big party, repeating the same story Trassi had told.

She smiled pleasantly at him when she concluded; his face had turned a dull red, and for a time he seemed speechless.

"I have copies of all the documents—"

"Just hold it!" Roxbury finally blurted. "Back up! You've known about this for weeks! Why haven't you mentioned it before?"

"Mr. Roxbury," she said gently, "please. If I had called your office and said I happened to have a suitcase of money that came from Mitch Arno, where would it be now?" She shook her head. "I had no idea you'd jump the gun and arrest the first suspect you got your sights on, and meanwhile, we handled this matter in a timely and orderly manner. I am prepared to deliver copies of all the documents to you at this time. Mr. Chenowith at Internal Revenue handled it for the government; Mr. Trassi acted on Mitch Arno's behalf. I'm sure that both of them will be happy to answer any questions you may have."

"I have questions, all right," he snapped, and began barking them at Maggie, the same questions Barbara had predicted he would ask. Maggie answered them all without hesitation.

Then Barbara handed the file folder to him. "Of course, we'll be available to answer any questions; however, I have advised my client to talk to you only in my presence."

"Why?" he muttered. "If it's all as aboveboard as you say, what's she got to hide?"

Barbara laughed. "Goes with the turf, Mr. Roxbury." She sobered again. "After you've discussed this at the office, and talked with the other principals, I expect you'll agree that you arrested the wrong man. Obviously, others learned that Mitch Arno was delivering a large sum of money in cash to his ex-wife. No one here knew it, but Arno's colleagues, his friends, or even his enemies could well have found out."

Roxbury's eyes narrowed, and abruptly he stood up. "We never suggested he did it for money," he snapped. "If what you're telling me checks out, it doesn't make a damn bit of difference in our case. We'll be in touch."

Frank escorted him from the office. As soon as the door closed behind them, Maggie said in a low voice, "You did it! They'll have to investigate those people now! They'll see that they're the ones with a reason to kill Mitch!"

"Maybe," Barbara said.

"Can't I tell the family anything?" Maggie asked. "Just a hint that things will work out?"

"They know I'm trying to get back support payments. Don't breathe a word more than that," Barbara said sharply. "For one thing, it's a court order and you could be held in contempt. But more important, we might need it later. If word leaks, I want to know who leaked it. If it leaks from the D.A.'s office, it will say a lot about how seriously they're taking this." She stopped; it was too complex to explain. If a little came out now, a little in a week or two, then a full disclosure, it might mean they intended to release Ray and go after persons unknown. If a rumor of unspecified wealth started to float around, it could mean they wanted to defuse it now, not have a surprise later. If they sat tight and nothing leaked, it could mean they really didn't consider it important to their case and would be prepared to deal with it later. Or . . .

She grinned at Maggie and spread her hands. "Anyway, from what I hear about the Arno family, it's a real talk machine set full speed ahead all the time. How long would it be a family secret?"

Reluctantly Maggie accepted that.

After Maggie left, and Frank was behind his desk again, his expression turned grim. "They won't buy it," he said flatly.

"I know. Roxbury thinks it's chalk dust."

"Well, he thinks you're trying to pull a fast one."

Alone later, he brooded about Roxbury. He had sounded very sure of himself when he declared the new development wouldn't make a damn bit of difference in his case. Frank had never met Ray, or any of the Arnos, and for the first time he wondered if Barbara had come to a conclusion prematurely.

By forcing Trassi's statement, Barbara had effectively given Mitch Arno an alibi for the murders of Thelma Wygood and the other Palmer courier in Florida, as well as for Gary Belmont's murder in New Orleans. Defending Cain, he mused, but what about the brother? They knew Mitch was a killer. How did they know his brother was not?

You never know for sure, he told himself sharply. So you risk a lot, take chances; that had been his life, too. But then he thought, this was different. He wasn't risking anything these days. He no longer had a damn thing to lose, he thought, surveying his office bleakly, but, Christ, she was way out there and the limb was fragile.

He became very still, remembering the laughter and happiness in her voice when she reported in from Mexico, from New York, from Denver; the sparkle in her eyes when they came home, the lightness of her step. And he wondered, had he acted for her sake when he asked her to come back years ago, or for his own? She had left once, packed her few things, cleaned out her bank account, and had taken off for parts unknown. And he had brought her back. For good or evil? It was one thing to walk because you decided to go that route, but quite a different matter to be forced out, to leave in disgrace. Or would that hidden engine that drove her think it was a pretty good trade-off? He leaned back in his chair with his eyes closed and cursed his helplessness, aware that she had to fight this battle alone.

19

All Monday evening Barbara pretended she was not listening for the phone to ring, and she learned how to make chicken breasts with green chilies. The sauce looked strange, but it tasted good.

Tuesday she didn't leave the apartment and pretended she was not listening for the phone. When it did ring, it was Bailey. He and Hannah were going to take a trip, he practically snarled; he would bill her for it. She didn't press him for details, but she thought, New Orleans in August, yuck.

She browsed through the children's cookbook for a few minutes, then began to walk.

He should be out of the mine by now. He should be back somewhere with a telephone handy. He should have called by now.

His call came at eight. "Hi," he said softly. "God, I've missed you."

She sank down into a chair. "Me, too. Where are you?"

"Boise. We just pulled in half an hour ago. I'll be out of here at dawn, home at eight or nine. Unless there's heavy traffic or something. If there is, I'll fly over it."

"Don't drive too fast. No, scratch that. Drive like hell."

He laughed.

After they hung up, she continued to sit with her hand on the phone, her eyes closed hard. Finally she roused. "And that's how it is, kiddo," she said softly.

He got home at eight-thirty Wednesday night. They didn't bother to eat, just tumbled into bed, and got up at midnight to scrounge for food, then back to bed.

On Thursday he told her the Staley mine was closed for good. "I dragged a couple of commissioners down with me and scared the shit out of them."

Then he said, "Up in the Canadian Cascades, I had plenty of time to think. It's beautiful country up there; we'll go back one day. I'd like to show you. Anyway, I got to thinking, what if you asked me to give up little jaunts like that, take up teaching or something instead. In time, a long time probably, but in time, after the honeymoon wore off and every day I had to face another classroom of kids who'd rather be out playing, or fucking their heads off, or something else, I'd come to resent my decision and blame the one I decided was responsible."

She looked at him in dismay. "I wouldn't ask you to give it up. You can't believe I'd ask that."

"No, I can't. But isn't that what I've been asking you to do? Give up the biggest part of your life? I don't know. If I have been, by implication or outright, I can't tell. If I have been, I'm sorry."

"But you said you hate what I do."

"What you get involved in, the people who might be dangerous, the risks you take. I'm afraid for you, and jealous of that part of your life because it takes you away from me. Out there in the wild I realized I'm a lousy test pilot's spouse."

She put her finger on his lips. "I have to show you something," she said. "We'll drive part of the way, then walk a little. Okay?"

She drove to the riverfront park, where they left the car and walked across the grass to the trail that followed the river for many miles. It was not crowded at one in the afternoon. Blackberry brambles were lush and weighted down with fruit on one side of the trail; the ground sloped to the flashing, sparkling river on the other.

"No hint about where we're going?" he asked.

"Not even a hint. Remember the great blue heron we saw that first day?"

He nodded; his hand tightened on hers.

After a walk of several minutes, she pointed to a trail through the brambles. "Up there," she said. It was not a very steep ascent; when they emerged, the Rose Garden was in front of them. She led him through it, and out the far side, past hundreds of blooming rose bushes; the air was heavy with perfume.

They crossed a street and went up several stairs, and before them was the Rose Garden Apartments complex. John looked at her curiously, but she didn't explain yet.

The apartments were laid out in three groups; a landscaping crew was at work putting down sod, planting bushes, some balled and burlapped trees. She headed for the apartments nearest the river. Four units of two apartments each faced one another across a courtyard with a swimming pool. Two more double units one floor up spanned the distance between them at the ends, enclosing the whole. She went to two doors, one leading to stairs, the other to the interior space between the apartments on the lower level. She unlocked the door to the stairs and they went up to a small landing with two facing doors, both locked. She opened the apartment to their right and led him inside to a short hallway with a closet on one side and an open door to the first bedroom on the other. Another short hallway led to the bathroom. Straight through was a hallway to the living room on the right and the kitchen on the left, open space now, with folding doors pushed all the way back. Beyond the kitchen was the door to the second bedroom. It was bright and airy throughout.

"What do you think?" she asked. He had been absolutely silent.

"I don't know what I'm supposed to think," he said in a curiously flat voice. "Small?"

"Yes, it is. But watch." Now she led him back out the way they had entered, and unlocked the second apartment, a mirror image of the first one.

She watched him walk through the rooms; in the kitchen he

turned to face her. "Two of them! My God, you're a genius! Two apartments side by side. Four bedrooms!" He was coming toward her as he spoke; he took her in his arms and held her, kissed her. "I had decided to rent an office and clear out my stuff, so there'd be room to move. This is a hell of a lot better. Two apartments!" He began to laugh, and she felt weak with relief.

RAY

20

Barbara smiled as she watched Shelley McGinnis walk toward her table in the Ambrosia Restaurant. Shelley had to be aware that eyes turned to follow her progress, but she gave no indication of it. She had grown prettier than ever in the months since she had moved to California in pursuit of a job; maturity, sadness, distress, were all becoming to her, although her outfit suggested anything but maturity. She was dressed in a pink raincoat and pink high-heeled boots. Her smile was radiant, belying her unhappiness at not finding a job here in Eugene.

"Hi," Barbara said when the younger woman drew near. "You look terrific, as usual."

"Hi. Bill keeps complaining about how gray the weather is, how miserable everything is, so I just brought bright and cheerful clothes this time. I have a yellow jacket that looks like sunshine. How are you?"

"Not bad." Barbara had talked to Bill Spassero quite a few times during the past months, just in passing usually, and she knew how miserable he was; he had made no secret of it. She wondered how many miles the two had traveled going back and forth, taking turns visiting, and how many triple-digit phone bills each had paid. "Let's order and then talk," she said. "Okay?"

"Sure." Shelley took off her raincoat to reveal a bright pink knit dress. "See?" she said complacently. Her cheeks matched the color almost exactly. Frank called her the golden-haired pink fairy princess, and that was just about right.

They ordered soup and salad, and then, waiting for it, Barbara asked what work she was doing now.

"I'm researching rights-of-way," Shelley said mournfully. "A lot of them. Hundreds and hundreds."

"Sam Bixby was an idiot not to take you on permanently."

"Well, you know. He interviewed me and asked me point-blank if I had any interest in trusts and corporate law, and I had to tell him no. He said the firm won't be handling any criminal cases in the future, and that was that."

"He said that?" Barbara asked, surprised. Shelley had not told her anything about the interview, which had taken place while Barbara and John were in Mexico. Shelley had worked as an intern for the firm for a year; most of the work had been done for Barbara.

"I thought you knew. He said the day Mr. Holloway retires, that's the last day they'll be associated with a criminal lawyer."

Barbara nodded. "I knew, but I didn't realize he was telling people that." The waitress brought crusty bread and herb butter. Barbara let Shelley carry the conversation until they finished eating and were ready for coffee.

Finally, with espressos before them, Barbara said, "I have an ulterior motive, as you probably guessed." Shelley leaned forward. "I'm mixed up in something that's going to be pretty messy in a few weeks, and I need help. But it wouldn't be permanent."

"I'll take it," Shelley said.

"Not so fast." Barbara laughed. "Can you get a leave of absence? Would it jeopardize your job?"

"I don't give a damn about my job! Rights-of-way! Good heavens! I'll take whatever you have."

"You have to know a little bit more before you make a decision. Just a few highlights for now, and then let's talk again before you fly back to Sacramento. Okay?"

Shelley's expression said she had decided already, but she nodded.

"Okay. I'm in a conflict-of-interest dilemma. . . ." Barbara gave her no more than a hint of the two overlapping cases, watching Shelley's face as she talked. Shelley was extremely intelligent, as she had proved during her internship, but she had little real experience yet; Barbara was uncertain how much of what she was relating needed more explanation. "So if you were on the scene, applying for jobs again, and sitting in on a couple of trials, then getting interested in this one, you would be in a perfect position to be my second counsel and fill me in on what you saw and heard. You would be doing it on your own, not in my employ, although there's no law that says you can't chat about things."

"I'll take it," Shelley said firmly.

They made a date for Shelley to visit Barbara's new apartment on Monday. "It has to be kept completely confidential," Barbara said; they both knew she was talking about Bill Spassero, who was in the public defender's office.

When they left the restaurant, the rain was pelting down; Barbara felt shabby next to the sparkling pink of Shelley's outfit. She laughed when Shelley opened an umbrella, transparent, with golden sunflowers hanging in space, aglow in the rain.

At home, she hung up her raincoat on the coat tree they had installed on the upper landing, then looked in on John, who grinned and waved, blew her a kiss. He liked for her to look in on him, and he never came to her office to do the same. His living room held his massive desk, a dining table and chairs, the television, and two easy chairs. They cooked in his kitchen, and she used hers to continue her lessons.

She went through the other door, past their bedroom, past her living room with reading chairs and lamps and bookcases, past her kitchen, and into her office, where no sound he made ever penetrated. She closed her door and stood at the window, gazing out through the trees, which looked ghostly in the rain, at the river, thinking about what Sam Bixby had told Shelley.

The next night at Frank's table, she brought it up when they were lingering over coffee. "Dad," she said hesitantly, "would you consider it abandonment if I struck out on my own?"

He blinked. "What do you mean?"

"I talked it over with John last night, and we both think I should have my own offices and stop using yours. It would be a stretch financially at first, but I think in time it would work out. You know how happy that would make Sam."

"Has he been at you again?"

"No. But to be truthful, I'm not very comfortable using your office space all the time. I can't stand the accusing look Patsy gives me."

Frank laughed. "I think it's a grand idea." Thoughtfully he said, "Patsy's problem is boredom. I've been thinking how good she'd be at organizing some of my book, retyping parts of it, proofreading it for me. It's just about ready to send off, and I keep finding reasons not to do the grunge work that needs doing. She'd love it." He eyed John diffidently. "You read it. What would you think about a title like *The Zen of Cross-examination*?"

They talked about the book he had been writing for the past five years, and Barbara kept giving him suspicious looks, unable to shake the feeling that somehow she had done what he had planned for her to do all along.

On Monday when Shelley arrived at the apartment, they went into Barbara's office and closed the door, and Shelley said she most definitely wanted the job.

"The situation has changed," Barbara said. Shelley's bright expression dimmed, and she looked near tears. "You see," Barbara said, "I'm going to start my own firm. Do you want a permanent job? As permanent as mine will be, anyway."

Shelley did not jump up and down, but it was obvious that she was pulling in unsuspected reserves of self-control. "Do I want it! Does an angel want wings! You don't have to pay me anything!"

"Well, let's start." Barbara had not told her anything in detail; now she did, starting with Maggie's seduction and abandonment, bringing it all up to date. "So Gilmore's dropped out of sight. Sylvia was approached by the FBI to drop charges, which she did, of course. Bailey got the lead pipe and the Belmont material down to the New Orleans police; nothing I have to do there. The D.A. decided the money is a side issue, and Ray's trial will start on December second. Between now and the trial date, you'll have to read every scrap I have—there's a ton of stuff—and become familiar with every detail so you'll know what to watch and listen for at the trial. But you won't be hired officially until the day of the closing agreement, when I discharge my obligation to Maggie. I can't cut her loose until I know that business is over and done with, and I don't dare show my face at the trial. I don't want even a suspicion of conflict of interest to arise, so it's going to be on your shoulders."

She scowled and added, "Meanwhile, Stover's been frightening the Arnos with talk of the death penalty, as opposed to copping a plea for a lesser offense."

Shelley had been making notes as Barbara talked. She looked up. "What about the fingerprints Bailey lifted? Isn't anyone chasing down those two men?"

"Nope. It's the one-armed-man syndrome. Except there are two of them, Stael and Ulrich, ex-cons. Stover's willing to bring them in, but only to muddy the water. He hasn't done a thing with them. He warned Ray that they aren't worth a damn, since no one can prove when they got in. That's the line the D.A.'s office will take if they're brought up."

Shelley looked shocked, and again Barbara thought how young she was, how inexperienced.

"Okay," Shelley said then. "I'll give two weeks' notice, and be done at the end of next week. I'll need an apartment here. Are there still any vacancies in this complex?"

There were three. She said she would take one today. "I'll need to be in touch with you every evening," she said. "That will be perfect."

"Perfect," Barbara agreed. "And I'll start looking for office space."

Almost shyly, keeping her gaze on her notebook, Shelley asked, "Would it offend you if I asked to decorate the offices? You know, pick out the drapes and desks and things like that?"

Barbara hesitated. Shelley was a very rich young woman with expensive taste who had never had to skimp or save a dime in her life.

"I won't go overboard," Shelley said hurriedly. "And no pink or anything like that. We could work out something about paying for it, if you'd just let me take care of that part."

"Done," Barbara said, mentally kissing her meager budget good-bye. They talked about what kind of space they would need, what they would need to start with, and then Shelley left to talk to management about her own apartment. When she walked out, her feet skimmed over the floor as she reverted to the fairy princess, who had no need for earthly contact.

21

From two until four, people had drifted in, oohed and aahed, had drunk champagne, and congratulated Barbara on the appearance of her offices, misplaced praise, since Shelley had been the interior decorator, but no one knew that yet. Shelley and Bill Spassero had been guests among many other guests. No one mentioned Bailey's invisible contribution—a state-of-the-art security system and a safe built into the wall behind bookcases.

The carpeting was a deep burgundy plush wool. Shelley had explained it with a helpless shrug. "Daddy wanted me to have it," she said. "It's his gift to both of us." The furnishings were Danish modern, pale gleaming wood with wonderfully simple lines. A couch covered with dark green leather and matching chairs were in Barbara's office; her desk was big, her swivel chair was high-backed, with a golden-tan leather seat cushion and armrests, and the clients' chairs were comfortable, with pale green cushions. A coffee table before the couch had an inlaid border of jade and ruby-colored stones. Three brilliant Chinese urns held plants, which Shelley swore she would take care of, and vertical blinds admitted soft light from windows on three walls.

"Shelley, how could you?" Barbara had cried after the furniture was delivered.

Shelley had already explained about the carpeting. She looked a little confused at Barbara's shock and dismay. "Don't you like it?"

"That's not the point. I love it, but I can't afford it!"

"Oh, that. Mr. Holloway said it was on him. Daddy gave me the carpet; your father gave you the rest."

"I can't let him do this," Barbara had said to John.

"I don't think you realize how much pleasure it gives him to be able to do it," John said.

That day Frank had come early and stayed until the last visitor left, and his pleasure had not been at all concealed. Now Barbara and John were alone in her office, sitting side by side on the couch, their feet on the coffee table.

"Good party," he said lazily. "Everyone's mighty impressed."

"Me, too," she said. "Other girls dream of dancing with Prince Charming. I dreamed of my own offices."

"Lucky girl," he said, taking her hand.

"I know." Then hastily she leaned forward and knocked on wood. John laughed.

After a moment she said, "You know I'm gearing up for Ray Arno's trial, don't you?"

"Just for the past three months."

"Well, it actually starts on Monday, and we'll have our closing agreement for Maggie the following Monday. That's cutting it terribly fine if the prosecution starts to steamroll and Stover doesn't slow it down. In any event, I'm going to be pretty busy from the start of the trial until it's over. Just a warning."

"Okay. Will it be over by Christmas?"

"I hope so. That's all I can say. I'm afraid there will be a lot of objections to the various lines I'll open; there may be a continuance."

John stood up and walked to the window, moved the blind aside, and gazed out. His children were due the day after Christmas for a week's visit. "I understand." He sounded distant.

"I'll gather up glasses and then we'll go eat." They picked up glasses and empty bottles together and she groaned melodramatically about having to wash everything, but he stayed remote.

Then the trial began. It was as bad as Barbara had feared; Shelley was outraged by Stover's performance. Her own performance was exemplary. Every day she reported in full, how people had appeared, how they had dressed; she commented on the jurors, on the judge's demeanor—everything.

Every night Barbara listened to the tapes. And that had to be done in real time, hours and hours of real time. On Thursday, four days into the trial, she asked Maggie to come to the office after court recessed for the day.

Maggie looked at her accusingly. She was staying in town all week, but she was not sleeping well, and she was more nervous than Barbara had ever seen her. "They're going to nail him," she said. "They keep adding more and more details to prove that no one else could have done it, and they showed the autopsy pictures and kept going on about how sadistic the attack was. They'll convict him!"

"They won't," Barbara said. "I told you, and I meant it. What do you want me to do?"

"What can you do at this point? Tell the truth? We should have done that at the beginning!"

"What did you say you wanted me to do months ago?"

"I wanted you to take Ray's case. But it's too late! Can't you understand that?"

"All right, today you asked me to take his case. But I can't simply agree and take over. Has Ray indicated that he would like to change his attorney?"

Maggie was on the couch, twisting her hands in a helpless gesture again and again. She became very still. "What do you mean?"

"Has he indicated dissatisfaction with his attorney?"

"Yes! He can see that Stover's not doing anything. He isn't blind."

"Now listen carefully, Maggie. Have you noticed a pretty young woman with a whole lot of beautiful blond hair in the courtroom every day?" Maggie nodded. "All right. Her name is Shelley McGinnis, and she has applied for a job with me. If I had a big case on hand that required a second attorney, I would hire her in a second. Tomorrow, during the first recess, Shelley will approach you and chat, and she will say how badly this case is being handled. You confide in her that there are fingerprints that no one is doing anything about, and she will advise you to tell Ray to get someone who will do something about them. She'll tell you to have Ray ask to see me, and to tell his attorney how unhappy he is. Got that?"

Maggie was stone still. She nodded.

"Okay. During visiting hour at the lunch recess, visit Ray and repeat what Shelley said, and tell him that she worked with me in the past. Tell him you asked me to take over, and I can't unless he requests it. Just tell him what Shelley says and urge him, if he needs urging, to ask to see me. Be very careful what you say. Your conversation will be taped. I'm counting on you to be very careful."

Maggie leaned back and closed her eyes for a moment. She drew in a deep breath, then another. "What else?"

"If Ray says he wants to see me, then you'll have to come and tell me that. Come straight over here after you talk with him. Maggie, you may be questioned about all this; probably it won't happen, but it might. It's important that you act on what Shelley says, that she solidified your doubts and worries. Can you do that?"

"God, yes!"

"Okay. Let's go over it all again. Then when you come to see me tomorrow, we'll take the next steps."

"It's really bad, isn't it? Is it too late?"

"They're rushing this through so fast, they could wrap up the state's side tomorrow, and that would be bad for Ray. They're on a downhill slope racing toward the bottom without any resistance at all, and probably feeling pretty cocky about the whole thing. I have to slow them down. I want the state to bring up the possibility of outsiders."

When they walked out through the hall to the reception room, Barbara was surprised to see Frank at the desk.

He greeted Maggie and held her hands a moment; after she left, he said, "Did you start wheels rolling?"

"Afraid so."

He was concerned, but he had expressed his worries already and did not push her again. "What I've been wondering," he said too innocently, "is if you'd let Patsy use your outer office over the next week or so. See, I hate to have her working on my private stuff downtown, and I couldn't bear to have her at the house. She'd want to straighten out my socks and sew buttons on my shirts. But she sure could sit at that desk and try to make an index for me." In a very offhanded manner, he added, "Of course, I'd have to hang around to consult with her now and then."

Barbara hugged him. He knew that getting a secretary who could be privy to what was going on right now was impossible.

Then he said thoughtfully, "You realize that if I have to do anything real, anything legal, I'd have to be an associate. Not just someone off the street."

"I don't think I could afford you," she said, also thoughtfully.

"We'll work something out. Am I in?"

"You are."

"Okay, about those subpoenas, someone will have to talk a judge into agreeing to an enjoinder for the witness not to leave the state until he testifies. I think I might be better at that than Shelley. It's hard to take a cream puff seriously."

"That little cream puff is doing one hell of a job," Barbara said fervently. "Did you get to yesterday's tapes yet?"

He nodded. "You're right. They want to wrap it up this week, and there's not a damn thing to stop them at this point. They're making a strong circumstantial case."

"Maybe after lunch tomorrow they'll tread water for a while," she said.

Although she had given up any pretense at cooking, she nevertheless insisted that they stick to their alternate days, and her meals were microwavable. That night it was chicken Kiev, which was actually pretty good.

"Another late night?" John asked as they finished eating.

"Afraid so."

"You look tired, and you don't even have the case yet."

"I know. This is not—repeat, not—the proper way to do it. First and last time for me." She got up to pour coffee. "Tomorrow all hell just might break loose. And from then on, I'll be involved," she said in a low voice. "You should be warned."

He nodded. "It's all right. Remember, I saw you at work before. I know pretty much what to expect. An absentee lover. But then, afterward, another honeymoon? The payoff's worth the wait."

The doorbell rang, and she started out. "That's Shelley. Time to go to work." She left, feeling him watching her out of sight.

"It's really bad," Shelley said in the office. "Today Roxbury brought in the Corvallis police and made the case that Mitch was in the area on legitimate business. And that no one but the Arnos knew he was here. He read a statement from Palmer, claiming that Mitch had worked for him for the past fifteen years, had been trustworthy and all that. Stover didn't challenge a thing. It wasn't even a deposition, just a statement. Roxbury brought in the first witness to testify about the fight eighteen years ago. He was rough with him. Treated him like a hostile witness with no cause. Then Stover tried to make him admit he couldn't really remember what happened so long ago. It was pathetic to watch him. He was rough, too."

"Was that the last witness? Was he dismissed yet?"

"Yes. It's all like that: they testify, Stover asks the wrong questions, and on redirect, they repeat what Roxbury wants the jury to hear, and they're out of there."

"Okay," Barbara said. "I talked to Maggie earlier. She'll be expecting you to approach her at the first recess."

The next day Maggie arrived at fifteen minutes before two; she was nearly breathless, from excitement or from running up the stairs to the office, or both.

"I did it. Stover tried to keep me away, he said he had to have a conference with his client, and I'd be interfering. Ray insisted on seeing me, and he wants to see you as soon as possible. He said he'd tell Stover to beat it, and he'd write a note to the judge to request a change of attorney." She said this without pause, the words tumbling almost incoherently.

"Good. Can you hang around for a while?"

"Yes."

"As soon as I can get in to see Ray, that's your cue, you go tell the Arnos that I'll want to talk to them. Ray's parents and James, that is."

Her phone rang and she picked it up. "Holloway."

A man said, "This is Clyde Dawkins, Judge Waldman's clerk. The judge would like a word with you. Can you hold a second?"

"Yes, of course."

Judge Waldman came on the line. "Ms. Holloway, a situation has arisen in court. Have you agreed to represent Mr. Raymond Arno?"

"His sister-in-law has asked me to represent him. I was going to talk to him later today."

"I would appreciate it if you could go there now and talk with Mr. Arno and make your decision. Is that convenient?"

"Yes."

"Very well. Then I want to have a meeting in chambers with you. Three-thirty. Is that convenient?"

"Fine. I'll be there.

"Well," Barbara said when she hung up. "It's starting. I'll go see Ray now, and you arrange with the Arnos to come over here at ten in the morning. Okay? And I'll want you at nine. Time to go to work."

Maggie was walking out when Barbara called Frank to tell him they were on, and to get Bailey over there that evening after dinner. "Marching time," she said. Frank laughed.

⟡

22

Ray Arno was handsome, even with deep shadows under his eyes and a tic in his cheek that seemed new enough to be bothering him. His hand kept edging up to it, as if feeling his cheek for something unfamiliar. He no longer looked younger than forty-seven. They shook hands and sat on opposite sides of the small conference table and studied each other.

Barbara knew he had been in Vietnam; although the war had been winding down by the time he served, he no doubt had seen horrors. He was a businessman, married with two children, the first of four sons in the Arno family, and none of his past experiences had changed him the way the past few months had done. When she had met him before, he had been open, unguarded, just puzzled. He had been trusting, had faith in the system—the criminal law system, the police—had believed in their mission to find the killer of his brother. Today he was withdrawn and watchful, wary and suspicious of her, of the conference room, this meeting. He had lost weight, and the shadows under his eyes were not as worrisome as the shadows that had appeared in his eyes, as if he had pulled himself back into a very dark place with a curtain between him and the world. His complexion, naturally a little saturnine, had paled to an unhealthy, lusterless grayed tone.

"Mr. Arno," Barbara said, "since I am not your attorney, we will assume that our every word is being recorded. Maggie tells me that you're not satisfied with the way your defense is being conducted and that you would like me to represent you. Is that right?"

His mouth tightened when she said they were being recorded, and his gaze flicked around the tiny room, searching for a hidden microphone or some other device. "That's right," he said. "Stover's an ass."

"Have you notified Judge Waldman of your wish to drop him, retain someone else?"

"Yes. I sent her a letter telling her that."

"You understand that she has to approve of the change at this late date?"

"Yes. Stover said I can't switch now, it's too late."

"We'll see," she said. "I'm on my way to a meeting with the judge. If she approves, I'll be back, and we'll be able to talk freely then."

He stood up; the look of total despair he had had earlier, while not erased, seemed a little less overwhelming.

Outside the jail, she drew in a deep breath before she got into her car; it was a cold day with the smell of wood smoke in the air. Eugene was the only city Barbara knew where wood smoke overcame the smell of automobile exhaust. She got behind the wheel and started to drive. Christmas lights shone from windows, twinkled, blazed; a line of cars inched along Willamette Street in a futile effort to find parking spaces close to the post office, which had its own line of customers on the sidewalk. She drove past them all to the courthouse.

There, after parking in the lot across Seventh, she went through the tunnel under the street and emerged in the lower level of the building, where she saw Bishop Stover watching the people entering as if on guard duty.

He strode forward to meet her, his face a dull red, his expression one of outrage and fury. He was in his fifties, a stocky man who would go to fat if he let up on the exercise and didn't keep a sharp eye on his diet. His hair was brown with a tinge of red, streaked with a little gray. "What the hell do you think you're trying to pull?" he demanded, stopping directly in front of her.

"Mr. Stover? How do you do?" She sidestepped him and continued to walk.

"You know damn well I'm Stover. You can't jump into my case and grab my client. You've been on the sidelines, coaching everyone all the time, haven't you? What for, Holloway? Arno's broke. Don't look to make a cent off him. You want to start a new office with a few headlines? Grab a little free publicity? Is that it?"

She looked him up and down contemptuously. "I'm sorry I can't stop and chat," she said. "I'm on my way to a command performance with Judge Waldman."

"So am I. I don't intend to get pushed aside and let you play your little game. You've had Folsum acting as your spy, and now McGinnis. You're too clever for your own good, Holloway. Go get your headlines somewhere else."

Very pleasantly, Barbara said, "I don't believe you look well, Mr. Stover. Perhaps you should check into the hospital, have a few tests."

"You're threatening me! My God, you're threatening me!"

"Don't be silly. Just passing the time of day. Now, if you'll excuse me, I should comb my hair, wash my hands before I meet the judge. See you in chambers, Mr. Stover."

Frank had said that Jane Waldman was a lady, and meeting her, Barbara understood exactly what he meant. She was fifty, but she could have been any age between thirty and sixty or even seventy. She was tall and slender, dressed in a mid-calf-length black silk dress with long sleeves; she wore a strand of pearls and pearl earrings. Her ash-blond hair was in a loose chignon. And her slender hands with long tapered fingers would have made an artist reach for his brush. She shook hands with Barbara and motioned toward the others in the room.

"I understand you've all met," she said. "Craig Roxbury, assistant district attorney, and Bishop Stover, defense attorney. Gentlemen, Ms. Holloway."

They were all very polite, shaking hands, taking chairs around a low coffee table set with silver coffee service and lovely bone china cups and saucers.

The judge did not waste time. She asked, "Ms. Holloway, have you consulted with Mr. Arno? And have you made your decision?"

"Yes, I have. If it please the court, I'll take his case."

"Before we continue, I must advise you that serious charges have been leveled in this office. Mr. Roxbury, please repeat your concern for Ms. Holloway's benefit."

He cleared his throat. "Yes, your honor. At this stage of the trial, I believe Mr. Arno is grasping at straws in an attempt to delay the outcome, to delay the trial until it is very close to Christmas, when he hopes the jurors will be more likely to be charitable. He has had ample opportunity to make a change such as this in the months past; to put it off until the state is nearly ready to rest is intolerable."

Judge Waldman nodded, then turned to Stover. "And your concerns?"

"She's been pulling strings behind the scenes for months," he said angrily. "I've done all the work, and she wants to step in and grab headlines. I agree with Roxbury that Arno's desperate, but the defense hasn't had its chance to tell the rest of the story yet. And she's using his desperation for her own purposes. She and Maggie Folsum cooked up this plot months ago, and she planted McGinnis in court to act as her spy, so she would know exactly when to step forward and make the power play." More belligerently, he said to Barbara, "If you have information concerning my client, it's your duty to let me in on it. You could even come aboard as part of my team. You don't have to grab him."

"You have the same information I have," she said coolly. "I just intend to use it, since you don't seem to grasp its importance."

Judge Waldman gazed at Barbara without expression. "Did you discuss this case with Ms. Folsum months ago?"

"Yes, I did. Maggie Folsum was already my client when she asked if I would defend him. I had to tell her no, that it might result in a conflict of interest. I didn't know at that time how either case would develop. She asked me again today, and since I will fulfill my obligation to her on Monday and I now see that no conflict could arise, I told her that if Ray Arno wanted me, I would talk to him about it."

Without pausing she continued, "Ms. Folsum has two major concerns. In August she and I met with Mr. Roxbury to inform him that Mitch Arno had brought a large sum of money in cash to the state, but his office apparently has chosen not to follow up that line of inquiry, and this alarmed her. She also said that since certain fingerprints she had given to the district attorney's office as well as to Mr. Stover appeared to have been overlooked or even deliberately put aside, she was even more alarmed. Today Ray Arno asked me personally to take his case, and I said I would if the change was approved by the court."

"Is Ms. McGinnis your employee?"

"No, your honor. She is a friend and she was a colleague in the past. She has applied to a number of firms for a position; she asked me for a job. I started my own firm only recently, and I had nothing on hand that required a second attorney as yet. I suggested she might fill in her time by observing as many trials as she could."

Careful, she told herself, aware of the judge's close scrutiny. "I shall hire Ms. McGinnis the minute I leave here. I know how intelligent and what an excellent observer she is. I think she will be invaluable to me in defending Ray Arno."

"You mentioned fingerprints," Judge Waldman said. "What fingerprints are you talking about?"

"Ms. Folsum told me she asked a detective to fingerprint Ray Arno's house last summer and that when the report came back, she gave it to the district attorney and to Mr. Stover. She said the detective had recovered prints of two ex-convicts in Ray Arno's house, but no one has brought them up at the trial."

"They're a red herring!" Roxbury said angrily. "They go nowhere! We investigated them, and they mean nothing!"

"Mr. Stover, did you intend to use the evidence of the fingerprints?"

"Yes, of course. Next week, when we have our turn."

"And which witness would have introduced them?" she asked politely.

"The detective," he said. His face had turned a darker shade of red.

"Have you subpoenaed him?"

"Not yet. I was waiting for the state to rest."

"Is his name on your witness list?"

"Not yet."

"I see." She leaned in toward the table. "Perhaps we should have coffee. I have a few more questions." No one moved or spoke as she played hostess, and although no one wanted coffee, they all accepted and murmured their thanks.

She asked about the money then, and Barbara gave her a very abbreviated account, aware of Roxbury's increasing fury as she spoke.

"Your honor," he said harshly, "that's a simple red herring. We looked into it. Mitch Arno didn't even have it, his lawyer did. It has nothing to do with the murder."

Judge Waldman regarded him thoughtfully for a moment, then turned to Stover and directed her remarks to him. "Since Mr. Arno has requested a change of attorney, I shall grant his wish. That is his constitutional right, of course, even if it delays the trial somewhat. And, Ms. Holloway, I shall not allow this trial to be delayed unduly. The jurors have every expectation of being through here before Christmas."

"What am I supposed to do, just bow out and let her take the stage?" Stover demanded.

"I expect you to cooperate fully with Ms. Holloway, to furnish her with all the information provided by the state, and to be of any other assistance possible. Ms. Holloway, I charge you with the duty to inform me if there has not been complete cooperation. Mr. Roxbury, your office will also cooperate with Ms. Holloway and provide any materials to which she is entitled without delay."

She asked Roxbury how much longer he intended to take. He

said bitterly that he had planned to rest the following day, but the delay meant he would need at least two more days. She consulted a calendar, then said with a sigh, "Very well. Mr. Roxbury will finish on Tuesday or Wednesday. On Monday, December sixteenth, I expect you to present the case for the defense, Ms. Holloway. That does not give you a great deal of time, but as I said, I want this jury to be finished with its work before Christmas. And as you said, Ms. McGinnis is an excellent observer. I shall instruct Mr. Dawkins to provide you with a complete transcript of the trial to date as soon as he can."

"Your honor," Barbara said, "if I find it necessary to ask additional questions of witnesses who have already testified, may I have them recalled, or must I subpoena them as defense witnesses?"

Judge Waldman considered for a moment, then said, "After you have gone over the transcript, show me the list of witnesses you want to recall on Monday morning. At what time on Monday will you be prepared to start your defense?"

"I can prepare my list for you by eight that morning and I can be in court by eleven."

"Very well. Monday morning at eight in here," Judge Waldman said. "I'll talk to the jurors and explain the new development, and we shall delay the start of Monday's proceedings until eleven o'clock." She looked at them severely and added, "This meeting is to be kept confidential. If any of you gives out a hint, I shall hold you in contempt and put you in jail."

By five Barbara was back at the county jail, back in one of the conference rooms, this time with her notebook and pen.

"I should have gone with one of the people you suggested at the start," Ray said unhappily when they were both seated. "You saw the condition I was in, still disbelieving, going along. I thought since I knew Stover—he's gone fishing with me, for God's sake! I thought he would work for me."

"It's done, Mr. Arno," she said. "No point in fretting about it now."

He seemed oblivious of her attempt to derail him, to start working. "At first you think it can't happen, not really," he said, looking over her head, at the wall, at the past, at nothing. "Then you think, well, it happens, but to other people, not you. Then, in the middle of the night one night, you think, why me? Why, God, what did I do to deserve this? You know? You warned me, and I simply didn't understand what you meant, as if you had been speaking a foreign language or something—"

"Mr. Arno—Ray! Please, there's no point in this. We have a little more than a week to prepare your defense. You have to help me; I can't do it alone."

"Just one more thing," he said; he gazed at her for a moment, then rubbed his eyes. "I'm sorry, but you see, my family . . . I can't say things like this to them. They're still in the opening phase—it can't happen, not here, not to us—and I can't seem to talk to them. They come in and say things like, It's just a big mistake, they'll see it's a mistake and turn you loose. But I've had my nights of asking God why it's happening, and that puts me in a different place from the family. It's as if I've finally seen into the pit, but they keep closing their eyes or turning away their heads. Today, when you showed up earlier, I knew you understood what I'm facing, you and the judge, a few others in court, but not my family. And, Barbara, I have to say this before you take over, today for the first time I felt like maybe I won't be tossed overboard into that pit. I'm grateful to you for coming, for taking me on. I just had to tell you that."

"Save your thanks for after the case is over with," she said; her effort to sound kidding and lighthearted fell a bit flat, but it was the best she could do at the moment. She patted his hands, folded on the table. "For now, please bear with me if I seem demanding and abrupt; tell me if you want a break. I really don't want this to become a new torment for you. It's just that the pressure of time is very much a factor."

"Shoot," he said.

At eight, going up the apartment stairs, she was overwhelmed by the fragrance of chicken and green chilies, one of John's specialties. He met her at the top landing and for a time he held her, his face pressed into her hair. Then he drew back slightly and said, "Dinner is being served at this very moment, madam."

She held on another second, until he took her by the shoulders and turned her toward the living room, where the table was ready. "Dinner," he said. "Did you have any lunch today?"

She had to think, then she shook her head.

"Dinner," he repeated. She thought the yearning look on his face must have matched her own, but they went in to eat.

When the first ravenous hunger pangs had been satisfied, she said, "On Monday we'll have the closing agreement and I'll be done with the Maggie Folsum business."

"Then what?"

"Tonight I have to collect Shelley and go to Dad's to consult. We'll all be dashing around for the next ten days. All the stuff I couldn't do in the past few months will have to be crammed into a little more than a week. It will take all of us, full-time, and then some."

"I meant what about the Palmer affair? You're not letting it go, I can tell."

A week after moving into the apartments, relaxed, with breathing space, she had decided that if they were to live together, there could be no secrets between them, and she had told him everything she knew and suspected about the case. She shook her head. "I'm not letting it go. I intend to force Trassi and Palmer to hand over Mitch Arno's killers."

He stared at her. "You'll need a bodyguard."

"Bailey's taking care of that."

"I'll go to Frank's with you tonight. I don't want you out at night alone, or just with Shelley. Don't even bother to try to talk me out of it."

"All right," she said. "But it's not a threat for now. Please believe me. I still have papers they need, and Trassi doesn't know the trap he's in. Monday afternoon he will, but not now, not yet."

Frank was relieved to see John arrive with Barbara and Shelley. "Go on in," he said. "There's Bailey driving up. I'll just wait for him."

They went into the living room, where Frank had a fire going, and both cats were on the couch, sprawled across most of it. "Beat it," Frank growled at them when he entered with Bailey. Neither cat stirred until he moved them.

"First," Barbara said as they were getting settled, "Judge Waldman gagged us all until the trial resumes on Monday. She doesn't want the jury speculating over the weekend about news stories of the change. I don't think the D.A. will find it to their advantage to leak anything yet. So we just might have the weekend without interference."

Barbara began to outline the following week. She had been planning the defense for months; now they could openly implement the plans.

"Starting next week," Frank said later, "no more restaurants. We'll eat here and I'll cook or we'll order carryout food. You, too, Shelley. No running around alone, no late hours driving by yourself." She was wide-eyed, and nodded emphatically. "Now, how about a snack and something to drink?"

Bailey was on his feet almost instantly. "How about that."

Barbara's gaze came to rest on John, who might have been carved from cold, hard stone.

23

Barbara accepted that she could never compete with the other professional women she met day after day, as far as clothes or hair or general appearance were concerned. She especially could never compete with Judge Jane Waldman, who that Monday morning was dressed in a mauve-colored sheer-wool knit dress with matching shoes. A simple gold chain and small gold hoop earrings finished her outfit; she looked more elegant than ever. Grumpily Barbara thought that she had tried; she had had her hair cut sometime in the fall. She couldn't remember when, only that for a while her own hair had looked wonderful, until she shampooed, and magically it had turned into her usual style, which was to say no style at all.

Craig Roxbury and Barbara had been admitted into Judge Waldman's chambers together, and this time the judge was sitting at her desk and motioned them to chairs across from her.

"You have your list?" she asked Barbara.

"Yes. It's only four names." She handed over the list.

"I have to warn you that I won't allow you to recross-examine these witnesses. If there is anything new to bring up from their various reports, you may do that, but you have the transcript, and we will not reopen the cross-examination. Is that understood?"

"Yes, your honor. However, there are two missing reports, one concerning what was found in Ray Arno's car when it was impounded, and the last page from the medical examiner's report."

"We turned over everything we have," Roxbury said. "If Stover lost the stuff, we can't help that."

"You will make copies of those two reports and see that Ms. Holloway receives them both this morning before court resumes," Judge Waldman said. She put on gold-framed glasses and looked over the list Barbara had handed her. "For the sake of continuity, I suggest that these four witnesses all be recalled on Monday, December sixteen. After that, of course, you will conduct your defense without further suggestions from the court. Is that agreeable?"

"Yes, your honor."

Judge Waldman took off her glasses and laid them down. "I have been informed that Mr. Stover was admitted to Sacred Heart Hospital late Saturday with chest pains," she said. "That is what I shall tell the jury. I don't want to sequester them at this season; they have shopping to do, other things to attend to. For that reason I am imposing a no-comment order from now until the case goes to the jury. I don't want stories in the newspapers, or television news concerning this trial. No press conferences, no news releases. The court will contact these four witnesses and recall them all for Monday, the sixteenth. I trust you will finish with them all on that day. And I trust you will finish the defense case by the end of next week."

The discussion continued until nine-thirty, when Barbara finally left the judge's chambers and walked across the street to the Federal Building, where Maggie met her at the entrance. Maggie was very nervous.

"Relax," Barbara said. "Now, as soon as I know beyond any doubt that there's no last-minute snag, you're no longer my client. You understand? I'll turn you over to Sunderman, who will handle the paperwork and arrange for a transfer of the money to your account."

She spotted Trassi standing at a table covered with handouts, facing away. "Excuse me a minute," she said, and walked to the table by Trassi. "They won't want you in there today, will they?" she asked him, picking up a pamphlet.

"No, of course not. Where are the printouts?"

She patted her briefcase. "I'll go in with Sunderman, but I won't have to stay long, I'm sure. The minute I'm done, I'll leave and hand them over."

"This is a farce. I have a plane to catch. Do you think I'll burst in there and cry foul? Give me the printouts."

"As soon as the signatures are on paper," she said. "There's Mr. Sunderman now."

At that moment a woman came to tell them that Mr. Chenowith was waiting for the group.

They were taken to the same room they had occupied before, under the same harsh white light. Both men began to pull papers from briefcases.

"Mr. Chenowith," Barbara said as he shuffled his stack of papers, "I have to be in court by eleven. I don't believe my presence is required here. Mr. Sunderman is representing Ms. Folsum in the matter."

He looked pained, but she had to assume that was his normal expression, unless he was conducting an audit with an unfortunate tax dodger caught red-handed.

"There is the matter of the amount of the arrears," Chenowith said. "Your original claim was for two hundred ten thousand dollars, and the money has since accrued interest; and there is the additional sum of thirty thousand dollars, which will be returned to Mr. Arno's estate. I have drawn up papers to the effect that Ms. Folsum will receive the original sum, plus the interest on that part of the money only. Is that satisfactory?"

"Yes. Absolutely. Mr. Sunderman, I no longer am Ms. Folsum's attorney of record. Now, if you gentlemen will excuse me. . . ."

Trassi was in the lobby near the entrance door. He walked outside and she followed. "It's done," she said. "Here's your package."

She took a manila envelope from her briefcase and handed it to him; he opened it and examined the contents as well as he could without removing anything. She waited until he closed it again. "Now, we're all finished," she said. "Good day, Mr. Trassi." She turned away at the same moment a young man in a windbreaker approached from behind him.

"Mr. Trassi?" he asked. The lawyer jerked around, startled, and the young man handed him a paper.

Trassi looked as if he had received a snake. He stared at the paper, then finally looked up at Barbara. "What is this? What are you trying to pull?"

"It's a subpoena," she said. "See you in court, Mr. Trassi."

She met Shelley in the courthouse at fifteen minutes before eleven. All the Arnos were milling about—James and his wife, David and his, Lorinne Arno, several of their various children, Mama and Papa; Maggie's daughters were with them, and it appeared that everyone in that cluster was talking at once. Gwen and Karen Folsum hurried to Barbara. They were both very handsome, tall like the Arnos, and with Maggie's lovely eyes and hair.

"Is Mother going to be here?" Karen asked.

"She may be delayed a few minutes, not for long, I'm sure," Barbara said. Mama Arno was approaching her. "Excuse me, I have to speak with Shelley a moment before we begin," Barbara said hurriedly. Talking with the Arnos was hard, she had learned on Saturday, when in desperation she had separated them and had talked to them one by one.

All the Arno sons were tall with dark hair and dark eyes, athletic, all like their father, who at seventy was still upright, strong, and vigorous. His face was deeply lined, weathered by salt spray, sun, wind; he had been a fisherman off the coast all his adult life until recently. His hands were very large and heavily veined. Mama Arno was five feet two and stout, not fat, but husky-looking; her hair was a soft golden blond with white roots. And her skin was unlined and as pink and creamy-white as a baby's. She liked to touch the people she was talking to, and since she seemed to talk to everyone within earshot at the same time, she was busy touching someone here, patting there, caressing another, smoothing down the hair, or straightening a collar. . . . Barbara had found it so disconcerting, she had kept her desk between them Saturday when they talked. The Arno clan all had the ability to listen to multiple conversations simultaneously, without any sign of confusion. And the wives had been trained over the years to participate in exactly the same way. Barbara could imagine what bedlam a big holiday must be in their households; sitting day after day silenced in court must have been a strain nearly beyond endurance for them.

Now, escaping Mama Arno, she drew Shelley aside and said in a low voice, "Trassi was served with the subpoena, and he's hopping mad. You might get in touch with Dad and let him know."

"Right. Roxbury handed over the two reports and snarled at me." She grinned. "He acted as if I had been Delilah to his Samson."

They talked a few more minutes, then people started to file into Courtroom B. Barbara entered and took her place at the defense table. Shelley left to call Frank.

Judge Waldman very politely introduced Barbara to the jury, and then she introduced the jurors to Barbara. Shelley entered and was introduced, and they started.

"Mr. Roxbury, your next witness, if you will."

He called Cory Sussman, a stooped man with a weathered face and thick gray hair, clearly nervous and unhappy about testifying. He kept glancing at Ray Arno, then at the rest of the family, as if apologizing.

After establishing that Sussman lived in Folsum, where he managed the Exxon service station and a small store, Roxbury steered him to the day of the fight between Mitch and Ray Arno.

"Just tell us in your own words about what you saw that day."

"Well, Papa Arno, he come into—"

"You mean Mr. Anthony Arno? Mitchell's father?"

"Yeah, Papa Arno. He come in to the store and bought a one-way ticket to Portland. . . ." It was the same story Barbara had heard many times, one the jury had heard twice already. He didn't add anything new to it.

"Mr. Sussman," Barbara said kindly when Roxbury was done, "you've known the Arno family a long time?"

"All my life," he said.

"Were the Arno boys fighting, brawling kids?"

He looked shocked. "Never were. Quietest bunch of kids on the coast."

"That day you've described, was Papa Arno bloody or dirty?"

He shook his head hard. "No way. Not at all."

"Was Ray Arno messed up, bloody and dirty?"

"Yeah, just like Mitch. Looked like they was both rolling in the mud and hitting each other hard."

"You said that Papa Arno got the bus ticket, and he was the one who put Mitch on the bus. Did you see Ray walking around that day?"

"He got out of the car and watched, maybe took a step or two toward the bus with them, but Papa didn't need no help."

"Was Ray wobbly and unsteady on his feet?"

"Yeah, maybe not as bad as Mitch, but he'd took a beating, too."

"Was Ray much bigger than Mitch in those days?"

He looked surprised. "Not bigger at all. They was all big boys, six feet or over, and strong. Fishermen, you see, strong."

"So you think they were pretty evenly matched if they had a fight?"

"Yeah, real even."

"And you think they looked about the same afterward?"

Now he shook his head. "No, ma'am. Not the same. Mitch looked whupped, and Ray looked like the whupper."

The next witness was Eric Rubens, a neighbor of Ray's. He had known Ray Arno for fourteen years, ever since Ray moved across River Loop One from him.

"Last summer, did Ray Arno ask you to keep an eye on his property while he was away for a few days?" Roxbury asked.

"Yes."

"Did you see him leave his house on the evening of Friday, August second?"

"Yes."

"At what time was that?"

"A few minutes after seven."

Barbara suppressed a smile. This witness was going to stick to the questions with the shortest possible answers. Let Roxbury pull teeth for a while.

Slowly, painfully, Roxbury dragged it out that Rubens had seen Papa Arno drive past at about seven and leave again almost immediately, and a few minutes later Ray drove out past him. In the same slow way he testified that he had been in his yard all day Sunday and had not seen any strangers around, had not seen any strange cars drive into Ray's driveway, had not seen anything out of the ordinary.

"Did you see lights come on in the Arno house each night of that weekend?" He said yes. "Friday night?" Yes. "Saturday night?" Yes. "Sunday night?" Yes. "Did you hear any sounds of distress, calls for help, yelling?"

"No."

"In other words, all weekend it was quiet over there, and you saw no one strange and heard nothing out of the ordinary. Is that correct?"

"Yes."

"And on Monday, did you see Ray Arno return home and enter his driveway?"

"Yes."

Pulling teeth, Roxbury got him to say that Ray had returned home around one in the afternoon and had left again about an hour later, then returned at about seven or seven-thirty. He had not seen him again that day or evening. When Roxbury nodded to Barbara, he was clearly glad to be rid of Eric Rubens.

"Mr. Rubens," she started, "your house is across the road from the Arno house, is that right?"

He said yes, then added, "Not straight across, down a piece."

"I have a map here of that area. Would you please show us where your house is, and where the Arno house is located?" Shelley was setting up a large map on an easel as Barbara spoke, and she turned toward it. "Maybe you could step down and point out the two properties." She looked at Judge Waldman, who nodded.

"You may step down, Mr. Rubens," the judge said.

He stood up and moved very deliberately to the map, studied it a moment, then pointed. "That's my place, twelve acres, and that's Ray's, six acres, down the road a piece."

"Before you take your seat again, could you explain how it happened that you were outside during those few days in early August?"

"I was selling apples," he said. "Gravensteins were in."

"And where was your stand?"

He pointed. "Had a stand right there, by the driveway."

"There are two more properties on River Loop One, before the name changes to Stratton Lane. Is that right?"

He said yes, and she asked him to take his seat again. Then, tracing the route on the map, she said, "So River Loop One turns off River Road, curves around past orchards, and finally ends here at the intersection with Stratton Lane and Knowles Road. Are those the routes most residents use to get to their places on River Loop One?"

"Mostly Stratton," he said.

"Is there anything on River Road to indicate that either Stratton Lane or Knowles Road joins River Loop One?"

He said no. "Stratton goes through the development, and Knowles goes past the school and has sharp turns. Not too many folks know about them, unless they live along there."

"Did you advertise apples in the newspaper when the crop came in?" Barbara asked.

"Yes."

"Were you at the stand most of the time when you had them for sale?"

He said yes.

"Did most of the customers come in by way of Stratton or by way of River Loop One?"

"River Loop One," he said.

"How far was your stand from the Arno driveway?"

"Four, five hundred feet."

"So, if a car came by way of River Loop One and turned in there, you wouldn't have seen it, would you?"

"Not likely."

"All right. You said lights came on every night that weekend. Did they come on Monday night, as well?" He said yes. "And Tuesday, Wednesday, all that week?"

He said yes. Every night.

"Can you explain that, Mr. Rubens? Do you know why they come on every night?"

He said yes, and she thought for a moment she would have to ask him to explain, but he continued. "There aren't any streetlights out there until you get in the subdivision. Most of us have lights on timers, or else on automatic, so they come on at dusk and go off in the morning. Every night."

"On Monday, did you talk to Ray Arno?"

"Yes. I picked up his mail on Saturday and took it over to him on Monday. We talked a little."

"How did he appear?"

"Same as always."

"Was he bruised, or cut? Did you notice any swelling on his hands? Anything of that sort?"

He said no.

"What time did you talk to him on Monday?"

"Seven-thirty, a little after. When he came home the second time and was putting his car in the garage."

"What kind of car was he driving?"

"Honda. Hatchback. Lorinne had the van."

"He was putting the car in the garage then? Did you see inside the car?"

He said yes. "He was taking stuff out to put it away—an overnight bag, cooler chest, things like that. We stood at the garage door and talked a minute or two."

She thanked him and listened to Roxbury make his same few points: Rubens had not seen any strangers, no strange cars, had heard nothing out of the ordinary.

Judge Waldman called for the recess then, and told the jurors that they must not talk about the case and they would resume at two.

Barbara and Shelley went to the office, where Patsy was at the receptionist desk, working on Frank's book. Frank, she said, was explaining to the magistrate that no one had singled out Mr. Trassi for special treatment, that all Barbara's witnesses were being subpoenaed and told not to leave the state. Patsy reported this perfectly straight-faced, knowing well that Trassi was the reason for all the subpoenas.

That afternoon Stan Truckee was the next witness. He worked in Ray's sports shop, had worked there for twelve years, mostly part-time. He was a gangly man in his fifties, with a crippled hand, the fingers drawn inward in a clawlike position. All Roxbury wanted from Truckee was the fact that Ray often took customers home with him to see his collection of flies.

"So, since you work only part-time, you have no way of knowing who he takes home with him, or when? Is that right?"

"Well, he's not real close-mouthed—"

"Just a yes or no, please. You have no way of knowing, do you?"

"He tells me—"

"Your honor, will you please instruct the witness to answer the question."

"Just answer the question, Mr. Truckee," she said kindly.

"No," he said. "Except—"

"The answer is no," Roxbury snapped. "Your witness," he said to Barbara.

Shelley had said Roxbury looked like an accountant, and at the moment he did, an accountant who had found a plus instead of a minus in the books. She smiled at him and stood up.

"Mr. Truckee, what exactly does your shop handle, what kind of merchandise do you sell there?"

"Fishing gear, hooks, lines, tackle, flies, lures, waders. Anything to do with fishing, freshwater or saltwater fishing."

"No baseball bats or golf clubs? Just fishing gear?"

"That's all. And we have customers from all over the world."

"Objection," Roxbury said. "The witness is advertising."

"Sustained."

"All right," Barbara said easily. "You just sell fishing gear. Let's talk a minute about the collection of flies Mr. Arno shows to some customers. Can you describe the collection?"

"Yes, ma'am. See, there are some people who have a real gift for tying flies, so real they would fool the insects' mamas. One of our suppliers is famous for his flies, he wins competitions, has private showings. And another one is a lady down in Medford, who gets her material from around the world—alpaca from South America, phalarope feathers from South Africa—"

"Objection!" Roxbury cried. "This is irrelevant."

"Overruled," Judge Waldman said. "You may continue," she said to Stan Truckee.

"Well," he said, "it's like that. Where common flies might use a copper bead, some of our suppliers use gold, real gold. Or instead of muskrat, they get wild boar, or instead of dying some pale fur orange, they get orange from an orangutan from Borneo. I mean, these are special, real works of art. And over the years Ray's built up a real collection of those flies. He mounted them in glass boxes, and he shows them at conventions, and sometimes he sets up a display at the shop."

"Does his collection have value for anyone besides other fishing enthusiasts?"

"Yes, ma'am. They're insured for a lot of money. They're all one of a kind, the best."

"All right. So he has customers who know about the displays and ask to see them? Is that right?"

"Yes, ma'am. Some regulars bring in new people and they can't wait to see them, they get real excited about them."

"If strangers come to the shop and ask to see the special collection, then what happens?"

"Well, he tells them when the next show's going to be, and where. Or when he intends to bring them in to the shop."

"To your knowledge, has he ever taken a stranger to his house to show off his collection?"

He shook his head emphatically. "No way. No, ma'am."

"Would he be secretive about such a thing?"

Roxbury objected and Barbara said, "You brought it up, that he might do it without telling anyone."

"I didn't say anyone. I said this witness has no way of knowing that."

"Sustained. Move on, Ms. Holloway."

She nodded. "Mr. Truckee, do you know how much Mr. Arno pays for the special flies?"

Roxbury objected, and this time was overruled.

"Yes, ma'am. I'm in on everything."

"You know all his suppliers?"

"Yes, ma'am."

"And most of his regular customers?"

"All of them."

"Do you set aside special lures and flies for special customers?"

"Yes, we do."

"And discuss in advance that a customer might like the new ones? Something like that?"

"Yes, ma'am. We talk about it."

"You talk about most of the business?"

"I'd say all of it."

"If you got a new customer who proved to be an avid fisherman who wanted only the best you had, you would talk it over with Mr. Arno?"

"Every time. We keep an eye out for the real fishermen."

"And he would do the same, mention to you that an avid fisherman had come in?"

"Yes, he would. We talk about the business all the time."

"And it would take an avid fisherman, a real enthusiast who was knowledgeable about flies, who would gain admittance to his private collection?"

"Unless he knows the difference between an English Gold Bead Headstone and a Glass Bead Caddis Pupa, there wouldn't be any point in it, would there?"

She smiled and shook her head. "I don't think so, Mr. Truckee. If such a customer came along, a new customer, would you learn about him?"

"Sure, I would."

"Mr. Truckee, without giving any names, can you tell the jury the last time that you know Ray Arno took a customer to his house to look at the collection?"

"Yes, ma'am. It was in May, early May. A customer, a regular, came in with two friends from Michigan, and they asked if they could see them. Ray said sure, and they all went out to the house."

She thanked him and sat down. "No more questions."

Roxbury snapped at him, "The days you don't work in the shop, you don't know who comes in for certain, do you?"

"I find out."

"You can't know unless Ray Arno tells you, and you have no way of knowing if he tells you everything, do you?"

Truckee looked puzzled, then shook his head. "No, not if you put it that way. But he tells—"

"That's all. The answer is no."

When Truckee left the stand, Roxbury called his next witness, Alexandra Wharton.

24

Alexandra Wharton was a large woman in her forties, five feet ten, one hundred eighty pounds, with dark brown hair, little makeup, dressed in a no-nonsense navy blue suit and white blouse. She walked to the stand, took her oath, and seated herself with a minimum of fuss, hardly a glance at the jury, and none at all toward Ray Arno.

Roxbury led her into her testimony quickly, and her story was simple. She went to the *Register-Guard* dock every night at two-thirty to collect bundles of newspapers, which she then distributed to route carriers.

"The corner of Stratton and River Road is the next-to-last stop I make," she said. "I always get there between five-thirty and a quarter to six, and usually the Dyson kids are there waiting and we transfer their bundle to their truck and I take off. That's Derek and Lina Dyson. She drives and he delivers the papers to the porches or the boxes out front."

"Do you recall what happened on the morning of Tuesday, August sixth?"

"Yes. I pulled in to the church parking lot, and the truck hadn't come yet, so I opened the back of my van and was getting the bundle ready for them when I saw headlights coming up Stratton. I thought it was the Dyson truck, but it wasn't. A gray Honda Civic came speeding to the corner and hardly slowed down at all, took the turn, and raced up River Road toward town."

"How far were you from the Honda?"

"No more than fifty feet."

"And you saw it clearly?"

"Yes."

"Did you see the driver?"

"Just that it was a man with dark hair; then it was gone."

"Could you see how he was dressed?"

"Not really. A dark sweatshirt or sweater is all I could see."

"What time did you see the Honda?"

"It had to have been about five-thirty. I got to my next stop at ten to six, and it's usually about fifteen minutes after I leave Stratton that I get up to it."

Roxbury was being silky smooth with this witness, showing not a sign of brusqueness or impatience. He drew her out slowly and carefully, covering every point with precision. She knew it was Tuesday, August sixth, because she had a dental appointment that day at nine, and the speeder had upset her and was still on her mind when she went to the dentist's office; she had mentioned it there, how kids who delivered newspapers in the dark were at risk from speeders.

Barbara did not interrupt, not even when he showed Alexandra Wharton a photograph of a car and asked if that was the one she saw speeding that morning. She said yes. He identified the photograph as Ray Arno's automobile and had it entered as a state exhibit. Soon after that he finished with her.

Barbara stood up and asked, "Ms. Wharton, was it still dark that morning when you got to Stratton?"

"Not real dark, but the sun wasn't up yet. Twilight."

"You said the speeding car had its headlights on, so it was dark enough to be using headlights?"

"Yes."

"Are there traffic lights at that intersection?"

"No, just a stop sign."

"Are there streetlights on the corners there?"

"No."

"Are there any lights at all?"

"Yes. The church has a lightpole; that's why I pull in there, so we can see what we're doing with the newspapers. And there's a light on in the grocery store across Stratton."

"A night-light in the grocery store? A dim light?"

"Yes."

"All right. When you pull in, do you turn off your headlights? Stop your engine?"

"Yes. Sometimes I have to wait for them, and the church light is enough. They can see me fine."

"Do you always pull in close to the church light?"

"Yes, so we can see what we're doing."

"Yes, of course. So the light was about fifty feet from the intersection, as you were. Is that correct?"

She nodded, then said, "About that far."

"And the automobile you saw was a gray Honda Civic? Do you know what year it was?"

Wharton hesitated, then said, "I wasn't thinking of what year it was or anything like that. I recognized it when I saw it, though."

Barbara nodded, then went to her table, where Shelley handed her a photograph; it was a montage of fifteen gray hatchback automobiles—a Honda, Toyota, Nissan. . . . The years ranged from 1987 to 1994. The individual cars were numbered, and there were no other identifying marks. She showed the picture to Judge Waldman, then to Roxbury, who leaped up and objected.

"On what grounds, Mr. Roxbury?" the judge asked.

"May I approach?"

Roxbury and Barbara approached the bench, where Roxbury said furiously, "This witness made a positive identification. That picture is just to confuse her, make her doubt her own eyes. All those cars look—"

Both the judge and Barbara waited for him to finish. When he didn't, Barbara said, "Alike. Is that the word you want? You had the witness pick out one from one. Let's see if she is that positive when there's a real choice."

"Are the cars identified somewhere?" Judge Waldman asked.

"Yes, on the back. Ray Arno's car is one of them, in fact."

The judge glanced at the back of the montage, then nodded. "Very well. Overruled, Mr. Roxbury."

Barbara took the sheet of photographs to the witness then and handed it to her. "Ms. Wharton, can you identify the car you saw in this collection?"

Alexandra Wharton looked confused at the number of cars on the montage, then she began to study them; she pursed her lips and a frown creased her forehead after a moment. It took her a long time, but finally she looked at Barbara and shook her head.

"I can't say for sure which one it was."

"Can you be sure it was a Honda?"

"No, not for sure, I guess."

"Can you say for sure it was a 1991 model?"

"No."

"How would you describe the car you saw that morning?"

"A little gray car, a hatchback."

"Thank you," Barbara said. "No more questions." She had the sheet of photographs entered, and watched the bailiff pass it to the jury foreman. And some of them would know in a second which was the '91 Honda Civic, she thought, satisfied.

Roxbury tried to undo the damage. Her memory when she identified the car in August had been clearer than it was now, after so many months. She had been certain at the time. Looking at so many gray cars was confusing. . . . He didn't help the situation and might have hurt it. Some of the jurors knew a Honda from a Toyota.

Roxbury called Anthony Arno next.

When Papa Arno's name was called, to Barbara's surprise and

consternation, Ray stood up; she heard a commotion behind her and twisted around to see James and David Arno also on their feet. Roxbury was shouting, and the bailiff was bawling for all to be seated. Judge Waldman raised her gavel, then gently put it down again; the jurors appeared as amazed as everyone else by this spontaneous display. They stared at Papa Arno, at the three tall sons, back to Papa Arno.

Then Judge Waldman said in her firm no-nonsense way, "Gentlemen, be seated. Please, there must be no further demonstrations of any sort in this courtroom."

Papa Arno had seemed unaware of his sons' actions; now he glanced behind him and nodded; it was as if his signal to sit down again was the one they needed. A guard had rushed to Ray Arno's side when he rose; he withdrew as Ray took his chair again. James and David Arno sat down, and only then was Papa sworn in.

Craig Roxbury turned a bitter, icy glare toward Barbara; she shrugged. If he believed she had had anything to do with that, she was certain he was the only person in the courtroom who did. The jurors regarded Papa with heightened interest.

On Saturday Papa Arno had said to Barbara, "A father should not have to testify against his son. Can they make me?"

"I'm sorry," she had said. "If you appear reluctant, not cooperative, they will call you a hostile witness and it would be worse for Ray. I don't think your testimony will be damaging."

"I am talking about the son I had, Mitch. I don't know anything about Ray that could hurt him."

After going over his testimony, Barbara had said, "Just tell the truth, Mr. Arno. The jury will know you're telling the truth."

And now Roxbury was leading him into the fight between Ray and Mitch nearly eighteen years ago.

"Mitchell Arno was married to Maggie Folsum. He claimed his marital rights with her and she was in tears. So you and the defendant forced him outside and beat him up. Didn't you?"

Barbara objected to his leading question; Judge Waldman sustained the objection, and Roxbury backed out of it and asked the same questions, one at a time.

"Did you and the defendant force him outside and beat him up?" he concluded.

"No, sir. Ray took him outside and they fought."

"Wasn't the defendant so enraged that he was uncontrollable?"

"He was outraged."

"Did you publicly disown your son Mitchell that day?"

"Yes, sir."

"Did the defendant tell Mitchell Arno that if he came back again, he would not be able to walk away next time?"

"Yes, sir."

"All right. Last summer on Friday, August second, did your son Mitchell return?"

"Yes, sir."

"Did you see him yourself that day?"

"Yes, sir."

"And what did you do?"

"I pushed him into the shed and told him he had to leave because there was a big party at the house. I told Mama to call Ray and tell him to wait for us. And we took Mitch to Ray's house in Eugene."

"So, aware of the threat the defendant had made, you delivered your son into his hands. Aware of his uncontrollable temper, his violence toward Mitchell—"

"Objection!" Barbara cried. "Improper questions, as the prosecutor knows very well."

"Sustained. Ask your question, Mr. Roxbury."

"You delivered Mitchell into the keeping of the defendant, who had threatened him in public at their last meeting. Is that correct?"

"I took him to Ray's house."

"Did you give him an opportunity to explain the reason for his return?"

"No, we didn't talk."

"Was the occasion of the party his older daughter's birthday?"

"It was her birthday."

"Did it occur to you that Mitchell had come to celebrate his daughter's birthday?"

"No, sir."

"Did you give him an opportunity to explain his presence?"

"No, sir."

"Did you talk to him on the drive to Eugene?"

"No, sir."

"How did you transport him to the defendant's house?"

"In the back of my truck."

"You shoved him into the shed, then you bundled him into the back of a truck, the way you might transport an animal. Is that correct?"

Barbara objected, and it was sustained. Roxbury had made the point, though. He hammered away at Papa Arno. No one had permitted Mitch to explain himself. No one had talked to him, except to tell him to keep away from the inn. Papa Arno didn't know what took place between Ray and Mitch after he left them. Finally Roxbury looked at the old man with open disgust and said no more questions.

"Mr. Arno," Barbara started, "what happened in February of nineteen seventy-nine?"

"Doris Folsum called Mama and said—"

"Objection. Hearsay."

"Your honor," Barbara said quickly, "this goes directly to the state of mind of Mr. Arno at that period. It explains his subsequent actions."

Judge Waldman looked thoughtful for a moment, then nodded. "Overruled," she said. "You may continue, Mr. Arno."

"Mama told me that Mitch was back at the Folsum house and had hurt Maggie." Papa Arno's face was set in rigid lines, but his voice was steady. He kept his gaze on Barbara and spoke in a low tone, pausing now and then, as if in pain. "We went up there and saw she was crying and had a big bruise on her face and on her arms. She said he raped her in front of the baby, that he hurt her down there. She said she told him to leave her alone and he knocked her down and raped her, and then hit her in the face." He looked down at his big hands clasped together on the witness stand.

"You said that he was back. Had he been gone?"

"Yes, ma'am. He left in the spring and came back in February."

"Did you know where he was during that time?"

"No. He just left one day."

"How old was Maggie when he left?"

"Sixteen."

"And how old was she in February when he came back?"

"Seventeen."

She led him through the rest of it.

"Why did you disown Mitch, Mr. Arno?"

"Because he brought dishonor to his wife, our daughter Maggie, and to our family. He no longer could be my son."

"You think of Maggie Folsum as your daughter?"

"She became the daughter we never had."

"In all the years since that day in February until last summer did you ever hear from Mitch?" He said no. "Did he send Christmas presents or birthday cards, or call, or get in touch in any way?"

"No. Not once."

"Why did you feel you had to get him away from Maggie Folsum's inn?"

"There was a big party, a family reunion. It was Gwen's eighteenth birthday, her graduation party, and all the family would be there—all the Folsums, all the Arnos, other relatives. There was a lot of bad feeling about Mitch, how he abandoned Maggie with two babies. I was afraid there would be terrible trouble if he stayed."

"When you took him to Ray's house, you said he was in the back of the truck. Why was that?"

"The truck was what I was driving. With a canopy on it. We

hauled a lot of stuff out to the party in it. I put a blanket back there for him to use if it got drafty. Only two of us could ride in the front."

"When you arrived at Ray's house, did he talk then?"

"We didn't stay long enough to talk. I just told Ray to let him stay until after the party, and we'd talk on Monday when we all got back. Ray said he would do that."

"Was Ray enraged?"

"No, ma'am. He was surprised, same as me. And disgusted by the way Mitch looked. Not mad or anything."

Slowly she then asked, "Mr. Arno, if you asked Ray to do something, would it occur to you that he might not do it if it was within his power?"

He looked surprised and shook his head. "No. Anything I asked, he'd do if it killed him."

"And you asked him to let Mitch stay in his house until you all returned home on Monday, when you planned to talk. Is that right?"

"Yes. He said he would."

"At what time did you get home on Monday?"

"About one-thirty or a little after."

"Did you call Ray?"

Roxbury objected. "Beyond the scope of direct," he snapped.

Quickly Barbara said, "This whole line of inquiry was opened by the state. I want to complete it."

"Overruled."

Barbara repeated the question.

"He called me. He said Mitch had left, that he had torn up the place first and then took off. I told him someone had broken in at my house, and he said he would come to our place right away."

"Objection!" Roxbury cried. "Irrelevant."

"Your honor," Barbara said, "this goes to the core of the defense. It is highly relevant."

Judge Waldman beckoned them both to the bench, and there, out of hearing of the jury, she asked Barbara to explain.

"Someone was looking for Mitch Arno, first at Papa Arno's house, then at Ray's, where they found him."

Judge Waldman frowned, tapping one finger lightly on an open notebook before her. After a moment she nodded. "I'll permit the question and answer, but if it turns out to be a red herring, or irrelevant, I'll so advise the jurors and have it stricken."

Barbara thanked her and continued to question Papa Arno. "Did you tell anyone else about the break-in at your house, or that Mitch had come back?"

"Yes. I called both James and David and told them, and we decided that Ray would call Maggie so she wouldn't be taken by surprise if he showed up at her place."

Barbara finished with him soon after that, and Roxbury stood up and walked around his table to approach the witness chair. In a soft voice he asked, "Mr. Arno, on the occasion that your two sons fought, and you then put your injured son on a bus and sent him away, did you at any time consider filing charges against him, or even reporting the incident to the police?"

"No, sir."

"Did you consider it a family matter, something to be taken care of within the family circle?"

"Yes, sir."

"Your testimony is that you consider Maggie Folsum to be your daughter. Is that right?"

"Yes, she's our daughter."

"And as your daughter, she is to be protected, shielded from harm, and avenged if she is mistreated—"

"Objection!" Barbara said. "That's a leading question if there ever was one."

"Sustained. Rephrase your question, Mr. Roxbury."

He bowed slightly to the judge, then asked, "Is it your belief that a daughter is to be guarded and protected by her father and her adult brothers?"

"Yes, sir."

"And do you believe that it is proper for a father and adult brothers to seek to punish anyone who brings harm or dishonor to that daughter?"

Barbara cried out an objection. "May I approach?" she asked.

"Your honor," Roxbury said smoothly, "I am merely trying to clarify the position Ms. Folsum holds within the Arno family. We all know that different cultures regard the honor of the family in vastly different ways—"

"Your honor—" Barbara called out, but before she could say more, the judge beckoned her and Roxbury to approach the bench.

"Your honor," Barbara said furiously in a low, intense voice, "he's deliberately introducing a cultural distinction where none exists. The Arno family is an American family from generations back, not part of some big Mafia family. This is an outrageous attempt to prejudice the jury against Ray Arno."

Judge Waldman nodded. "Mr. Roxbury, I am sustaining the objection, and I want you to back away from that line of questioning. We will not have a jury racially or culturally prejudiced in this case."

But the damage had been done, Barbara knew. The jury had been prejudiced even if only infinitesimally. When Roxbury resumed his redirect, she watched him closely, aware that he was far more dangerous than she had originally assumed. His move to characterize Ray Arno as a stereotypical Italian-honor-crazed brother was as smart as it was reprehensible. She had no doubt he would allude to it again before this trial was over.

❖

Today the media were on hand, newspaper and television reporters as well as cameras; there had been little interest in the case before Barbara's entrance. Frank bantered with the reporters good-naturedly, the way he always did, and Barbara said simply, "Of course, Ray Arno didn't do it. And no comment beyond that."

Then Frank drew her aside in a huddle with John and Shelley. "They'll go on to the house," he said. "We have a date with Trassi."

Bailey was waiting at the curb in Frank's Buick. "Hilton," Frank said.

"What's up?" she asked. "How did it go today? Will Trassi be held?"

"You kidding? He was given a choice: stay put or answer to an arrest warrant and face thirty days in the pokey for every hour he's out of state. He's not happy. Might say he's boiling over, but it's hard to tell with him." Frank clearly was quite amused. "No New York lawyer should come to the boonies and try to outtalk a judge. Gets their back up for some reason."

She grinned. "So what's up now? This meeting?"

"Not sure. I told him no private talks except in your office, or in a public place. He opted for the Hilton bar. We'll see. I made a reservation."

Bailey drove them to the hotel and even got out to walk to the door with them, looking over everyone on the way. They took the elevator to the second floor, where Frank motioned toward a bar. "He didn't want the top floor, too open," he said.

The bar was dim, noisy, and crowded; after they were shown to a table at the back of the room, Frank excused himself to give Trassi a call. When he returned, they both ordered wine; Trassi appeared before it was served. He was stiffer than ever, and in the faint light, his complexion suggested that he had probably died since the last time Barbara had seen him.

"Mr. Palmer wants to talk to you," he said curtly.

The waiter brought the wine, and Trassi snapped at him, "A telephone."

No one spoke while they waited for the telephone. A pretty young woman was playing very good jazz on a piano; there were loud voices, an undercurrent of lower-pitched voices as counterpoint, now and then bursts of laughter. . . . Barbara sipped her wine.

The waiter returned with the telephone and plugged it in, retreated again. Trassi dialed a number; apparently an operator came on, and he gave his room number and name, then he waited.

Finally he said, "Trassi," then handed the phone to Barbara.

"Hello," she said. "Barbara Holloway."

"Ms. Holloway, in the company I keep, when you make a deal, you honor it. What are you after now?"

She was very surprised at his voice; it was deep and almost lilting, with just a touch of a brogue, enough to sound charming. "I kept my end of the deal," she said. "I delivered everything I said I would."

"Let's not play games," he said. "Let Trassi go, release him from the subpoena, and let's be done with all this business."

"I can't do that," she said. "I'm afraid he has to testify, and the only way we can be assured of his presence is by subpoena."

"What do you want?"

"I want the two men who killed Mitch Arno, and the one who handled them."

She was watching Trassi as he said this; his expression did not change by even a flicker. Dead man, she thought again.

Palmer paused only a second, then said easily, "I'm afraid I don't have any idea what you're talking about."

"If you don't, then you have some very dangerous loose cannons in your organization," she said. "You should be warned about them and take measures before they do you grave harm."

"I understand that you have a great number of admirers, Ms. Holloway. I confess that against my will and my determination not to be drawn into their circle, I have found myself joining them. I found myself helpless to resist admiring and, yes, appreciating your cleverness and dedication in pursuing the interests of your former client. I trust you wouldn't now nullify all the very fine work you've done or jeopardize her future enjoyment of her new wealth through any indiscretion, however minor it might appear." He sounded pleasant, musing aloud as he went on. "I didn't order the world we find ourselves in. I never would have made it such a dangerous world for the indiscreet."

"I can assure you, I am very discreet," she said coolly. "Now, if there's nothing else on your mind, I have to go. I have work to do. Good-bye, Mr. Palmer."

"Oh, I don't think we're through yet, Ms. Holloway," he said, sounding almost lazy. "Let me talk to Trassi."

She handed over the phone and picked up her wine. Trassi said, "Yes." After a moment he said it again, then hung up. Without another word he rose and left the table, walked out through the lounge.

"Good wine," Barbara said. "Good music, too." She was glad Frank couldn't see how clammy her palms were; she hoped he didn't notice that her hands were trembling.

"Let's get the hell out of here," Frank said.

It was very late when Barbara went to bed that night. The last thing she did was look in on Alan Macagno, who was reading a book in the other apartment, John's apartment. When Bailey said Alan would be staying over for the next few nights, John had said dubiously that he supposed someone could sleep in the extra bedroom on his side. "He isn't being paid to sleep," Bailey had said. And

Alan hadn't looked a bit sleepy at two-thirty; he had looked like a college kid cramming for an exam. He would prowl around a little now and then, he had warned Barbara, but he'd try to be quiet about it.

For the duration of the trial Shelley was staying at Bill Spassero's townhouse, where security was okay, Bailey had said after looking it over. And every morning a driver would pick up Frank and Shelley, then come to collect Barbara and take them all to court together.

She was unable to account for the way she barely had time to close her eyes before the alarm went off, and how she dragged through the morning routine of shower and breakfast, only to come wide awake instantly when court convened. Another one of Pavlov's dogs, she thought, disgusted; bell rings, saliva flows, except in her case it was adrenaline.

Roxbury called his witness, and they began.

Winnie York was a young woman, handsome without being pretty, sensibly dressed in a navy wool skirt with a pale blue cardigan, low heels, her only jewelry a single strand of cloisonné beads.

Roxbury led her through the preliminaries quickly: she was thirty-four, had been born in Newport, and had lived there until she was about sixteen, and she had known all the Arnos and the Folsums. Now she was employed as a sales representative for a publishing company; her territory was the Northwest. She had been transferred to Portland in the spring this year, after working in California for a number of years.

"Please tell the jury what happened last May," Roxbury said. He was being very pleasant to this witness, not rushing her, not pressing.

"Yes," she said. "During a regional book fair here in Eugene, one of the girls I had known as a child suggested we get together for dinner with a couple more old friends. We did that, and went to a microbrewery pub. I hadn't been back to the coast or heard from any of them for nearly twenty years, and they talked about who married whom, children, divorces, gossipy things like that. One of them mentioned Maggie Folsum, and I asked if she had had the baby and if it had been a girl. Maggie had been pregnant when I left. They told me about Maggie and Mitch, and how Ray had beaten him up, and that whole story. I hadn't known any of it. I said that it was a wonder Ray hadn't killed Mitch then, that if he had known about Mitch and Lorinne, he probably would have killed him." She gave her testimony in a steady, uninflected way, as if she had rehearsed it until all the emotion had been wrung out of the words. She kept her gaze on Roxbury throughout.

"What happened next?"

"Sue grabbed my arm and shook her head. A man and a woman had come out of the next booth and walked past us. When they were gone, Sue said that was Ray and Lorinne. I hadn't recognized either of them."

"Did they hear your conversation?"

Barbara objected, and it was sustained. He rephrased the question.

"At the time did you believe they had heard your conversation?"

"Yes. We were not speaking in whispers; we might have been a little loud at times, recounting the past."

"Ms. York," Roxbury said then, his voice dropping to an almost confidential level, "exactly what did you mean by what you said, that if he had known about Mitch and Lorinne, he might have killed Mitch?"

For the first time she hesitated, and her voice was less steady when she answered, "I meant that Mitch had slept with Lorinne several times."

"How did you know that?" Roxbury asked softly.

"Mitch told me."

Roxbury nodded to Barbara with a smug expression. "Your witness."

At first Ray Arno had gone very still when Winnie York was testifying, then he had started scribbling notes. Barbara glanced at them and nodded.

"Ms. York," she said, "let's back up a little to the summer of 1978, the summer that you moved away from the Oregon coast. You said you were almost sixteen? When is your birthday, Ms. York?"

"October twenty-ninth."

"So you were fifteen that summer. Were you a friend of Maggie Folsum, in classes together?"

"No. Not really. She was older, a year ahead of me in school."

"Were you a friend of Lorinne Talbot, now married to Ray Arno?"

She shook her head. "No. She was a lot older. I knew who she was, that's all."

"Eighteen years ago Newport was a much smaller community than it is today, wasn't it?"

"Much smaller," Winnie York said, nodding.

"And Folsum is quite a bit smaller than Newport, isn't it?"

"Yes."

"In those days, before you left, did the local residents pretty much know what was going on in one another's lives?"

"It was a tight community," Winnie said after a brief pause. "I doubt there were many secrets."

One of the women on the jury nodded slightly.

"Were there places where the young people, kids in their teens, hung out together? Danced, played music, things of that sort?"

"Yes, a couple. In Newport, not in Folsum."

"Did Mitch Arno hang out with the young crowd?"

"Sometimes." She had grown cautious now and was watching Barbara intently.

"Did he hang out after he married Maggie?"

Winnie hesitated, then said, "Sometimes."

"Can you tell us exactly when and where Mitch made his comments about Lorinne?"

She shook her head. "I don't remember."

"Well, we know from testimony that he left the area early in May that year, so it must have been before that. Is that right?"

"I guess so."

"All right. Were other people present who heard him?"

"I . . . No. Just me."

"Were you a good friend of his?"

"He just liked to talk to me."

"Do you know how old Mitch Arno was that spring?"

Roxbury objected on the grounds of irrevlevance.

"But it's relevant," Barbara said. "If Mitch Arno was making claims of conquest, we have a right to know something about the circumstances."

"Overruled," Judge Waldman said.

"Do you know how old he was?" Barbara asked again.

"Twenty-two," Winnie said in a low voice.

"And you had become his confidante when you were fifteen? Is that what you're telling us?"

"I . . . He said there weren't many people he could really talk to, and he liked to talk with me."

Barbara nodded and went to stand by her table. "Did the two of you leave the group and go off to talk alone?"

"Sometimes," Winnie said in a very low voice.

"Do you recall now what led up to his comment about Lorinne?"

"Yes. I said I wouldn't see him alone because he was a married man with a pregnant wife. He said the marriage was a big joke; as soon as the baby was born, it would end. He said Ray told him he'd beat the crap out of him if he didn't do right by Maggie, and he laughed and said if Ray knew about him and Lorinne, the times they had gone to bed together, he might try to make him marry her, too, and turn him into a bigamist."

"Did Mitch say he loved you?"

She looked startled, then ducked her head and gazed at the table before her. "Yes, he did."

"Did you believe him?"

"Yes."

"Did he tell you he was going away?"

"Yes."

"Did he say he wanted to take you with him?" It was a long shot into a very dark place, but she asked it and didn't hold her breath for fear someone would notice.

"Yes," Winnie said in a near whisper.

"Did Mitch Arno seduce you when you were a fifteen-year-old girl and he was twenty-two?"

Winnie hesitated and Roxbury yelled an objection. Before Judge Waldman could respond, Barbara said quietly, "I withdraw the question."

Instead, she asked, "Did he borrow money from you?"

"Yes."

"And did he pay you back?"

She shook her head. "No."

"After Mitch left in early May, did he get in touch with you at any time?"

"No."

"Did he tell you good-bye?"

"No."

"Did he lie to you?"

"He lied."

"All right. Last May, when you met your friends at the brew pub, did the conversation continue after Ray and Lorinne left the restaurant?"

"Yes, for a long time."

"Did anyone refute what you had said about Mitch and Lorinne?"

She nodded. "They all did. They said people would have

known, but besides that, she was too old for him. He couldn't have been more than thirteen when she left to go to college, and she never was back much after that." She stopped, but looked as if there had been more, and Barbara waited for her to continue. "They said he just liked young girls, very young girls."

"Was his nickname brought up?" Barbara asked when Winnie stopped again.

"Yes," she said faintly. "They used to call him Mitch the Cherry Picker."

"Thank you," Barbara said. "No further questions."

After a brief recess, Roxbury called the next witness: Judith Ludlum. She was seventy, bent with osteoporosis, and she had sharp features, a long bony nose, sharply pointed chin, frail-looking wrists and fingers. Her hair was gray, in a frizzy perm; she wore bifocals.

She stated that she lived in Corvallis, where she owned and managed an apartment building, two quads for college girls. Her voice was high-pitched and wavery.

"Do you recall a time when Lorinne Talbot lived in one of the quads?" Roxbury asked.

"Yes, back in the seventies, seventy-seven and seventy-eight. Two years."

"Is there a particular reason for you to recall her?"

"Yes, there is. I thought she would be a steadying influence on the younger girls. She already had some degrees and she was going to Monmouth to get her teaching certification. She must have been about twenty-eight then. The others were all real young, hardly old enough to be away from home."

"Was she a steadying influence?"

"For a while I thought so, but then I changed my mind."

"Why was that?"

"Well, she got engaged, you know, and they were out all hours, her and Ray Arno. Then she took off with his brother Mitch for a weekend or two. I changed my mind, all right."

"Tell us about when she took off with his brother Mitch," Roxbury said softly, glancing at the jury as if to make certain they were listening.

"Well, I live downstairs in the building, and the quads are on the second and third floors. All women, no men allowed except in the front room. This was on a Friday, in early April; I was out front weeding in the daffodils when a man drove up, and he began to blow the horn. I don't allow that. If they come for a girl, they can go in the front room like civilized people. I was just starting to go over and tell him to stop. I thought at first it was Ray, but it wasn't. I heard Lorinne yell out the window at him. Mitch, she called him, and she told him she was coming. Then I heard her tell one of the other girls she'd be back Sunday night, and she came out with her suitcase and got in the car. He leaned over and kissed her, and they took off."

"That was on a Friday afternoon?"

"Yes, before dark; I was still out weeding."

"Did you see her come home on Sunday?"

"Yes. I heard the car stop out front, and I looked out just to see if someone was about to come in. It was late, after ten, and they were in the car kissing and hugging. Half an hour or longer. Then she came in all smiling. And he took off."

Roxbury nodded gravely. "I see. You said she went with him more than once. Can you recall another time?"

"Yes. A few weeks after that. She put a lot of camping stuff in her own car that afternoon, and he called her on the telephone. One of the girls told her it was Mitch on the phone, and she came down to talk to him. She said she would meet him as soon as she got off work. She didn't come home that time until Sunday late."

"You didn't see them together that time?"

"No. I just heard her ask him where he was, and she said she knew where it was, and would be by as soon as she got off work at nine. I thought at the time that was a pretty late hour to be meeting someone, but I didn't say anything to her."

"Did you overhear anything else she said to him?"

"Yes." Her lips tightened until they nearly disappeared. "She said, 'Don't tell Ray anything.' I thought maybe she was fixing to break off with Mitch and was afraid he might tell his brother about them and their meetings."

Roxbury finished with her soon after that, and Barbara stood up. "Ms. Ludlum, you said at first you thought it was Ray Arno blowing his horn that afternoon, then you saw that it wasn't. What made you change your mind?"

"Well, I got a good look at him," she said. "I got up and walked to the end of the hedges, where I had a good look at him."

"Could you see him or the car he was driving before you walked to the end of the hedges?"

"Not much. Just a glimpse of the car, dark, like the one Ray usually drove, that's what made me think it was him."

"When she got in the car, did he put his arms around her?"

"No. Just leaned over and kissed her."

"Did he kiss her on the lips?"

"I don't know."

"Well, did she turn toward him?"

"Not much. She knew I was watching."

"Was she facing the windshield, the front of the car?"

"Yes, like I said, she knew I was watching."

"Yes, you said that. All right, when she came back on Sunday night, what were you doing at the time?"

"Watching television in the front room."

"But you were able to hear the car drive up and stop? Is that right?"

"Yes, I heard it."

"Then what did you do?"

"Like I said, I got up to have a look, to see if anyone was coming in."

"Where did you look from? The windows in the front room?"

"No. I went to the hall and the front door; there are two windows by the door, one on each side."

"Was it very dark outside?"

"It was after ten, yes, dark."

"Did they have the dome light on in the car?"

"No. They wouldn't do that, not with all the hugging and kissing and such."

"Were they parked under a streetlight?"

"No. There isn't any light out there."

"I see. How far back is your front door from the curb?"

"I don't know. I never measured it."

"Let's reconstruct your property," Barbara said pleasantly. "Is there a porch?"

"Yes."

Step by step Barbara drew from her a description of the house and the landscaping in the front. Finally she said, "So there are bushes, a hedge, several trees. Forty feet? Is that about right?"

"I don't know. Maybe that's about right."

"Was there a porch light on?"

"Yes."

"All right. Was there a light in the hall where you were standing?"

"No."

"So you left watching television to stand in the dark hallway, where you looked out past the porch light, past shrubs and trees, to a dark car at the curb. Ms. Ludlum, what could you actually see in the car under those conditions?"

"Enough," she said indignantly. "I could see them just fine."

Barbara shook her head. "Were you watching television again when she entered the house?"

"Yes. I could see her fine. I turned on the hall light by then."

"Do you usually stay in the front room with the door open to the hall?"

"Yes, of course. I have to know who's coming and going."

"Oh, I see. The other time you mentioned, you said Lorinne had put camping gear inside her car earlier. Is that right?"

"Yes, a sleeping bag, a pack of some sort."

"Did you answer the phone when the call came for her?"

"No. I was in the front room. One of the girls picked up the phone."

"But you could hear what was said?"

She hesitated, then said yes.

"Were you watching television that afternoon?"

"Yes, but the sound was turned real low. I could hear her."

"You testified that she asked him where he was, and said she knew where that was. Do you know where she met him?"

"Yes, at the Black Angus Motel."

"Before, you said she knew where it was. Is it now your testimony that she mentioned the motel by name?"

Ludlum's lips tightened even more and she nodded, then said almost defiantly, "Yes. The Black Angus."

"Is there an extension phone in the front room?" Barbara asked coolly.

"Yes, of course."

"Ms. Ludlum, in fact, didn't you listen to part of her conversation on the extension phone, up to the point where she asked you to hang it up?"

"I can explain that," Ludlum said swiftly. "Sometimes the girls upstairs don't hear if someone yells for them to come to the phone, and it stays off the hook for hours. I wanted to make certain she took her call and then hung up, that's all."

"Did you hear what Mitch told her when she said she would meet him after work?"

"No, that's when she came to the door and said to hang up the phone."

"Did you hear her say for him not to tell Ray something in particular?"

"Just not to tell him, not to call him."

"So, after you hung up the telephone, you continued to listen to her half of the conversation?"

"I could hear every word."

"Do you know where she went camping that weekend?"

"No."

"Did you see her with Mitch that weekend?"

"No, of course not."

"Did it make you angry for her to tell you to stop eavesdropping on her private call?"

"I was doing my duty, trying to keep my house respectable, that's all."

Barbara gave her a scathing look, then took her seat. "I have no further questions for this witness."

26

Lunch that day was a hurried business in Barbara's office. Bailey was waiting for her with a report on the neighbors of Victor Radiman, the next witness; she read his report as she ate a sandwich.

"Good job," she said. "All right, Roxbury will wrap it up today, and we'll have the rest of the week to get our act together. Anything yet on Palmer?"

"Nope. Hasn't budged," Bailey said. "And Trassi hasn't had a visitor yet, but he's burning up the telephone lines."

Frank walked in and looked over the remaining sandwiches. "Got it," he said, giving Barbara a Xerox copy of an inventory. "Took a court order, but I got it." He had a police report of the possessions that had been taken from Radiman the night he was arrested, which had been the first night that Ray Arno had spent in jail. Frank helped himself to a sandwich while Barbara scanned the list he had handed her.

Then they were back in court and Victor Radiman was called. Roxbury was brusque with him, as if he wanted the jury to know he had little sympathy for this witness, but it was necessary to hear him out.

Radiman was a florid-faced man in his late forties, with the telltale broken veins in his cheeks and the bulbous nose of a heavy drinker who suffered from rosacea. He was a scaler for a lumber mill, he said. He kept his gaze fixed on Roxbury, listening intently to the questions, then turned to address the jury when he answered in a too-loud voice. His story was that he had been arrested on the night of August sixteenth for disorderly conduct and had spent the night in the Lane County jail.

"Tell the jury what happened that night," Roxbury said.

"I was trying to sleep and I kept hearing this guy sort of moaning and making noise. He woke me up and I couldn't get back to sleep. I could hear him crying and saying he was sorry, that he didn't mean to do it, and praying for God to forgive him, things like that."

"Can you repeat his exact words?" Roxbury asked harshly.

"Some of them. He said, 'I didn't mean to hit him that hard. I didn't mean to kill him. I couldn't help it. I'm sorry. God, I'm sorry. Dear God, forgive me, I'm sorry.' Then he said, 'God, have mercy on his soul. Have mercy on my soul.'" His voice was not only too loud, the words were curiously uninflected, almost flat, turning the prayer into a recitation that could as easily have been a laundry list.

"Then what happened?"

"I yelled at him to shut up, and after that he was quieter, but he kept praying for a long time."

"Do you know who that man was?"

"It was the defendant over there. Ray Arno."

"Was he in the same cell with you?"

"No. I saw him in a cell when they took me to lockup. I noticed because he looked wild and like he'd been crying. His eyes were red, like they get when you've been crying. And one of the other guys in my cell said he was in for murder."

"You got a good look at him, at Ray Arno?"

"Yes. And I heard him like I said."

Roxbury sat down.

"Mr. Radiman," Barbara said, standing at her table, "what were you arrested for that night?"

"Like I said, disorderly conduct."

"That's the charge you pleaded guilty to, but what were you charged with by the arresting officer?"

Roxbury objected. "Prejudicial," he snapped.

"No, it isn't," Barbara said quickly. "There is no one clear definition of disorderly conduct; what constitutes disorderly conduct is in the eye of the beholder, and since Mr. Roxbury brought it up, the jury has a right to know precisely what is meant in this situation."

She was allowed to continue, but Radiman shook his head. "All's I know is that my lawyer said if they asked me if I was disorderly, I should say yes, and I did."

"I have here the arresting officer's report from that night," Barbara said, picking it up. "Let me refresh your memory." She showed the report to the judge and to Roxbury, then read from it: "Suspect was in a drunken state; the television was on loud enough to hear from the street; his neighbors—" She stopped and said, "I'll leave out the names of the neighbors who brought the complaint." Judge Waldman nodded, and Barbara read the rest of the report: "His neighbors complained that other times when they asked him to turn down the volume, he threatened to set his dog on them. When they knocked on his door on the morning of August seventeenth, he shoved one of them off the porch and used loud and abusive threatening language. Plaintiffs then called the police. . . ." She looked up at Radiman and said clearly and slowly, "The arresting officer charged you with drunkenness, with maintaining a public nuisance, with assault and battery, and with resisting arrest. Do you recall those charges, Mr. Radiman?"

He shook his head. "I said I was probably disorderly and that's what I was guilty of."

"Did you pay your neighbor's doctor bill as a result of that incident?"

"Yeah, I agreed to pay it."

"What time of night did all this take place?"

"I don't remember."

"The arresting officer has the time on his report, Mr. Radiman. It's given as twelve-forty A.M. Do you recall that now?"

"It wasn't that late."

"And it says here that you were booked into the Lane County jail at one-ten in the morning. Do you recall that?"

"No. It wasn't that late."

"I see. So everyone else has the time wrong. Do you recall what time was right?"

"No. I don't remember."

"After a person is taken to jail, there is a certain routine that they follow, isn't there? Fingerprints are recorded, an inventory of possessions is made, things of that sort. Do you recall being searched and fingerprinted?"

"Sure."

"Do you recall being taken to a cell where there were others already locked up?"

"Yes. I was drinking earlier, but by then I was pretty sober."

"Were lights on all through the jail?"

He hesitated, as if trying to remember, then nodded. "Not real bright lights, but there were lights."

"Lights in the various cells? Really? At two in the morning? Are you sure, Mr. Radiman?"

Roxbury objected. "Witness has already answered the question."

"But perhaps he misspoke," Barbara said.

"Overruled," Judge Waldman said.

Radiman was watching Barbara as closely as he had watched Roxbury. When she repeated the question, he nodded. "I could see in the cells just fine."

She smiled slightly, although his loud, flat voice was starting to grate on her nerves; then she turned her back to pick up a second report. "I have here the inventory of your possessions from that morning. Do you recall signing it?"

When he didn't reply, she faced him again. "Did you hear the question?"

"No, I didn't. Your back was turned and you were mumbling."

"Sorry," she said. "Do you recall signing the inventory of your possessions on that occasion?"

"Yes," he said.

Still facing him, but holding the sheet of paper in front of her mouth, she asked clearly, "Why do you play the television so loud that it can be heard from the street?"

He fidgeted a little, glanced at Roxbury, then at the jury, and finally said, "Can you ask the question again? I didn't catch it all." His face, florid to start with, was a darker red.

She repeated the question, and he said angrily, "I don't play it that loud. They're just troublemakers, looking to make trouble for me."

She covered her mouth again and read from the list of belongings the police had taken from him the night he was arrested: "A wallet, and the amount of money in it, credit card, driver's license, change, pocket knife, keys, hearing-aid battery pack and hearing aid . . ." She put the list down and asked him, "Did you sign the inventory for those items?"

He hesitated again, then nodded. "I signed something. I don't remember what it was."

"When did you tell the police that you had heard Mr. Arno talking in the next cell?"

"I don't know, after a day or two."

"Was it after you retained an attorney? As a result, were the charges reduced to disorderly conduct?"

Roxbury was shouting his objection before she finished the question.

This time, with a look of sharp rebuke, Judge Waldman sustained the objection.

Barbara nodded and turned to her table again; then facing away from Radiman, she asked, "How long have you used a hearing aid?"

She had to repeat the question, and he flushed even darker and said, "I hardly ever use one. Just for movies."

"In fact," she said coldly, "you are an expert lip reader, aren't you?"

"I can hear you."

"But not if I cover my mouth, can you?" she said, covering her mouth.

"I can hear you," he said angrily.

Keeping her hand in front of her mouth, she asked, "What time is lights-out in the jail?"

"I can hear you, I said," he snapped.

"Then answer the question," she snapped back, even sharper.

When he made no response, Barbara said to the judge, "Please direct the witness to answer the question, or else admit he couldn't hear it." When she turned to look at the judge, Radiman did, also.

"Did you hear the question, Mr. Radiman?" Judge Waldman asked clearly.

"No. She's playing tricks with me, trying to trap me."

Before Barbara could say anything, Judge Waldman asked, "Mr. Radiman, did you at any time indicate to the police or the district attorney's office that you suffer a hearing loss?"

"I don't," he said. "Not really. Just a little bit at movies."

Judge Waldman leaned back and nodded to Barbara. "You may continue."

She studied Radiman for a second, then said, "No further questions for this witness." She hoped the jury read her meaning: what was the point, since he had impeached himself already?

Roxbury tried to salvage something. "Do you have more trouble with some voices than with others?" he asked.

"Yeah. Soft women's voices are harder than men's. High voices, like hers, are the hardest to hear." He inclined his head toward Barbara, who grinned.

"Are you certain you saw Ray Arno in his cell the night you were booked?" He said yes emphatically. "And are you certain you could hear his voice clearly, hear his words plainly?" He said yes, in an even louder, more assertive voice.

Roxbury read from his notes: "I didn't mean to hit him that hard. I didn't mean to kill him. I couldn't help it. I'm sorry. God, I'm sorry. Dear God, forgive me, I'm sorry." He looked up at Radiman. "Were those the words you heard that night?"

"Yes, they were. Plain as I heard you right now."

"Try a question facing away from him," Barbara suggested. Roxbury yelled an objection, and the judge used her gavel to make them both behave.

"The jury is instructed to disregard counsel's remark," she said sharply.

When Roxbury finished with Radiman, Judge Waldman summoned Barbara and Roxbury to the bench.

"We will have a recess at this time, and I want you both in chambers in ten minutes," she said.

Returning to her table, Barbara saw Matthew Gramm at the rear of the courtroom, standing near the door with his arms crossed over his chest. Gramm was the district attorney. Roxbury rushed to him, and they left together.

"What's up?" Frank growled when she cursed in an undertone.

"Don't know. But Gramm's in on it, and we're due in chambers in ten minutes. I want you to go with me. If they're trying to pull a fast one at this late date—"

"Don't panic until you see the fire," Frank said.

Today Judge Waldman did not serve coffee; she had not taken off her judicial robe, and was seated at her desk with the visitors' chairs arranged in a semicircle across from it. Gramm and Roxbury nodded at Frank and Barbara, and that ended the civilities. If Roxbury could have been described as an accountant with fair accuracy, Gramm would have fitted anyone's description of a wrestler, which he had been in his youth. He was fifty-five, sandy-haired and tanned, and large in every dimension, with thick shoulders and a deep chest, over six feet tall, well over two hundred pounds, and most of it muscle. He worked out, he liked to tell people; athletes got flabby if they didn't continue to work out all their lives. He was not flabby.

"Mr. Gramm has filed a motion requesting a short continuance of the trial," Judge Waldman said crisply. "Mr. Gramm, will you explain please."

"Although this is highly irregular, which we admit," Gramm said easily, "under the circumstances, we are compelled to ask for a delay. A witness has come forward today—this morning, in fact—with a statement of such gravity, it cannot be ignored. We are forced to investigate, and our investigation will cause a brief delay in the proceedings."

"A surprise witness!" Barbara exclaimed in disbelief. "You've got to be kidding! With no discovery? Please!"

Ignoring her, Gramm addressed the judge. "This witness called my office earlier today, and came in person three hours ago. She has made a formal statement in which she swears she saw Ray Arno throwing a large bundle into the McKenzie River at eight o'clock on the morning of August sixth. At this moment we have divers in the water, searching for the bundle."

Barbara made a rude snorting sound. "Is your witness certifiably blind? A partner for Radiman?"

"Our witness," he said smoothly, "is Marta Delancey, the wife of California senator Rolfe Delancey."

For a moment no one moved, then Gramm reached into his briefcase and withdrew a folder, which he handed to Barbara. "Her statement," he said, not quite smiling, but close enough for her to want to kick him. "I already handed a copy to Judge Waldman." He turned back to the judge then. "Of course, we will call her even if we don't find the bundle, but it would be a dereliction of our duty not to search for it."

"How long a delay are you requesting?" Judge Waldman asked. She had been cool at the start of the meeting; now she was icy.

"Two days only," he said. "Mrs. Delancey said the bundle appeared quite heavy. It could have been weighted with something, and it is quite possible that it has not moved very far."

Frank and Barbara both began to make objections, and the judge heard them without interruption; then she said, "I will grant the continuance for two days only. Presumably, Mr. Roxbury, in the event that a bundle is found, you will then want to call a witness to identify the contents. I warn you to have any discovery in the hands of the defense by Friday morning when we resume. You will not be permitted to rest the state's case until the defense has had an opportunity to examine all the evidence you uncover, and statements from all the witnesses you intend to call to testify."

"Your honor," Barbara said very quietly then, "this development means that the defense very likely won't be able to conclude during the period we agreed upon earlier."

"I'm afraid that's correct," Judge Waldman said with some bitterness. Evidently she was already considering what the news of a delay would mean to the jury panel.

"They can use this hiatus exactly as if we had rested," Gramm said. "It shouldn't make a bit of difference to them."

Judge Waldman regarded him silently for a moment. "Don't push too hard, Mr. Gramm," she said. "I'll inform the jury that we will be in recess until Friday morning." She stood up. The meeting was over.

27

They had read Marta Delancey's statement in Barbara's office. A glum silence had followed. "She was a local girl," Frank said thoughtfully. "Can't recall her maiden name, but she married Joel Chisolm, and after he died, she latched on to the senator. She's on committees, boards of directors, things of that sort. Respected."

The silence had settled again, until Barbara broke it the next time. "Shit!"

Now she was waiting for Ray to be delivered to the conference room at the jail. Her father was having a tête-à-tête with Sylvia Fenton, and Bailey and Shelley had been dispatched to dig up what they could about Marta Delancey.

Ray was almost bouncy when he entered the small room and sat down. "Wow! You did a real job on that creep today."

She shrugged. "He was easy. Ray, do you know Marta Delancey?"

He looked blank, then shook his head. "Why? Who's she?"

"Of course, we knew Marta after she married Joel Chisolm," Sylvia said to Frank.

They were in a small sitting room, Sylvia, Joe, and Frank, having a glass of wine and some very fine spiced shrimp and lobster tidbits. The room was overcrowded with furniture, as were all the rooms in the mansion, but it was an intimate setting, and the artwork had been held to a minimum here. Only one wall had paintings, Picassos, and the tables had space for the Waterford wineglasses, after some of the knickknacks had been rearranged. Lovely crystal fish and Dresden bowls of candies, a hand-beaten copper bowl of agate marbles . . .

Joe Fenton had a little bit of fuzzy white hair, hardly enough to cover his scalp, and fuzzy white eyebrows; his eyes were bright blue, and his cheeks as pink as any Santa's. He was wearing a gorgeous Chinese brocade jacket and old worn house slippers. Sylvia had on a silk sari in a wild red print. On the table at her elbow was a silver bowl with a lot of rings in it; the gemstones flashed and glittered as if with an inner life.

"Joel Chisolm was an idiot," Sylvia said complacently. "He got an MBA, and God alone knows how he managed to get through the courses—we always thought Marta did the work for him—and they went off to New York for him to make a million or two, but he was mugged and killed. What else do you want to know?"

"What about her, Marta? Tell me about her."

"Marta Perkins, gold digger," Sylvia said promptly. "Greta, Joel's mother, wanted to kill her when she snatched little Joel. She told me all about it. I reminded her that people had talked about me that way, and she pooh-poohed that, said this was different. And maybe it was." She looked at her husband, who was beaming at her.

"The Chisolms made a fortune in wood products," Joe Fenton said then. "They had three kids, none of them able to tie their own shoes, so there was a lot of disappointment in that house. But they had hopes, always had hopes, you see. Marta's father was a working logger, worked for the Chisolms, in fact. She was a pretty girl, I remember."

"She tried to snag you," Sylvia said with good humor.

"When was that?" Frank asked.

"Oh, we were married by then. And she was married to Joel. Fat chance she had, but she gave him the eye plenty. He would have been a better catch than Joel, you understand. Anyway, they got married and after five or six years moved to New York, and a few months later, his father died from a massive heart attack. No warning symptoms or anything, just keeled over one day. Poor Greta was devastated. Her kids were a mess and she was a widow. She hit the bottle, and that and prescription drugs did her in within a few months. Found dead one morning. So the kids suddenly inherited a lot of money. There's Harry, he's up in Portland, I think, with his third or fourth wife, and broke. And Connie, who's off in Italy, last I heard. And Joel was mugged and shot soon after his mother died; after he and Marta came home and cleaned out the old house; they took everything worth a cent and moved it all back to New York, and probably had a big yard sale. Harry and Connie fought like devils to prevent it, but Greta had left the house and everything in it to Joel. She told me that Joel needed money, that things just seemed to go wrong for him. The rest of the estate, stocks and such, was split three ways. I don't believe any of them ever spoke to one another after that." She speared a piece of lobster and ate it, then went on. "So there was Marta, a very pretty widow with a fortune of her own. She's smart, got herself a college degree in history, I believe, and she learned how to eat with a fork and everything. She married the senator within the year. And he has an even bigger fortune. She's done well, little Marta Perkins."

By the time Frank left, he felt he knew more about Marta Perkins Delancey than any tabloid reporter could ever uncover. At the same time, he felt that all this information was as useful as a tabloid story that proved the aliens had landed.

Rain moved in before dawn on Wednesday, not a hard, driving rain, just insistent and continuous, and it was still like that when Barbara and Bailey left her apartment before nine. She drove to I-5, onto Highway 126, through Springfield, past Weyerhauser with its loathsome smoke curling up to merge with the clouds and turn them a dirty yellow, then the straight shot toward the McKenzie River bridge. She didn't exceed the speed limit; when the bridge came into sight through the relentless rain, Bailey said. "Twenty-two minutes."

She slowed down. Ahead, on the other side of the bridge, a turnoff access road wound down to a parking area near a small beach where the river was shallow and not too fast for swimming, although the McKenzie was always so cold, summer and winter, that warnings about hypothermia had to be repeated year after year in the hottest weather. Now the beach was crowded with official cars; a dozen men in waterproof ponchos, under umbrellas, were standing around, a camera crew huddled by their own van. . . . There were two drift boats in the water.

Barbara didn't stop; she felt sorry for the divers in the swirling frigid water. Today the river looked black; the sky at treetop level and the steady rain dimmed what little light there was at this time of year. She hoped that Gramm and Roxbury were freezing their asses off down there in the rain.

"Tell me where to turn for the cabin," she said. She had been there once, but on a sunny fall day, and the road had been easy to spot.

"There it is," Bailey said a minute later.

She made the turn off the highway onto a county road, and the forest closed in on both sides immediately. They had been in farmland until now—fields, pastures, filbert orchards, farmhouses—but here the forest took over with massive fir trees that blotted out the sky.

"Third turn on the right," Bailey said, watching closely. The next turn put them on an even narrower road that twisted and climbed through the forest. There were driveways, but the cabins themselves were invisible. "There," Bailey said. She turned onto a gravel driveway, and ahead was the Marshall cabin.

"Okay," she said, and started backing and filling until she was heading out again. It would be faster going out, she knew; it took ten minutes to get back to the bridge, then another twenty minutes to return to Eugene.

Neither commented again until she parked at the office on Sixth. "It's a fuckup," he said then.

"You got that right," she agreed unhappily.

Late in the afternoon she visited Ray. "How are you holding up?" she asked.

He looked very tired and worried. "Okay, I guess. I've tried and tried to come up with a time I might have run across Marta Delancey, and there's just nothing. I never saw her in my life."

"Did you know her first husband? Joel Chisolm. They were still married eighteen years ago, just about when you were opening your shop. Could he have been a customer?"

He shook his head. "Good God, eighteen years ago! Chisolm. You mean the lumber-company people?"

"He was one of the sons."

He shook his head more emphatically. "I don't believe the Chisolms mingled much with the Arnos. I never met him, never even saw him that I'm aware of."

"Were you keeping records back then? Would his name be in your books if he bought anything from your shop?"

"No. Probably not. I learned about good records later, the first time I was audited, five or six years into the business." He leaned forward then and asked harshly, "Why is she doing this? What's in it for her?"

"I wish I knew," Barbara said.

"I didn't throw anything in the river," he said with great intensity. "She didn't see me. I didn't kill Mitch. But right now I feel like I'm losing my mind. A strange woman can come forward and convict me with a lie. Why is she doing it?"

Barbara reached across the table and took his hand. "I know all that, Ray, and you're not convicted yet. Try to relax, get a little rest while you can."

Some of the tension left him; she knew, because she could almost feel it flowing into her through their joined hands.

That night Frank ordered food from Martin's. Too busy to cook, he said, they'd have to make do with second best. Martin had prepared roast duckling in a sweet and hot mustard sauce, asparagus tips with herbed butter, a potato-leek casserole. . . . Binnie had added one of her specialties: raspberry cream tarts in hazelnut crust.

John didn't stay long after they had dessert and coffee; he was working hard to wrap up his report on the Canadian mine, which he had to finish before Christmas.

She walked to the door with him. "This is a bitch," she said. "But it won't be much longer. Promise."

"Better not be. If I'm sleeping when you get in, wake me up." Then, in a whisper, he added, "If Alan's sleeping, leave him alone."

Frank was just bringing in a carafe of fresh coffee when she returned to the dining room. "Let's talk about Marta Perkins Delancey," he said. "After I talked with Sylvia, I spent some time with Bud Yates, up at his place in Pleasant Hill. He suspected I wanted to pump him, and when I said it was about Marta, he said pump away." Bud Yates was one of his old friends, older than Frank, and retired now.

"Bud was the Chisolm attorney for a good many years," Frank said. "And he gave me an earful. Between him and Sylvia, I reckon I got the whole story. After Marta hooked Joel, they stayed in Eugene for a few years and went through his money, took it down to zilch. Then Marta got an itch to move to New York. So off they went. Greta, the mother, was heartbroken, and the money problem got worse. She hated Marta with all her soul, and probably with cause. Anyway, after the father died, Joel began talking about his marriage being a mistake after all, and Greta bought it. Joel and Marta came home to discuss things. He said he was going to leave Marta and live in the family house with his mother. That's when she added the clause to her will, leaving it to him, and everything in it. It had priceless antiques the Chisolms had collected and she had added to, things like that. She told Bud that she knew Joel was irresponsible about finances, but at least he would have the house and its contents, and maybe after the divorce he would find a nice local girl and really settle down. She also said that Joel was in desperate trouble and that she had made him a big loan. Something to do with brokering phony stocks. Two weeks after they left again, with a big check, Greta died. Harry, the other son, accused Marta of poisoning her, but nothing came of it. Alcohol, sleeping medications, and tranquilizers, that was all, and his accusation was treated as sour grapes.

"After the estate was settled, they had this fancy mover come in, crate up everything, and haul it off to New York, and they put the house in the hands of a real estate company and left town. Two weeks later, Joel was shot in the street and killed. They had gone to a play and were on their way to a supper club when it happened. Marta was not injured."

He stopped and regarded Barbara with a knowing look. "Sylvia said they used a mover who specialized in handling expensive goods, one based in New York."

"Oh, my God! Palmer?"

"Possibly. She didn't know the company name."

Barbara remembered Ray's question and repeated it: "What's in it for Marta? Why would the wife of a United States senator come forward to commit perjury?" She shook her head. "We have to try to find the link between her and Palmer. Your job, Bailey, whatever it takes. And I need some ammunition by Friday."

Bailey groaned. "You know we can't dig deep that fast."

"Whatever you can find. And, Bailey, a three-way link maybe: Marta, the senator, and Palmer. See what you can find about Joel's death." She frowned, thinking, then said slowly, "She knew about Palmer's moving business eighteen years ago. Was it operating then the way it is now, a little business deal of moving something to cover up the real transaction? In that case, maybe a murder?"

Frank made a throat-clearing noise, which she ignored. She knew he hated it when she went leaping over obstacles blindly. She turned to Shelley. "Your work is in Portland. Find Harry Chisolm and talk to him. Did Joel ever go fishing? Buy stuff from a local shop? That line. We may want him to testify, but you'll have to judge that. Remember, a bad witness is worse than no witness, and if he hates Marta enough, he might be a very bad witness. But we need to know. I'll want dates, when Marta and Joel left town here for New York, when and where Ray opened his shop. . . ."

When she got home, John was sleeping. She stood inside the bedroom door for a moment, then quietly left again and went to her office, where she sat at her desk and thought about time. All this business about Marta was cutting into the hours she had budgeted for other things. She swiveled in her chair to examine the calendar on her wall. Christmas was on a Wednesday. Would Judge Waldman take the entire week off, or just Tuesday and Wednesday? What she wouldn't do, she had made clear, was sequester the jury at this point, nor would she work them on Christmas Eve or Christmas Day. Barbara did not believe the judge would send the jury into deliberation on Monday, two days before Christmas.

And John's children were due the day after Christmas. He had motel reservations at the coast, for them to see Keiko the whale. And a day planned in the mountains, sledding and snowboarding. A day in Portland to visit the science museum . . . Plans for shopping for their presents.

She closed her eyes hard; then, very roughly, she cursed Palmer and Marta, and finally she opened her briefcase, pulled out papers, and started to work.

⟡

At four-thirty on Thursday Barbara and Frank joined a group of people in the forensics lab. There were detectives, forensic personnel, Matthew Gramm and assistant D.A. Craig Roxbury, and now Frank and Barbara gathered around a long table that held a shallow black plastic pan, such as a photographer might use for developing large negatives. A stark white light glared on a black plastic bag in the pan. The table was covered with a white plastic-coated sheet of paper, and there was a second shallow pan, empty.

Two cameras were recording everything, one on a fixed tripod, the other handheld by a photographer who moved in and out among the assembled witnesses.

The black plastic bag was heavy-duty, industrial strength, fastened by a wire that had rusted and fused together but was so brittle that when the forensics technician cut it, it broke in several places. There were a few small slits in the plastic bag, and it was still partly filled with water; when it was opened, the water ran out into the pan.

The technician was wearing elbow-length rubber gloves and a rubber apron. Carefully he opened the bag and held it open for the photographer, then he reached inside and drew out the contents, moving slowly, stopping frequently for the pictures. A sodden stained shirt, black slacks, black shoes, filthy white socks, very brief briefs, a pair of leather work gloves, a second pair of canvas gloves, a lead pipe like the one Mitch had carried in his duffel bag, six big rocks. The technician identified each item as he pulled it out and laid it in the pan. After the plastic bag was empty, he examined the pockets of the slacks and the shirt, all empty.

"Ms. Holloway, Mr. Holloway," the district attorney said then, "may we have a word? Outside, in the corridor."

They followed him and Roxbury to the hall.

"Obviously, they can't do anything with that stuff until it dries out," Gramm said. "We can't tell if those stains are just muddy water or blood at this point. What I propose is that we ask Judge Waldman for another postponement, until Monday morning. By then we'll know something about this evidence. Is that agreeable to you?"

Barbara nodded. "You understand that you're asking for this delay, not I."

"I know that," he said curtly. "I informed Judge Waldman as soon as I received word that the bag had been found. She wants to see us in chambers. She said as soon as we had opened it, to come over directly; she'll be waiting."

She was at her desk, toying with gold-framed glasses, with a calendar before her. Her nod was frosty and her words were clipped and sharp when she said, "Please be seated." As soon as they had taken chairs opposite her, she turned toward Roxbury. "What do you propose to do?"

"Well—" he started, but Gramm interrupted him and answered.

"Your honor, we regret very much this unforeseen development, but we all are experienced enough to know that sometimes the unexpected does occur."

Judge Waldman shook her head at him. "Mr. Gramm, no speeches. We are all experienced enough to know that an enraged jury panel is a bad jury panel. How they will vent their displeasure is an unknown factor. Will you introduce this new evidence, and how long will it take?"

"We need until Monday," Gramm said bluntly. "We can't examine the items until they dry out, and that will take a day or two."

Judge Waldman was tapping her fingers on the calendar.

"Your honor," Gramm said then, "we have an alternative to propose. It would be highly irregular at this point, but we would consider a plea bargain with Mr. Arno, let him admit to manslaughter, and be done with the whole thing. Those clothes, the incontrovertible testimony of the next witness, Mrs. Delancey, is overwhelmingly convincing. To drag out these proceedings further serves no purpose whatever."

Judge Waldman looked at Barbara.

"Impossible," Barbara said. "Ray Arno didn't kill his brother."

"Can you speak for him?" Judge Waldman asked.

"I'll talk with him, but he won't accept a plea bargain."

"In the event that we continue with the trial," Judge Waldman said, addressing Roxbury, tapping the calendar, "how long do you expect to take with Mrs. Delancey, and then with any follow-up witnesses you require?"

"Half a day with Mrs. Delancey, half a day with follow-up," he said. "Providing defense counsel doesn't drag things out the way she's been doing."

"I already have a lot of questions for Mrs. Delancey," Barbara said. "I don't think the state will rest until the middle of next week." She added thoughtfully, "It would not be fair to the defense or to the jury for us to start and then be interrupted by the holidays. Such a break in the continuity of the defense case would be grievously damaging."

Judge Waldman put on her glasses and looked at the calendar, frowning. "What I propose," she said after a moment, "is to let you recall the state's four witnesses next week, then recess until the day after Christmas. I'll advise the jurors of this schedule and warn them that we could continue into the New Year, and that if we do, they should be prepared to work half a day on New Year's Eve, then off for New Year's Day, and back the following day. And I warn both sides now that the jurors are not going to be happy about this."

Gramm and Roxbury both raised objections, politely, but with some force, and she heard them out. If Arno would not accept a plea bargain, and he needed time to think about it, they wanted the trial postponed until after the first of the year. She rejected their arguments. Then Barbara said, "Your honor, would it be possible to let them know that this delay is not a sinister machination of the defense?"

"I object to such a statement being made to the jurors," Roxbury said. "That would be grossly prejudicial."

"I shall consider carefully what I tell them," Judge Waldman said dryly.

Ray Arno leaned back in his chair and studied Barbara with a disbelieving gaze, then he turned the same incredulous gaze on Frank. He shook his head. "I told Bishop Stover on day one that I didn't do anything and wouldn't plead to a lesser charge, because it would be a lie. Nothing's changed. Why are you bringing it up again?" His handsome face had become ravaged-looking, and strangely more attractive than before.

"Because Gramm made the offer before the judge," Barbara said. "That makes it more or less binding. You would get twenty years, or we could go for a lower number and argue about it; in any event you'd be out on parole in seven or eight years at the most. On the other hand, under the sentencing guidelines, you could get life without parole if you're found guilty, or you could even get the death sentence."

"So those who are guilty get the breaks, and the innocent get life, or the final shot in the arm," he said bitterly after a moment. He was very pale. "I didn't do anything, Barbara. I won't say I did."

Gil Wilkerson, one of Bailey's hired guns, was waiting to drive them home when they left the jail. It was raining very hard.

"My place," she told Frank. "I'll give Bailey and Shelley a call, meet back at your place around eight. We'll scrounge up something to eat first."

She heard John's printer at work when she let herself into the apartment; he came to the small landing to meet her and help her off with her coat.

"You're shivering," he said. "Let's have a hot drink. Irish coffee?"

"God, yes! But first I have to get out of these clothes." Then, a few minutes later, in her jeans, sweatshirt, and sneakers, she called Bailey and Shelley, and finally she sat at the table, sipping Irish coffee, and told John about the new developments.

His forehead furrowed, the way it did when he was troubled, and the scar on his face drew up his mouth in a crooked grimace. "You won't even start your case until the day after Christmas?"

"No." Then she said, "I told Dad we'd eat here. I have to go to his place at eight. I'll see what we have."

"I'll do it," John said. He quickly went into the kitchen, and she understood that he needed time to think.

She felt almost numb as she gazed at the living room, at his massive desk spread with maps, opened books on end tables, pages of printout on the couch. . . . She looked down at the steaming coffee and took another sip. Not too much, she thought, and realized she had eaten nothing all day, not since a hasty breakfast. Her system was miswired, that was the problem; she never got the signals for hunger or fatigue or . . . John had stopped rummaging about in the kitchen.

"Barbara," he said, his back to her, his posture stiff and even hostile-looking, "you can't really believe a man like Palmer has a woman like Marta Delancey in his pocket. Aren't you taking a gamble a little too far?"

"I do believe it," she said. "And it's a gamble, but not mine. It's Ray's gamble. He's innocent!"

"She saw him, recognized him, fingered the place where he dumped the bag, and they found it there, or nearby." Now he turned to look at her. His face was expressionless, the way it became when he was unwilling to reveal his thoughts, his feelings, a way that revealed everything by concealing too much.

"She's lying," Barbara said.

"Someone's lying. This whole case started with a big lie, and it's gone on from there. You got it into your head from the beginning that it's a single case, the Palmer affair and Mitch's murder, but maybe they're really not connected. Can't you even consider the possibility that there's no connection? The murder might be a family affair; most murders are."

"And sometimes they aren't that simple."

"Have you considered that if you're right, if Palmer can send in a senator's wife to do his dirty work, no one here is safe, no matter if you have armed guards? Have you considered what it would mean to bring two kids into an armed camp where they could become targets?" The scar on his face flared, then turned livid. His mouth drew up, and abruptly he spun around and stalked from the kitchen. "I don't think I'm hungry. I'm going for a walk."

She didn't move as she heard him at the coat tree, then going down the stairs fast and hard; she heard the outside door close with a bang.

He had not returned when Bailey rang the bell with his characteristic signal; she had made herself a sandwich but after a few bites had put it down. She tossed it into the garbage. When she went down, swathed in her heavy poncho, it was still raining hard. He would get soaked, she thought distantly, and hoped he would come home and take a hot bath, hoped he had ducked inside somewhere to brood over a beer or two, that he was not out tramping around in the weather.

In Frank's living room, Barbara reported on the day's events and the new schedule. Both Shelley and Bailey groaned. Batting a thousand, Barbara thought.

"Forget Harry Chisolm as a possible witness," Shelley said glumly. "He thinks Marta's guilty of whatever sin has been reported, starting with the Fall of Rome. But he said that Joel Chisolm never went fishing in his life and he, Harry, never did, either. He was able to give me some dates—when Joel and Marta got married, when they moved to New York, when they came home for the father's funeral, and then again a couple of weeks before their mother's death, and so on. He said all the antiques went straight to an auction house." She pushed her report across the table to Barbara.

"Also," she said, "I talked to Lorinne and went over old photograph albums with her. We found pictures of the various places where Ray's had his business, starting with day one. She let me have copies made of the snapshots. They're in here, too. Then," she said, "I did a little research on the various sites, what they were like when Ray was there, things like that, and what they are now. There have been a lot of changes since he started in 1978."

"Why?" Barbara asked.

"I thought that if Marta Delancey is lying, she might not know where Ray's shop was back then, what it looked like. I was surprised by it; that's what sent me searching."

She opened her file folder and drew out the pictures. "See, a corner in a warehouse in an area that was zoned industrial. It was temporary, but still, there it is."

"Good work," Barbara said, studying the photograph. "You've had yourself a real day, earned your keep plenty."

Shelley beamed at her and blushed.

The corner in the warehouse looked like a dismal, poorly lighted space with a picnic table that kids might have used to sell lemonade.

Bailey had been less successful. "Okay," he said, "the cops were suspicious of Joel Chisolm's death, but they didn't have a thing to go on except a gut feeling. Joel and Marta left the show at ten after eleven and decided to walk three or four blocks to the supper club, where Joel had made reservations earlier that day. After a block, a car drove past them and stopped, and two guys got out. One of them grabbed Joel's arm and snatched the wallet from his coat pocket; the other one shot him in the head. No one could describe the guys, happened too fast, they said." He spread his hands. "Gut feeling says it was a setup. Hard facts, zilch."

"Any link between Marta and Palmer? Did he move the family heirlooms?"

"Don't know. They're trying to find out, but it might take days, weeks. That was a long time ago, remember."

Barbara frowned. "So, unless and until it's proved one way or the other, we go on the assumption that he did, that he and Marta were acquainted, and she used his services."

Bailey nodded noncommittally. "She and the senator were married nine months after Joel bit the dust. According to interviews, they had met years earlier. Two kids: a son by Joel, a daughter by the senator. One of the successful marriages, not a word of scandal, Caesar's wife, all that." He shrugged. "We need a little time, Barbara. You know how it goes. They'll make her out to be Mother Teresa."

She did know, and ignored his complaint. "So Palmer's got something on her that makes her jump when he gives the word. Why would he get involved? Why now? He doesn't want Trassi and his two goons implicated, for openers. Is that enough to bring out a big gun like Marta?" She stopped, considering, then said, "Trassi could be making demands. Maybe he's hanging on to the printouts until Palmer gets him out of this mess. He must think that Ray will take the plea bargain. They must believe they have an unimpeachable witness." She looked at Frank and asked, "Is that how most lawyers would think at this point?"

"A plea bargain is a powerful inducement to deal," Frank said after a moment. "Trassi knows that." Slowly he went on. "Most attorneys who aren't trial lawyers would say, 'Take the deal.' Many trial lawyers would say the same simply because there isn't enough time to refute Marta's statement, to discredit her. Stover was ready to deal even without her testimony. They could be counting on you to dig as much as you can in the time allotted, and then conclude that you can't impeach her. And, Bobby, maybe you can't. We know things from the old boys' network, but they aren't worth a tinker's damn in court. If you can't impeach her, can't convince the jury that she's lying, will she carry the burden of a conviction with her testimony? That's the question. They must think the answer is yes, and that you will arrive at the same conclusion."

At twelve Bailey and Barbara drove Shelley to the townhouse and he saw her safely inside; then he drove Barbara to her apartment and went up with her, ostensibly to have a word with Alan Macagno, but she knew it was to see her all the way in, not leave her at the outside door. Armed camps, she thought; Pete McClure had arrived at Frank's house at eleven to spend the night in his living room.

John and Alan were watching a movie, which seemed to involve a lot of men on horses, a lot of dust, and a lot of shooting. A pizza tray was on the table.

John left Alan and Bailey and followed her into the other apartment. He didn't get closer than arm's length. "I put pizza in the fridge," he said. "It needs a minute in the microwave."

"Thanks. Maybe later."

"Coffee's in the carafe. Are your feet wet?"

She looked down, then nodded. "I'll change. How about yours?"

"Okay. Well, back to justice, frontier-style. Don't work too late."

She watched him walk stiffly through her hall, through the landing, into his own hall, then vanish into the other living room, where the gunfire sounded like corn popping.

❖

29

If Barbara had kept a diary, what she would have written for Friday was: *Notified Judge and Roxbury, no deal. Rain.* For Saturday it would have been: *Reports, work. Rain.* Sunday: *Work. Rain.*

What she would not have written was an account of the strange new behavior that had developed between her and John. Either they clung to each other like desperate teens or they were as distant as polite, well-mannered acquaintances. No middle ground. Ominously, neither of them had referred even once to his outburst of Thursday, or to the new schedule she had to observe, or to the trial in any way.

On Monday, Marta Delancey was sworn in and seated herself gracefully. She was tall with broad shoulders, very handsome in a salon-finish gloss from head to foot. Her hair was an indeterminate color between blond and brown, cut stylishly short, with a few wisps down on her forehead. Her jewelry was discreet—small pearl earrings, a pearl necklace against a pale blue silk blouse that was exactly the right color to go with her dark blue silk suit. Her blouse matched the blue of her eyes.

Roxbury led her through her past history, her marriage to Joel Chisolm, his untimely death, and her later marriage to the senator from California. He had her list the various committees on which she had served, those on which she was presently active. It was all very impressive. Her voice was pleasant, carrying without being strident or overly forceful as she answered his questions concisely.

Barbara could tell nothing about what the jury was thinking. The members were as unreadable as petroglyphs on granite walls.

"Mrs. Delancey," Roxbury said, finally getting to the point, "are you acquainted with the defendant, Ray Arno?"

"Not really. I have seen him two times in my life."

"Will you please tell the court the circumstances of the first occasion on which you saw him."

"Yes. It was in the fall of 1978. My late husband and I were in Eugene visiting his mother. We were strolling, looking in windows, and noticed a new shop, The Sporting Chance. Joel, my late husband, said he would try to find a gift for his brother there. It was a fishing supply shop, and Joel knew nothing about fishing; therefore, he engaged the young man at the counter in a rather lengthy conversation. I knew even less about fishing than Joel did, and I was not interested in the conversation, but I found the proprietor very interesting. He said he had recently opened the shop and business was not very good, but he had great hopes for the future. He was very handsome and, frankly, I studied him quite a bit, enough to make him uncomfortable, I'm afraid. I realized I had embarrassed him, and stopped, of course. When we left the shop, I turned and wished him luck, and he said thank you. He was the defendant, Ray Arno."

"Was he very different from the man you see today? Has he changed very much since then?"

"He's hardly different at all. He might be a few pounds heavier, but he looks almost exactly the same as he did then."

"Would you have been able to pick him out of a crowd?"

"Objection. Speculation," Barbara said.

It was sustained, and Roxbury moved on. "Mrs. Delancey, please tell the court the circumstances of the second time you saw the defendant, Ray Arno."

"That was last August. I had come to Eugene to visit my mother, who is quite ill and resides here in a nursing home. On the morning of August sixth, I decided to take a drive up in the mountains. I left early that morning, and I was on the McKenzie Highway, heading east, when I saw a car stopped on the bridge ahead. I slowed down, thinking the driver might need assistance. Then, just as I had driven onto the bridge, a man came from around the back of the car, carrying a large plastic bag that appeared to be heavy. He lifted it over the bridge railing and let it drop into the water, and then he looked in my direction, as if he had not previously heard my approach. He seemed startled, and for a second or two he didn't move, just looked at me. I had drawn up almost even with him by then. Suddenly he hurried to the driver's side of his car and got in and drove away fast, toward Eugene. I recognized him, although I didn't know his name then. I don't believe I had ever heard his name, but it was the same man I saw in the fishing shop, the defendant, Ray Arno."

"Are you positive it was Ray Arno you saw on the morning of August sixth?"

"Yes."

"Do you recall what time that was?"

"About eight."

"Do you recall what kind of car he was driving?"

"I don't know makes and models, but it was a small gray car with a hatchback. I watched it out my rearview mirror as he drove away."

She was a very good witness, Barbara had to admit silently; her answers were fluent and to all appearances unrehearsed. Roxbury asked what she had done after seeing Ray Arno, and she answered readily.

"I was troubled by what seemed to be illegal dumping, but I was here because my mother was having a crisis, and by the time I returned to visit her later that morning, I'm afraid I let the matter of Mr. Arno slip my mind. I was trying to decide if I should take my mother to California, where I could visit with her more often, weighing the pros and cons of moving her away from doctors and nurses she had grown fond of, a comfortable setting with other residents she had become friends with. It was a difficult decision, one that occupied my thoughts for the remainder of my visit. I forgot about Mr. Arno."

"Did you read about the murder of Mitchell Arno?"

"Not at that time. I was gone before it was reported in the local newspapers, and I didn't know anything about it."

"And what made you come forward now?"

"I was visiting again last week. I try to get up here as often as possible. I came across an account of the murder; it was summarized when Ms. Holloway joined the defense case, and there was a picture of Ray Arno. I remembered seeing him on the bridge that day, and I knew I had to tell what I had seen."

Roxbury finished with her soon after that, and Judge Waldman called for a short recess. That morning the courtroom was filled to capacity; Marta Delancey's appearance had made the news both locally and nationally.

"Mrs. Delancey," Barbara said after the recess, "your testimony is that you first saw Ray Arno in the fall of 1978. Can you be more precise about the date?"

"I'm sorry. I don't think I can. We were back and forth between Eugene and New York several times that fall. On one of those trips, but the date. . . ?" She shook her head. "It was a long time ago."

"I understand. Nineteen seventy-eight was a momentous year in your life, wasn't it? Was your son born that year?"

"Yes, January twenty-eighth."

"And your father-in-law died unexpectedly in March. Is that right?"

"Yes."

"Then, in October, your mother-in-law died, also unexpectedly. Is that correct?"

"Yes."

"Was there an investigation regarding her death?"

"There was. It was determined that she died from an accidental overdose of a prescription sleeping medication."

Barbara picked up a paper from her table. "This is the official report following the conclusion of that investigation." She showed it first to the judge and then to Roxbury, who looked bored and resigned. It was admitted. "According to the report here, Mrs. Delancey, the autopsy report attributed her death to a high level of alcohol in her system, in combination with the sleeping medication, antidepressants, and tranquilizers. Do you recall that?"

"Yes," Marta Delancey said in a low voice. "She had become very depressed that year. I believe her children, and I, all made a statement to that effect."

"Yes, your statements are included. Your statement also says that you and your late husband visited Mrs. Chisolm two weeks before her death, that you arrived on October fourth and left on October seventh. Is that correct?"

"Yes."

"Did you accompany your late husband and your mother-in-law when they went to her bank and arranged a loan?"

Roxbury was on his feet with an objection instantly. Judge Waldman was frowning at Barbara, who said, "Your honor, I am trying to pinpoint exactly when Mrs. Delancey might first have seen Ray Arno."

"Please rephrase your question," the judge said crisply.

"Mrs. Delancey, did your late husband have business to attend to with his mother on that visit in early October?"

"Yes. It was a business trip."

"Did they spend time on both days of your visit conducting their business?"

"Yes."

"And did you visit your own mother while they were doing that?"

"I did."

"In fact, did you spend the nights of October fifth and sixth in your mother's house?"

"Yes. Her health was failing, and I wanted some time with her."

"You flew all the way from New York City to Eugene in order to spend two days with your mother? Is that what you're telling us?"

"Yes. I didn't know at the time how ill she was, and I had a nine-month-old baby back in New York. I was torn between them. After I reassured myself that she was in no immediate danger, I was eager to return home."

"Was your mother employed at the time?" Barbara walked to her table and picked up a sheet of paper. She looked at Marta Delancey, who was watching her closely.

"I really don't remember when she retired."

"Wasn't she given a luncheon in 1982 and presented with an award for thirty years of service with the Lane County government?"

"I don't remember when that happened."

Barbara nodded and said, "I have a photocopy of a newspaper account of her award and her retirement, dated December third, 1982. Would that refresh your memory?"

Marta Delancey shook her head sadly. "What happened was that my mother began to suffer from a debilitating illness that was intermittent for several years before it progressed so much that she could no longer hold her position."

Her point, Barbara thought almost in admiration. "I see," she said, putting down the photocopy of the newspaper account. "So on that first occasion in October of 1978 you arrived in Eugene at seven or later in the evening on the fourth, your late husband and his mother were occupied with business the following two days, during which time you stayed with your mother; then you left Eugene at ten in the morning on the seventh. Was there an opportunity for you to stroll and shop during that brief visit?"

Marta Delancey glanced at the police report Barbara was still holding, then said, "I don't think so. It must have been when we came back later that month."

She continued to be very calm and poised, to all appearances unruffled and quite willing to be as cooperative as possible. A good witness for the prosecution. Painstakingly, keeping her own voice as pleasant and conversational as Marta Delancey's, Barbara led her through the next visit, following the death of Greta Chisolm.

That afternoon Barbara summarized: "So you flew back to Eugene on October twentieth, and the funeral was not until the twenty-fifth. In the intervening days, there was the reading of the will, and many discussions about the new codicil that Mrs. Chisolm had added on October fifth. Did Harry Chisolm retain his own attorney to represent his interests?"

"Yes. It was a very emotional time for everyone. We all felt it was best to let attorneys handle all the details."

"Was Harry Chisolm not only shocked and stunned by his mother's sudden death but also furious that she had left the house and furnishings to your late husband?"

Roxbury objected fiercely, and this time asked permission to approach the bench. Judge Waldman motioned him and Barbara to step forward.

"Your honor, this is harassment, pure and simple. Innuendos that are certain to be prejudicial. This witness is not on trial here, and what happened nearly twenty years ago is irrelevant."

"But she said she first saw Ray Arno nearly twenty years ago," Barbara said reasonably. "I just don't quite see when that was possible."

Judge Waldman considered for a second or two, then she said, "I'll permit you to continue, but I don't want you to rake up old scandals and gossip. And I direct you to rephrase your question with that in mind."

After Roxbury and Barbara returned to their tables, Judge Waldman said, "Sustained. Counsel will rephrase the question."

"Mrs. Delancey," Barbara said then, "did Mrs. Greta Chisolm leave her house and furnishings to your late husband?"

"Yes."

"Was the codicil added to her will on your previous visit in early October?"

"I believe so," she said. "That was Joel's business and hers. I didn't know she had done that until after she died."

"All right. So the funeral was on the twenty-fifth. Did you have an inventory made of the furnishings before you returned to New York?"

"Yes, of course."

"Was that done by a local person?"

"I don't know. Joel handled it."

"Did all three of the Chisolm children oversee the inventory?"

"Yes. Harry and his sister had some personal belongings they wanted to recover, and naturally there was no question about that. Those items were not included in the inventory."

"How long did it take to inventory the furnishings?'

"I don't remember precisely. A day, perhaps two days."

"Were you all staying in the house during this period?"

"No. Harry had his own residence and was staying at home, and his sister chose to stay with him."

"So the inventory might have taken two days, and you remained in the house during that time, and that brings us up to the twenty-seventh of October. Is that right?"

"I really don't remember how long it took. Possibly not two whole days."

It was slow, and there was always a risk that the jury would get too bored to keep listening, but for the moment they were following closely, maybe intrigued by the witness or by the timetable Barbara was constructing. She could tell little about them; it made a difference not being there from day one, not being there for jury selection. They were an unknown quantity to her now.

"When did you return to New York?" Barbara asked.

"A few days after the inventory was made."

"I see. There was a third catastrophic event in your life that year, wasn't there? Was your late husband shot and killed on a sidewalk in New York City on December thirteenth?"

Marta Delancey looked down and said yes in a low voice.

"During the ensuing investigation did the police ask you to retrace your steps for several weeks prior to that incident? And didn't you tell them that you had returned to New York on October twenty-ninth?"

Marta looked startled momentarily, then nodded. "Yes, that was my statement. At the time, of course, I remembered it very well."

"Of course. And did you make one more visit to Eugene between the twenty-ninth of October and the time of your late husband's death?"

"Yes. When the movers crated up the furnishings, we supervised them. In November. We didn't go shopping then, we went the day after the inventory was made in October. Joel said he needed a distraction, and we left the house for several hours."

That was good, Barbara thought. Marta had seen the timetable narrowing to nothing and had taken steps to fix it. A good move.

Barbara nodded, as if satisfied. "So on the twenty-eighth of October you and your late husband took some time off and went shopping. Is that right?"

"Yes. Not to shop, actually, just to get out of the house."

"When did Harry Chisolm and his sister remove their personal possessions from the house?"

"Immediately following the inventory. I believe it was early the next morning. We went out soon after they left."

"Were there servants in the house?"

"No, they had left several days earlier."

"Did you just lock up the house and go out for a stroll?"

"No. My husband made arrangements for a security firm to maintain a watch in the house until we had the furnishings moved. An empty house is too tempting to leave unwatched."

"I see. Do you recall what company was used for security?"

"No. My husband took care of it. I know a guard arrived before we went out."

"Was he instructed not to let Harry Chisolm or his sister enter the house?"

"I don't know."

"You said earlier that your late husband was interested in buying a gift for his brother. Was that not the case?"

"Not really. He was being ironic, I think. He just wanted to get out, to get his mind off the past week, I think."

"In fact, had there not been a number of very emotional scenes that week, a lot of tension and turmoil?"

Barbara waited for Roxbury to object, but he remained silent, and Marta answered almost sadly, "There was a lot of tension. It was an emotional week. Losing the second parent in such a short time had everyone's nerves frayed. Joel was in a highly emotional state and he said he had to get out and get some air. We drove, then we left the car and walked past some shops in south Eugene. I don't recall exactly where. I don't even know what kind of shops they were, and that's when we spotted the new shop and went in, just to be doing something."

"While he was being shown fishing gear, what did you do?"

"Just wandered around the shop a little. I was not interested in fishing equipment."

"Did you pick up items, examine them at all? Just to keep yourself occupied, perhaps?"

"I might have done so. Probably I did."

"Were there other customers in the shop?"

"Not that I recall."

"Are you certain it was The Sporting Chance shop that you entered that day?"

"Yes. My husband commented on the name. He liked it. That's really why we entered, the name sounded interesting."

"Were you standing near your husband and Mr. Arno when you began to study Mr. Arno?"

"No. I might have been near the door, or across the shop. I don't remember where I was standing, only that I was bored and that I found his face interesting and very handsome."

"How far from Mr. Arno were you when you observed his face?"

"Not far. Fifteen feet or so. It was a small shop."

"And how was the lighting?"

"It was quite good. I could see him clearly."

"Did you ever see him again between then and this year?"

"No. I have a very good memory for faces, and names as well. I would remember if I had seen him again. Besides, following the death of my husband, my trips to Eugene were solely to visit my mother."

"Are you certain you entered his shop that day in October, and not the next month when you and your late husband returned for your last trip together to Eugene?"

"Yes. You reminded me by mentioning the police report concerning Joel's death. In November we were very busy supervising the crating of the furniture. There was no time for shopping."

"You said 'crating' again. Did each piece have to be crated up?"

"Most of them. They were very valuable antiques. And we had to check each piece against the inventory list. We didn't go out shopping on that trip."

"Who moved the furnishings, Mrs. Delancey? Was it the Palmer Company from New York?"

Roxbury objected that it was irrelevant, and his objection was sustained, but she had seen a flicker of startlement in Marta Delancey's eyes. If Barbara hadn't been watching closely, she would have missed it. But finally she had shaken the witness just a little.

"Mrs. Delancey, when you came to Eugene last August, did you fly in?"

"No. I drove."

"Up from California? That's a long drive."

"I often do if the weather is pleasant."

"Where did you stay while you were in town?"

"One of the motels off I-5."

"Can you be a little more precise?" Barbara asked, just a touch sharper than she had been before.

"I'm afraid not," Marta said, still at ease, still trying to help.

"Usually when I come to visit my mother, I simply stop at a motel and sign in, often with a fictitious name because I don't want any publicity about my visits, and I don't want to become involved in any social obligations or interviews, anything like that. When I visit my mother, that's all that's on my mind."

"I see," Barbara said. "What name did you use in August?"

"I don't remember," Marta said regretfully. "Once I said I was Mary Pickford. Another time I registered as Jane Austen. I just pick a name at random because I want to remain anonymous. And I pay in cash. I've been doing that for many years."

Barbara let her disbelief show, then asked coolly, "When you visit your mother at the nursing home, do you sign in with a fictitious name?"

"I seldom sign in," Marta said. She made a little gesture with her hand, as if waving away gnats. "One time, reporters got wind of my visit and they pestered my mother afterward, and it was traumatic for her. Many of us with long-term residents in the home don't bother to sign in; we just visit and leave again."

"So there's no record of your visit to Eugene in August? No motel record, or nursing home record, or credit card record?"

"I'm afraid that's right," Marta said. "There's just my word that I was here and why." She said this with absolute self-confidence mildly tinged with regret.

"Have you used the same method for your present visit?"

"No. I don't drive up when the weather might turn bad. I flew into Eugene last Wednesday and rented a car. I didn't have a hotel reservation yet. I had a slight headache and went to the lounge for a cup of coffee and an aspirin, and there I picked up a newspaper someone had left and I read about the murder and I realized that I couldn't keep this visit private and anonymous. I called my secretary and asked her to make a reservation for me. I'm registered in a local hotel under my own name."

Once, many years earlier, before Barbara had passed the bar exam, she had watched Frank question a witness, then abruptly stop, and she had asked him why he hadn't nailed the guy. "Being a trial lawyer is nine-tenths facts and evidence and knowing it by heart backward and forward, and one-tenth intuition," he had said. "But when that one-tenth clamors for attention, you listen hard before you utter another word. That's the part that wins or loses your case."

Her intuition was telling her to stop. She wasn't going to crack Marta Delancey open, and she had become aware that the jury was developing a great deal of sympathy for Marta. Barbara wouldn't have been able to say how she knew that, just that it was so. It would not benefit her to play the heavy now, to pound away.

Very politely she said, "Thank you, no further questions."

It appeared that everyone in court was astounded by her stopping without even trying to refute Marta's positive identification of Ray Arno on the bridge, and maybe that was a point, she thought. Ray had scribbled a big *Why?* on his notepad. She whispered, "I'll explain after we adjourn." She didn't know if she could explain to his satisfaction, but she had been reassured by an almost imperceptible nod of approval from Frank.

30

That night Barbara dreamed: She was standing in a sleety rain, watching divers at work in water so clear, she could see their every movement. The water kept freezing over with a thin layer of ice that acted as a magnifier and did not obscure her view; then a wave would come and the skim of ice would crack and break and float away, only to re-form after a second or two. She could have told the divers to come out, to look from the surface, that they didn't need to enter the water, since it was clear enough to see every rock on the bottom, every bit of floating seaweed, tiny fish darting, but her dream self did not move, did not speak. Eddies formed and vanished. She leaned forward in an effort to see them more clearly. Then fear and wonder seized her as she realized they were faces. She struggled to turn away, to close her dream eyes, but her dream self was frozen in place, leaning over, then falling toward the water, toward the watery faces.

She snapped awake, still caught in the deep-dream paralysis, until a shudder passed through her; she was freezing, soaked with sweat. Carefully she slipped out of bed, groped for her robe, and padded barefoot to the bathroom. Her face was streaked with tears, her hair clung to her sweaty forehead and cheeks, and she was shaking with a chill. Even as she tried to recapture the dream, it vanished from her mind, leaving only a dull headache.

That morning the courtroom was as packed as it had been the day before, but without the air of expectancy that Marta Delancey's appearance had roused. Last night's television news had shown Marta getting into a limousine, being whisked away after her testimony; she had returned to California. An item in the morning paper, more commentary than news, had suggested that she had been the state's star witness, that her testimony had been devastating to the defense, which was not expected to recover.

As the jury was being brought in, Shelley whispered that Bailey said there was an FBI agent present. Then Roxbury brought in his next witness.

Harrell Trainer was twenty-eight and looked years younger, a little ill at ease at his role in the trial but extremely confident when he began to talk about the underwater search. In excruciating detail Roxbury had him describe the procedure, the strategy of a water search in a fast-moving river, and finding the plastic bag.

His fifteen minutes of fame stretched out to over an hour, but that was incidental; he looked very proud when he left the witness stand. Barbara did not ask him a single question.

A laboratory technician was next. Gus Moxon was a stout man with a pale complexion and a very grave demeanor, with deep worry lines in his forehead. He had been in charge of cataloging the items recovered. It had been his responsibility to see that the items were air-dried and that all the water was collected to be analyzed.

Roxbury had him identify the various items: a pair of shoes, socks, underwear, shirt. . . . The articles of clothing were all in separate, tagged plastic bags.

Roxbury finally got to the gloves and had them identified: two pairs of gloves, one leather, one canvas. Then he held up the plastic bag with the lead pipe. There was a profound hush in the courtroom as he described it—hollow, lead, two feet long—and asked Moxon if he had identified it and cataloged it. Moxon said yes after thinking about it for a second.

"And can you tell the court what is in this bag?" Roxbury asked, holding up one more plastic bag.

"Yes, sir," Moxon said. "Detective Ross Whitaker removed those items from the pipe. There's nine pounds of metal washers, two steel key rings, and a piece of nylon line."

Roxbury had a few more questions, and he got the same kind of slow, thoughtful answers.

When Barbara had her turn with Moxon, she asked, "When did Detective Whitaker dismantle the pipe?"

He thought about it, then said ponderously, "We put it in the drying room with everything else until everything was good and dry on Sunday, and then they tried to recover prints, and did other tests, and then he took it apart and I cataloged the washers and key rings and the nylon cord at that point in time."

"Thank you," she said. "No further questions."

The glance Roxbury gave her was deeply suspicious, as if he sensed a trap and could not quite fathom how it would be sprung.

⟡

They ate lunch at Frank's house that day. He had made a pot of chicken soup over the weekend, and he brought out a loaf of good French bread.

"Bailey, are you sure the printouts are still in the hotel safe?' Barbara asked.

"Never sure about anything," Bailey said. "What I know is that Trassi put the stuff in the safe, and the guy who stands to earn a buck hasn't alerted us that he's taken it out again."

Bailey's beeper went off. He cleaned his bowl before he ambled away to the study to return the call.

"Palmer's on a plane heading toward Seattle," Bailey said in the doorway a minute later. He grinned at Barbara. "A herd of guys will pick him up at SeaTac and hang on him like burrs."

"If they lose him, I personally will go on a vendetta," she said. His grin broadened. After a moment, almost absently, she stood up and headed for the stairs, not because she had anything in particular to do up there but because she had to move.

"When she gets restless like that," Shelley said in a near whisper to Frank, "I feel like I should start pacing, too. But I'm too hungry."

The forensics investigator, Detective Ross Whitaker, was a slightly built man in his forties; his hair was black and straight, and he wore eyeglasses with black frames. Neatly dressed in a charcoal gray suit, a blue tie, black socks and shoes, he looked studious and sincere, rather like a Mormon missionary.

For the benefit of the jury Roxbury had Whitaker describe his education, his police training, his specialized forensics training, his duties. . . . Barbara would have been willing to stipulate all this; she knew Whitaker's credentials were flawless. But Roxbury went on and on with him, with numbing exactitude.

They had recovered no usable fingerprints, he said when Roxbury finally got around to the evidence. The water in the bag had trace amounts of blood, and the bloody water had soaked all the items, so that they all had the same traces of blood; the blood was in Mitchell Arno's blood group. There had not been time for DNA tests. They had recovered hair samples, which were not incompatible with Mitchell Arno's hair.

Roxbury tried to get him to state that the hair samples matched Mitch Arno's hair, but he would only say they were not incompatible.

"Did you find hair samples that were not incompatible with Ray Arno's hair?" Roxbury asked.

"Yes, sir."

"Detective Whitaker, why did you take the lead pipe apart?"

"After we examined it for fingerprints and trace evidence, we saw that both key rings had bits of additional trace material wedged in them. We took it apart to examine the key rings more thoroughly."

"Your honor, at this time, I ask permission to show a video we made of the procedure," Roxbury said then.

Barbara objected; she had not seen the video yet. Judge Waldman called for a recess, and she and the attorneys met in her chambers to view it.

On the television screen in the judge's chambers, they watched the scanning of the entire pipe when it was still intact. At both ends large key rings had been used to hold the nylon line in place. At one end the line was unbroken and had been slipped between the coils of the key ring wire; on the other end the cord had been knotted, then the ends burned and fused together to hold the second key ring securely. Whitaker, wearing latex gloves, cut the line to free the key ring at one end. He picked it up with tweezers and put it on a dish, with a short piece of the line still attached. He tilted the pipe, and the washers slid out in a neat row. He pulled the line through the pipe, slid the second key ring off and placed it on another dish.

"There's more," Roxbury said then. "We wanted to reconstruct a pipe to inform the jury of the process, and to show the weapon complete." He looked at Barbara as if expecting an argument. She merely shrugged.

The scene shifted to a desktop that held packages of washers, a length of pipe, a roll of nylon line, and two key rings. Whitaker's hands were ungloved now. He moved swiftly and surely. First he stretched out the line and cut it, then slid a washer on it and centered it, then he doubled the line and slipped it through the holes in one package of washers after another until the line was filled, like a string of beads. The first washer acted as a stopper for the rest. He inserted the string of washers into the pipe far enough that several of them were visible at the other end, and he worked the loop at that end between the coils of the key ring. He pulled the string tight, placed the second key ring on the other end of the line, and tied a knot to hold it in place. He fused the knot with a cigarette lighter and then cut off the excess line. The entire process had taken only a few minutes. The four-pound lead pipe had become a more lethal weapon that weighed thirteen pounds.

"Satisfied?" Roxbury asked smugly.

Barbara nodded. "Nasty," she said. "Very nasty."

When court resumed, it was nearly four o'clock. He would take half a day with follow-up, she thought derisively, and listened to Roxbury inform the jury about the video they were about to see.

Barbara watched the jurors as they watched the video. One of the women began to look ill when the implication of what she was seeing struck her. One of the men, who had appeared sleepy and even bored that morning, had come wide-awake, his eyes narrowed in concentration.

Roxbury resumed questioning Whitaker after the video ended. He showed him various bags, the washers, the key rings, the cord, and finally the pipe itself. "Is this pipe we just saw being assembled like the one you took apart?" He held up a pipe and handed it to Whitaker, who said yes.

"Did you assemble this pipe?"

"Yes, sir."

"Where did you get the materials you used? The washers, pipe, all of the items?"

"At a local home builder's supply house."

"You just walked in and bought all those items, no questions asked?"

"Yes, sir."

"Detective Whitaker, when you examined the key ring on the end of the pipe more thoroughly, what did you find?"

"There were bone fragments wedged in between the coils of the ring. And there were traces of skin tissue and head hair also wedged in the loops."

"Can you determine if the skin tissue is from the scalp?"

"Yes, sir. The hair follicles of the skin tissue indicate that it was from the scalp, and there were three hair fragments, also from the scalp."

"If that pipe had been wielded with enough force to crush the skull of a man, would you expect to see bone and tissue fragments lodged in the loops of the key ring?"

"Yes, sir, I would."

"And that's what you found, bone and skin. Is that correct?"

"Yes, sir."

When Roxbury said he was finished with this witness for now, Judge Waldman excused the jury for the day with her usual strict admonition about talking about the case or watching any news broadcast or reading about it.

Barbara reassured Ray Arno that she would be by later to discuss the day, and the days to come; he looked very gloomy. Then his guard collected him, the spectators began to disperse, and Frank said in a low voice close to her ear, "Your office. We have a visitor coming by around six. Carter Heilbronner."

Carter Heilbronner was with the FBI, maybe the head of the

Eugene office, maybe chief of operations of the entire Northwest; she never had found out exactly what his place in the hierarchy was. And he, no doubt, would want to know how she had managed to reel in R. M. Palmer, she thought with satisfaction.

31

Barbara and Frank talked to Ray briefly in the conference room and then had Bailey take them to her office, where she regarded Carter Heilbronner. He was tall and well built, about fifty, with brown hair and brown eyes, and a crisp no-nonsense air about him. He sat on the couch, crossed his legs, and looked relaxed and reflective. He had said no, thank you, to coffee or wine, to anything she had to offer.

"Ms. Holloway," he said, "your questioning of Mrs. Delancey has stirred up quite a bit of interest. I believe you've never worked in Washington, have you? It's like a big spiderweb. I watched a documentary about spiderwebs once, very interesting and complex structures. If you touch a strand anywhere on it, the vibrations are carried to every strand, and the spider hiding in her corner knows exactly where the original touch occurred, and even if it's something she has to do something about. If it's prey or predator, or too big and threatening, or too insignificant to bother with, even if it's a suitor come calling. Her response to the touch is instant, or so nearly instant as to make no difference. Amazing creatures."

Barbara waited.

"If you get Palmer out here, what are your plans?" Heilbronner asked.

"I'll subpoena him."

"I thought that was the case. Others thought not. So I said, what the hell, I'd come around and ask." Obviously he had not said that; it was not his style, and he even smiled faintly, but he was serious when he said, "You've got the web in motion, Ms. Holloway, a lot of telephone lines are vibrating. You're an unknown factor to most people, of course, but since we did work well to the same ends previously, it was decided that I should ask you a few questions and make a request."

Not quite mockingly she said, "You realize that at this point in the defense case, I may not be at liberty to answer your questions. Do I get to ask questions, also? Or is it to be one-way?"

"Ask," he said. "Of course, I may not be at liberty to answer."

She grinned and settled back. "So ask already."

"Do you have a basis in fact for asking Mrs. Delancey if the Palmer Company moved the furniture? Or was it a wild shot?"

"It wasn't a wild shot," she said.

"I thought not, but others . . . If you get him on the stand, do you intend to bring up her name again?"

She shrugged. "Do you know where Stael and Ulrich are?"

"Yes."

"Are you keeping them under surveillance?"

This time he shrugged. "I would be very careful if I were you." He regarded her soberly. "I must tell you, Ms. Holloway, that if a federal agent advises an individual that certain actions would result in obstruction of an official investigation, that individual would be held responsible if he or she persisted in those actions and did indeed cause an official investigation to go awry."

"I saw that same documentary about the spiders," she said. "Every night the spider rebuilds the web, whether it was torn apart by a stick or any natural event, or hardly touched at all; overnight it gets rebuilt in a virtually identical structure. Isn't that interesting? If you're really determined to be rid of the web, you should step on the spider."

He recrossed his legs and tented his fingers in a contemplative way. "You can't step on this particular spider. All you can do is stir it up and get in the way. Perhaps even suffer a dangerous bite."

"A murder charge or two is a serious effort toward eradication, Mr. Heilbronner."

"You can't make it stick. We're not interested in local murders, as you well know. Go after Stael and Ulrich, and Trassi, if you have the ammunition. I hope you get them. Our request is that you do not subpoena Palmer. And I advise you that we will consider it obstruction if you do." He spread his hands apart, palms up. "Don't start something you can't finish, Ms. Holloway. Any more questions?"

"Am I likely to get any more answers?"

"Probably not."

She spread her hands in a gesture that mimicked his. "No more questions."

"I have one," Frank said suddenly. He had been watchful and very still until now. "Off the subject, I'm afraid. An old friend of mine, Sylvia Fenton, told me an interesting story recently. Seems a con man tried to take her for a big pile and she called bunco. Then, strangely, the FBI asked her to drop the charges. Seems she got to worrying about the con man out there bilking other old ladies, and it's really preying on her mind that she went along with the FBI. She got it in her head that he might be FBI, too, and since he's a crook, someone should know about him. I told her to let it be and I'd see if I could find out anything about it." He looked as guileless as a child. "Carter, she's afraid she made a mistake, and she thinks that guy belongs in the pokey. And Sylvia can be a handful when she sets her mind to it."

Heilbronner's thoughtful expression became as innocent as Frank's. "I'll tell you an interesting story. Confidential, of course. Seems one of the offices back East thought a man had information for them, and they were planning to interview him as soon as he returned home from a trip, but an unfortunate drive-by shooting occurred; he was hit and killed instantly on his doorstep. End of story. Tell your old friend not to worry about him, Frank."

Very gravely Frank said, "I'll tell her his conning days are over. Thanks."

Heilbronner stood up. "I've kept you from your dinners long enough. I'll be on my way. Maybe, with luck, the rain has let up. You know, they expect flooding." He pulled on his raincoat, and they all walked through the hall to the reception room. "Every winter I think I'll ask for a transfer to someplace where the sun shines once in a while, then every summer I think this is the only place to be." They shook hands all around, and he left.

Bailey emerged from Shelley's office.

"You've got to get in touch with Jolin," Barbara said. "Tell him they're investigating Palmer, big-time."

"What we have to do is collect John and beat it to my place and eat," Frank said.

Bailey left to get the car, and she said accusingly, "You know Heilbronner came to find out how much we know, and you practically told him everything."

"But we had to find out how much Gilmore talked," he pointed out. "Not much, apparently, but it set them in motion. Besides, he already knew we were on to Palmer and Delancey. Come on. Bailey must be around front by now."

Frank called Martin and ordered whatever Martin recommended. "Half an hour," he said, hanging up the phone in the kitchen.

They sat at the dinette table, and Barbara filled in Bailey about Heilbronner's visit. "So call Jolin and tell him Gilmore's dead, and they're going after Palmer on the QT. And that Stael and Ulrich are probably in the area somewhere."

"You still want to serve the subpoena?" Bailey asked.

"I have to think about it," she said.

"Well, you've got a little time. His plane was an hour and fifteen minutes late, fog. And Seattle's fogged in tight. Nothing's moving. Palmer headed for an airport motel. He'll be stuck there until sometime tomorrow, more than likely."

Suddenly John spoke. He had been listening silently, not moving, not touching the wine Frank had put before him. "He told you Stael and Ulrich are around?"

"Not in so many words," Barbara said. "But that was the message."

John's face was almost totally without expression; his scar was a pale line, his mouth straight. She knew what kind of effort it took for him to do that, and she reached across the table for his hand. It was unresponsive to her touch. "We expected them," she said. "We thought they'd turn up, remember?"

"Gilmore's dead; two killers are loose out there; Palmer's on his way. When do the fireworks start?" he said tonelessly. "How many more bodies do we get to count? What's the score to date?"

Bailey stood up. "Use the study phone?" he asked Frank, carefully not looking at Barbara or John.

"Help yourself," Frank said, also standing. "I aim to set the dining room table."

They both left the dinette, and Barbara pulled her hand back from John's. "You know we're taking precautions," she said. "Do you have any suggestions to add to what we're already doing?"

"You can't guard against a drive-by shooting or a bomb or a guy on a roof with a rifle. I had a suggestion months ago; you chose not to listen."

"I told you then why that wouldn't work; nothing's changed. If I'd told them, they wouldn't have Major Works or Jolin, or Gilmore, or the other company back East, or the Palmer Company connection. They'd have Maggie and Ray, period." She shook her head. "I can't change anything now, it's done, and I'm on the roller coaster until it stops."

"I know you are," he said softly.

The doorbell rang, and he stood up. "That's probably Martin. I'll catch a ride home with him. You have work to do here; I have work to do there."

Frank admitted Martin, and they took the food to the dining

room. Barbara walked to the front door with John. Neither spoke now. Martin came back and said sure, he'd be glad to give John a ride, and they left together.

When she got home to the apartment that night, it was after eleven; Alan Macagno was reading a book in the living room; John was in his office, with his door closed. She went into her own office and closed the door behind her.

"Detective Whitaker," Barbara asked the next morning in court, "would you say that some of the tests you ran were inconclusive?"

"Not really," he said. "We put in a lot of overtime on that material."

"I'm sure you did," she said. "But you said earlier that you could not do DNA tests because of time limitations. Is that correct?"

"Yes."

"And all you could say about the hair samples you found was that they were not incompatible with Mitchell Arno's hair, and neither were they incompatible with Ray Arno's hair. Is that correct?"

"Yes."

"How does a person pick up hair samples from someone else, Detective Whitaker? Do you have to use their comb, for example?"

"No. If you brush against someone, or sit in their chair or their car, you might pick up hair fragments. They're all around, even floating in the air."

"I see. From testimony, we know that Mitchell Arno was in Ray Arno's house for a period of time. Would you find it surprising that he had picked up some of Ray Arno's hair on his clothes?"

"No."

"Did you find other hair samples that were not similar to either Ray or Mitchell Arno's hair?"

"Yes."

"Did you try to match them with anyone else's hair?" He said no, and she asked why not.

"Because there's no way of knowing when or where they were deposited on any of the material."

"How many different types of hair did you find?"

"Five."

"And they are all unidentified? Is that correct?"

"Yes."

"You also said that you found no usable fingerprints. Does that mean you found some that you could not identify?"

"Yes. Not complete prints, just smears, and some partial prints."

"Did you try to identify the partial prints?"

"I tried."

"Where did you find those partial prints?"

"On the washers."

"How many fingerprints did you recover altogether from the washers?"

"Seventeen partial prints."

"And you examined each washer individually?"

"Yes."

"Did you try to match those partial prints to Ray Arno's fingerprints?"

"Yes, I did."

"And could you make a match with any of them?"

"No, there wasn't enough to work with."

"Did you try to match them to anyone else's fingerprints?"

"No."

"When you tried to match them to Ray Arno's prints, did you think you had enough to work with?"

"It was a long shot, just a faint possibility, so I tried."

"Did you try to make a composite print? Put two or more of the partials together to try to obtain a complete fingerprint?"

"Yes, I tried that."

"And it still didn't match Ray Arno's prints, is that right?"

"I didn't even know if I had partials of the same finger," he said.

"My question was: Did the composite print you assembled match Ray Arno's fingerprints?"

"No, I couldn't match it."

"And did you try to match it with anyone else?"

"No."

"So all you were interested in was matching your partial prints to Ray Arno's fingerprints, wasn't it?"

Roxbury objected; it was overruled.

"That isn't the case. I would have sent it to the FBI lab if I had recovered enough for a positive identification," Whitaker said.

"You stated that you had forensic training with the FBI. Is that correct?"

"Yes, I did."

"Isn't if a fact, Detective Whitaker, that the FBI labs can take partial fingerprints and make a composite print that then can be used for identification purposes?"

"If they have enough material to work with."

"Is that a yes answer?" she asked coolly.

"Yes."

"Did you send your partials to the FBI to see if they could do that in this instance?"

"No."

"Why not?"

"I didn't have enough for them to use."

"But you thought you had enough to try it yourself at one time, didn't you?"

"I tried."

"Did you think you had enough that you might get an identifiable composite fingerprint?"

"It was a faint possibility, that's all."

"Is that answer yes, Detective Whitaker?"

"Yes, I thought I might have enough."

He hadn't lost his detached, neutral demeanor, but she knew she had pricked him. "How long would it take for the FBI laboratory to report back on such a task, making a composite print from partials?"

"I don't know," he said.

She had him describe the procedure: photographers would take pictures and enlarge them, then fingerprint experts would try to match whorls and ridges in a complex jigsaw puzzle.

"You wouldn't expect a report overnight, would you?" she asked then. He said no. "In a week?" He said no.

"When did you recover the partials?" she asked then.

"A few days ago," he said.

"Please, let's be precise," she said coldly. "You had to let everything dry before you began your examinations. You had to go out and buy the materials to assemble a facsimile of the pipe. You had to have a photographer and a video cameraman come in. Is all that correct?"

"Yes."

It took time, but she got him to admit that he had recovered the partial prints Sunday evening at about seven or eight o'clock. He had gone out to eat while the photographer made the enlargements, and had worked with them from about nine until after midnight.

"So you spent a few hours at a job that FBI technicians might spend weeks on, and you decided you couldn't make a match with Ray Arno's fingerprints. Whose decision was it not to send the material to the FBI lab to see if their technicians might have more success?"

"It was my decision," he said flatly.

Slowly she walked to her table and stood by it, then asked, "Detective Whitaker, if you had recovered those partial prints back in September, or even October, would you as a matter of routine have forwarded them to the FBI laboratory for possible identification?"

Roxbury objected, and this time his objection was sustained.

"Is it a matter of routine forensic investigation to forward partial fingerprints to the FBI for possible identification?" she asked deliberately.

"Sometimes we do, yes."

"What determines the instances when you do?"

"If the identification is crucial to a case, we would send them in usually."

"And you decided without consultation that those partial prints were not crucial to this case? Is that what you're telling this court?"

"I decided there was no point in sending them in, yes."

She regarded him for a second; then she went to the evidence table and picked up the pipe he had assembled.

"You described in great detail what you found in the key ring at one end of the pipe. Was there any material, any trace material at all, in the other ring?"

While he didn't really refuse to answer any of her questions, it took a long time before she got him to say the material at the other end of the pipe had been leather, pigskin, and that it was discolored not so much by the stains from bloody water as from age and wear.

Before the lunch break, Judge Waldman summoned Barbara and Roxbury to the bench, and asked somewhat wearily how much longer Barbara planned to take with this witness.

"Your honor, I'm sorry, but you can see how it's going with him. I need a shoehorn to pry out basic information." She glanced at Roxbury. "You could speed things up by telling him to stop dodging, no one's after his scalp."

"You're just picking apart every word of his testimony," Roxbury snapped.

"I'll keep picking away," she snapped back, "until we hear the full report of his findings, all the things he conveniently left out in direct."

Judge Waldman shook her head at them both. "Mr. Roxbury, it would be helpful if your witness would simply answer the questions more directly." Then she said to Barbara, "And I hope you will finish with him before we adjourn today."

As if to emphasize her point about time, she allowed only an hour for lunch, an hour Barbara spent pacing back and forth from her office to the reception room.

Whether it was because Roxbury spoke sharply to him, or he simply foresaw many more hours of cross-examination looming, Detective Whitaker stopped dodging that afternoon and answered her questions directly.

He stated that the canvas gloves and the leather gloves were new, both size large. As work gloves they were readily available. The leather gloves were cowhide, and he had found traces of pigskin in two seams of the leather gloves.

"Detective Whitaker," she asked, "would it be fair to say that the person who wore those leather gloves handled the same object that left pigskin traces in the key ring?" He said yes.

"Can you speculate, based on your experience, what that object might have been?"

"Yes," he said to her surprise. "I believe it was a handgrip for the pipe."

"Are you familiar with such an object?" He said yes, and she asked, "Did you find such an object in the plastic bag?"

"No."

She held up the pipe he had put together. "Would it fit over the end of the pipe and be tight against the edges?" He said yes. "Would you expect the sharp edges of the pipe to fray the pigskin?"

"it might get worn down that way," he said cautiously.

"You testified that the pigskin fragments indicated that the pigskin was old, discolored by age, not merely stained by water and traces of blood. Would you say the pigskin handgrip had been used more than once on a pipe such as this one?"

Roxbury objected finally, and it was sustained.

She worked around the objection, and Whitaker admitted that the fragments of pigskin had been frayed and worn thin, and the discoloration was due to both age and staining by lead.

It was nearly four-thirty when Barbara thanked the witness and sat down. Roxbury went directly to the problem of the handgrip.

"Is it not possible that such a grip would be useful for other purposes? Such as at the end of a sickle for cutting brush and weeds?"

"Yes, it would work for that."

"Or even as a grip for a fishing rod?"

"Yes."

After Roxbury was finished with his redirect examination and Whitaker was dismissed, Judge Waldman asked Roxbury if he had another witness.

"May I approach?" he asked. Wearily she beckoned him and Barbara to the bench. "I have another witness," he said in a low voice.

"You've got to be kidding!" Barbara exclaimed.

"Who?" the judge demanded.

"An FBI agent, to explain more fully about partial prints and composites," he said.

Judge Waldman said, "No. If you have concluded your case, the state may rest at this time. We have heard quite enough about composites and partial prints to understand the matter."

"Your honor," he said, "she's left the jury thinking Whitaker shirked his duty, that his investigation was less than thorough. I don't believe that's a fair assessment, and it's misleading and prejudicial—"

"Rest your case," Judge Waldman said.

32

When Barbara, Frank, and Shelley left the courthouse, Barbara could not suppress a groan. Fog eclipsed Skinner Butte; it hid the upper floors of the Hilton Hotel, it pressed down on the bank under construction across the street and wrapped the world more distant than a block away in ghostly shrouds. Lights were haloed everywhere, sounds muted. The fog was insidious; no clothing could keep it out. It was cold and penetrating, chilling to the bone. Bailey was at the curb, with the Buick door open, a scowl on his face.

"John said for us all to come up to the apartment," Bailey said at the car door. "He's got a surprise." He sounded only marginally less gloomy than Barbara felt.

As soon as they were inside the car, and Bailey was waiting for a chance to enter traffic, Barbara asked, "Where's Palmer?"

Bailey took his time answering. The traffic was creeping as if following invisible tentacles that had to test each inch of road ahead. "Vancouver, Washington," he said after making his turn off Seventh. "Nothing's moving from the North Pole down to the middle of California. Fog all the way."

John's surprise was dinner: his specialties of green chili and cheese enchiladas; do-it-yourself tacos, with many bowls of various fillings; a beautiful salad with green and red peppers and slivers of red onions, white mushrooms, and black olives; black beans and rice. . . . He was as anxious and nervous as a newlywed serving in-laws their first meal in his house.

Cornering him in the kitchen, Barbara whispered, "Thanks."

"Can't compete with your old man," he said, "but I hated the idea of your being in and out of the fog all night."

She kissed him. "It's wonderful."

The first witness to be recalled the next morning was the medical examiner. At first glance it appeared that Dr. Tillich was a frail old man, but that was deceptive. He was going on seventy, but he was sinewy and muscular without a trace of fat, a runner who ran a mile every day. As he regarded Barbara through thick lenses, his attitude suggested that he had not been surprised in fifty years, and didn't expect to be surprised now.

"Dr. Tillich," she said, "good morning." He nodded. "I won't keep you long today," she said. "There are just a few points I'd like to clarify. Have you had the opportunity to review your report, refresh your memory?"

"I have."

"In your report you wrote that Mitchell Arno's death could have occurred anytime between Sunday night, August fourth, and before noon on Tuesday, August sixth. Is there any scientific or medical reason for choosing one of those periods over another for the time of his death?"

"There's no reason to pick one over another."

"Dr. Tillich, is it usually possible to tell how long before death the victim has eaten a meal? And even what that meal had consisted of?"

"Often that is the case. However, where serious trauma is inflicted, the digestive process slows or even comes to a stop in some cases."

"Based on your autopsy findings, can you tell us what Mitchell Arno's last meal was and how long before his death he ate it?"

"Not precisely. The stomach contents indicated a meal based largely on meat protein, partially digested, as it would have been during a two- to three-hour period following consumption. There was little further digestion following that, indicating severe trauma had occurred. Also, he had been drinking beer, within minutes of the severe trauma. It had not been assimilated to any extent."

"Later, in your report, you wrote that based on the amount of swelling present and internal hemorrhage present, you estimated that his right arm was broken and that he suffered the injury to his testicles two to three hours before death. Is that correct?"

"It is."

"So, he had his meal, then two or three hours later he was drinking beer when he was attacked, and two to three hours later he died. Does that sum up the times correctly?"

"Yes, it does."

"Would the initial attack, the breaking of his arm and the trauma to his testicles, have caused unconsciousness?"

"More than likely. He would have been in shock and incapacitated, at the very least."

"In your original report you provided drawings of the wounds on Mitchell Arno's feet. Do you recall that?"

"Yes, of course."

"I'd like to go into more detail about those lacerations and other wounds at this time," she said. He had included the injuries in his report; no one had referred to them when he first testified. Now she picked up his drawing from her table and showed it to him. "Is this the drawing you made of Mitchell Arno's feet?" He said yes, and she turned to the judge and said, "Your honor, I had an enlargement made of this drawing, and would like Dr. Tillich to use it in order for the jury to see more clearly what he is talking about."

Shelley set up an easel and placed the enlarged drawing on it, several views of both feet. Dr. Tillich left the stand to position himself before the drawing, then used a pencil as a pointer as he explained his marks.

"I'll start with the heels," he said. "Here, there are two cuts on the left heel in the upper region." He had found slivers of glass from a lightbulb in both heels, but only two had cut through the skin.

Barbara stopped him to ask if those cuts had bled, and he said yes, a little.

Then he said concrete dust and particles were embedded in both heels.

The soles were both embedded with slivers of fir bark, the sort that comes from bark mulch; there were several bruises where the deceased had stepped on sharp gravel, and there were bits of cedar splinters in both soles. The upper parts of the toes and the tops of the feet had splinters of cedar, and several deeper lacerations from gravel cuts, and they had fir splinters and embedded dirt.

"Did those wounds on the toes and upper fleet bleed?" Barbara asked.

"No. They occurred after death."

"From the nature of the lacerations and the glass cuts, can you surmise how the deceased received those wounds?"

"Yes. He was dragged through the glass and then over concrete. The cuts and the embedded concrete are in parallel lines, and concrete dust was on top of the glass fragments. Then he was dragged after his death, facedown this time, across rough cedar, flooring maybe, and over fir bark mulch and peaty dirt. Again, all the lacerations and cuts are in parallel lines. He walked through the bark mulch and gravel, and his weight caused the gravel to bruise his soles."

She thanked him and asked him to resume his seat. After he had done so, she asked, "When you perform an autopsy, do you also examine the deceased's clothing?"

He said yes, and explained that he would look for holes, entrance or exit holes for bullets or sharp weapons, for possible tears that would help explain and identify various wounds.

"What did you find on the deceased's clothes?"

"The lower legs, the bottom three inches in the back of the jeans, had slivers of lightbulb glass, and some concrete dust. The front of the jeans legs, the lower three inches, had embedded cedar, fir bark mulch, and dirt. There were slivers of cedar on the front and the back of the jeans and the shirt."

"Dr. Tillich, if the deceased had been conscious and struggling, would you expect the cuts on his heels to be parallel?"

"No," he said promptly.

"How high would you need to lift an inert man in order for the lower three inches of his jeans to scrape the floor, and only his heels to show signs of being dragged?"

Roxbury objected that this was beyond the scope of the doctor's expertise. No one knew the condition of the deceased at that time. His objection was sustained.

"Dr. Tillich," Barbara said slowly, "in your previous statement, you said that the deceased's hands were burned after his death, and that the flames had reached as high as his wrists. Is that correct?"

He said yes.

"Was flesh and skin sloughed off his wrists or hands?"

"Where they were in contact with the floor when they burned, some tissue sloughed off," he said. "And there was a small track of tissue two inches long trailing from one hand area."

"What about the rest of the cabin? Any burned tissue anywhere else?"

"No."

"As a medical examiner, do you sometimes try to reconstruct the events at a homicide to clarify in your mind the sequence of actions, how it might have happened?"

"Yes, I usually do that."

"Can you do it for the jury in this instance? There is a dead man lying facedown, with his hands outstretched over his head. How could you lift him in such a way that only the tops of his feet drag on the floor, in such a way that you don't slough off the burned tissue from his wrists or hands, in such a way that his hands, necessarily dangling down from his body, avoid contacting the floor? Can you reconstruct that scenario, Dr. Tillich?"

Roxbury had started objecting halfway through this, but she persisted to the end. For the first time, Judge Waldman used her gavel, not a heavy-handed banging, a tap only.

"Object!" Roxbury said furiously, red-faced. "Same grounds as before. Beyond the scope, not his expertise."

"But it is within his scope," Barbara said coldly. "This is what he often does, as he stated, and this time we do know the condition of the man being moved. He was dead."

During this exchange Dr. Tillich leaned back in his witness chair, frowning thoughtfully. Waldman overruled the objection.

Before Barbara could repeat the question, Dr. Tillich said, "I don't know how one person could have moved him without leaving a trail of tissue and blood."

"Could two people have done it, one grasping each arm, lifting him under the armpits?"

Roxbury objected on the grounds that it was sheer speculation. The objection was sustained.

"Back in your autopsy room, having only the evidence of the dead man and his clothes, during your attempt to reconstruct what had happened at the crime scene, did you surmise that more than one man had moved the deceased?" Barbara asked.

Roxbury objected, but this time Judge Waldman allowed the question.

"Yes," Dr. Tillich said. "That was my first assumption."

Barbara nodded. "In your original testimony you stated that you could tell approximately how long before death the deceased had suffered various injuries. His broken arm, for example, had time for a great deal of swelling to take place, and the fingers were swollen to a much lesser extent. Is that correct?"

"Yes."

"Did he have blood under his fingernails? Could you tell?"

"I examined them; there was no blood."

"Would the deceased have been able to use his hands in a meaningful way at the time he received the final, fatal blow?"

"The right hand, absolutely not; the left hand, I doubt it."

"Would he have been able to grasp a stick or any other object and write his name with his left hand?"

"It would be most unlikely."

"Just one more detail, Doctor," she said then. "When you examined the deceased, did you find any teeth marks or claw marks on his leg or on the jeans?"

He said no, and she thanked him and sat down.

Roxbury came on hard then. The doctor was not at the scene when the deceased was injured and moved, was he? He couldn't know how the defendant handled the body, could he? Hadn't he seen domestic pets, cats and dogs, carry objects, move them, play with them, leaving no teeth marks?

Barbara kept thinking she had laid the first stone in the structure she had to build.

After a brief recess, the next witness was Detective Gil Crenshaw. He had been one of the detectives sent to search Ray's house and car. He was a heavyset man in his thirties, with blond hair so pale that it looked white. It was cut short, in almost a skinhead effect, and he squinted as if he needed glasses.

Barbara had the schematic of Ray's house placed on the easel and now pointed to it. "Detective Crenshaw, you testified in some detail about your search for additional bloodstains, out here on the back patio, along the stepping-stones to the garage, and in the garage itself. Did you examine the front walk?"

"We looked it over," he said.

"But did you give it the same kind of painstaking examination you gave the other areas?"

"I looked it over and didn't see anything."

"Did you test it with chemicals the same way you tested the garage and stepping-stones, and the patio?"

"No, I didn't."

"Why not?"

"The defendant said they always used the back entrance, and that's a long walk around the front to the driveway. It didn't seem likely that he would have dragged the victim all that way when it was so much closer to a car from the back door."

The house was laid out in such a fashion that the front walk from the driveway passed two bedrooms, then the living room, to the main entrance. The garage was detached and set back even with the edge of the patio, and reached by slate stepping-stones from a redwood deck and patio. Barbara pointed to the drawing of the house and garage, then asked, "Would a stranger to the premises be able to tell how much closer the car would be to the back entrance? It isn't evident from the road, is it?"

Roxbury objected, and his objection was overruled.

"You'd have to walk around it to tell," the detective said.

"Is that front walkway concrete?" He said yes. Then she asked if there was concrete anywhere else on the premises.

"The garage floor is concrete," he said.

She picked up his report and asked politely if he could summarize his findings regarding the garage floor.

"There wasn't any blood," he said.

"In your report did you state that the floor was dusty and dirty, with old oil stains, and no evidence of having been disturbed for a long time?"

"Yes, I wrote that."

"All right. Did you fingerprint the house?"

"No, we didn't."

"Why not?"

"It wasn't the crime scene. And the defendant admitted his brother had been in the house. There wasn't any point in it."

"Did Ray Arno tell you he found evidence of a scuffle when he returned home from the coast that weekend?"

"Yes, he said that."

"But you determined that no crime had been committed there. Is that correct?"

"We knew the cabin was the crime scene," he said doggedly.

"Did he tell you his father's house had been broken into over the same weekend?"

"Yes, he told us that."

"Did you investigate the break-in?"

"I asked his father some questions."

"Did you fingerprint his house?"

"No."

"Why not?"

"They had changed the locks, there wasn't anything to find there. Too many people had been in and out."

"Did you remove the vacuum cleaner bag from Ray Arno's house?"

"We did."

"What did you find in it?"

"Just the usual dust and stuff, and a little bit of glass."

"Glass from a lightbulb?"

He said yes.

"Did you remove a shovel and a garden spade?"

He said yes.

"Did you find any forest duff, forest dirt, or fir needles on either of them?"

He said no, and she quickly went down the list of things they had not found: no lighter fluid, no charcoal starter, no bloody clothes, no shoes with forest dirt embedded in them, no pigskin handgrip, no plastic sheeting. . . .

"Did you remove a gasoline can with approximately a gallon of gasoline in it?"

"Yes, we did."

"Why?"

"We knew an accelerator had been used on the victim; we didn't know yet if it was gasoline or something else."

"Did you notice a lawn mower in the garage, or a tractor in the barn?"

"Yes."

"Yet you thought a can of gasoline might be incriminating? Is that what you're telling us?"

"I thought it might be evidence," he said. He was squinting at her, ignoring the jury, and he looked a little flushed. He was so fair that any flush at all on his cheeks was apparent.

"Did you search Ray Arno's car?"

He said yes, and she asked him to tell what he had found. A gum wrapper, a boy's sock, a soda can, some comic books, a library book, the usual tire tools and spare tire.

"After you removed those items, did you proceed to vacuum the car?" He said yes, and she asked him if he found bits of glass from a broken lightbulb, forest dirt, fir needles, bark mulch, forest duff, trace evidence of plastic sheeting, or blankets. He said no to each item.

She asked if he found bloodstains, and he said no.

"Detective Crenshaw, in your entire search did you find any incriminating evidence?"

"Yes, the bloodstains in the family room."

"When you questioned Ray Arno, did you consider him to be not only the prime suspect but the only suspect in this case?"

His flushed deepened perceptibly. "No. We never make an assumption like that."

She shook her head at him, then said to Roxbury, "Your witness."

"Detective Crenshaw," he said briskly, "on what day did you question the defendant and search his house and car?"

"Saturday, August tenth."

"And on what day was the deceased killed?"

"Early morning, on Tuesday, August sixth."

"Was the defendant alone in his house during those intervening days, to your knowledge?"

"Yes, he was."

"With plenty of time to get rid of incriminating evidence?"

"Objection," Barbara said. "Speculation."

It was sustained.

"Were there any visible signs of a struggle in the house—broken furniture, forced entry, anything of that sort?"

"No, sir."

"If the deceased had been wrapped in a plastic sheet, something of that sort, would you expect to find traces of blood in the car? Or anywhere else?"

She objected; there had been no evidence of the use of a plastic sheet or anything of that sort.

"You brought it up," Roxbury snapped.

"Only to indicate that there was no evidence of such a thing," she said calmly. "If I had brought up a teleportation device, would you now suggest he might have been moved with it?"

Roxbury wanted to argue about it, but evidently the judge didn't want any more argument; she sustained the objection and almost brusquely asked the prosecutor to get on with it.

He was surly when he asked the detective, "Do you know how the victim was transported from the defendant's house to the cabin?"

"No, sir, I don't."

As soon as he was finished with the detective, Barbara said no further questions, and Judge Waldman recessed for lunch.

The fog had not lifted: it was even denser than it had been earlier, and everyone was edgy. Palmer was still holed up, Bailey said, no planes were flying, little traffic was moving. There was a mammoth pileup on I-5 down around Medford. A bright spot was provided by Patsy Meares, who had ordered duck soup, along with potstickers and spring rolls with shrimp filling. She ate with them that day, as reluctant to go out into the fog as Barbara was.

Lieutenant Stacey Washburn had been the lead detective in the case, heading the joint special homicide investigation team made up of county and city detectives.

Washburn looked hungry; he always looked hungry. He was lean with sharp features, and black hair and eyes. His teeth were bad, which might have accounted for his hungry look; they were crooked, and his bite probably was terrible. Frank said rumor had it that because his temper was fierce, the only way he could testify in court was by taking a tranquilizer first. In the witness chair he appeared relaxed and at ease now.

"Lieutenant Washburn, during your investigation of the murder of Mitchell Arno, did you become aware that he had carried a large sum of money into the state?" She could hear a ripple like a collective sigh pass through the spectators; this was the first mention of money in the case.

"Yes."

"When did you learn about the money?"

"Back in August. I don't remember the exact date."

"In your testimony you stated that Mitchell Arno had been driving a Lexus automobile that had been wrecked and recovered by the police in Corvallis. Do you recall that?"

He snapped his answer, yes.

"Did you go to Corvallis at any time to inspect the automobile?"

"No. I talked to the officers by phone."

"Did you interview Mr. Stanley Trassi, the attorney representing Mitchell Arno regarding the large sum of money?"

"Yes."

"In person?"

"Yes."

"Did you talk with R. M. Palmer, the man Mitchell Arno was working for?"

"Yes, by telephone."

"Not in person?"

"No. He's in New York."

"Did you request a sworn deposition from Mr. Palmer?"

"No. I took his statement over the phone."

"Do you know when the Lexus was repaired and released to Mr. Palmer's representatives?"

"No."

"Were you aware that fingerprints from Ray Arno's house had been collected and delivered to the district attorney's office?"

"I learned about them."

"Did you do an independent check on those fingerprints?"

"No."

"Did you do a follow-up investigation of the men identified through those fingerprints?"

He said no, more sharply.

"When did you become aware that such fingerprints existed?"

"Back in September sometime."

"Perhaps we can refresh your memory for exact dates. In your report you state that you talked to the Corvallis police officer on August tenth. And it says that you talked to Mr. Trassi about the Lexus on August twelfth. And on September second you learned about the fingerprints. Are those dates in your report correct?"

"If they're in the report, they're correct."

"All right. So you knew a very expensive automobile had been wrecked, possibly stolen, and that Mitchell Arno had been wandering around on the coast. Did you at any time consider a different reason for the murder of Mitchell Arno than the one you proceeded to pursue?"

"No. His business had nothing to do with his death, that was our conclusion."

"On August twenty-sixth you learned that a large sum of money might be involved in the case. Did that make you consider a possible different motive for the murder?"

"No."

"Then, on September second, you learned that two unknown men had left fingerprints in Ray Arno's house. Did that make you reconsider his story about possible intruders, and about his father's statement that his house had been broken into as well?"

"No."

"At any time from the moment you entered the case until the present did you consider an alternative suspect?"

"We considered all those other things and decided they were not relevant."

She nodded. "So your attention was focused on Ray Arno from the start, and you did not allow yourself to become distracted by anything that might conflict with your first assessment. Is that correct?"

He said no, it was not. He was angry now, but still controlling it. "There are always false trails that have to be looked into, false leads, and we investigated them all."

"But not to the extent of obtaining a sworn deposition from Mr. Palmer, or examining the Lexus in person. Did you ask the Corvallis police to make a thorough search of the automobile?"

"No. They reported that they had looked it over. I didn't see any need to do anything else about it."

"Do you know who collected the Lexus after it was repaired?"

"No. The car wasn't part of my case."

"I see." She went to her table and picked up a photograph of the shallow grave near the cabin. It was one of the first pictures that had been taken, and showed the grave and one foot exposed quite clearly. She asked him if he recalled it. He said yes.

"Did you find any evidence of an animal? Any footprints or droppings, anything of that sort?"

"No, we didn't."

"Yet in your report you stated that it was obviously the work of an animal. Why did you conclude that, Lieutenant?"

"In my experience," he said coldly, "I've found that that's what an animal would do. It smells blood and digs for it."

"Then why didn't it dig in the area where there was a great deal of blood? That's the right foot exposed, isn't it? Wasn't the only blood from the head wound, and a trace amount on the left heel?"

Roxbury objected that she was piling on questions and not giving the witness a chance to respond. Judge Waldman sustained the objection.

Barbara didn't belabor the point, but moved on to the name scrawled in blood inside the cabin. She produced the photograph and showed it to the lieutenant. "Did you have an enlargement made of this picture in order to study it more thoroughly?"

He had not done that.

"I did," Barbara said. She found the enlargement on her table and showed it to him, then to the judge and Roxbury, and had it admitted. "Lieutenant Washburn, those letters were scratched into dried blood, weren't they?"

"I don't know how dry it was," he said. "We know it was not flowing any longer."

She pointed out the flaking and cracking, and the fact that the blood had not flowed back into any of the markings, and he admitted that it had been dry when the letters were written.

"Yes," she said. "Further, whatever was used to write those letters made scratches in the wood floor, didn't it?"

He said yes, the floor had been marked.

"Would that have been a metal object? A nail or a key, possibly the point of a knife, something like that?"

"I don't know what was used."

"Did you find a nail or key, or even a sharp stick, with blood on it?"

"No."

"Would it have taken a bit of strength to scratch through the dry blood hard enough to mark the flooring?"

"Not much," he said. "The cedar's old and soft."

"Would a man with a broken arm and broken fingers on his other hand have been able to do it, in your opinion?"

"Yes, certainly."

"Would a dead man with a broken arm and broken fingers have been able to do it?" she asked scathingly.

He tightened his lips and Roxbury objected stridently. Judge Waldman frowned at Barbara and told her to rephrase her question.

"You heard the testimony that the head wound was the only wound to produce blood, and that the head wound was instantly fatal, that the brain stem had been broken, his skull crushed. He had no awareness, no cognitive function; he was dead. Are you telling us it is your opinion that he survived long enough for the blood to dry first, and then he scrawled his name in it with a sharp object that then disappeared?"

"That's how it must have happened," he said darkly.

She shook her head. "You mean that's how it had to have happened for your scenario to work, don't you?"

"Objection! She's arguing with the witness."

Very coldly Barbara said to Washburn, "You gave three possible reasons for burning the deceased's hands after he was dead. You said, first, to mutilate the body. Was the deceased's face marked, his nose broken, teeth knocked out, anything like that?"

"No. His face was untouched, except where it came in contact with the floor."

"Were there any other signs of mutilation on his body, not connected with the beating he received?"

"No."

"All right. Then you said possibly it was to torture him. Are you still of that opinion? That you can torture a dead man?"

"The killer might not have known he was dead at that point," he said.

"With his head crushed in as it was?" she said incredulously. "All right. Then you suggested that the killer might have wanted to burn down the cabin, hide the evidence of the crime through arson. With all the incendiary material around the cabin, would anyone have tried to burn it down in that grisly fashion?"

"Nobody sane would," he said harshly.

"I agree. Lieutenant Washburn, did you consider a fourth possible reason for burning his hands? That the killers might have wanted to obliterate his fingerprints?"

He shook his head. "No. That didn't seem reasonable."

"Did you consider a possible reason for sparing Mitchell Arno's face, his mouth and nose? That someone might have wanted information from him?"

"No."

When Barbara was finished, Roxbury had Washburn restate that they had investigated the business that had brought Mitchell Arno to Oregon, and they had concluded that there was no connection between that and his murder. Everything to the contrary was simple speculation.

Then Roxbury said, "Lieutenant Washburn, you've had many years of experience in police work. During those years do you recall instances when the perpetrators of crimes left incriminating evidence behind in a way that looked as if they did it on purpose in order to be apprehended?"

"They do it more often than people suspect," Washburn said. "Either consciously or unconsciously."

Barbara objected. "This is really getting into the area of abstract speculation," she said. "Philosophy 101."

"I agree," Waldman said. "Sustained. Move on, Mr. Roxbury."

"Would you find it surprising if the perpetrator and not the victim had scratched those letters, that name, in the blood in the cabin?" Roxbury asked, with a sly glance at Barbara, as if awaiting her objection, now that his point had been made.

Since his point was exactly the one she intended to come back to, she held her peace.

"I would not find that surprising at all," Washburn said.

After Washburn was dismissed, there was a brief recess, and then the last state witness to be recalled came forward. He was a police officer from Corvallis. His testimony had been brief and not very informative earlier. Today he looked a little nervous, as if he was afraid he had been found negligent somehow.

She smiled reassuringly at him. "Officer Trent," she said, "I have just a few questions for you. Do you recall the incident of the wrecked Lexus and the subsequent events?"

"Yes, ma'am."

"You testified that you went to the garage to inspect the car, and you found the title transfer in the glove compartment. Was the glove compartment locked?"

"Yes, ma'am. The officers who found the car said it was locked up, so I took a locksmith with me, and he got it open."

"You testified that you then called Mr. Palmer in New York. Did you reach him?"

"I left a message on an answering machine, and he called me back in fifteen minutes, at seven-thirty our time. Ten-thirty his time. He told me the car was supposed to go up to Washington State somewhere, and he wanted to know about the driver, if he was okay. He said his lawyer, Mr. Trassi, would come around to take possession of the car."

"When the car was in the possession of the police, did you make a thorough search of it?"

He looked puzzled, then shook his head. "No, ma'am. We looked in the trunk, just to make sure it wasn't carrying something illegal. After I talked to Mr. Palmer, it seemed like it was a legitimate delivery arrangement. No one had been hurt, and the guy who had driven it must have walked away after he ran into a tree. No one filed a complaint and it didn't seem like police business, more like insurance business."

"All right. When Mr. Trassi arrived, did you go with him to inspect the car?"

"Yes, I did. I had to make sure it was the right car, and he didn't know the town, so I went with him."

"Was the car locked when you went with Mr. Trassi to inspect it?"

"Yes, ma'am. We couldn't get inside, but he said it was the right car, and he had the license number and some papers that Mr. Palmer had faxed to him. I was satisfied that the Palmer Company was the owner, and he was their lawyer."

"But Mr. Trassi didn't have a key for it, is that right?"

"No, he didn't."

"Where was the car at that time, Officer Trent?"

"In a lot we use up in Corvallis, the back lot of a mechanic's shop. Mr. Trassi said he would have the car towed to a repair shop, and I told him it was in the best one in town, and he decided to let them fix it there." He added, "Besides, nothing was open anyway, it being on a Saturday. That's when he said he'd just leave it where it was. He didn't want to hang around and see to having it towed on Monday."

"Could the car be driven at that point?"

"No, ma'am. Looked like the left front wheel was bent, and the radiator was leaking pretty bad, and the left headlight had to be replaced. They had to order parts."

"But the damage was all to the exterior, is that right?"

It was clear that he was puzzled by her questions, but he answered readily. "As far as I could tell, the inside was in near perfect shape, except the radio and CD player were gone."

"Thank you, Officer Trent," she said then. "No more questions."

He was surprised and evidently relieved. Roxbury had no questions, and Officer Trent was dismissed.

Judge Waldman told the jurors again not to read about the case or watch television news concerning it, not to talk about it, and then she wished them all a Merry Christmas, and announced the court would recess until December twenty-sixth.

⟡

33

"What I thought we might do tomorrow," Frank said in the kitchen, preparing dinner, "is put up a tree and decorate it. Those damn-fool cats are old enough now to leave the ornaments alone, I hope." Last year, as kittens, they had undecorated the tree repeatedly and joyously.

"We should put our tree up," Barbara said. John had bought a tree, which was standing in a bucket of water in the storage space under their stairs.

"Is it really true that criminals, perps," Shelley asked, "often leave really incriminating evidence behind?"

"You bet," Frank said, slicing a beef filet into strips. "This guy goes into the bank and passes a note to the teller, the usual thing—I have a gun, give me money. She gives it to him and then gives the note to the police. It's on the back of one of his own deposit slips."

"Another guy goes into a jewelry store," Bailey said then, "and while he's waiting for another customer to get finished and skedaddle, he's playing with his car keys like there's nothing on his mind. So he takes a bag full of diamonds and stuff out and leaves the keys on the counter. Then the poor sucker goes back for them, and the clerk says he has to go to lost and found, and he walks to the back of the store and into the arms of the cops. True," he added.

They were all laughing by the time Frank told another story. "A guy bashed his wife in the head and put her behind the wheel of the family car and pushed it off a cliff, perfect accident. Except he took pictures of the whole thing and turned in the film to a local processing company to have it developed."

No one drank much of the wine; Barbara had several hours of work ahead, and so did Shelley, and Bailey was antsy about Palmer in his motel in Vancouver. He hadn't asked again if she still planned to subpoena him if he entered the state, and she still hadn't made up her mind. That was something they had to discuss after dinner.

After they finished eating, John volunteered for kitchen duty. "You all have to have your conference," he said. "I'll clean up."

Barbara suppressed a smile at the "you all." Every once in a while his Southern roots poked through, not often, but when he addressed a group, there it was, not slurred as one word exactly, but close enough to betray his origins.

He began to busy himself in the working part of the kitchen, and Bailey asked bluntly, "What do you want us to do about Palmer?"

"What do you think, Dad?" Barbara asked.

"Heilbronner's a good man," he said. "I don't think he'd steer you wrong. The real problem that I see is if you implicate Palmer without enough to make it stick, he will squirm free, and he might drag Trassi out with him. A confused jury is not a pretty sight when you've got a defendant depending on you." He paused, and she waited. "As of today," he continued, "you've probably got Ray off the hook, but the question is, if you try to go too far, will the jury decide you're throwing dust in their eyes? Palmer might be that kind of distraction for them."

Barbara nodded slowly. She turned to Shelley, whose eyes had grown very round as she listened to Frank.

"Do you think Ray's really off the hook?" Shelley asked.

Frank answered, "She laid the foundation today for serious doubt in their minds, and she'll build on that foundation day by day. Reasonable doubt, remember, is all it takes, and what she's giving them and will keep giving them is a tad more than just reasonable doubt. It would be a mistake to undo that doubt, maybe, by trying to do too much."

What she really wanted was to hang Palmer along with his henchmen, Barbara thought, but she had to agree with Frank.

She said, "If Trassi comes to think that Palmer is making him a sacrificial lamb, what are the chances he'll do something drastic?"

"Turn state's evidence? Something like that?" Frank asked. "Hard to say. The way it looks to me is that he's so deep into Palmer's business, there's little chance he can just walk away from it. But if the feds want to deal? I don't know. He's too much an unknown player, not like Gilmore. He was pretty predictable."

Barbara was aware that John had stopped moving in the kitchen, that he had become as still as stone. And this conversation had taken a turn that was reminiscent of the talk they had had months earlier concerning Gilmore.

Decisively she said to Bailey, "Tell your people not to serve the subpoena. We may still want it later, but not now."

They continued to discuss the case, and Barbara was aware that John had become busy again in the kitchen, and she was aware later when he went to the living room, where he would read until they were through.

When she went to bed that night, John was waiting for her. They made love in silence, with an intense and terrible urgency.

The next morning she waited until she heard Alan leave before she wandered to the kitchen in her robe and slippers. John was reading the newspaper at the table. He put it down when she walked in.

"Still foggy?" she asked, helping herself to coffee.

"More than ever."

She shivered. "Yuck." She put bread in the toaster. "I wonder if *yuck* is just a euphemism for *fuck.*"

"Barbara, we have to talk," he said quietly.

She sat down opposite him, feeling as if the chill fog had entered the apartment, after all. "I know."

"From what I heard last night, you can get Ray off now with what you have. You don't need to drag in Trassi and Palmer."

"I can't go partway and then stop."

"You mean you won't."

She shook her head. "Put whatever slant you like on it. I can't do it."

His face twisted into a grimace; he was not hiding that morning. That was more frightening than if he had become stone-faced. He was letting her see a dangerous side, a dark and mean side. "Won't you try to see it the way I do?" she asked in a low voice. "I can't just say maybe two other guys did it and not give the jury more than that. Ray wouldn't be free of suspicion. It would follow him forever, even if we got an acquittal, and there's no guarantee that we would."

"I've been trying to see it your way from the beginning," he said angrily. "My eyesight's failing me, though. All I can see is you on a personal crusade of some kind." He rubbed his hand over his eyes, as if had meant that literally. "Your job is to get Ray off, but you're forcing Trassi and Palmer into a corner without a clue about how they'll react. They're killers, for God's sake! I can't bring my kids into this mess, put them in jeopardy. You know that."

"I do know," she whispered. "John, I'm sorry. God! I'm sorry."

Abruptly he jerked up from his chair and crossed the room, then with his back to her he said, "I'm meeting them in L.A. I'll take them to Disneyland or something, camp out, go to the desert. I don't want them in Oregon for even a second, not with those two killers on the loose. I called Betty and arranged a different flight for them."

"Can't you just postpone their visit?" she asked after a moment. She felt stunned, shocked into mindlessness.

"To what end?" he demanded, facing her now. "I can't tell them to forget it and we'll make it up later. They're in school, remember? Spring break? God only knows what you'll be mixed up in by then." He rubbed his eyes again. "You don't need me hanging around. I'm just in the way here. But my kids need me, and I need them."

She wanted to protest, to cry out that she needed him desperately, more than his kids did. They had their mother and each other and a loving stepfather. She wanted to reach for him and hold him, to explain that she had not planned this, had not wanted it to happen this way. She felt that even language had deserted her; there were no words to express what she wanted to tell him. When she found her voice, she was surprised at her own question, not one that she wanted to utter. "Will you come back?"

Now his face became expressionless, rigid with control. "I need a little time to think," he said. "I may drive on up to Canada after they leave."

"You're driving? When will you go?" It wasn't panic, she thought bleakly; it was desolation, despair, misery that made her voice sound strange.

"I couldn't get a flight on Christmas or Christmas Eve, and I have to be there by four on the day after Christmas. That's when they're due in. I can't risk a delayed flight then. I have to drive down. I'll leave in the morning, give myself plenty of time to fight the fog most of the way."

She stared at him. He had made plans, made preparations, called his ex-wife. . . .

"Aren't you going to say anything?" he demanded. "No more explanations?"

She shook her head.

"Then hear me out," he said harshly. "I wondered at first if you were doing this on purpose, to test me, make me choose. You built your case on a big lie, and if you had played it straight from the beginning, we wouldn't be here like this now. But you had to play the avenger, you and your bloody sword. I don't really think you did it deliberately, cornered me to force a choice, but it happened. You crossed that line, and you're still on the wrong side, scheming, conniving, covering one lie with more lies."

"Just hold it a minute," she said furiously. "I didn't put Mitch in Ray's house and I didn't send two murderers there after him. And I sure as hell didn't assume that one brother killed another, and then put on blinders to everything that pointed somewhere else.

The day the law treats the Ray Arnos exactly the same way it treats the Trassis and the Palmers, then you can talk to me about morality, but until then, just shut the fuck up!"

"You keep saying things like that, but the way I see it—"

She was on her feet without being aware when she had risen; she was at the hall without being aware when she had moved. "Let me tell you something," she said icily, interrupting him. "At this moment I don't give a shit how you see things. If I had butted out, Ray would have been arrested anyway. Nothing I could have said or done would have prevented that. The state had an easy win, and they weren't going to mess around looking for complications. He would have been found guilty of murder preceded by torture. That's the reality. He probably would have gotten the death penalty. That's how the real world works when you're a nobody. But your cozy little Christmas with your children would not have been bombed out. Well, get your ass on the road, beat it down to La-la Land, and have yourself a dreamy vacation. Don't let reality get in the way."

"Goddamn it, Barbara! Can't we even talk about it!"

"No!" She was at the end of the hall. "You don't have the authority to pass judgment on me or what I do. You don't know shit about how justice works in this country. Just fuck off!"

She stepped out onto the landing, and she saw Bailey at the bottom of the stairs. "I'll be ready in half an hour," she snapped. She went to her bathroom and closed and locked the door. Then she started to shake.

It was a day just like the rest, she told herself that afternoon; she had more work than she could get through, more reports to read, more testimony to study, more pretrial statements to go over than she had time for. The days would be okay. And dinner with Frank, Shelley, and Bailey, that was okay, normal. Then more work to do; but after that, the long nights.

At four-thirty she had Bailey drive her home, planning to change clothes and then go to Frank's to help with his Christmas tree.

"I'll wait," Bailey said in the car, gazing straight ahead.

She didn't blame him. He had not referred to the scene he had overhead that morning, and she knew he never would, but he was uncomfortable now, and would be more uncomfortable if another scene started in his presence. Bailey was very proper in many ways; domestic problems alarmed him, and he would go to great lengths to be somewhere else when one occurred.

The apartment felt empty, deserted. On the table was a large gift-wrapped box. The card had no name, simply the words in John's precise writing: *I love you.* Moving as if the box contained something very fragile, she picked it up, carried it to his office, and put it on his desk, then walked out and closed the door.

PALMER

34

"Of course," Frank muttered to the Things, "he couldn't bring his kids into this mess." He had known for days that John had a tough decision to make, but he had reasoned that he would simply put off his kids until after the holidays, after the trial was over, and then he and Barbara would take off for a delayed visit. He suspected Barbara had thought the same thing.

An awkward moment had come when she said that was enough work for the night, time to go home. Hesitantly Frank had suggested that she could move a few things over, use her old room upstairs, and she had looked distant and unapproachable. "Too much trouble," she had said. He knew from past experience that she would not talk about it, not now, maybe never.

They were all as jumpy as cats, although at the moment the two cats on the floor looked about as jumpy as bricks. Thing One had rolled over on his back, all four legs sprawled out in impossible angles, and Thing Two was draped partly across him, playing dead. But until the fog lifted, until they knew something about what

Palmer was up to, where his stooges were, what plots were being concocted behind closed doors, the people involved would be on edge, and Barbara would be over there alone most of the time.

On Friday afternoon Barbara, Shelley, and Frank were discussing the batting order of the witnesses; Bailey was waiting for their final decision, not bothering to take notes yet. He would be in charge of getting witnesses to court. Some of them, he had warned, would rather go fishing. Barbara's phone buzzed and she crossed the office to get it; Patsy would not have put a call through unless she thought it important.

"Barbara," Patsy said, "there's a man on the line who said to tell you he's calling from Vancouver, and that you want to talk to him. Do you?"

"Yes indeed. Thanks, Patsy." She covered the mouthpiece and said, "Palmer."

He came on the line and said hello when she said, "Holloway." Frank came to her desk and she held the phone away from her ear for him to hear.

"Ms. Holloway, I understand the fog is lifting. I want to know if you intend to subpoena me if I set foot in your state. If you do, of course, I'll stay on this side of the river, but I really have some business to discuss with Mr. Trassi, and this is an awkward situation."

His voice, lilting, mellifluous, charming, sent a chill through her. He sounded almost amused.

"I won't subpoena you," she said.

"Mr. Trassi tells me I shouldn't trust your word, but, Ms. Holloway, I do. I have given a good deal of thought to the various aspects of our dealings and I have concluded that you don't actually tell falsehoods, although you may curl the truth around the edges a bit—but don't we all? To demonstrate my trust, I'll even tell you my travel plans. I shall drive down there with a companion, and register at the Hilton when we arrive. I have a reservation, of course. Then, after a bit of refreshment, may I call you again, to arrange for a brief face-to-face meeting? I find it helpful to talk in person whenever possible. Don't you?"

"We can arrange to meet," she said.

"Good, good. Has the fog lifted in your area? I understand driving can be difficult and slow in the present conditions. But never mind. We will drive slowly and with great care. Until later, Ms. Holloway. Tomorrow, possibly." He paused, then very smoothly he said, "It may be late when we arrive. Would you mind if I call you at this number?" He gave Frank's telephone number. "Yes, probably that would be best." He hung up.

Frank returned to his chair near the ornate coffee table, and Barbara leaned back in her desk chair. "Well," she said. "Well, well." She was icy. He knew Frank's number.

"I'll wire you," Bailey said.

"No way. He's not a dope. He'd never fall for that. Did you notice that he didn't say anything actually? Do you suppose he really trusts me to keep my word about the subpoena?"

"Maybe," Frank said. "In any event, I doubt a subpoena would hold him if he wanted to leave. Then, safely out of the state, maybe out of the country, he'd fight it with a pack of attorneys based in New York."

"Well," she thought, rising, "back to work." An hour later, after she had explained exactly what her game plan was, and which witnesses she wanted early and why, they were interrupted again. This time Patsy said Mr. Heilbronner was in the outer office.

Frank's eyes narrowed, and he said to Shelley, "You and Bailey better head for your office. Carter doesn't like an audience. I'll go fetch him."

Barbara felt the same anger that Frank had revealed. Those sons of bitches were bugging her telephone! When Frank left to bring Heilbronner back, she went to her desk and sat behind it.

Frank and Heilbronner came in, and she motioned toward the chairs. "Good afternoon, Mr. Heilbronner," she said coolly. "What can I do for you?"

He looked taken aback at her tone. He sat down and crossed his legs, regarding her. Then he said, "We're not tapping your phone, Ms. Holloway. His? That's different."

"In any event, it's still my private conversation that got put on a tape somewhere."

"Sorry," he murmured. "Would you consider a wire?"

"No. What else?" The last thing she wanted was for the FBI to tape a private conversation between her and Palmer, she thought savagely.

"Ms. Holloway, from his comments, I take it that you've had dealings with Palmer before."

"I've spoken to the man one other time in my life," she said coldly. "And you probably know about that conversation. He wanted me to release Trassi." She suspected that Palmer had used a secure phone for the first call; he had said too much not to have taken precautions.

"His remarks suggest there's more than just releasing Trassi on his mind," Heilbronner said. "What did he mean, you curl the truth around the edges?"

"Mr. Heilbronner, you have the records with our dealings concerning Maggie Folsum and Internal Revenue. You know very well that I had to request certain documents that ultimately came from Palmer, through Trassi. At present I am in the middle of a defense case, and I don't have time to involve myself in your investigations."

"I understand," he said. "I would like a formal interview with you following your conversation with Palmer, however."

"And I am at liberty to refuse your request."

"You are, but it could be to your advantage not to do so."

"Carter," Frank said then in a conciliatory tone, "when we find out when and where she'll meet him, we could let you know and you could drop in at the house for a glass of wine afterward. Christmas cheer, that sort of thing. Certainly not a formal interview, just a friendly chat."

Heilbronner was watching Barbara; she shrugged. "That would be pleasant," he said. "Yes, I'd like that." He stood up. "I know you're busy, sorry to interrupt. I'll expect a call."

Frank walked out with him.

When he returned alone, she demanded, "Why?"

"Because he knows where Ulrich and Stael are," Frank said. "And God help us, we don't."

Palmer's call came at eight that night. Barbara waited for the answering machine to take it, then picked up the receiver. "Holloway," she said.

"It wasn't a bad drive at all," Palmer said. "In fact, the hills were quite lovely wreathed in vapor, very picturesque. I'm afraid it has closed in again, however. Perhaps we could meet at the reception desk at the hotel here at eleven tomorrow morning? Quite public and open. We can decide then where we can share a cup of coffee and have a quiet conversation. Is that acceptable, Ms. Holloway?"

"I'll be there."

"Very good. Don't worry about paging me or anything. I'll recognize you. Until eleven. Have a pleasant evening."

"Eleven, Hilton front desk," she said after hanging up. Bailey nodded. He would have his own crew on hand, she understood, and he would be there himself, but she really didn't want to know the details.

Bailey had already reported on Palmer's arrival, at six-fifteen, with a Ms. Fredericks, who Palmer had said was his secretary. He had a suite; she had a single room on a different floor. Palmer had met Trassi in the bar, where they had a short talk and a drink, then both had gone back to their own rooms, where they remained. Trassi had ordered dinner in his room for one; Palmer had ordered for two. Trassi had not yet removed anything from the hotel safe.

That night she dreamed she was driving a very large truck with more gears than she knew what to do with; she was driving too fast when a deer appeared on the road ahead. She manipulated gears, but the truck simply sped faster and the deer did not move. She groped for the brake pedal and couldn't find it, then she got on the floor to search with her hands for the brake. She was speeding faster and faster, and ahead the deer gazed at her with luminous red eyes and did not move. She came wide awake, shivering, sweating. She was clutching her rock, the rock John had given her nearly a year ago.

She put it down on the bedside table and groped for the clock, turned it so she could see the hands. These nights she had been facing it away, not willing to register the time—two o'clock, three, four. . . . It was five after five. She got up to go to the bathroom, get a drink of water, wipe her sweaty face. Alan came to the hall almost instantly when she left the bedroom.

"It's only me," she said.

He withdrew, back to John's apartment, John's living room.

When she returned to bed, she again faced the clock away.

At eight Jory Walters relieved Alan. If Alan looked like one of the youths who always seemed to be hanging around at the mall, or riding a bike around town, Jory would be at home in a group of football linebackers. She had never heard him utter a sound that wasn't in direct response to a question; he simply nodded that morning and settled down on the couch with a newspaper. He had brought hers up as well, and she settled at the table with coffee and her own newspaper, and they read in silence.

At fifteen minutes before eleven they left the apartment and Jory drove her to the Hilton. He drove around the hotel to enter the underground parking level, where he could pull up within a few feet of the back entrance. Another escort opened her door and hustled her inside swiftly, then walked by her side up the stairs to the ground level, past the many convention rooms, a large lounge with a dozen or more groups of comfortable furnishings, couches and easy chairs with only a few people occupying them, although a lot of people seemed to be drifting aimlessly about.

As they approached the reception desk, a man in a dark suit turned her way, then walked toward her. "Ms. Holloway, good morning. I'm Palmer."

She knew he was fifty-two, but he looked younger, with curly auburn hair and blue eyes with a lot of crinkly smile lines, and very white teeth. He was trim, with a salon suntan. He didn't offer to shake hands, but his smile was broad, as if he really was glad to see her.

"Good morning, Mr. Palmer," she said, as pleasantly as he had spoken.

"Since the fog has come back so densely, and it is such a cold and dismal fog, I suggest we have our talk here in the hotel. Perhaps in the big lounge you passed on your way in. Or there's a coffee shop, a little noisy and crowded, but it would do."

"The lounge is fine."

"Good. You pick the chairs, since I more or less picked the setting. Fair enough?"

She nodded, and led the way to a couch and chairs with a coffee table, situated almost in the center of the big room.

"Don't you want to take off your coat?" Palmer said to Barbara. "I'm afraid this hotel, like so may of them, overheats the space terribly."

She took off her raincoat, and he was at her side helping her instantly. Holding the coat, without glancing around, he motioned to someone. A woman strolled to them. "Ms. Holloway, Ms. Fredericks," Palmer said. "She'll be happy to hold your coat for you, and your purse, if you don't mind. Not far away, and not for an instant out of sight, certainly. Just over there."

Barbara shrugged and handed the woman her purse. She was blond, in her forties, and had on too much makeup. She was dressed in a severe black skirt suit, with shiny black boots to her knees. Wordlessly she took the coat and purse across the lounge and sat down.

Barbara sat down, and Palmer sat across a table from her.

"Your maid travels with you?"

Palmer shook his head, smiling. "Not even my secretary, just a private investigator I hired for the occasion. She assured me that she could tell if you had a wire on your person, something about earrings, or a necklace, possibly a lapel pin, or buttons. I trust her to know her business, but I feel I must ask anyway: Are you wired?"

"Of course not. Are you?"

He laughed. "No, my dear Ms. Holloway."

"Mr. Palmer," she said, "another time, when I am not engaged in a trial, perhaps we can meet over tea and crumpets and have a nice cozy conversation, but at present I really am quite busy. What do you want?"

"Tea and crumpets," he said musingly. "My accent, of course. My mother would have tea and soda bread, and my father the crumpets. Irish and English, they fought constantly. I wanted to see you in person. Your photographs don't do you justice. I'm afraid Trassi is not a very good judge of women; he described you as a dragon lady. I like dealing with women, personally. Charm and business do mix quite pleasantly. I want to retain you, Ms. Holloway. I pay extremely well, and the work would be negligible, but it would be comforting to know you're on hand if needed. Perhaps for only a year, perhaps longer. We could talk later about renewing our relationship. One hundred thousand dollars for one year."

She studied him thoughtfully. "You know I'll turn you down, and then what? Subtle threats?"

"Yes, I know," he agreed, smiling again. "I'm a bit fey, you see. A legacy from my mother, I imagine; she was never deceived in her life to my knowledge. What do you want, Ms. Holloway? Everyone wants something; everyone has something he or she wishes to keep. What do you want?"

"I want Trassi, Stael, and Ulrich."

"I see. Suppose I hand you Stael and Ulrich."

She shook her head.

"Do you have enough to get them on your own? I rather doubt it."

"I have what I need."

"But not enough to go after me? How unfortunate for you, how lucky for me." He leaned back in his chair. "My father was a simple man, Ms. Holloway. He had a truck and he moved people, not far usually, from one address in Brooklyn to another, sometimes all the way to the Bronx, or even Staten Island. It was very hard work. And it was a pain. People complained that a waffle iron was missing or a chair was scratched, petty details that were annoying, over and over. Together we changed direction, thirty-one years ago it was. We became specialists. Over the years the business has become very successful. I can move anything and do, and I never ask questions about the origin of what I move. I feel strongly that it's not my business to inquire; I'm not a detective agency. But over the years I have come to have a reputation for reliability, you see. I insure what I move, and I deliver. Always." He sighed. "A reputation is a precious commodity, Ms. Holloway, as I'm sure you're aware. But something quite strange started happening in the past few months. Quite strange, indeed. My staff has suffered certain losses, not irreplaceable, but still, bothersome. And a customer is starting to get very anxious about a delay in a certain shipment, and not only that, but the entire question of confidentiality has arisen in an irksome manner."

Briskly Barbara said, "Mr. Palmer, I told Trassi what I wanted at our first meeting. He delivered, and so did I, exactly as we both agreed. What has come up between you and him since then does not concern me. I have not breached the confidentiality of our transaction, and I don't intend to. When we first talked, you and I, I told you what I want: Trassi, Stael, and Ulrich. That has not changed, and I won't need to go into a matter that is concluded as far as I'm concerned in order to get them."

"You can't have Trassi," he said then, his voice flat and very cold now.

"I already have him," she said. "If he skips, an arrest warrant will be issued and he will be brought back to face a contempt charge. Of course, he understands this quite well. He'll never work as an attorney again, and whatever problem you have with him you will have to solve without me. Now, I really do have things to do. Such a busy season, you know."

"Ms. Holloway, I made you an offer. I'll deliver Stael and Ulrich with whatever you need to convict them. I doubt you have enough to do it without help. But, understand, turnabout's fair, now, isn't it? I can also offer you to them, don't you see?"

She laughed. "Not very subtle, after all, Mr. Palmer. You know very well that too many others are in possession of my facts." She stood up.

"I cried like a baby when my mother died," Palmer said softly. "I was eighteen. My father was very embarrassed by such a display, of course, being English as he was. When he died, I was thirty, and I wept again. The Irish are very sentimental, I fear. How Irish are you, Ms. Holloway? I can see the English in you, but Irish? I wonder if you would weep in public as I did."

35

Half an hour later she, Frank, and Carter Heilbronner sat in Frank's study with the drapes closed and few lights on, as if this really were a friendly get-together of old pals.

"He wants me to release Trassi. He offered to exchange Stael and Ulrich, with whatever evidence I need to nail them, for his favorite attorney," she said. "He threatened me, and he threatened my father. What more do you want?"

Heilbronner was watching her closely, and she appreciated now the reason Frank had arranged the lighting as he had. Her face was in shadows. She had washed her hands, but she felt an almost irresistible urge to go wash them again, harder.

Heilbronner was sitting comfortably, his legs crossed, his hands at ease on the arms of his chair. Frank was in his old brown chair that was gradually falling apart, and she was in a wing chair with a high enough back that she could rest her head against it. Heilbronner brought his hands together and steepled his fingers.

"Ms. Holloway, I need a little information. For instance, why did Palmer go along with your scenario and release that money to Ms. Folsum? That would be a good place to start, I believe. I've read all the statements and talked to Mr. Chenowith at Internal Revenue, and, frankly, it doesn't really work. Does it?"

"I can't divulge confidential matters that concern my client," she said. "But I can tell you another story that you may find interesting. Then we can come back to that. Agreed?"

He nodded.

"Years ago," she said, "young Marta Chisolm and her husband, Joel, moved to New York City. His mother hated Marta and was very upset with the marriage. Following the death of her husband, she became depressed and relied for a time on sleeping pills, tranquilizers, and alcohol. Then Joel said that his marriage was over, that he was coming home to live with her, and she dropped the dope and booze overnight. She changed her will, leaving a fortune in antiques and an expensive house to him, with the expectation of having him with her once more. Marta and Joel came to town for him to obtain a loan from his mother, and oversee the change in the will, and to confirm that the marriage was ending. Sometime during the next two weeks something happened to Joel's mother, and she once more turned to drugs and alcohol, and this time she overdosed and died. Joel came into a very large inheritance, as well as the house and the antiques. Then he was shot and killed, and Marta was very rich."

When she paused, Heilbronner said coldly, "None of that is news. What are you getting at?"

"Marta was restless with her rather dull husband," Barbara said, as if he had not spoken. "She had met a man named Palmer, and no doubt at that time he was devastatingly charming and irresistible. What I'm suggesting is that she, with Palmer's help, planned to kill Joel's mother as soon as possible after she changed her will. Marta was in the house long enough to substitute something deadly, or maybe simply too potent to be taken with alcohol. Also, I'm suggesting that, back in New York again, she called her mother-in-law and said forget it, no separation was taking place, Joel would never return to Eugene, she would never even see her grandchild. Then she waited for the inevitable, which came about as planned. Soon after that Joel was shot and killed by unknown assailants."

Heilbronner wanted to speak, but she held up her hand and said sharply, "Wait a minute. What I'm suggesting is that someone could find the original inventory of those antiques, as well as the original insurance policies that covered them; both of the other children had copies, and so did their lawyer. That someone could find the appraisal, and the auction records, and find out how much of what was inventoried was actually sold then. A real investigation might reveal that Palmer sold a lot of priceless antiques privately at some later date and pocketed the money. His payment. And from that time to this, Marta Chisolm Delancey has been his to use when the occasion arose." Very softly she said, "It must be extremely important to get Trassi off the hook, for him to use such a big card in such a small case as the Arno murder."

For a time Heilbronner didn't move. Then he tapped his fingertips together almost delicately, it seemed. "Can you impeach her, beyond question?"

"Yes."

The silence lasted longer then, until Frank said meditatively, "I think the question now is, If you hook Calpurnia, do you also snag Caesar? Interesting little problem, isn't it? Carter, I suggested coffee a while back. Maybe now's a good time to reconsider."

"Coffee would be good," Heilbronner said.

His face was turned toward Barbara, but she felt certain he was not seeing her. Frank left and they were both silent for a time, until Heilbronner said, "You don't have an iota of proof, I take it."

"Adding one plus one plus one; local gossip; a good dose of intuition and guesswork; end results," she said. "And perjury."

Frank returned with a tray. "Way I see it," he said, "a map's worthless unless you know two things—where you stand, and which way is north. But if you know those things, then it's dot-to-dot child's play. I don't keep up with politics the way I should, I'm afraid. I wonder how many committees Delancey's on, how much power he's gained in the past fifteen or twenty years. Cream?"

Heilbronner rose and walked to the window, pulled the drape aside, and stood gazing out.

Barbara accepted a cup of coffee from Frank, watching Heilbronner. After a moment she said, "You've read the statements and findings; you know I agreed to pursue Mitch Arno for his ex-wife and recover long-past-due child support. I did that, and as far as I'm concerned, that whole matter is history. At present, my only concerns are staying alive, keeping my father alive, and exonerating Ray Arno. He is a textbook example of an innocent bystander."

Heilbronner let the drape fall back into place and turned once more; he went to the table and added cream to a cup of coffee, then sat down. "I understand," he said almost absently. After another moment he focused on her again, sipped his coffee, then said, "One of the theories that has arisen, Ms. Holloway, is that you or Maggie Folsum found the money along with something else that had great importance to Palmer, and that you used the other item or items to force him to deal. This suggested that it was not his own money, of course; he would have been more reluctant to relinquish his own money. But, as you say, the past is done, history. He recovered his item or items, you accomplished your mission for your client, and it's over. Theories come and go, but we have the official record, statements, the IRS final agreement, and I see little profit in trying to ferret out each and every detail of historical incidents."

Then Frank said bluntly, "Carter, there are a couple of little items that do need clarifying. Where are Stael and Ulrich? Palmer has made threats; they're his hired guns. Be nice to know where they are."

"Yes," Heilbronner agreed. "They were not very high-priority, I'm afraid. I don't know where they are. In Oregon, last seen in Portland, over a week ago. I'm afraid we've been more preoccupied with the senator's wife, and the reason for her appearance here, than with Palmer's hired hands."

Frank nodded. "Seems to me that there's been a lack of attention to several things. Losing a guy back East to a drive-by shooting; losing two ex-cons who are about to get accused of murder. One way or the other Trassi is dead in the water. I hope, Carter, that when all the bodies are laid to rest and the dust settles, Mr. Palmer isn't going to be the only one to walk away untouched. I trust there's no one with a vested interest behind the scenery manipulating priorities, making decisions about what is or isn't important enough to keep an eye on. You know, someone in an oversight position second-guessing fieldwork."

Heilbronner's face was expressionless. He set his cup down and got to his feet. "It's been informative and interesting talking to you both. Thanks. I'd better be on my way. I know you have work to do, and so do I. Fieldwork can be demanding—Saturdays, Sundays, holidays, no letup. Communications break down; people in the head office are out partying while you're in the field slogging away. I'll be in touch."

He shook hands with Barbara, then left with Frank, talking about the fog, about Christmas shopping still to do, about nothing.

Later that day she moved into Frank's house. Whether she was trying to protect him or be protected in his house didn't matter.

"You think you can't possibly get through the days sometimes, but then the day's over and you did it," she whispered that night to Thing One, who was half on her lap and half on the couch. He grunted when she spoke. Both Things grunted a lot, the first cats she had ever heard make that particular noise deep in their throats, as if trying to speak. She stroked the cat and watched the fire, wishing for tomorrow, wishing for Christmas to be over.

Frank came in, trailed by Thing Two, and sat opposite her; the other cat tried to get into his lap. It was grunting, too.

"Rain's moving in," Frank said. "Maybe that will be the end of the fog for a time. Sylvia asked us over for eggnog and a cookie tomorrow. I said okay. I'll eat the cookie and drink the eggnog, and you can tramp around her hills in the rain. Deal?"

Tomorrow, Sunday. "Sure," she said. "Sounds good."

And so she got through Sunday; Sunday night, tired from climbing hills in the rain, she slept undisturbed by dreams. You do get through the days, she thought. You really do.

She worked Monday, and most of Tuesday, Christmas Eve. She visited Ray on both days, and, strangely, she felt almost envious of him; in jail over the holidays, his family pretending a cheer they couldn't be feeling, yet he was enduring the season in better shape than she was. She could envy him his faith, she thought, and envy his big family that was so supportive and comforting, even if they all talked at once.

Frank spent most of Christmas Eve in the kitchen, preparing dinner for Shelley and Bill Spassero, and Bailey and his wife, Hannah. A party, Barbara thought bleakly, putting on a long skirt and cashmere sweater, her party clothes.

Christmas night she stood in her upstairs room at the window, gazing at the city lights through the rain that continued to fall steadily. She had thought John might call, then had decided there was little point in it. What could either of them say, except "Merry Christmas"? And tomorrow, back to court, back to the real world. What a long holiday. Then, looking at the lights shimmering through the rain, she whispered, "Merry Christmas."

Court was not filled to overflowing that morning, the day after Christmas. No doubt, the usual hangers-on would wander in eventually, but the media had lost interest again since there were reports of flooding in the valley, and the immediacy of floods at the holiday season would make for more human-interest features than a humdrum murder case, at least for now. After the lunch recess, they would be back, Barbara knew. The jury was not happy to be in court again—that was evident from some dour expressions. Tough, she thought, and called her first witness.

Douglas Herschell was in his thirties, prematurely balding, a stocky man with a large open face and a good-natured grin. He was a machinist, he said, at a chicken-processing plant in Pleasant Hill, fifteen miles south of Eugene. He lived on Stratton Lane with his wife and a seven-year-old son.

Quickly Barbara led him to the first week of August. "Please tell the court what was different about that week," she said.

"Yes, ma'am. We were putting in new machines and we had to be on hand earlier than usual, by six in the morning, every day from the fifth of August until the middle of the month. It was hard because I had to get up at four-thirty and leave the house at a quarter after five. I was late the first two days," he said, then grinned sheepishly.

"What time did you leave the house on those two days?"

"Five-thirty."

"On the morning of Tuesday, August sixth, you left your house at five-thirty in the morning, knowing you were going to be late for work. Did you speed a little?"

"Probably did," he admitted.

"What kind of car were you driving, Mr. Herschell?"

"An eighty-nine Toyota Tercel," he said promptly.

"And what color was that car?"

"Gray."

She showed him the picture of fifteen gray hatchback cars, and he pointed to his. She had him initial it, had it passed on to the jury, then said no more questions.

Roxbury picked at him, but he didn't change a word.

Moving right along, Barbara thought, and called her next witness, Sally Arno. Sally was thirty-nine and married to James Arno, Ray's brother. Blond and dimply, a touch overweight, she had the contented expression of someone not obsessed with appearance. Her hair was showing touches of gray, and she was leaving that alone, obviously not concerned.

"When you and Lorinne Arno prepared a lot of food to take out to the family reunion at Folsum, why did you do the cooking at your house instead of hers?"

"Well, she had been painting and cleaning most of July, she does that in the summer when school's out—she's a teacher, you know—paints her cabinets, waxes the floors, cleans everything when school's out, and I said it would be a shame to leave a mess for Ray to deal with." She smiled at Ray, then at Lorinne, sitting among the spectators. "And we knew we'd leave a mess. Someone would have to clean it all up, and I was going to be home, but she was taking her kids down to Gold Beach to visit her folks right after Maggie's party. So I said let's get together at my place and cook, and I'd have all the next week to straighten up again and she wouldn't have a mess to face when she got home again."

Two of the women on the jury were looking at Sally with understanding; they knew what it meant to leave a mess for a man to clean up.

"Did Ray Arno pick up your husband, James, and the two of them drive to the coast together that weekend?" She said yes, and that they had arrived before nine-thirty.

"Do you recall the spring of 1978?"

"Yes, very well."

"Will you please tell the court what was going on with the Arno family in April that year?"

"James and I were engaged, and Ray and Lorinne were, too, and none of us had any money. David and Donna were married by then, and they were really broke. And Mitch never had a cent in those days, and Maggie was pregnant. I mean, things were tough. Then Papa Arno said he knew about a fishing boat that was good and sound, and he could buy it at a really good price, but it needed a lot of work; it had been let go a long time, I guess, and it needed varnish, parts replaced, woodwork redone—just a lot of work. He said if the boys wanted to do the work, he'd buy the boat and they could fix it up and he'd sell it, and they could keep all the profit. We were all trying to save up a little, and the boys jumped at the chance. So starting on the last weekend in March and every weekend in April, we all headed out to the coast and worked on the boat."

Barbara let her ramble on and tell it her way without interruption. One weekend, she said, Lorinne had called to say her car was having a problem with the brakes and she wouldn't be able to drive over. Everyone else was there already, and Mama Arno said that since Mitch wasn't doing a lick of work on the boat, he could drive to Corvallis and pick up Lorinne and bring her over; then Ray would drive her home again on Sunday night. Mitch drove Ray's car and got her.

"Do you know when they arrived, what time it was?"

"Yes, before dinner, and we ate at six."

"What happened the last weekend of April, or the first weekend of May? Do you recall that time?"

"Yes. We were done with the boat, it was the first weekend in May that we didn't have that on our minds anymore, and we were all going camping, David, James, Ray, Lorinne, another couple of friends, and me. Lorinne had to work late, until nine, but she said for us to go on and get the camp set up and she'd drive over as soon as she got off work. That same day, Mitch called me and asked if I'd lend him some money. He said he was in trouble, he'd borrowed money from a girl, and her father threatened to throw him in jail if he didn't pay her back right away, but I didn't have any money to lend him and I said so. Anyway, Lorinne showed up at the campsite and she told me that Mitch had asked her for a loan, and said the same thing, he was in trouble, and he said he'd go to Ray for it if she couldn't help out. She said she worried what it would do to Mama Arno if he got in more trouble, and of course, Ray would have told her, so she gave Mitch fifty dollars."

"Did Mitch pay back the money, to your knowledge?" Barbara asked.

"No. In fact, that was the weekend he took off altogether."

"Do you recall what time Lorinne arrived at the campsite that night?"

"Yes. It was about an hour's drive, and it was pretty dark, so we were watching for her, and she showed up by ten. Then we ate and played cards and like that."

When Roxbury did his cross-examination, he tried to back her down about dates and times, but she simply wanted to explain things more fully.

Two down, Barbara thought when she did her redirect, and then thanked Sally and excused her.

After a brief recess, she called Walter Hoven. He had not wanted to testify and resented being called, and had been furious about being served with a subpoena. He was sick, he had said angrily, and he had nothing to tell the jury anyway, and it was a fucking waste of his time.

He was sixty-one, heavyset, with a permanent frown that had been fixed so long, his face had become rearranged with deep scowl lines.

"Mr. Hoven, where were you employed in the fall of 1978?" she asked politely.

"Valley Warehouse," he snapped.

"What was your position there?"

"Manager."

"Where was the warehouse?"

"West Seventh Place."

Bit by bit she drew out of him a description of the area at that time, a warehouse district across the road from fields, with the train tracks not far away, railway sidings crisscrossing the roads and fields, no sidewalks, nothing for consumers, just warehouses.

"Did you have occasion to meet Ray Arno in the fall of that year?"

"Yes."

"Will you please tell the court how that came about, what your association with Mr. Arno was at that time."

"He wanted to rent space. I rented it to him."

She had known he would be difficult, but gradually she became aware of a growing sympathy toward her from the jury. A mean witness could do that, she thought, and asked her questions patiently, and he answered, begrudging every word.

Ray Arno had looked for space to rent because the shop he had counted on having was not yet available, and he had goods due to arrive through the fall. He had rented the corner of the warehouse from September tenth until December first. Barbara showed him the pictures Lorinne had provided, and he admitted that that was the warehouse, that was the space Ray had rented. It was a dim corner with a fold-away table, and rough board planks on concrete blocks stacked with boxes. Fishing gear was spread out on the table.

"Did he show you his business license?" she asked.

"Yes. Wouldn't have rented the space to him otherwise," he said.

"Did he have customers come to the warehouse?"

"No. Not allowed."

"Did he have a sign in his window?"

"There wasn't no window for a sign, and it wasn't allowed anyway."

"When did he actually move out of the warehouse?"

"Last day of November. Didn't get through until the next day, and he paid for an extra day."

There were a few more details, but she had what she had wanted from him and turned him over to Roxbury soon after that.

Roxbury asked coldly, "Do you know where his shop was at the time?"

"No."

"Do you know that he didn't open his shop that fall?"

"No."

"Isn't it possible that he had his shop, and used the warehouse to store excess merchandise at the same time?"

Barbara objected, speculation. It was sustained.

"Do you know where he was when he wasn't in your warehouse?" Roxbury asked.

Hoven's face was a dull red; he looked ready to erupt in anger, but he simply snapped, "No."

"Was he there all day every day?"

"No."

"So he could have been in a retail shop, selling his wares," Roxbury said sharply.

Barbara objected; it was sustained. Roxbury was dogged, though; he knew as well as Barbara that this witness was devastating to his case.

When Roxbury finally finished, Barbara said, "Mr. Hoven, you stated that Mr. Arno was not in the warehouse all day every day, but isn't it true that your agreement with him was that he was to be there to receive his shipments in person?"

"Yes. I told him I wouldn't do no unpacking or checking orders, wouldn't be responsible for signing for it, none of that. He had to do it."

"And isn't it true that his shipments were arriving through the month of September and into October?"

"I don't know when they came," he said sullenly.

"But the agreement was that he would receive his own shipments in person. What did he use the table for?"

"He opened stuff and counted it, spread it out to check things. Then he put everything back in boxes. Not allowed to leave things out on the table."

She let it go at that. It was time for lunch.

It pleased her when they left the courthouse to see Hoven struggling furiously in the midst of several reporters and photographers. He was not restraining his language any longer; obscenities were loud and coarse. Camcorders were getting every second of it, and that night on the news, there he would be for the world to see. Word had gone out that he had contradicted Marta Delancey's testimony, impeached her.

Norman Donovan was Barbara's first witness that afternoon. He was a bespectacled man in his fifties, now in management at the big mall across the river. In 1978, he testified, he had been manager of a strip mall in south Eugene. His testimony was precise and to the point.

Ray Arno had rented a store in the mall, but the then-current tenant had not been able to vacate as planned during the first week of September. Ray had been upset; he had his business license, and he had taken a Yellow Pages ad and had cards and invoices printed already, all with that address, so it was out of the question for him to look for a different location. The tenant had not moved out until the middle of November; management had redecorated, the sign painter had done the windows, and the last day of November and the first of December Ray had moved his goods in and taken possession.

"Was there any one particular cause for worry for Mr. Arno?" Barbara asked.

"Yes, there was. He had planned to be in the shop early in September and he had a lot of stock due to arrive starting at that time and for the following few weeks, on into October. He didn't know where to store it, until he located a warehouse that would rent him a small space temporarily."

When Roxbury did his cross-examination, he pressed the same points he had with Hoven: Donovan didn't know where Ray was all that time, he didn't know if he was selling his merchandise out of a different shop, did he?

When Shelley stood up and called on Maggie, there was a ripple of interest in the court. They looked like Girl Scouts, Barbara thought, watching. Shelley had tamed her gorgeous abundant hair into a chignon and had dressed in a very simple dark blue suit, with a dark red blouse, and she wore simple gold hoop earrings. Maggie's hair was drawn back and held at the nape of her neck with a bone clasp, and she was dressed in an equally simple suit, gray, with a gray blouse. Neither of them looked at all nervous.

Shelley took her through her history with Mitch and the Arno family quickly and briefly, then focused on the events following the Monday after the party.

"Do you know what time Ray Arno called you that night?"

"Yes. The call was recorded at eight-thirty."

"At what time did you return his call?"

"A few minutes after twelve, from the hotel in Folsum."

Shelley produced both records of the phone calls and had them admitted. "When Mr. Trassi approached you in the hotel on Tuesday morning, why didn't you talk with him?"

"I was too upset. I believed that Mitch had done that to my inn. I didn't think I could discuss him with anyone at that time."

"Why did you stop believing that?"

"The deputy sheriffs said it was the work of at least two people, and the detective I hired confirmed that. He said two people had done it, and one of them was left-handed."

Point by point Shelley took her over the events concerning the money, hiring Bailey to fingerprint the house, the meetings with Sunderman, and then with the Internal Revenue representative. Maggie was a good witness. At no time did anyone mention how much money was involved, and Roxbury's objections were few and of little consequence.

"Following the initial meeting with the Internal Revenue Service, what did you do?"

"The next working day Ms. Holloway and I had a meeting with the district attorney and told him about it. That was August twenty-sixth."

"When you received the report about the fingerprints found in Mr. Arno's house, what did you do with it?"

"I gave a copy to the district attorney, and one to Mr. Arno's former attorney."

Shelley turned to Roxbury then and said, "Your witness."

"Ms. Folsum, when the defendant told you Mitchell Arno was at his house, did you express fear? Beg him to keep Mitchell Arno away from you?"

"Objection," Shelley said coldly. "Leading question based on a false premise."

"Sustained."

"Did the defendant tell you he would protect you from his brother, as he had done before?"

"No."

"If you had asked the defendant to defend you as before, would you expect him to do so?"

"Objection. Speculation." It was sustained.

"When you informed the defendant that your bed-and-breakfast had been wrecked, did you tell him you suspected Mitchell Arno had done the damage?"

"Yes."

"Was he enraged?"

"No. He was very sad, and worried about my safety."

Roxbury hammered at her, making the point that the Arnos had their own code of justice; a daughter and sister had to be protected, that Ray as the eldest son had that obligation: to protect the cherished sister.

Without exception, Shelley's objections were sustained, and Maggie remained calm and refused to be rattled.

Barbara had suspected that the state intended to play down the money Mitch had carried; the fact that there had been no leak concerning it had reassured her that they had accepted the IRS agreement, as well as the various statements, and that it was a closed issue. She was not surprised that at this time Roxbury never once referred to it. He was going to play his other card: the Arnos were not like the jury panel members, they pursued justice Mafioso-style.

"The Girl Scouts came through with flying colors," Barbara said to Frank when Maggie was finally excused and Judge Waldman called for a recess. Barbara walked to the women's room with Maggie and Shelley, and inside, they both started to shake. She laughed and put her arms around them, drawing them in close. "I do that, too," she said. "But never in court. You were both swell."

Then, back in court, still on schedule, moving exactly as planned, she called Bailey. He was not dapper, she thought as he was being sworn in, but he was presentable in a brown suit she estimated to be about fifteen years old and a red-striped tie from some historical period. He had shined his shoes, she noted with approval. She would try to remember to compliment him on that bit of heroism.

She had him give an account of his training and experience: the police academy in California, work with the San Diego Police Department as a detective, special FBI training, then his move to Eugene and going into business as a private investigator.

She went straight to their visit to the bed-and-breakfast and the photographs he had taken. He identified the pictures and they were admitted as evidence. "What did you conclude about the damage done to the inn?"

He said two people had been searching, and explained how he had determined that one was left-handed. "It wasn't the pattern for malicious vandalism; they were looking for something."

"What is the difference between malicious vandalism and a hasty search?"

He explained: malicious vandalism involved scrawling obscenities here and there, spray-painting walls, breaking windows, defecating on beds, urinating on carpets, flooding the place, and it wouldn't involve the entire building, because that was too much work. The inn had been searched methodically from top to bottom; it had been fast and they hadn't cared how much damage they did, but there hadn't been any of the personal touches of malice.

"On Saturday, August tenth, did you receive a call from Ms. Folsum?"

He said yes, and recounted what he had done.

"Did you receive a report from the FBI?"

"Yes. On August twenty-ninth the report came back and I made a copy for my files and gave the original to Ms. Folsum on the following day, August thirtieth."

"Do you have that report?" she asked. He said yes, and she asked him to summarize it for the court.

"One set of prints," he said, referring to the report, "belongs to a man named Jacob Stael, who goes by the name of Bud, address unknown, believed to reside in New York City. He has a criminal record, served seven years in New York State for assault and battery. Another set belongs to Jeremy Ulrich, also of New York City, also with a criminal record, for armed robbery. Both men are employed by the R. M. Palmer Company of New York City."

"Is either of them left-handed?" Barbara asked then.

"Bud Stael is left-handed."

"Do you have photographs of those two men?" she asked.

He did.

Roxbury objected strenuously when she asked that the pictures be admitted. There was no foundation for introducing two new characters, he said meanly.

Barbara asked to approach, and at the bench she said, "Those two men will be identified by various people as the defense case proceeds. We will demonstrate that they were in the area throughout much of August, as well as in the Palmer office when Mitchell Arno retained Mr. Trassi."

"Picking out a man from a single picture isn't admissible," Roxbury snapped, "as she well knows."

"Not like picking out a single car from a single picture?" She turned to Judge Waldman. "We have witnesses who will testify that they picked out these men from among a group of mug shots."

Judge Waldman looked thoughtful for a moment, then said, "I'll sustain the objection at this time, but if your witnesses testify as you state, then you may introduce the photographs after the proper foundation has been laid."

She thanked the judge and resumed questioning Bailey.

In his cross-examination, Roxbury wanted to make three points, and he drove at them harshly. "Did you recover other fingerprints that were not identified?" Bailey said yes. "It is just an opinion, isn't it, that the inn was subjected to a search?"

"It was a search," Bailey said.

"According to the official police report—"

"Objection," Barbara said. "Improper cross-examination. No one has introduced an official report on the damage. It was not part of discovery."

"I have it right here," Roxbury snapped, holding up a sheet of paper.

Barbara shook her head. "But you didn't supply the defense with a copy, did you, Mr. Roxbury?" She thought she was being very reasonable, and even sweet, but his flush of anger suggested that he didn't agree.

"Enough arguing," Judge Waldman said. "Overruled."

Barbara's exception was noted, and Roxbury continued.

He tried to give Bailey a hard time, but in Barbara's opinion, it would take a nuclear explosion to accomplish that.

When Bailey left the witness stand, Barbara called her final witness for the day.

Gene Atherton was a pale, nervous man who had confided to Barbara that he had never been in court before, and worried that it would be an ordeal. She had reassured him as much as possible, but now, today, it appeared that his worst fears had surfaced once more. For a moment he seemed to forget how to spell his name.

In a conversational tone, she invited him to tell the jury where he worked and what his position was. She kept her tone easy, almost soothing, as she drew him out about working in a motel; he began to relax a little.

He worked as desk clerk in one of the Gateway motels off I-5, and had been there for nine years.

"I suppose with so many people arriving and leaving constantly, you don't particularly remember any of them after a time has passed," she said. "Is that correct?"

"Usually," he said. "There's no reason to remember most of them."

"But if something unusual happens, then later on you might recall one or more of your guests. Is that right?"

"Yes, it is."

"Do you recall any of your guests from last August?" she asked, still easy.

"Yes, very well."

"And is that because something unusual happened to make you remember them?"

"Yes, it is."

"Please tell the jury about that, Mr. Atherton."

He hesitated, evidently not knowing just where to start. "You mean from when they checked in?"

"That would be fine," she said. "Just tell it in your own words."

"Well, two men checked in late on Saturday night, August third. They called first for a reservation and gave a credit card number and said they'd be late and to hold a room. So they checked in, and they said they were tired, ready for bed. New Yorkers, they sounded like, and I thought the time difference, jet lag, something like that, was bothering them. They said they'd be there three or four days, maybe longer, maybe not." He paused, watching Barbara for a sign of approval, a clue that this was okay. She nodded at him.

"The next morning they were up and out early, before I got off work, even. I work from ten at night until seven in the morning. I saw them take off."

Barbara interrupted him then. "Mr. Atherton, before you continue, just a few questions to clarify what you've already said. What is the procedure when a call for a reservation comes in, with a credit card number?"

"Whoever takes the call reserves the room and then puts the card through the machine for verification, he initials the charge information, and that's that."

"All right. So you had that information, a name and credit card number. When they sign in, what is the procedure?"

"They have to sign, or one of them does, in the registration book, and give the license number of their car and a home address, and sign the credit card charge slip. One of them did that."

"Did you get a good look at them?"

"The one who signed them in, I did. The other one was looking over maps, the tourist information in the rack. I didn't see him as well."

"You said they were New Yorkers. Did the one who signed in give a New York address?"

"Yes, but it was the way he talked that made me think New York—you know, the accent."

"What were they driving?"

"A ninety-three Honda Accord, dark blue, with an Oregon license plate."

"Do you know the number of the license?"

He produced a photocopy of the registration with the license number and read it.

"All right. Did they stay the few days they had said they might?"

"No. They stayed until the morning of August fourteenth."

"On Sunday morning, August fourth, you said they left very early. Do you know when they returned Sunday night?"

"Yes. I saw them drive in at two-thirty in the morning."

"Were both of them in the car?"

"Yes. The reason I noticed the time," he added, "was that I was thinking if they were still on New York time, it was like five-thirty in the morning for them, and it had been a long day for them."

"Mr. Atherton," Barbara said, "so far this sounds like very routine motel business. What was it that made it memorable, made you remember them in such detail?"

"It wasn't then," he said hurriedly. "I mean, they didn't do anything to bring attention. It was a couple of weeks later, when a credit card investigator came around. The card was stolen, you see, and the company was looking into it. They ran up a pretty big bill, eleven days, meals. And it turned out that the license plate on the car was stolen, too, and the car was stolen. They asked all of us questions, and it was still recent enough that we could remember, and after we answered their questions, it's like we'll never forget now."

"Did you describe the men for the investigator?"

"Yes."

She asked him to describe the two men and he did, but his description was not very detailed until he said, "The one who signed in was left-handed."

"Did you identify them by looking at photographs?"

"Not then. He didn't have any. Later, another private investigator came around with a book of pictures, and I picked them out."

"Can you tell the jury about the book of pictures? What was it like?"

"Thirty pictures maybe, in a book, like a photograph album."

She went to her table and picked up the album and showed it to him. "Is that the book of photographs you looked through?"

He leafed through it, then nodded. "That's it."

The pictures were all of ex-cons, dressed more or less the same in sports shirts open at the throat. Their ages ranged from about thirty to about fifty and there was nothing to make one stand out from another. A good mug book that Bailey had assembled over the years. "From those pictures you were able to identify the two men who checked in on August fourth?"

"Yes. One of them was the guy who signed the registration, him I knew right off. I wasn't that sure about the other one, like I said. But I picked out another picture and I told the investigator I thought that was the second man."

"Then what did you do?"

"Well, the investigator asked me to put my initials on the back of the pictures, and I did."

Now Barbara picked up the photographs she had wanted to introduce earlier, and she asked Atherton to look at the initials. "Are those the initials you wrote there?" He said yes, and she showed him the pictures. "Are those the two men you identified?"

"Yes. That one for sure," he said, pointing. "That one I think is the other man, but I wouldn't swear to him, not like the other one."

Barbara asked to approach the bench then, and she and Roxbury stood before the judge and spoke in low voices. "There is peel-off tape on the back of those two photographs," Barbara said. "The pictures were provided by the criminal justice department in New York City, and have a certification stamp and signature. May I identify the men, or must I introduce yet another witness to do so?"

Judge Waldman took the pictures and peeled off the tape, then showed them to Roxbury. "Will you stipulate the authenticity of the photographs?" she asked him.

It was clear that he wanted very much to say no, but after a moment of hesitation, he shrugged. "So stipulated."

Judge Waldman nodded to Barbara. "You may identify them."

Back at her table, Barbara said, "Let the record show that the witness identified Jacob 'Bud' Stael as the man who signed his registration book on the night of August fourth, and tentatively identified the second man as Jeremy Ulrich." She had the pictures admitted and passed them to the jurors, and when they were done looking, she said, "Your witness, Mr. Roxbury."

37

It was ten-thirty when Bailey and Shelley left that night. The rain was hard, relentless, although it was not very cold.

"You planning to be up a bit longer?" Frank asked Barbara in the living room. Alan was in the dinette with his book.

"Awhile," she said. "I'm working on my closing argument. Maybe I'll even get a draft of it down. What about you?"

"What I aim to do is take a very long bath, snuggle with a book for half an hour, and then sleep. Sounds pretty good, don't you think?"

She grinned and nodded, then stood up and walked to the hall. "I'll tell Alan he might as well come share the fire with the monsters; I'll be up in the office." Both golden cats were stretched out full-length as close as they could get to the fire without singeing their fur. In the corner the Christmas tree glowed and sparkled, untouched this year, every ornament in place. She almost regretted how fleeting childhood was for cats. Well, Alan could enjoy the fire and tree; she would leave the lights on it for him. She had taken only a few steps when the doorbell rang, long and piercing, as if someone was holding a finger on the bell. She turned toward the door; Bailey? Had he forgotten something? Then, magically, Alan was passing her. He motioned her back to the living room, and Frank grabbed her arm. Alan went to the front door, looked out the peephole, then came to them, just inside the living room doorway.

"Trassi," he said.

"Alone?" Frank asked.

"Didn't see anyone else, but there's shrubbery out there."

"Let's turn on the floodlights," Frank said, walking into the hallway. "Ask him what he wants; I'll do the lights."

Alan nodded and returned to the door. "Mr. Trassi, it's pretty late. Won't this keep until morning?"

Frank flipped the switch for the outdoor lights, and as if on signal, gunfire erupted. Five, six shots, as loud as cannons. The cats streaked past Barbara, up the stairs. She was immobilized, and Frank stood with his hand on the light switch, as motionless as she was. Alan now had a gun in his own hand, and he was opening the front door.

"Just back up," he snapped. "Palmer, put the gun on the step, then back up, or I'll shoot you. Now!"

"Call nine-one-one," Frank said to Barbara, and he hurried toward the door. She ran to the kitchen phone and made the call.

"Tell them two men are down, maybe three," Frank yelled as she spoke into the phone. "We need an ambulance."

The dispatcher wanted her to stay on the line, to keep talking, but she put the phone on the stand, and ran to the door. Trassi was leaning into the front of the house, with Alan patting him down, holding his gun very steady as he did. He motioned Trassi away and told Palmer to walk very slowly toward the house. Then Barbara saw two men lying in the rain, with blood all around them both. Frank was kneeling by one of them; he stood up, walked the few steps to the other one and did the same thing, knelt down, felt for a pulse.

"One of them might still be alive," he said. "Maybe a couple of blankets."

She ran to get the blankets. Stael and Ulrich, she thought, Palmer had killed Stael and Ulrich. He had delivered them to her doorstep, just as he said he would. Fighting hysteria, she groped in the linen closet for blankets, then hurried back to the front porch. Frank covered the two men on the ground.

"Do you suppose we could get inside out of the rain?" Palmer asked then. "I'm afraid Mr. Trassi is exhibiting signs of shock."

Trassi was shaking violently. His skin was blue-white, even his lips.

"Are they clean?" Frank asked. Alan said yes. "Get inside," Frank snapped to Palmer. Already, the wail of a siren was all around, the noise reverberating against the low clouds. Up and down the street, lights had come on; people had come to doorways, some all the way out to the street, huddling under umbrellas. "We'll go in, too," Frank said. "You okay out here?"

Alan said sure, and leaned against the house on the porch, out of the rain. Barbara thought irrelevantly how different he looked, no longer the friendly kid delivering a pizza, or one of the youths riding a bike aimlessly around. He looked like a man Bailey would hire and trust to do his job. His gun had vanished again.

Inside, Frank said, "You want to put on some coffee? This might take a while." He ushered Trassi and Palmer into the living room, where they drew near the fire, both of them soaked. Frank was only slightly less wet. She hurried to the kitchen to make coffee, saw the phone again, and hung it up. The siren sounded as if the ambulance or police car, or both, had turned the corner of their street.

After the initial confusion of uniformed officers asking questions, of medics whisking both men away to the hospital, Lieutenant Lester Cookson arrived with two plainclothes detectives and asked what was going on. Without hesitation, Palmer said, "I shot them both."

Trassi was huddled in a chair with a blanket around him, still shaking, but less violently now. His color was better, more white than blue; he looked terrified. Palmer was seated comfortably in another chair close to the fire. His clothes were steaming; he had turned down Frank's offer of a blanket.

"We'd better go to the station and let you make a statement," Lieutenant Cookson said.

"I prefer to explain in front of Ms. Holloway and Mr. Holloway," Palmer said coolly. "They should know what happened on their doorstep, don't you think?"

Just then Bailey arrived, and after a little argument between Frank and Cookson, he was admitted.

"Why not?" Palmer said. "The more the merrier." He watched one of the detectives open a laptop computer, and he shrugged. "Tell me if I speak too fast. Earlier this evening Mr. Trassi and I had dinner together. Mr. Trassi is my attorney, and it was a business meeting and meal. Afterward, we met Ms. Fredericks, who is a private investigator in my employ. The three of us boarded an elevator together to return to our rooms, but we were stopped on the second floor. Two men boarded; they grabbed Mr. Trassi's arms and dragged him off the elevator, and were hustling him toward the stairs when the doors closed, and we began ascending again. They were Stael and Ulrich, both of whom I employ now and then, and, frankly, I was quite alarmed. I told Ms. Fredericks to lend me her gun, a forty-four I believe it is, and at the next floor I left the elevator and ran down the stairs, hoping to catch up with the kidnappers. I could hear them in the stairwell, and I followed them to the lower-level parking garage, where I glimpsed all three of them on the opposite side of the area. They got into a car, and I got into my own car, and was close enough to catch up with them at the street exit. I followed after them out into the street, quite worried, and not knowing what other course to take, except to keep them in sight until they stopped somewhere, and then confront them."

He spread his hands in a gesture that suggested helplessness. "I had no idea of their intentions, of course, nor any idea where they might be going or what was being said in their car, and the rain was very hard. It was difficult just keeping them in sight."

He might have been describing a jaunt to the beach, he was so self-assured and at ease. Watching him, Barbara again felt the chill that his presence had brought on before. His voice was almost hypnotic in its rhythmic cadences.

"When they turned into this street, I didn't know where we were," he continued. "I saw a car pull out of the driveway at this house, and they pulled in. I stopped at the curb down a way and came after them on foot. Stael and Ulrich shoved poor Mr. Trassi to the door, and they both stepped behind bushes; Stael had a gun in his hand, and that's when it occurred to me that this could be the Holloway residence."

He frowned and said with an air of apology, "I'm afraid it gets a little confusing now. I was close enough to hear Stael say something like, As soon as the door opens, we rush them. No one's going to walk away. I'm not repeating his words verbatim; he was using very vulgar language and I see no point in echoing his exact words; however, that was what he meant. My worst fears were confirmed." He looked at Trassi and shook his head. "He was quite helpless. After all, Stael was holding a gun on him.

"My next move was to step forward and call out, 'Bud, for the love of God, stop this. Put that gun away and get out of here before someone gets killed.' Just as I spoke, many lights came on, and the two events, my voice coming from behind him, as well as sudden lights all around, made him panic, I'm afraid. He spun around and started shooting. I shot back. And Ulrich had drawn his gun from his pocket, and I shot him also. Perhaps unnecessarily, but at the moment it was quite a reflexive action," he added. A very slight smile curved his lips for a moment, then he added, "Mr. Trassi did the only sensible thing. He threw himself flat on the ground when the shooting started."

He was going to get away with it, Barbara thought then. Trassi would back him up, and Palmer would come out a hero who had saved the lives of her and her father, and Alan. He looked at her, and she could almost hear him say, "I delivered them right to your door."

Trassi added a few details: Stael and Ulrich had meant to rush the door as soon as it opened. They knew there was a security system, and it had to be opened from inside. They both had silencers on their guns, and they would have killed him, too. They wouldn't have left a witness. In a high-pitched and tremulous voice he confirmed Palmer's story. He didn't look at Palmer once.

It wasn't long after that when the lieutenant said, "Thank you, Mr. Palmer. I still have to ask you and Mr. Trassi to come downtown with us, but it shouldn't take long."

"I understand," Palmer said. "I shall be of any assistance possible, of course. I wonder if it would be permitted to go back to the hotel long enough to change clothes first? I did get rather wet, you know, and poor Mr. Trassi must be even wetter, and neither of us in heavy coats. I am reluctant to leave the warmth of the fire."

Cookson spoke with two officers and they left with Palmer and Trassi. At the doorway Palmer turned back toward Barbara and ducked his head in a little bow. "I so regret such unpleasantness outside your door. I apologize." She did not say a word.

After they were gone, Cookson said to Frank, "We have a crime-scene tape up, and a car will be parked out front overnight. A television crew is out there now and it's going to get worse. I'd like to keep them off the property until we've had a chance to look around in daylight."

With everyone gone, the house secured again, Frank said bitterly, "Christ on a mountain! Rush the door, shoot everyone in the house! Lunatics!"

"They weren't going to get in," Alan said. "No way was I going to open that door. I meant to give Bailey a call and have him drive back over."

"That's how we set it up," Bailey said. "Once the security system goes on, no outsider gets in unless he's escorted by me or one of my guys."

"That wasn't the plan, anyway," Barbara said. "The plan worked exactly the way Palmer arranged it. He set them up and then killed them. He delivered them to me. That's his business, special deliveries. Guaranteed." She became aware of Frank's appraising gaze and stopped.

Alan nodded in agreement. "By the time I got the system off and the door open, Palmer was at Stael's side. I think he put his hand over Stael's on the gun and fired twice. I heard two more pops from the silenced gun after Palmer stopped shooting."

Bailey and Alan went to check out the house then, to make certain nothing had been opened during the confusion, and Frank put his arm about Barbara's shoulders in the living room.

"You going to be okay the rest of the night?"

"Sure," she said. "Safest night so far with a cop car parked out front."

Later, wide awake in bed, she was remembering John's bitter words: *How many more bodies do we get to count?* Thelma Wygood, the other Palmer man in Miami, Belmont in New Orleans,

Mitch, Gilmore, now Stael and Ulrich. In spite of the warmth of the room, the warmth of her blankets, she couldn't stop shivering.

She never had believed in evil as a thing in itself. People did evil things, usually for understandable reasons, money or power to gain possession of what they coveted, or keep what they possessed, to exact revenge. . . .

But evil infects some people, she thought, it gets in the system and stays like a virus that is never killed, that might lie undetected for years and then surface again, a virus that is so contagious that those who have even casual contact with the carrier are endangered; no one is safe in its presence, and it spreads like a plague.

Any accommodation strengthened evil, a wink, a nod, a hurried glance away, a minor deal, a favor accepted or returned, a denial of word or act, the slightest compromise—they all added to its power, because such evil was very aware of its ability to ensnare, and finally enslave, those who accepted it. Those it used might be unthinking, unaware whose cause they served, but evil was never unaware; it used its tools when it needed them, discarded them when their usefulness ended, and never without full awareness.

She had met evil for the first time, she realized, and she was afraid of it. She was afraid of Palmer, and he knew her fear.

In her mind she heard his softly spoken words, almost purring, *I don't think we're through yet, Ms. Holloway.*

He had offered her a deal, to deliver Stael and Ulrich, and he had carried out his part even though she had said no. But she had dealt with him before, over the money for Maggie and the return of the program. They were not through yet.

Frank looked terrible and the next morning, drawn and old, as if he had not slept, and she looked like death itself, but they reassured each other that they were fine, just fine.

"Things are happening," he said at the table. "Story's out, of course, but no names attached. Ulrich was DOA, Stael died an hour later in the operating room. The usual, names withheld pending notification of next of kin. Jane wants us in chambers when we arrive in court. I expect the good judge is a bit upset, and no doubt Gramm and Roxbury are, too. The press is out there clamoring, as expected. Palmer's given a couple of interviews, modestly downplaying his part in saving our lives. Let's see, what else?"

"Eat," Barbara said, regarding her toast with disfavor.

"If you will, I will," he said.

Alan admitted Bailey, who said that Stael and Ulrich had been driving a stolen car, and had phony ID. Stael's gun had been fired twice.

"How do you find out stuff like that?" Barbara demanded, watching Bailey eye her toast in a predatory way. She pushed it toward him, and he took it.

"Got connections," he said.

He said he had sent someone to pick up Shelley, and Alan would stay in Frank's house until relief arrived, any minute now. It was understood that he was planning to stick close to Frank and Barbara all day.

Then, outside, she ignored the press being kept behind the crime tape; two uniformed officers cleared a path through the reporters to Bailey's car parked at the curb. It wasn't raining, although the sky was gray and low. "Remember that old horror movie," Barbara said glumly, getting into the car, "*The Day of the Triffids*? There was one scene where the monsters were all pressed against a fence, cornstalks gone wrong, something like that. There they are in the flesh."

"Now, Bobby," Frank said, waving good-naturedly at the reporters.

At the courthouse they went straight to Judge Waldman's secretary, who said the judge would be there in a minute or two. Gramm and Roxbury were both waiting also. The district attorney looked unhappy, and Roxbury was grim-faced, chewing on his lip. Everyone nodded to everyone else; no one spoke.

Inside chambers, Judge Waldman was behind her desk, not yet in her judicial robe. She was frowning and not in a good mood. Her voice was crisp and cold when she invited them to be seated.

"Ms. Holloway, Mr. Gramm has requested a continuance in the trial, and his concerns must be addressed. Mr. Gramm, please explain your reasons."

"Your honor, in light of the double shooting in front of Mr. Holloway's house last night, and the fact that the two men have been identified as Stael and Ulrich, both of them named in court yesterday, the state is forced to ask for time to investigate this incident, to ascertain if it has any bearing on the case being tried. The jury must be aware of the shooting, and could not help but be influenced by such knowledge. We don't feel it would be fair to Mr. Arno to continue with so many uncertainties."

Judge Waldman looked at Barbara.

"Absolutely no! Hold Mr. Arno in jail for another delay? They had months to look into the Stael and Ulrich connection."

"Mr. Palmer and Mr. Trassi have been very cooperative," Gramm said quickly, "and will continue to cooperate, but it will take a few days to get information that could be vital. We're not planning for a lengthy delay."

Barbara shook her head. "I object to any delay whatever."

"We would be willing to reconsider bail for Mr. Arno," Gramm went on, as if she had not spoken. "I agree that to hold him in jail for the continuance probably isn't necessary."

Before Barbara could object again, Frank said musingly, "Bail? I don't think so. Of course, if the state is willing to drop the charges and, further, to make a public statement of apology and exoneration for Mr. Arno, that would be a different matter."

Gramm flushed. "Based on the information we had, the state acted with all due propriety. No apology is called for, and we can't consider dropping any charges until we complete our investigation."

"I'll fight it through every appellate court," Barbara said.

"That's won't be necessary," Judge Waldman said firmly. "Mr. Gramm, the court denies your request for a continuance. You have had sufficient time to investigate those two men. I spoke with the jury this morning, and since the names of the men were not released, they don't know who they are, and they will not be influenced by the scant news they might have seen or read. I shall speak to them again at the end of the day, of course. Court will convene in ten minutes."

Walking down the corridor toward the courtroom, Barbara said, "I want to be like her when I grow up."

"I think that's a possibility," Frank said. "Course, you'll have to take up clothes shopping."

They met Shelley, and before she could ask a question, Barbara said, "Later." She told Ray the same thing; they would talk later.

Her first witness was Peter Stepanovitch. He was thirty-five, a salesman for an electronics company in Portland, a job that required a lot of travel, he said importantly.

"Do you recall the first week of August?" Barbara asked, and he said yes. "Tell the jury what made that week memorable for you," she said.

"You see, on the third I had to fly to Chicago, so I drove to the airport and put my car in long-term parking, like I always do. I flew back home on the eleventh, and the car was gone. Stolen."

Barbara nodded. "I see. Did you recover your car?"

"Yes, on the fourteenth, the police called and said they had it. They found it outside Corvallis on the night of the fourteenth of August."

"What kind of a car is it, Mr. Stepanovitch?"

"A ninety-three Honda Accord, dark blue."

"And what condition was it in when you recovered it?"

"Well, it wasn't wrecked or anything like that, but it was filthy, like they'd been using it for camping. The trunk had a lot of dirt, and fir needles and stuff like that, like you get out camping. And there were a lot of beer cans in the back."

"Was there anything else unusual about the car when you recovered it?"

"Yes, there was. The license plates weren't mine. At first there was a little confusion about whose car it was, and the police called the wrong guy, because of the plates, but we figured it out with the motor-identification number. The crooks switched plates to make it harder to spot, I guess."

"Did you make a note of the wrong license plate number?" she asked.

"Yes. When they called and said they had a car, they gave me the number and I wrote it in my notebook."

She asked him to repeat the number for the jury, and he recited it without looking in his notebook. It was the same number the motel manager had given.

Barbara turned then to Roxbury and said, "Your witness." He said, No questions. She thanked the witness, and he left the stand.

She called Michael Murillo.

Murillo was twenty-seven, married, and lived in Corvallis, where he worked for the repair shop that had received the wrecked Lexus. He described the shop and yard with a high security fence, topped with barbed wire, where the police put impounded cars, and cars that had been involved in wrecks. He remembered the Lexus very well, he said, because it was first one he had seen up close like that, and then to see it brand-new and already smashed up, he wouldn't forget it.

"What did they do with the Lexus?"

"They towed it to the back part of the yard and left it there. We all just looked it over."

"Was it locked?"

"Yes."

"Just tell the jury what happened with the Lexus after that, Mr. Murillo."

"Okay, I mean, all right. First a policeman and a locksmith came and opened it up and found papers. They locked it again and left. Then, late in the day, the cop—the policeman—came back with a lawyer, Mr. Trassi, and said he was in charge of it. And he, the lawyer, wanted to have it moved, but there wasn't any way to do it that late on a Saturday, so he said to just fix it enough to run, and they'd take care of the stereo and CD player back in New York. And we said that we didn't know what it needed, and in any case, we'd have to order parts and it might be a week to get them. He said to do it as soon as possible and give him a call when it was ready. He said he'd call us back with a number where we could reach him. So we ordered the parts and got it ready to run again."

Barbara stopped him there. She smiled at him reassuringly. "Just a few details before you continue," she said. "When Mr. Trassi arrived, did he have a key for the car?" He said no.

"While the car was being repaired, did your mechanics do anything to the interior?"

He shook his head. "They just got it up and running."

"Where was the car being kept during the time it was at the shop?"

"Until we got the parts, it was out in the yard; then they moved it inside to work on it."

"Is the shop inside the security fence?"

"Yes, and there's a night watchman. We keep cars that are going to be used in trials, so we have to keep everything pretty much locked up."

"All right. So you got the car ready to run again, then what happened?"

"I called Mr. Trassi on the thirteenth, late—we were about to close—and he said someone would come for it the next day. On the fourteenth a guy came to get it."

"Were you present when someone collected the Lexus?"

"Yes. I work in the office mostly; I do the calling, ordering, all that kind of stuff. So I was the one that signed it out."

He went on to say the man had walked in, but he had seen a dark blue Accord pull away, and he thought the man had been driven there in it. He described Ulrich, then said he had picked him out of the album Bailey had shown him; he had initialed the picture, and now he identified it again.

"Did he have a key for the car?" Barbara asked. He said yes.

"Did he have any papers of authorization, or the title, anything like that?"

"He had the title transfer, and he had a letter signed by Mr. Trassi saying he could take it."

When Barbara finished with him, she turned to smile at Roxbury. He glowered at her.

Barbara's last witness before the lunch recess was Gloria Reynolds, who lived in the Blue River district. She said she and her husband had advertised a cabin for sale the first week of August, and two men had come by to look at it early on Sunday, August fourth, before ten in the morning.

"They took one look and said that wasn't what they were after," she said. "Didn't even bother to get out of the car or anything, just one look."

"Can you describe the men or the car they were driving?"

"A dark blue foreign car, that's all I can say about it. But they were from back East, real abrupt-speaking. One had a map and the classifieds, the other one was driving. They had on suits, I remember, dark suits. Not like fishermen, like we thought might be interested." She sniffed, then said, "They were rude, too. Said, 'Where's the Marshall place?' Just like that. So I told them how to find it, and they left without a thank you or anything."

"Where was the cabin you had for sale?" Barbara asked.

"Just across the road from our place, a real nice little A-frame, walking distance to the river, easy to get to. A real nice little cabin. It's sold now."

Barbara produced the classified ads with the A-frame listed, and Gloria Reynolds said that was their ad. "The one immediately following it is for the Marshall cabin," Barbara pointed out. "Is that what they indicated they would look at next?"

"Yes. I told them to go back to the highway, down a mile or two, and turn right. The Marshall place is at the end of the gravel road down there."

In his cross-examination, Roxbury asked how many others had inquired about her cabin without bothering to go inside, and she said several. He demanded to know how many of the others she could recall with such detail, and she said a few, but none of the others had been so rude, so she remembered those two best. Her lips tightened when she said that, as if she now would not forget him, either.

Did she know anything about those men, he demanded, whether they had been agents for someone else, for example? If they were real-estate agents? If they were bankers? She said no, all she knew was what she had said. He gave it up with that.

Lunch was a seafood salad and crostini, ordered by Patsy. Between bites Frank and Barbara told Shelley and Patsy about the shooting at the house. Afterward, Barbara thought how strange that they all had to keep reminding one another to eat. Shelley was horrified and frightened, indignant and furious, in a combination that kept changing, as she flushed, then turned pale, then flushed again.

"But that's so . . . so . . ." She swallowed hard. "He's the devil," she whispered.

No one disputed her. Then Barbara said briskly, "Okay, next comes Trassi."

She watched as Trassi was sworn in. In her mind he had become the little gray man, and today he was grayer than ever, and he looked shrunken, as if fear had drained something vital from him. At one time she had thought to keep him on the stand for a whole day, or even more than one, wringing denials from him; then, considering how restive the jury had become, she had decided not to go that route, but to drive directly to the points she wanted to make.

After Trassi had stated his background, she asked him to recount his association with Mitchell Arno, and he gave the same statement he had made at the IRS office, in almost exactly the same words as he had used then. She admired his memory.

"All right," she said. "Because the various dates tend to become confusing, I have prepared a timetable to help the jury keep them straight." She turned to see Shelley setting up the easel with a very large calendar printed on heavy cardboard. The dates began with the middle of July and went through August into the first week of September. There were strips of peel-off tape on many of the dates. She went to the calendar and said, "On the nineteenth of July you stated that Mitchell Arno approached you in the anteroom of the Palmer Company in New York and asked you to represent him. Is that correct?" He said yes, and she peeled off two strips on the nineteenth, revealing the name Trassi in green lettering and under it Mitch's name in red letters.

"Were there others in the anteroom that day?" He said yes, and she asked if Stael and Ulrich had been there.

He hesitated momentarily, then said, "I didn't know them by name at that time, but they were there."

She peeled off two more strips over their names, both in dark blue. She asked, "Was mention made of the delivery of the Lexus in their presence?" When he said yes, she took off another strip and there was a cutout of a sleek black automobile, very small and elongated to fit. When he admitted that the money had also been mentioned, she uncovered the final icon, a yellow suitcase with a dollar sign on it. And that filled the space.

She backed away from the calendar in order to let the jury see it more clearly, then she said, "The next day you met with Mitchell Arno was on the twenty-sixth of July. Is that correct?"

He answered her questions, and she peeled off more tape on the twenty-sixth, to show Mitch's name, Trassi's, the automobile, and the suitcase.

"During the following week were you in contact with Mitchell Arno?" He said no. "Were you in contact with either Mr. Ulrich or Mr. Stael?"

"No," he snapped.

"All right. From testimony, the next time we know anything about the Lexus was on August third, the day you went to Corvallis to claim the car for the Palmer Company. Is that correct?"

He said yes; his answers were getting sharper, his eyes narrower as he watched her peeling off the tape. His name, the suitcase, and the car were revealed on Saturday, August third.

"Did you know who would actually pick up the Lexus and drive it back to New York?"

"No."

"Did you know that Mr. Ulrich and Mr. Stael were in the state? That they had checked into a motel in Eugene that evening?"

"No!" He wasn't loud, but his voice was high-pitched and strident.

She peeled the tape from their names on August third, then regarded the calendar for a moment: Trassi in green, the blues of Ulrich and Stael, the yellow suitcase, and the sleek black Lexus.

"Did you take possession of the title transfer on August third?"

He hesitated, then said yes.

"Did you at any time have a key for the Lexus?"

"No!"

"You were on the coast at Folsum to see Ms. Folsum on Monday, August fifth, weren't you?" He said yes and she took off the strip of tape. "And Tuesday, August sixth?" Another strip came off. "And you had not yet delivered the suitcase and the money?" She revealed the suitcase.

"All right. Then you came over to Eugene and stayed here until the fifteenth." A row of green Trassis marched across the dates, on to the next line. Under his name the blues of Stael and Ulrich were revealed as if in lockstep until August fourteenth. "In your statement you said you had to delay your departure until the legalities of the transfer of the funds for Ms. Folsum were settled. When were you informed that Ms. Folsum and her attorney insisted on talking directly to Mr. Arno about the settlement?"

"I don't know when it was," he said. "I don't remember the date."

"Mitchell Arno's body was discovered on Friday, August ninth," she said. "Following that, did you agree to arrange for the necessary documentation to prove to the authorities the legality of the transfer of funds to Ms. Folsum?"

"Yes, I did."

"Then you left Eugene and returned to New York on the fifteenth." She regarded the calendar. "And on the previous day, the fourteenth, Mr. Ulrich picked up the Lexus, presumably with Mr. Stael, but since that is less certain, we don't show his name here." Ulrich and the Lexus were both revealed under Trassi's name on the fourteenth.

"Mr. Trassi, when did you give the title transfer to Mr. Ulrich?"

He blinked, then shook his head. "I didn't."

"Were you given the tittle transfer when you identified the Lexus."

"Yes."

"What did you do with it?"

He frowned, as if trying to remember. "I mailed it to the Palmer Company in New York."

"Oh? Why? Were you not put in charge of the car and its recovery?"

"I didn't know who they would send to get the car, but whoever it was would need the title, so I mailed it to the office."

"I see. When did you do that?"

"I don't remember just when it was."

"Well, did you use the post office at Folsum?"

He hesitated, then said no. "I mailed it in Eugene."

"So it must have been on or after Wednesday, August seventh. Weren't you afraid that was cutting it rather fine, since the car was due to be ready in just a few days?"

"I mailed it back to New York," he said. "I thought they could handle it any way they wanted to."

"What about the letter of authorization you signed for Mr. Ulrich to pick up the car? When did you give that to him?"

"I didn't sign it for any particular individual," he said. "I mailed it with the title."

She regarded him for a moment without comment, then stood by her table. "Mr. Murillo's testimony is that he called you on the thirteenth, late in the afternoon, to inform you that the Lexus was ready to drive. Do you recall that?"

"Yes, he called me."

"Did you inform Mr. Ulrich that it was ready?"

"No. I didn't talk to him. I didn't even know he was in the area."

"Do you know how he found out the Lexus was ready?"

"No, I don't."

"Did you tell Mr. Murillo that someone would collect the car the next day, the fourteenth?"

"I probably did. I don't remember."

"Did you tell the front desk at the hotel that you would be leaving on the fifteenth?"

He was watching her like a snake; his eyes were almost glazed over with his intense stare. "I might have told them. I don't remember when I checked out."

She nodded, then turned to shuffle through some papers on her table. "I have a certified copy of your billing record from that stay, Mr. Trassi." She showed it to him. "Is that your signature?" He said yes. "According to this, you made no long-distance call to New York on the thirteenth. But there is one for five P.M. on the fourteenth. Is that right, to your recollection?"

"I don't remember particular calls," he snapped.

"Did you meet with Mr. Stael and Mr. Ulrich on the evening of the thirteenth, or the morning of the fourteenth, of August?"

"No! I didn't even know they were in the state!"

Barbara regarded him for a moment, then turned away and said, "Your witness, Mr. Roxbury." In the last row among the spectators, she saw Palmer; he smiled very slightly at her. The expression was so fleeting, it might not have happened at all, but she knew he had smiled, that he knew where she had led Trassi, and it amused him. Shaken, she sat down and listened to Roxbury try to undo some of the damage, to disconnect Trassi from Stael and Ulrich. She couldn't stop the thought, looking at the little gray man on the witness stand: he was a dead man. He had outlived his usefulness.

39

Although Roxbury was rather good with Trassi, the calendar spoke louder than he did. Trassi said, responding to his questions, that there were often half a dozen employees in the Palmer anteroom; they were a delivery service and had to keep people on hand most of the time. Some of them had familiar faces, most did not, and he knew none of them personally.

"Were you in a position to give any of those men direct orders at any time?" Roxbury asked.

"Never! I am Mr. Palmer's attorney for contracts, things of that sort. I have nothing to do with the day-by-day affairs of his actual business or the men who work for him."

"When you mailed the transfer title and the letter of authorization back to New York, who did you send it to?"

"The office manager, Mr. Henry McClaren. I told him that I didn't expect to be in the area when the car was finished, and it would be best to handle it from the main office."

"On the thirteenth of August, when you were informed that the Lexus was ready, did you notify anyone else?"

"Yes. I took a walk, and then realized that my number was the only one the garage had, so I placed a call to the main office and left a message that the car was now ready to be picked up."

It wasn't very good, Barbara thought, just the best he could do without more advance planning. When she started her redirect, she came back to the evening of the thirteenth. "The garage notified you late in the day, nearly five, I believe. Then you took a walk. At what time did you call New York?"

"Right away after I went out," he said. His color had improved under Roxbury's handling, but he was wary and gray again.

"So it had to be later than five, six possibly?"

"I don't know what time it was."

"All right. Of course, that would have been after eight or nine in New York. Was the office open at that hour?"

"No."

"Do you know what office hours they keep in New York?"

"No. I have nothing to do with any of that."

"Presumably your message was heard the following morning, if no one was there when you left it. Wouldn't you agree?"

Almost sullenly he said he didn't know anything about that.

"Do you know when the title transfer and authorization, as well as the key, were sent to Oregon, and then given to Mr. Ulrich and Mr. Stael?"

"I said I don't know anything about that."

"Yes, you did. Do you believe that the company sent someone else out here with those items in advance? Would that be a reasonable explanation?"

Roxbury objected that she was arguing with the witness, and harassing him. "He said he doesn't know," he snapped.

"Sustained," Judge Waldman said. "Please move on, Ms. Holloway."

She harassed him just a little longer, then said no more questions, and he was dismissed. Barbara watched him hurry out of the courtroom, past Palmer, without a glance in his direction.

The judge gave her usual warning to the jury and everyone else not to discuss the case, and she left, but she was going to talk to the jury, she had said. And Barbara had to spend time with Ray. She had gone over all her questions with him already; it was time to warn him about the line of questioning Roxbury would take.

"A couple of hours," she told Frank. "If someone can pick me up around eight or eight-thirty, that should be time enough."

They were standing outside the courtroom door; Barbara glanced around, but Palmer was not in sight. Down the corridor, held at bay, the press was waiting, and a crowd of people were leaving work. Everything looked entirely normal, but, Barbara realized, she was as apprehensive as Bailey. "Let's beat it," she said, steeling herself for the reporters.

That night Barbara and Shelley talked about her character witnesses; they were an impressive lot. A church member or two; a counselor from the juvenile rehab center; a teacher from a local high school—Ray did a lot of volunteer work with troubled youngsters, took them fishing, taught them to fly-fish, supplied the materials they needed. . . . He and Lorinne were active in church work, community affairs. . . .

She and Shelly were talking in the study when the phone rang, and she heard Clyde Dawkins on the machine. She raised her eyebrows at Shelly and picked up the receiver.

"Ms. Holloway, I'm sorry to disturb you at this hour. Judge Waldman asked me to call to see if it would be possible for you to be in chambers at eight-thirty in the morning."

"Yes, of course," she said. He said thank you and hung up.

"Now what?" Barbara got up and went out to find Frank; he was as mystified as she was. A few minutes later she told Shelley she might as well go on home; Shelley knew exactly what to do the following morning, and she was prepared.

"Something's happening," Bailey said. "Gramm and a detective talked to Palmer and Trassi around six, for about half an hour. Palmer and Trassi had dinner in the hotel after that, then they cleaned out Trassi's safe and took stuff up to his room. He might have handed over the program finally. While they were at the front desk, Palmer told the desk clerk to get two first-class reservations on a flight tomorrow to New York. He went to the Hult Center to see the show, and Trassi went out twice to use a pay phone. My guy said he looks like a chicken that can't find his head. Now he's in his room trying to get a call through to a New York number; he stopped going out to do it, just using his own phone. No dice, so far. He gets a machine and hangs up, then tries again in a few minutes."

No one spoke for a time, until Barbara shrugged and said, "Palmer's up to something, but God knows what. Meanwhile, we stick with the scenario we've got. I don't give a shit if they both fly to Bermuda at this point. Let the cops haul Trassi back later."

A little later, alone with Frank, Barbara said, "Palmer must have told Trassi he'd back him up, but he won't. He can't admit they knew Stael and Ulrich were here. If he does, he drags the entire company into a mess."

Frank nodded. "That's the choice you gave them: throw Trassi out for the wolves, or risk an investigation of the whole outfit. Evidently the police aren't going to hold Trassi right now, but they'll have to look into it, ask the office manager questions about the title transfer and letter. What would you bet that's the call Trassi's been trying to get through—to the office manager?"

"And he's suddenly unavailable. Think they'll question him by phone?"

"I doubt it. Not this time. They'll send someone. It's going to take a week or longer to get answers."

"By now Trassi understands he's being scuttled," Barbara said softly, "no matter what Palmer might have told him earlier. Now what?"

"God knows," Frank said. He watched her pace about the living room restlessly, and he was well aware that she knew, as he did, that if Trassi decided to deal with the police or the FBI, she was still at risk. And to save his skin, Trassi might have to deal.

The next morning, when he came around to drive them to the courthouse, Bailey said glumly, "Trassi skipped a while ago. He drove his rental car to the Eugene airport and got on a plane heading for New York, by way of Denver."

There was nothing to say. So Palmer would have two first-class tickets to use. Maybe he meant to take the Fredericks woman home with him. Barbara shrugged and pulled on her coat. "Showtime," she muttered.

At eight-thirty in the morning on a Saturday, the courthouse was a bleak, echoing shell. The coffee shop was closed, barred; the room for the jury pool was sealed off; the law library was closed; no bailiffs scurried about; no police officers milled about waiting to be called.

Judge Waldman's secretary was at her desk on the second floor, looking sleepy, and no one else was in sight. Barbara turned when she heard footsteps coming along behind her and Frank; Roxbury was hurrying toward them, his cheeks flushed by the cold morning air.

The secretary buzzed the judge, and Clyde Dawkins opened the door and motioned them to come in. Judge Waldman was at the coffee table, where the fragrance of coffee was welcome.

"Please," she said, "make yourselves comfortable." She poured coffee for them all and handed out the cups before she spoke again.

"As you know," she said then, "I spoke with the jurors yesterday after we recessed. The foreman, Mr. Tomlinson, speaking for them all, made an unusual request. He asked if it would be possible to conclude the trial today and give them the case to deliberate by tomorrow afternoon. He said they quite definitely do not want to disrupt another holiday and have to return after the first of the year, and the others agreed with him, without exception. I told them I would have to think about it, and discuss it with counsel."

Before anyone could speak, she held up her hand. "I questioned them in a group, and then individually, to try to determine whether they have been discussing the testimony, and I don't believe they have. This is simply a unanimous decision they have reached. They want to be done with this."

"They've made up their minds," Roxbury said in a grating voice.

"It could become a mistrial," Barbara said slowly. "Have they been reading the newspapers, watching TV news? Talking to people outside?"

"Perhaps," Judge Waldman said, "although they denied it. If they've made up their minds, they gave me absolutely no sense of how they intend to go with the evidence. I believe Mr. Tomlinson. They want to be done with it. They want to enjoy a remnant of the holiday without the trial hanging over them."

Her turn, Barbara thought then, sipping her coffee. She put the pretty little cup down and said, "I can be finished by the end of the day today."

Barbara was aware that she would be cutting her defense short, aware also that to do otherwise would risk alienating the jury even more. A jury already in rebellion could jump erratically. She looked at Roxbury, who was gnawing on his lip, frowning. He appreciated the problem as much as she did, she knew. If he was the one to drag it out beyond the close of the day, would the jury retaliate? The jury might already blame the prosecution for the many delays, for ruining their Christmas and now threatening their New Year. He knew that Ray Arno would take the stand that afternoon. How much tough questioning had he planned for Ray? How short would he have to cut that? No one spoke as they waited for his response.

"I have to say that I never heard of a jury dictating terms. Not like this." His tone suggested that the judge could shape them up, keep them in line if she chose. "I'll go along. If she can close the defense today, the state will go along as much as possible, but no guarantees that we won't go overtime."

"I'll explain that to them," Judge Waldman said. "Now, for the closing arguments. I propose one and a half hours for each side; I'll need at least an hour for my instructions, and they can have the case by the lunch recess." She looked at Barbara and Roxbury in turn. "Is that acceptable?"

Barbara thought of the pages and pages of closing argument she had already prepared; she suspected that Roxbury had at least as many pages ready. Cut it down to one and a half hours. She glanced at Frank. He nodded and she did, too. "I can handle that," she said. Then she thought, poor Shelley; she had planned to take all day with her character witnesses.

"Half a day!" Shelley cried. "Just half a day! Good heavens! Who can I leave out?"

"Look at it this way," Frank said, "you don't leave out anyone so much as you leave out a few selected tidbits. Let's have a look at your list and your questions." He sounded as comforting as a family doctor who knew panic when he saw it and could put an end to it before anyone else even recognized it as panic. He sat down with

Shelley at the defense table, and they looked over her list. Barbara went to speak with Ray, who was already in the holding room at the courthouse.

Shelley's last witness before they recessed for lunch that day was Michael Conroy, a thirty-year-old high-school teacher. He had testified that Ray Arno took four boys at a time out fishing, that he taught them how to fish, and something about responsibility, about life, loyalty. . . . "He changes their lives," he said.

"How do you know what he does with them out fishing?" Shelley asked.

"Because I was one of four he took responsibility for fourteen years ago, and they tell me about it now. It's the same thing that I experienced with him then. Of our four, two of us became teachers, one's still in graduate school, a postdoctoral physicist, and one's a cook in a very good restaurant. But we were all headed for trouble when he took us in hand. So are the kids he takes in hand today. His boys, those he guides, don't get into trouble."

Then, after lunch, Barbara had Ray tell about the past summer, when Mitch showed up at his house, what happened afterward. Ray was a good witness for himself, careful, just emotional enough, transparently truthful.

"Mr. Arno," Barbara asked, "did you consider it your duty to protect Maggie Folsum last summer?"

"No," he said. "She's a very capable young woman who is quite able to take care of herself."

"But you felt it your duty eighteen years ago to protect her? Is that right?"

"Yes. She was defenseless, with an infant of her own, and little more than a child herself, and my brother had threatened her, had even hurt her. I felt responsible for my brother's actions and for ensuring that he didn't hurt her again. I felt it my duty then to get between my brother and my sister."

"When you spoke to Maggie Folsum after you returned home and found that Mitch had left your house, did she tell you about the vandalism done to her bed-and-breakfast inn?"

"Yes."

"Did you assume that Mitch had done the damage there?"

"Yes."

"What was your reaction? Did you vow to get even with him, to punish him yourself?"

"No. I talked to my father, and we agreed that if Mitch turned up again, if he actually had wrecked her inn, we would have him arrested and charged. I told Maggie to stay with other people, not be alone at the inn, just in case he returned."

Barbara led him through the past years, the spring he and his brothers had worked on the boat at the coast, his engagement to Lorinne, when he went into business for himself, the problem with the warehousing of merchandise before his own space was available. She showed him the pictures of Stael and Ulrich and asked if he had ever seen either of them; he said no. Quickly she went over the state's case with him, and he denied being on the bridge the morning Marta Delancey claimed to have seen him; he denied ever being near or in the Marshall cabin. . . .

She had allowed herself two hours with Ray, leaving the same amount of time for Roxbury. At the end of her time, she asked, "How long were you with your brother Mitch after your father left him at your house?"

"Ten minutes at the most. I showed him through the house, told him to clean himself up, to help himself to food, and that I would be back on Monday, probably around noon, and we would have plenty of time after that to talk."

"Did you see him alive again after that?"

He shook his head, and in a low voice said, "No. He was gone when I returned home."

"Did you fight with him?"

"No."

"Did you kill your brother?"

"No!"

That night both Shelley and Barbara were glum, and no amount of reassurance from Frank could lift their spirits. "Look," he said, "you both did a bang-up job today. Shelley, you had your witnesses so primed that if you'd cut them off in half the time you took, they still would have put the halo in place and lighted it. And, Bobby, they crowned him with a halo, and you showed that it was a perfect fit. No more could have been asked of either of you if you'd taken a week."

"Well," Barbara said after Shelley left, "I'll go take an ax to my closing argument. An hour and a half! God!"

But she found it hard to concentrate. Trassi had vanished in Denver. His plane had arrived there on time, apparently, but Trassi had not arrived in New York. No one had followed him past the departure gate in Eugene; there had been little reason to do so, and the Major Works men who were keeping an eye out for him in New York said he had not been aboard the continuation of the flight. Denver was one of the big hubs; he could have taken off in any direction from there. Later, the Fredericks woman had driven Palmer to Portland, where he had caught his nonstop to New York alone. Now, with the whole Palmer crew gone, Barbara should have been able to relax and concentrate, she kept telling herself. But, instead, she was as tense as a prima donna waiting for the curtain call.

She then stared at her computer screen filled with pages of closing argument. *Everyone goes away,* she thought. *Disappear without a trace, one and all.* She closed her eyes hard when she realized she was no longer thinking of Trassi or Palmer, either. Then, furiously, she began to red-line her prepared text.

40

Sunday morning. Everyone looked sleepy and tired, and except for the Arno clan, the courtroom was nearly empty when Roxbury started his closing argument.

"Ladies and gentlemen, no oratory today, no flowery speeches, or appealing to your sympathy; today the facts will be sufficient, and just the facts. You have been attentive and patient throughout this ordeal of a trial, and now I ask only for your attention for a short while longer. The facts will demonstrate that the defendant, Ray Arno, in cold blood and with malicious intent to inflict the greatest pain possible, murdered his brother.

"It is a fact disputed by no one that Ray Arno attacked his brother in a vicious fight eighteen years ago, and at that time threatened his life if he ever returned to the area. . . ."

He laid out his argument with cool precision. "There is no need to speculate about mysterious strangers with mysterious motives; the facts speak for themselves," he said. "Ray Arno was incensed that people were talking about his wife and his brother. Did the defendant find his brother in his own bed, using his belongings as if he had a right to them? Did Mitchell Arno intend to move back into the family circle and give new cause for more gossip? We'll never know what transpired between the two brothers on that fateful Monday when the defendant returned from the coast and found his brother usurping his place. . . . He buried his brother and put various items in the plastic bag to dispose of them—the lead pipe murder weapon, his brother's clothing. But then fate stepped in and a witness saw him on the bridge. We know she saw him that morning; she identified him positively, and she pointed out where he had thrown the plastic bag. And we found it.

"We found the plastic bag exactly where it had to be, where it had been for months."

He took his full hour and a half, and finally summarized: "The defendant beat up his brother years ago, and threatened to kill him if he returned. He admits to feeling responsible for the safety of Maggie Folsum, to feeling responsibility for the actions of his brother. We all know that in many families, protecting the honor of a sister, a niece, a mother is the prime responsibility of the males of the family, especially the oldest son. I suggest that Ray Arno feels this responsibility to an extreme. He alone had the opportunity to commit the murder. He had a motive. He was the last person known to have been with Mitchell Arno, and he killed him and tried to hide the crime."

After a ten-minute recess Barbara stood up. "Mr. Roxbury is quite right in that there is no need for oratory this morning," she said. "You have heard the testimony and you have seen the evidence, but there is a difference in our approach to that testimony and evidence. Mr. Roxbury would have you examine and consider only the evidence that supports his case, and I want you to examine and consider all of it. It happens, ladies and gentlemen, that the same evidence often yields more than one interpretation. When it was generally believed that the earth was flat, the only evidence most people saw supported that assumption. Evidence to the contrary was there; it was simply not recognized. And so it has been with this case; the evidence is there and for a long time it went unrecognized, its meaning lost. Today, I want you to consider all the evidence.

"First, let's examine the state's case."

She pointed out that one witness had not been able to pick out Ray's car from others that were more or less similar. And she reminded them of the witness who had confessed to speeding past the corner of Stratton and River Road in another similar car. "When most of us look at a flock of birds, unless we are avid birdwatchers, we might say they were simply little gray birds," she said, smiling faintly. "To a real bird-watcher, they might be sparrows and finches, wrens and juncos, and so on. To most of us one little gray bird is very much like another; to most of us one little gray car is very like another. And we know who did drive past the corner that morning."

Another witness, she went on, could not have seen Ray in his cell, not at two in the morning, and he could not have heard him praying and confessing, since he suffered a severe hearing loss that had been demonstrated in court. A third witness had misinterpreted what she had seen when Lorinne got into a car with Mitchell Arno eighteen years ago, and misinterpreted what she had heard on the telephone.

One by one she demolished the state's witnesses, and then she came to Marta Delancey. "It happens that we sometimes misinterpret what we hear or see," she said slowly. "We hear what we expect to hear and see what we expect to see, and there is no sinister intent; it is a simple human failure. However, there are times when misstatements are harder to understand or explain. Mrs. Delancey said positively that she saw Ray Arno in his shop, that she studied his face to the point of embarrassing him, that her husband commented on the name of the shop displayed on the window, that she browsed through the merchandise and picked up and put down items there. None of this could have happened. Ray Arno did not yet have his shop. By the time his shop opened in December of 1978, Mrs. Delancey's first husband was dead. Her testimony was that she returned to Eugene only to visit her mother, never to do any shopping, and especially she would not have had an occasion to visit a sports shop. This cannot be put down to a misinterpretation of what she saw or heard." Barbara read from her testimony, all positive statements about Ray, and his shop, and the visit there with Joel Chisolm.

"Ladies and gentlemen," she said, putting down the transcript, still speaking very slowly and carefully, "if you find that a witness has spoken falsely, has distorted the facts, or has not recalled accurately what has been offered as truthful testimony, you are entitled to disregard all of that person's testimony. To do otherwise would be unjust, since you have no way of knowing where factual testimony starts and stops."

She was being cautious because she knew the jury had been sympathetic to Marta Delancey and might not take kindly to her calling the woman a liar. She continued. "I don't know what Mrs. Delancey saw on the bridge that day. I don't know the state of her mind at that moment, concerned as she was about her mother's health. I don't know the state of her mind when she returned and read the account of the murder in the newspaper and saw Ray Arno's picture.

"I do know that she could not have recalled him from the time she said he so impressed her in his sports shop. And if part of her testimony is demonstrably wrong, the rest of it is suspect also."

She moved to the calendar then, and pointed. "Now, this is when we first hear of Mitchell Arno in the recent past, talking to Mr. Trassi in the Palmer Company anteroom on July nineteenth. Present were Mr. Ulrich and Mr. Stael. So on that day, these four people and a stenographer all knew that Mitch Arno would be carrying a large amount of money to Oregon."

Using the calendar, she outlined the following days and weeks and tracked down the known movements of Trassi, Stael and Ulrich, the Lexus, and Mitch. "We don't know where Mitchell Arno was or what he was doing in the period from the twenty-sixth of July until August second, when he was found on the coast. . . ."

She moved away from the calendar and said, "Let's pause here and ask a few of the questions that all this raises. First, of course, what were Stael and Ulrich doing in Eugene? Why was Mitchell Arno taken to the cabin? If Ray had killed him, there was no need to go there. He knew he would be alone in his house for a week. He has five acres of ground, plenty of places where a body could be buried, with no questions asked. But if others had been looking for and then found Mitch Arno, they had no way of knowing when they would be interrupted. They needed a secluded place.

"Why was Mitchell Arno's face untouched? In the fight between the brothers, they had both been bloodied, faces and hands. But Mitchell's face was spared this time. I suggest that it was to make certain he could talk. A broken jaw would interfere with talking.

"Then, the actual physical act of moving him must be considered. Could one man have dragged him through broken glass in such a way that only his heels scraped the floor? Then he was dragged again, after he was dead, and this time he was dragged face-down with only his toes and the tops of his feet scraping the floor. Could one man, acting alone, have accomplished that? I suggest that you try acting it out when you start your deliberations, to see just how impossible that would be.

"Next, consider the weapon. This was not a crime of uncontrollable passion; this was premeditated, the isolated cabin was selected in advance, the weapon was assembled in advance with care. It was a weapon designed to inflict a great deal of damage; the parts had to be purchased, and this was done by someone who knew exactly what he was doing. You heard the testimony about the pigskin fibers, and the opinion that a leather holder, a handgrip, had been used on the pipe. In other words, this was a professional weapon assembled by a professional in his own field.

"Why two pairs of gloves if there was only one killer?

"Why burn the hands of a dead man? Consider, he had no identifying clothes; he was wearing his brother's clothes. He had no papers, nothing to identify him, except his fingerprints, and they were burned off.

"Now, as to the time of the attack and the murder. We know that Mr. Stael and Mr. Ulrich arrived in Eugene on the third of August, Saturday. When could they have left their fingerprints in Ray Arno's house on surfaces that had been washed, painted, waxed in July? Not before Saturday night, certainly. But isn't it likely that on Sunday, after preparing the setting for the crime to come, they then went looking for Mitchell Arno, and they found him Sunday evening, two hours after his last meal, in his brother's house?

"What did they want from him? He had already turned the child-support money over to Mr. Trassi; that was the arrangement from the start. When he was found, he had only the clothes on his back, and the Lexus was missing, presumably stolen by joyriders. Is that all he could tell them? Did they accept it?

"We know that on Monday Maggie Folsum's bed-and-breakfast inn was ransacked, ruthlessly searched. If they had found what they were looking for, would they not have left the area instantly? Why did they remain in the motel, risking discovery of a stolen car and stolen credit cards? I suggest they did not find what they were after, and that the only other place to search for it, whatever it was, was in the Lexus itself. But the Lexus was behind a security fence in Corvallis and could not be entered, could not be driven away."

She returned to the calendar and pointed to August eighth. "On Thursday Mr. Trassi was informed that Ms. Folsum demanded a meeting with Mitchell Arno, that she could not accept the past-due child support without adequate proof that it was legitimate. And on the following night, as the result of an anonymous phone call, Mitchell Arno's body was found. There were no tooth or claw marks, no animals tracks, nothing to indicate that an animal had dug up and raised one foot from the grave. And on that night, in the blood that had dried and hardened, the name Arno was scratched with a tool that dug into the floor under the blood. Why?"

She walked back and forth before the jury as she spoke now; they were rapt in attention. "I suggest, ladies and gentlemen, that Ms. Folsum's demand to see her former husband in person made it imperative that his body now should be found. No one had paid much attention to the Lexus; it was simply a business deal that had gone bad. But an investigation into the whereabouts of Mitchell Arno might bring about an impoundment of the car, might bring about a real search of it. So, in spite of the care that had been taken earlier to make identification of the body difficult or even impossible, it now became necessary to have it discovered and identified. And the Lexus remained in the background, considered irrelevant, a minor crime that the Palmer Company and their insurance company would handle. No one had inspected the interior with care, and no one did now. The investigation of murder was focused solely on Ray Arno; the Lexus was ignored.

"Then, Mr. Trassi agreed to provide the necessary documentation to substantiate the legality of the transfer of money, but still he did not leave the area immediately. And, in fact, he didn't leave until the day after the Lexus was actually released."

She pointed again to the calendar. "On the fourteenth, Mr. Stael and Mr. Ulrich left the motel; Mr. Ulrich took possession of the Lexus, and the following day Mr. Trassi checked out of his hotel. And all three men and the Lexus vanished from the area."

She shook her head and said slowly, "But there are a few questions to be answered about those last two days they were still here. Who told Mr. Ulrich that the Lexus was ready? How did he get possession of the title transfer and letter of authorization? And most important of all, how did he get a key?"

She stopped moving and said quietly, "The last person who had the key was Mitchell Arno. I suggest that the person who killed him took that key." She began to pace again, moving very slowly back and forth before the jurors, holding their attention.

"What happens when you buy a car? The dealer has two keys and gives them to the new owner. He doesn't keep one for himself. So, no doubt, Mitchell Arno started out with two keys. If joyriders, as the state suggests, stole the car, they had one of the keys, but Mitchell Arno still had the other one, and then Mr. Ulrich had it."

She turned to regard Ray then. "You've observed Ray Arno day after day in this court; you've observed his family. You saw and heard his friends and colleagues, the teachers and church members;

you've heard about the kind of life he and his wife lead, the good work they do, their involvement with their community. Everything you've heard and seen about him reinforces the simple truth that he is a good man who is not a killer. . . ."

She spent the rest of her time talking about Ray and his family, and finished by saying, "He was caught up in a series of events that had nothing to do with him. He was carrying out his father's request, to provide a haven for his brother for a weekend until they could gather and discuss the situation, and he knew nothing of the other players who were in the field with their own sinister agenda. Ray Arno was a truly innocent bystander in the deadly drama."

Judge Waldman was as good with her instructions as Frank had predicted she would be, and then they were all sent away for the lunch recess, to return at two-thirty, at which time the case would go to the jury.

Barbara and Frank had talked about the problem of lunch for the whole Arno crew, and agreed that a restaurant was out of the question. There were fourteen people to feed in an hour, an impossible task for any restaurant. They ended up going to Frank's house, where Patsy had arranged with a caterer to provide sandwiches and salad for an army. And the Arnos talked, reassuring one another that it had gone well, reassuring Barbara that she was the best lawyer they had ever seen, reassuring Patsy that the sandwiches and salad were fine. But they were all nervous, and Lorinne burst into tears when Mama Arno said she should eat something.

Barbara felt as if she had to scream, go somewhere alone and scream. She kept thinking of the hurried explanations, the scanty summation. . . . "I didn't even mention reasonable doubt," she said to Frank.

"Not your job, and Jane told them all they need to know about it. Relax, honey. You did a great job. I didn't believe you could wrap it all up in such a short time, but, by God, you did. Relax."

Then it was time to return to court, time for the real waiting to begin. Judge Waldman gave the jury their final instructions and sent them out, then she said to Barbara, "If the Arno family would like to wait in the lounge down the hall, they are welcome. I believe we can have coffee brought in."

"She thinks it's going to be fast," Frank said as the judge left the bench. "And I think she's right. That jury wants to go home. The lounge?"

Barbara nodded. Ray was escorted out to a holding room, and the rest of his family made their way to the lounge, where they began to talk again. There had been more spectators that afternoon than earlier, but they were all barred from the lounge. Roxbury had vanished.

"Barbara," Maggie said hesitantly, "it did go well, didn't it? Mama and Papa are so up about it. They're convinced that Ray will go home with them today. They're planning a big party for tonight."

Barbara patted her arm. "I think it went well," she said, and wished she felt the same confidence. If only she had not left out so much. She should have protested the time limit, she thought then. Would it be grounds for an appeal? She wanted to ask Frank, but not now, not with the whole family present, watching. How could they do that? Watch everything, hear everything, and keep talking, too?

She heard snatches: ". . . one of those range turkeys, a bronze something or other. Best you ever tasted . . ."

". . . a spiral, honey-baked ham . . ."

"And mashed rutabagas. You know how much he likes them."

"He says he has to go shopping for presents. . . ."

"We should take him out fishing, first chance. Remember how he needed to be out on the water after he came home from the army?"

". . . so much new stuff to be sorted through. We're just leaving it for him. He'll need to do things like that."

"The kids will be fine with us, and you both need to get away for a while. He's so pale."

Barbara closed her eyes and thought about the coast, a rocky stretch of beach with no one in sight, no one in earshot, a place where she could scream and scream. Frank touched her arm and she jumped, startled.

"Bobby, it's all right," he said. "It really is."

But what if it isn't? she wanted to cry. What if I lost him after all the promises I made? What if the jury believes Marta Delancey in spite of everything? She looked across the room and met Maggie's gaze. What if I got the money for her, and lost Ray? She'll hate me. I'll hate myself. What's the money worth if he's lost? This is what John was afraid of, what he meant. He hates this—lying, cheating, conniving—and he's right. Nothing good can come out of a lie. My entire case was based on a lie. . . .

Frank put his arm about her shoulders and squeezed, then he moved on to talk to Papa Arno.

At a quarter to five they were summoned back to the courtroom; the jury had a decision.

She felt frozen as she watched the ritual; the sheet of paper passed from Mr. Tomlinson to the bailiff, who took it to the judge. She put on her glasses to read it, then took them off again and asked the foreman if the jury had reached its decision.

"Yes, your honor. We find the defendant, Ray Arno, not guilty."

Then it was bedlam. As if she knew the Arnos could no longer be contained, Judge Waldman spoke over their cries and laughter and shouts. She thanked the jury and dismissed them, and told Ray he was free, and she left the bench as if unaware of the circus taking place in the courtroom.

Everyone was hugging everyone else, crying and laughing. Ray grabbed Barbara and hugged and kissed her. Roxbury wormed his way through the group and shook Barbara's hand, then walked out, and the jurors came to shake Ray's hand, and talk and talk. They wanted to talk as much as the Arnos. Again, Barbara could hear only snatches of what was being said, as one after another of the Arnos hugged her. Ray and Lorinne were both crying, surrounded by brothers and wives and children, hardly giving him breathing space; Maggie's daughters were holding Shelley; all three were jumping up and down, laughing and crying. . . . Mama Arno was hugging the jurors, crying, thanking them. . . . She invited them to dinner on New Year's Day, all of them.

Then Frank was at Barbara's side; he touched her cheek gently, and she realized her face was wet with tears.

"It's contagious," she said, and groped in her purse for a tissue.

"I reckon it is," he said, surveying the hordes of people who could no longer control themselves. He grinned. "Let's move this circus out before I start blubbering."

41

The Arno party was both raucous and reverent; food appeared in an endless stream of casseroles and pastries, pasta dishes and salads, hams and smoked turkeys. . . . And they all talked and laughed and joked and wept. The party was in James Arno's house; it was the biggest house available, and it was crowded with family and friends in every room, all of them eating and talking. No one ever finished a sentence, and no one minded. They all touched one another a lot, hugged one another, patted, caressed, loved one another without reservation.

At ten-thirty Barbara, Frank, and Shelley said good-bye and escaped into the foggy night. Ray, Lorinne, and Maggie came out with them to the car, where Ray shook hands with Frank, kissed Shelley again, and then held Barbara's shoulders for a moment before he wrapped her in a bear hug.

"I'll never forget you, what you did for us. Never," he said huskily.

When he released Barbara, Maggie said, "I just want to say, you have a room at the inn anytime you want it, anytime at all. You're family now. On the house, just like the rest of the family."

Then, finally, they were inside Frank's Buick, leaving. None of them said a word as Frank drove Shelley to Bill's townhouse. Shelley got out but hesitated at the side of the car. Barbara rolled down her window and said, "I don't want to see your face until the day after New Year's. Get some sleep. Rest."

Shelley nodded. "You, too." Suddenly she leaned over and put her head in and kissed Barbara's cheek. "Thanks, Barbara. Just . . . thanks. It's the best holiday of my life suddenly."

She turned and ran to the door, where Bill was standing, waiting for her. Frank started to drive. After a moment he said, "When we get home, let's have a bit of that good Courvoisier I've been saving for lo, these many years."

Later, in front of a fire in the living room, with one of the Things grunting on her lap, she tried to sort through the days to come, the things she still had to do—write a report for Major and Jolin, start a search for a secretary, go over the accounting with Bailey, clean up her own files, move back to her own apartment. Change the lock on her door.

She bit her lip. Change the lock. Move his things to his apartment, hers back into her place, although there was little of hers to move back. Suddenly she wondered, was the price too high?

Frank got up to poke the fire, the other Thing complained at being moved. The Christmas tree glowed, the fire was comforting, the cognac was excellent, and, outside, the fog pressed close to the house.

And she was thinking of the things she had intended to accomplish. Palmer was spinning his new web; she had given him an out, defended him even. She shuddered: defending the devil. All his company had to do was deny receiving the title transfer and letter of authorization in the mail, and the suspicion would land on Trassi, who had vanished, probably to Argentina or the Riviera, or who might even be dead now. Palmer had delivered the rest of the program to his client, who no doubt was celebrating as merrily as the Arno family.

This whole affair had started with a monstrous lie concocted by Major/Wygood; a tissue of lies had followed, and the trail from there to here was littered with bodies. Far from feeling elated, jubilant over her victory in court, she felt as if she was sinking into gloom and despair. She felt uncertain about her own actions, uncertain how far she was capable of going to save a client, win a case. She didn't even know why she was doing this, what she was trying to prove, if anything. Was the price too high?

"Bobby, let's talk a minute," Frank said quietly, back on the couch with the Thing settled in again, grunting.

She looked up, startled by the realization that he had been watching her, maybe even tracking her thoughts.

"You saved a man's life this past week. You don't have to explain the ins and outs of it to Shelley or me or Bailey or Jane Waldman or Bill Spassero. We all know. And you can't explain to a hell of lot of other people who will never know. That's how it is." He held up his hand to forestall anything she might have said. "There was a time when I was about your age, when I still believed the law was holy writ, and I would have fought the devil himself to keep it pure. Then, one day, I came to understand that laws are written by people like me, like us, fallible people, biased people, who are incapable of writing holy law. On that day, I came to realize that justice takes precedence over the imperfect laws we swear to uphold. And, Bobby, your sense of justice is very fine. You're going to brood about cases now and again, try to replay them in different ways over and over—that can't be helped, it's your lot in life. But your instinct for justice won't be fettered by imperfect laws, and you have to live with it. You'll pay the price more than once, and you'll have black nights, but you'll go on doing what you have to do." He stood up. "And what I have to do is get some sleep. Good night, honey."

She watched him walk from the room; both cats stretched, yawned, and followed him.

The main thing is to keep busy, she told herself, and she kept busy. She talked to Jolin, and then to Major, who begged her to come to the island, at her convenience, to discuss the whole case. She hesitated only a moment, then said yes, she would like that. Jolin was especially interested in the fact that the FBI was looking into Palmer's connection to Senator Delancey, who, he said, was chairman of a joint telecommunications committee.

She had her accounting session with Bailey, who said he would send a guy to change her locks if she wanted him to. Next week, after the first of the year. She started to sort files and worked on her final report to Major Works.

Late in the afternoon she went to her own apartment to see what needed doing there before she could move in again. She came to a dead stop when she saw the desiccated Christmas tree in a bucket.

Upstairs, she walked through both apartments, touching things lightly as she passed them—John's oversized desk, his chair, his robe over a chair in the bedroom. Next week, she told herself, and left again without moving anything.

New Year's Eve she went to a party at Martin's restaurant, where many of her old clients greeted her like a long-lost kinswoman. Everyone danced at Martin's parties; everyone sang. Hot and sweaty, she sat down to cool off, and she spied Maria Velasquez dancing and realized that Maria could be her perfect secretary. She had done a little work on Maria's behalf once, and knew the young woman was capable and smart, and with a little training, she could become for Barbara what Patsy was for Frank. She grinned at the idea, and at the next break in the music she offered Maria the job and hired a secretary. And, she chided herself, this is the way you bow out, ease yourself out of the filthy law business. Then she danced with Martin.

She didn't stay long after the midnight countdown. "Happy New Year," she whispered, pulling into Frank's driveway. All over town fireworks were exploding, guns were being fired. It was raining hard again, and Frank's car was not in the garage yet. He was ringing in the New Year with old friends and might be late, he had warned her. "Pretend you don't notice if I come staggering in in the wee hours."

She didn't bother with an umbrella, but pulled her coat over her head and dashed the few feet from the garage to the front porch. Then, as she was unlocking the door, she heard a soft voice, "Happy New Year, Ms. Holloway. No, don't stop. Let's get inside and dry ourselves. I'm afraid your Oregon climate is rather wretched." Palmer had stepped out from behind the large azalea shrub at the porch; he grasped her arm and propelled her inside the house.

He was all in black, a long raincoat, black hat, gloves, shoes. He was holding a gun with a silencer. "Ah, this is better," he said. "Living room." He drew her with him to the living room and looked around approvingly. "Take off your coat, Ms. Holloway, and please sit on the couch, and I'll see if a new log will rejuvenate the fire. I do appreciate a fire on a rainy night such as this. Does it ever not rain here?"

She pulled off her coat and put it on a chair back, then started to sit down.

"Not at the end. Why don't you center yourself on the couch? I think you'll find that more comfortable."

"What do you want?" She sat down in the center of the couch, where nothing was in reach. Both cats wandered in; one joined her, the other one went to sniff at Palmer's feet and legs. He ignored it.

"You didn't really believe we were finished, did you? I find that hard to accept." Slowly he took off his coat, holding the gun steady as he pulled one arm free, then he shifted the gun from one hand to the other to free his other arm. He was wearing a black turtleneck sweater and black jeans; he didn't take off the black gloves. "Now, please, don't move while I tend the fire. I'm afraid I got a chill out there in the rain, and I'm sure you must be feeling chilly as well."

When he opened the fire screen, and then reached for a log, she tensed, but he smiled at her and said, "Nothing foolish, Ms. Holloway. I really would rather not shoot you; that's not part of the scenario, but if I have to change the action, improvise, then, of course, I shall do so. I think in the leg. No lasting damage that way, but something memorable. You see, I don't intend to do you any real harm tonight, but I must have your cooperation." He poked the fire, and moved away from it as the log blazed up. "Ah, how pleasant a fire is. Part of our heritage, I suspect, it satisfies the atavistic in our psyche."

"What is your scenario?" she demanded. There, in the middle of the couch, with a goddamn cat halfway in her lap, she felt totally immobilized.

"I have come to think of you as my own personal death angel, Ms. Holloway. You know her, the mythic figure that appears when a death is imminent? Those who move into her sphere are doomed, and no one knows the breadth of her sphere until too late. She appears with awesome beauty and awesome power, and often seems unaware of the deaths that follow her path. She herself is always unaffected by the deaths she foretells. A powerful figure indeed, one to be feared and avoided if at all possible. I believe in her with all my soul." His voice had taken on the lilt of a balladeer; he looked relaxed, at ease as he remained standing near the fireplace with the golden cat at his feet. "My dear mother told me all the old legends, of course, and she told them as true stories, but she also said that the only way to win the struggle that is life was by confronting our fears and banishing them. I have found that a useful homily."

"We have no unfinished business," Barbara said coldly. "We

both said at the start exactly what we wanted, and we both delivered what we said we would. We are through."

"No, not through, not quite. You see, there is also the pesky matter of reputation. I'm afraid mine has suffered greatly in the past few months. My organization has been decimated. I have lost valued friends, allies, and employees, and I fear that word will get around that an insignificant woman in a mudhole of a Western town was the agent for the destruction of a powerful machine. That won't do, you must understand. I can't refute one by one the malicious gossips who would relish such a revelation. And not many of them share my belief in the death angel, I'm afraid. We have lost our sense of wonder and awe; myth no longer moves us or explains the world to us. No, people will say I let a small-town female lawyer wreak havoc and did nothing in return. In my business, as in yours, one's reputation must be jealously guarded at all times."

"But you don't intend to do me any real harm," she said bitingly.

"That's correct. Soon, I imagine, your father will return from his revelries. I told you I wept when my father died; I did. Without shame, I wept."

Barbara felt a wave of ice crash over her. The Thing on her lap stirred and complained. Then it raised its head, listening. The Thing at Palmer's feet was listening, too.

He raised his gun and said, "Shh."

Both cats relaxed again and Palmer said, "Even they are appropriate. Early-warning systems. How very convenient." He smiled at her. "And I see you already grasped my intentions. You are a very intelligent young woman, very intuitive. I suspect there is a lot of the Irish in your blood. I sensed it before, of course. Yes, the scenario. Your father will return and if you call out to him, he will come into the living room here; if you don't call out, he will come. So we don't have to concern ourselves with getting him to walk through the doorway. And when he does, I'll shoot him. Will you weep for him, Ms. Holloway?"

"How many people can you shoot before you run out of plausible-sounding explanations?"

"No explanation will be required. Mr. Palmer is celebrating a joyous New Year's Eve party in California. Many important and influential people will attest to that. And by the time they get around to investigating the truth of the claim, I will be there, and express my shock and horror in an appropriate manner. You, of course, will relate this evening's events in great detail. But, Ms. Holloway, no one will believe you. I'm afraid I shall have to inflict the small amount of damage to your person that I alluded to earlier. No lasting damage, you understand. A blow to the head, enough to raise a bump; then I shall bind you and leave you to watch your father bleed to death. I fear the blow to your head and shock will unbalance your mind. You see, the death angel herself cannot be killed; we shall see if her mind can be destroyed. You, of course, will assume a new role, that of avenging angel, and our little private game will continue until the day comes that you will have to be restrained. I won't forget you, Ms. Holloway; I shall send you flowers periodically, dark red roses. Which is worse, Ms. Holloway, death or the destruction of a superior mind?"

She didn't speak or move. He was leaning against the mantel, alert and watchful, and she realized that he was studying the room in swift appraising glances, taking his eyes off her only for a second or two at a time, fully aware each time she moved a finger.

"The lines I had imagined for you now," he said, "are the platitudinous cries of desperation: you are mad, or, you can't get away with this. I underestimated you. Instead, you're trying desperately to think what you can do to thwart my little playlet, not wasting time with foolishness. I admire that. I truly admire you, Ms. Holloway."

She visualized the space behind the couch, a long narrow table that held the cognac bottle on a tray with several glasses, a lovely crystal candy bowl that had never been used for anything but special Christmas mints, cut flowers in a vase, a lamp. . . . All behind her, out of reach. At both ends of the couch were tables with lamps, a few books, out of reach. Pillows on the end of the couch, out of reach. Palmer was eight feet away, still at the mantel, and equally distant were three easy chairs and other end tables, out of reach. The Christmas tree in the corner had not been turned on; in the shadows it appeared strangely menacing, out of place here.

The fire crackled, and outside there was the sound of continuing fireworks. She became aware that Thing One was no longer as relaxed as pudding but felt tense under her hand, as if she had communicated her own fear and tension. Then both cats lifted their heads again, listening, and this time they both rose and trotted from the room. She realized that they, and she, had heard Frank's soft whistle. More fireworks exploded closer.

Palmer raised the gun again, also listening.

"Firecrackers spook them," she said.

"It's time to reset the stage," Palmer said, his voice no longer easy. "I think you'll be more comfortable in the middle chair, over there. Move."

She shook her head. "No."

"Don't start being tiresome now," he said in a hard, flat voice. He reached under his sweater and brought out a blackjack with a leather strap, which he slipped over his wrist. He took a step away from the fireplace; the gun now pointed at her legs.

She tensed, ready to spring up and away. He planned to tie her to the heavy chair, she understood, one she couldn't turn over, couldn't move. She slid closer to the edge of the couch as he took another step toward her.

Then he stopped, listening again. There was the unmistakable sound of a door being unlocked.

"Bobby, you still up? It's me," Frank said at the front door. At that moment the lights went out.

She twisted and rolled even as Palmer closed the space between them. She grasped a pillow and flung it toward him, continued to roll to the floor, and felt the sweep of air as the blackjack whirred past her head.

She scrambled to the end of the couch, around it; the fireworks had entered the house, not with great explosive booms, but with pops and a compression of air. She raised her head to see a man's shadow in the doorway; behind her she heard a gasp and then the sound of Palmer falling heavily.

"Bobby! Are you all right? Bobby!"

Frank was on his knees at her side, examining her face by firelight, and she shuddered and grabbed him hard. "All right," she gasped. "I'm okay." She realized that someone else had entered the room and she stiffened. "Who's there?"

"Carter Heilbronner," Frank said, holding her. "It's all right." The lights came on again, and she could see the FBI agent.

They sat in the study, where Frank put a glass of brandy in her hand; his hands were shaking more than hers. She told him all of it, and they sat in silence afterward.

Burned into her retinas, into her mind was the last image of Palmer she had seen, black from head to foot, a shadow outlined by firelight, leaping toward her, rising from the flames.

Much later Carter joined them. He accepted brandy gratefully and sank down into a chair, and Barbara told him what she had already told Frank. Her hands were no longer shaking, but her voice wavered now and then as she spoke, and once it failed her altogether.

"I get the picture," Carter Heilbronner said. "We had him under surveillance, of course, and we knew when he made the switch in San Francisco. He flew in, went to the men's room and changed clothes. Another man, dressed like him, walked out and got into a limo and left. Our man in San Francisco called the office here to say Palmer had boarded a plane to Eugene. He got in at eleven-twenty; there was a car waiting for him in the short-term lot, and he drove off in it, with a tail. He left the car near the train station and came the rest of the way on foot, and my guy was trying to locate me for instructions. When I got here, we decided to wait until Frank showed up. We thought Palmer might be waiting for him to get home to do anything, and we were afraid if we rushed the place, he'd shoot you. It wasn't the easiest of calls."

Carter said he had an agent wave down Frank when he rounded the corner coming home, and the agent told him to keep driving on past the house, not to pull into the driveway, in case Palmer was watching. Then they huddled. They had to call off the security company, get in through a window, and let Carter get to the dark dining room. He did that part because he was familiar with the house, he said. Frank whistled for the cats, to alert Barbara that she was not alone any longer, to prepare her to act, and so the cats wouldn't give it away that someone had entered the house. As soon as Frank opened the front door, called out, an agent pulled the main light switch, and Carter moved in from the dining room.

"And so it ends," Carter said heavily. "Sometimes you have to step on them, after all." He drained his glass but did not yet stand up. "Frank, Barbara, we've removed the body, and we'll clean up your place tomorrow—today. I'm afraid he shot up the couch a little. You deflected his aim with that pillow just fine, by the way. Anyway, nothing happened here tonight. One day next week, or the week after that, the body of an unidentified man will wash ashore somewhere on the coast; meanwhile Mr. Palmer is enjoying a holiday with friends in California. No doubt, in New York there will be meetings and discussions about what to do with the business, the outstanding contracts. We would like very much for those meetings to go forward. Without Palmer the web will disintegrate and blow away in the wind, but before it's gone, we'd like to pick up as many of the pieces as we can. We believe some very important people are involved, some important projects are still in the works, and we'd appreciate the opportunity to gather in the tatters and remnants. We need your cooperation to do that. No one knows that the FBI is interested in the activities of the Palmer Company, so there's still the chance to go forward with our investigation. No one will know where Palmer is, what happened to him, and our guess is that they will try to continue with business as usual while they wait for his return."

Barbara moistened her lips. "Where's Trassi?"

"He had a fatal boating accident off the Virgin Islands."

She closed her eyes. "They're all dead," she whispered. "All of them." Death angel.

"Not all; the web spinner is dead, but those who are left don't know that yet. Will you cooperate?"

She nodded, then said huskily, "Yes."

"Carter," Frank said, his voice almost as husky as Barbara's, "when you take the couch and rug away, don't bring them back."

Carter Heilbronner nodded. "We're all pretty exhausted. I'll be off." He stood up and walked to the door, where he paused to say to Barbara, "It's really over. No one else is going to bother with you; they'll have too many other things on their mind."

She stands at her window in the dark upstairs bedroom and watches the city lights through the rain as they glitter, fade and brighten, then go out one by one.

Dawn comes very late in January in a process that is so gradual, it is hardly distinguishable. Shades of gray, interchangeable. She is thinking how it started with a monstrous lie, and ended with an equally monstrous lie. Thinking: *death angel,* he was the angel of death, he, Palmer. All he touched withered and died.

And now she believes in evil, believes in the devil; he touched her and changed her. He knew her fear and cherished it, played with it, nurtured it.

She remembers what John said: she got obsessed with her cases, put everything on the line. A year ago it was John's life on the line, and together they won. Strange that he didn't mention that, that she gambled with his life, won. And she can never mention it, never refer to it in any way, but it was strange that he didn't. Would he read about this case, know that she gambled and won again? The dragon's dead, she thinks, I killed the dragon. She presses her forehead on the cool window.

"But the price is too high," she whispers to the gray dawn, the gray room. She feels as if she has crossed a threshold that she never suspected was in her path, that on this side of it she has become as ageless as the death angel, that she can never grow older or more alone than she is at this moment.

ABOUT THE AUTHOR

Kate Wilhelm is the author of more than two dozen novels, including *The Good Children, Justice for Some,* and three previous Barbara Holloway thrillers, *Death Qualified, The Best Defense,* and *Malice Prepense.* Her fiction has been translated into many languages and received such honors as the Prix Apollo, the Nebula Award, and the Kurd Lasswitz Awards. She and her husband, Damon Knight, helped found the Science Fiction Writers of America organization and the influential Clarion Writers Workshop, at which they taught for many years. They and their family live in Eugene, Oregon.